ROME'S EXECUTIONER
VESPASIAN II

Robert Fabbri read Drama and Theatre at London University and has worked in film and TV for 25 years. He is an assistant director and has worked on productions such as *Hornblower*, *Hellraiser*, *Patriot Games* and *Billy Elliot*. His life-long passion for ancient history inspired him to write the VESPASIAN series. He lives in London and Berlin.

ROME'S EXECUTIONER
VESPASIAN II

ROBERT FABBRI

CORVUS

First published in hardback and trade paperback in Great Britain in 2012 by
Corvus, an imprint of Atlantic Books Ltd.

This paperback edition published in Great Britain in 2012 by Corvus,
an imprint of Atlantic Books Ltd.

20 19 18 17 16 15 14

A CIP catalogue record for this book is available from the British Library.

Paperback ISBN: 978 1 84887 914 0
E-book ISBN: 978 0 85789 676 6

Printed and bound in Great Britain by Clays Ltd, Elcograf S.p.A.

Corvus
An imprint of Atlantic Books Ltd
Ormond House
26–27 Boswell Street
London
WC1N 3JZ

www.corvus-books.co.uk

For my aunt Elisabeth Woodthorpe
who has always been there for me.

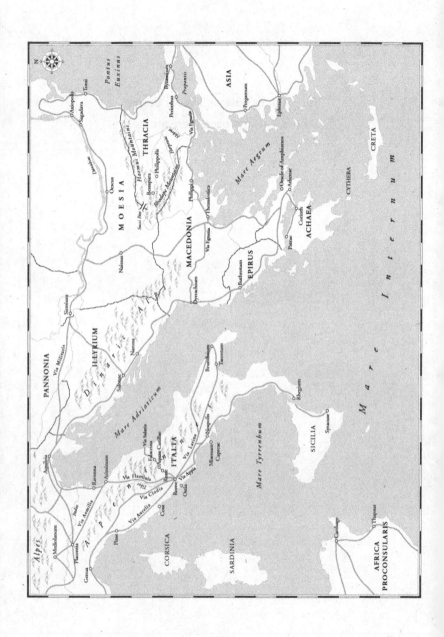

PROLOGUE

ROME NOVEMBER, AD 29

A STACCATO CLATTER – hobnailed sandals striking wet stone – echoed off the grimy brick walls of an unlit alley on the Viminal Hill up which two cloaked and hooded figures made their way at a brisk walk. The deep, moonless night had been made yet more oppressive by the first fog of winter, which had descended upon the city earlier that evening; condensed by smoke that oozed up from the countless cooking fires of the densely populated Subura below, it clung to the men's damp, woollen cloaks and swirled in their wake as they passed. Guttering, pitch-soaked torches held by each man provided the only light by which they could navigate their way through an otherwise all-enveloping gloom.

Both men were aware that they were being followed but neither looked back, it would only have slowed them down, and besides, they were not in any imminent danger; judging by the stealth and even pace with which their pursuers were trailing them, they were being tracked by spies, not thieves.

They hurried on as fast as was possible, picking their way past heaps of rubbish, a dead dog, piles of excrement and an unfortunate victim of a street robbery lying, groaning faintly, in a pool of his own blood. Not wishing to share the dying man's fate they passed by without a glance and pressed on up towards the summit of the Viminal. Here the wider residential streets benefited from the occasional patrols of the club-wielding Vigiles, the Night Watch. However, the two men knew they would have to avoid the attentions of that branch of Rome's law enforcement; they could not afford be stopped and questioned and had purposely chosen a direct route from their starting point on the Palatine Hill through the lawless alleys of the Subura to the

Viminal so as to avoid, for as long as possible, the wider and more patrolled thoroughfares. In travelling so late at night and so conspicuously unguarded they would immediately arouse suspicion and the success of their errand depended, in part, upon arriving at their destination unchallenged and without being followed.

In an attempt to shake off the pursuit they broke into a run and made a few quick turns left and right, but, in the effort to keep up, the following footsteps gained on them; they were now plainly audible above the smog-dampened cries and the ceaseless night-time rattle of wagon wheels and horses' hooves that emanated from the stew of human desperation and misery simmering below in the Subura.

As they turned another corner one of the men looked at his companion. 'I think we should take them before we go any further,' he hissed, pulling him into a doorway.

'If you say so, sir,' the other man replied evenly. He was older than his companion, with a full black beard just discernible beneath his hood in the torchlight. 'And how would you suggest we go about it? From the sound of their footsteps I would say that there are four of them.'

A look of irritation passed over what was visible of the younger man's round face, but having known his companion for nearly four years he was used to his impeccable manners and deference; he was, after all, still a slave.

'No real plan, just up and at them as they pass,' he replied, quietly unsheathing his *gladius* beneath his cloak. The carrying of swords in the city was the privilege of only the Praetorian Guard and the Urban Cohort; it was the main reason why they wished to remain unchallenged by authority.

The elder man smiled at the impetuousness of his young friend as he too unsheathed his gladius. 'The simple plans are often the best sir, but may I suggest one slight refinement?'

'What?'

'I'll stay here with both the torches and you hide yourself on the other side of the alley and then take them from behind as they come for me; that will give us a good chance of evening the odds.'

Bridling somewhat at not having thought of such a simple ruse the young man did as his companion suggested. He pulled out a short dagger from his belt and waited, with a weapon in each hand, invisible in the treacle-dark smog, wondering how his companion had managed to shield the glare of the torches.

A few moments later he heard voices at the end of the alley. 'They turned down there, I'm sure of it,' the leader growled to the man next to him as they rounded the corner. 'They know we're on to them, they've speeded up ... What the—'

Before he had time to finish his expletive a flaming torch flew through the air and hit him on the side of the neck, scraping burning pitch over the oily wool of his cloak and his hair, both of which caught alight instantly. He screamed maniacally, dropping to his knees as his head became engulfed in a fireball, filling the already heavy atmosphere with the sharp acidic smell of burning hair and fibre. His associate had just enough time to take in the fast-moving turn of events before feeling the razor-sharp point of a gladius punch into the base of his chin and out through his left ear, half severing his jaw, filling his senses with unimagined pain and his windpipe with hot blood. He fell to the ground clutching at the wound and sprayed a thick, dark mist from his mouth as he rattled out a long, gurgling scream.

The younger man leapt from his hiding place straight at the two following spies, trapping them. The new threat bearing down from out of the shadows behind them was too much for men used to covert work and taking their victims by surprise in murky alleys; they threw down their daggers and, silhouetted by the flames from their still writhing leader's burning cloak and tunic, dropped to one knee in token of surrender.

'You cowardly little maggots,' the younger man sneered, 'sneaking around after us. Who sent you?'

'Please, master, we mean you no harm,' the nearest man begged.

'No harm?' the younger man seethed. 'Then this is no harm.' With a straight military thrust he jabbed his gladius into the spy's throat and through the spinal cord; the man slumped to the ground without a sound, dead. His one remaining colleague looked aghast at the fresh corpse and pleaded with his eyes for his life. He lost control of his bladder and started to sob.

'There's a chance of a way out of this for you,' the young man insisted. 'Tell us who sent you.'

'Livilla.'

The young man nodded, his suspicions evidently confirmed.

'Thank you,' his bearded companion said, coming up behind the kneeling spy. 'But obviously we can't let you go.' He grabbed the man's hair, pulled his head back and abruptly slit his throat, then threw him, convulsing, to the ground. 'Now finish him off, sir,' he said pointing to the smouldering leader whimpering on the ground, 'and then let's get on.'

A quarter of a mile later, without further incident, they reached their destination: an iron-studded wooden door in the lamp-makers' street, close to the Viminal Gate. The bearded man knocked three times, paused and then repeated the signal. After a few moments the shutter in the door slid back and a heavily shadowed face peered through to inspect the new arrivals.

'Your business?'

The two men pulled back their hoods and brought their torches closer to illuminate their faces.

'I am Titus Flavius Sabinus and this is Pallas, the Lady Antonia's steward,' replied the younger man. 'We're here for the arranged meeting with Tribune Quintus Naevius Cordus Sutorius Macro of the Praetorian Guard on business that concerns only the lady and the tribune.'

The shutter slammed shut and the door creaked open. Leaving their torches in the holders on the wall outside, Sabinus and Pallas entered a small, dimly lit room, which, in comparison to the oppressive gloom they had travelled through, seemed warm and homely. Scattered around the bare wooden floor were a few folding stools and a couple of tables upon which oil lamps flickered. At the far end, in front of a curtained doorway, was a plain wooden desk; two more lamps at either end of the desk provided the only other light in the room.

'The tribune will see you shortly,' the door guard said curtly.

He was dressed in the uniform of the Praetorian Guard when on duty within the bounds of the city: a white-bordered black tunic, belted at the waist; and a white toga, under which a gladius hung from a baldric slung over his shoulder. 'Your weapons please.'

Reluctantly they handed their swords and daggers to the guard who placed them, out of reach, upon the desk. Having not been invited to sit, Sabinus and Pallas stood in silence; the Praetorian walked over to the curtained doorway and took up position there, hand on gladius hilt, his blank, pale-blue eyes staring at them steadily from beneath a mono-brow.

From beyond the curtain came the unmistakable sound of a woman being pleasured. The guard showed no emotion as the soft moans gradually escalated, becoming shriller and longer, culminating in a loud cry of ecstasy that was abruptly cut short by a series of sharp, hard slaps; the woman started to sob but was silenced by a crashing blow that evidently knocked her out cold. In the ensuing quiet Sabinus looked nervously at Pallas who remained as impassive as the guard; being a slave he was used to being treated as part of the furniture and knew better than to let his emotions play on his face.

The curtain was abruptly swept aside; the guard sprang to attention. Out of the doorway stepped Naevius Sutorius Macro, a huge, barrel-chested man, well over six feet in height, in his late forties, dressed only in a Praetorian tunic, belted at the waist. His thick, tightly muscled forearms and legs were covered in short, wiry, black hair, great tufts of which also sprouted from beneath the collar of his tunic. Square-jawed, thin-lipped with dark, calculating eyes and hair cut short, military style, he was a man who exuded authority and the desire for power.

Pallas remained inscrutable but smiled inwardly; he could see that his mistress had chosen the man well for what she had in mind. Sabinus found himself snapping to attention even though he was no longer under military discipline. A flicker of amusement passed over Macro's face, he was used to having that effect on people and enjoyed the superiority that it made him feel.

'At ease, civilian,' he drawled, enjoying the young man's discomfiture at having made a fool of himself. 'You know who I am otherwise you wouldn't be here. Introduce yourself and then tell me why the Lady Antonia has seen fit to send me a young man of no importance and a slave to bear her message.'

Sabinus choked back the rage that he felt at the deliberate insult and drew himself up and met Macro's eye. 'I am Titus Flavius Sabinus and this is—'

'I know who the slave is,' Macro interrupted tersely, easing himself on to the stool behind the desk, 'it's you that interests me; where's your family from?'

'We are from Reate; my father was the pilus prior centurion of the second cohort of the Twentieth Valeria Victrix and fought under our beloved Emperor in Germania before receiving a medical discharge. My mother's brother, Gaius Vespasius Pollo, is of senatorial rank and was a praetor seven years ago.' Sabinus stopped, pitifully aware of just how mediocre his family was.

'Yes, I know Senator Pollo; I used to be his client but he was too weak and ineffectual for what I want from Rome, so I did him the dishonour of repudiating him. A family insult you might wish to address some day?'

Sabinus shook his head. 'I'm here solely on the Lady Antonia's business.'

'Well, nephew of an ex-praetor, what are you to Antonia?' Macro's eyes bored into Sabinus'.

'My uncle is in her favour,' he replied simply.

'So the little fish of an ex-praetor seeks the protection of the great she-whale and in return he does her dirty work and his nephew is promoted to the lofty rank of messenger. Well, messenger, sit and deliver your message.'

Sabinus took the invitation, grateful that he no longer was being made to feel like a naughty schoolboy having to explain himself to his *grammaticus*. 'I do not bear the message, Tribune; I am here only to add authority to the voice of a slave. Pallas has the message.'

'Authority?' Macro scoffed. 'I suppose the good lady thought that I would not listen to a slave? Well, she was right, with or without "authority" why should I listen to a slave?'

'Because if you don't you might miss an interesting opportunity,' Pallas said quietly, looking straight ahead.

Macro stared at him in disbelief, a quiver of rage shook his body. 'How dare you speak to me, slave?' he said with quiet menace. He turned back to Sabinus. 'An interesting opportunity you say, go on.'

'I'm afraid that I can't tell you, Tribune, it was to Pallas that she entrusted the message, you will have to listen to him or we shall leave.' Sabinus' heart raced as he felt that he had over-stepped the mark by pushing Macro into a corner.

Macro remained silent, torn between wishing to know what the most powerful woman in Rome could want with him and not wishing to compromise his *dignitas* by listening to the words of someone so beneath him. His curiosity won. 'Speak then, slave,' he said finally, 'and make it brief.'

Pallas looked at Macro and then flicked his eyes towards the guard standing behind him.

'Satrius Secundus stays, slave,' Macro said, understanding the gesture. 'He won't betray any confidences; he's my man to the hilt, aren't you Secundus?'

'To the hilt sir!' the Praetorian barked.

'As you wish sir,' Pallas agreed, making a mental note of the man's name to give to his mistress upon his return. 'The Lady Antonia sends her greetings and apologises for not inviting you to her house and doing you the courtesy of speaking with you in person, but she feels sure that you will understand that there should be no evidence to connect the two of you, for the safety of you both.'

'Yes, yes, get on with it,' Macro said, disliking the smooth-talking Greek intensely.

'My mistress' feud with Sejanus is no secret to you, sir. She now feels that she has the ability to bring this feud to an end, and expose Sejanus to the Emperor as a traitor bent upon usurping the Purple.'

Macro raised an eyebrow. 'That is quite a claim. What proof does she suppose she has to convince the Emperor of this alleged treachery?'

'Although she has for some time now been collecting evidence of Sejanus' disloyalty it does not amount to a full case against him; a few documents corroborated by hearsay and speculation, but nothing solid, no witnesses, until now.'

'A witness?' Macro was intrigued. 'What testimony will he be able to supply?'

'My mistress naturally hasn't taken me into her confidence on that matter.'

Macro nodded.

'However,' Pallas continued, 'he is not a citizen; he won't be testifying under oath, his testimony will be extracted under torture in front of Tiberius himself.'

'How does she imagine she can get this man to the Emperor when we Praetorians control all access to him?'

'This is where the Lady Antonia needs your help and she has this proposition for you: help her to bring down Sejanus and in return she will see to it that you become the next prefect of the Praetorian Guard.'

Macro's eyes gleamed momentarily; he brought himself under control and smiled thinly. 'How can she guarantee that?'

'If the word of the Emperor's sister-in-law is not enough then consider this: when Sejanus falls, and fall he will, the new prefect of the Guard will have to step in immediately to control the rank and file and to execute officers who remain loyal to old regime. This will have to be set up in advance and will cost money, a lot of money, which you don't have. The Lady Antonia will provide you with what you need to buy the loyalty of key officers for when the time comes; meanwhile you work out who you will need to buy and start to cultivate them.'

Macro nodded his head slowly. 'What about the problem of getting your witness to the Emperor?'

'With all due respect sir, my mistress considers that to be your problem; she suggests that somehow you get yourself transferred to Capreae.'

'Oh, does she now?' Macro sneered. 'As if it could be easily done just by putting in a transfer request.' He fixed Pallas with an icy glare and studied him for a few moments; the Greek remained, as always, unreadable. 'What is to prevent me', Macro continued slowly, 'from going to Sejanus now and telling him all that you have said? I wouldn't give much for your life or the lives of this ex-praetor's nephew and his family, would you?'

'No, sir, but then I wouldn't give much for your life either after you told him.'

'What do you mean?'

'I mean that the very fact that you agreed to see us will give him cause to doubt your loyalty; he will assume that this time you were just not offered enough, but next time you may well be. I think that we will all be dead if you go to him.'

Macro stood and slammed his palm down on the desk. 'Secundus, sword!' he shouted, grabbing a sword from the desk. The guard instantly drew his gladius and rushed at Sabinus and Pallas.

'Ennia!' Pallas shouted.

Macro raised his hand to stop his man. 'Hold,' he commanded. Secundus obeyed. 'What has my wife got to do with this?' Macro growled.

'Nothing at the moment sir,' Pallas replied flatly. 'She is in very good company and no doubt enjoying herself.'

'What do you mean, slave?' Macro was becoming visibly agitated.

'Soon after you left your house this evening the Lady Antonia sent a litter for your wife Ennia with an invitation to come and dine with her and her grandson Gaius; of course she could not refuse such an honour. We left as she arrived, and she will stay there until our safe return, so it may be advisable to have Secundus escort us.'

Macro tensed as if ready to fling himself at Pallas and then flopped back down on to his stool. 'It seems that you leave me little choice,' he said softly. He looked up at Pallas with hatred burning in his dark eyes. 'But believe me, slave, I will have the balls off you for this insolence.'

Pallas knew better than to express an opinion on that subject.

'Very well,' Macro said, collecting himself. 'Secundus will escort you back. Tell your mistress that I will do as she asks, but I do it for myself, not for her.'

'She did not expect anything else from you, sir; she is well aware that this is an alliance of convenience. Now, with your permission we shall leave.'

'Yes, go, get out,' Macro snapped. 'Oh, one question: when does Antonia want to get the witness before the Emperor?'

'Not for at least six months.'

'At least six months? You mean he's not in Rome?'

'No, sir, he's not even in Italia. In fact he hasn't even been captured yet.'

'Where is he then?'

'Moesia.'

'Moesia? Who's going to find him there and bring him back to Rome?'

'Don't concern yourself about that, sir,' Pallas replied, turning to go, 'it's all in hand.'

PART I

PHILIPPOPOLIS, THRACIA,
MARCH, AD 30

CHAPTER I

VESPASIAN EASED HIS weight cautiously on to his left foot,
trying not to rustle the dead leaves or crack any of the twigs
that carpeted the snow-patched forest floor. He had covered the
last few dozen paces with hardly a sound, his breath steaming in
front of him as he tried to lower his heartbeat after a long chase.
He was alone, having left his companions, two hunting slaves
borrowed from the royal stables, a couple of miles back to follow
on slowly with the horses as he stalked his wounded prey on foot.
His quarry, a young stag, was close now; the trail of blood from
the arrow wound to its neck he had inflicted earlier seemed
fresher, a sign that he was gaining on the slowing animal, weak-
ened by loss of blood. He pulled back the string of his hunting
bow and brought the fletched end of the arrow to his cheek,
ready to release. Hardly daring to breathe, he took another
couple of steps forward and peered around, looking through gaps
between the crowded trees for any sign of dun-coloured fur in
amongst the umber and russet hues of a forest in winter.

A slight movement in the corner of his eye, off to the right,
caused him to freeze momentarily. He held his breath as he
slowly turned his stocky frame to face the source of the distraction. About twenty paces away, half-hidden in the tangled
undergrowth, stood the stag, motionless, with blood-matted
withers, staring dolefully at him. As Vespasian took aim it
collapsed to the ground, making the shot unnecessary. Vespasian
cursed, furious at being denied the excitement of the kill after
such a long chase. It seemed to him to be a metaphor for the past
three and a half years that he had spent in Thracia on garrison
duty, since the quashing of the rebellion. Any promise of action
would always fizzle out to nothing and he would return to camp,

frustrated, with an unbloodied sword and sore feet from chasing a few brigands around the countryside. The harsh truth of the matter was that the Roman client kingdom of Thracia was at peace and he was bored.

He had not always been so; the first year had been reasonably interesting and fulfilling. After mopping up the remnants of the Thracian rebels, Pomponius Labeo had marched the V Macedonica, most of the IIII Scythica, the cavalry *alae* and the auxiliary cohorts back to their bases on the River Danuvius in Moesia, leaving Publius Junius Caesennius Paetus, the prefect of the one remaining auxiliary Illyrian cavalry *ala*, in command of the garrison. Vespasian had been left in nominal command of the two remaining legionary cohorts, the second and fifth, of the IIII Scythica; although in practice he deferred to the senior centurion Lucius Caelus, the acting prefect of the camp, who tolerated him but made it plain what he thought of young upstarts placed in positions of command solely because of their social rank.

However, Vespasian had learnt a lot from Caelus and his brother centurions as they kept their men busy with field manoeuvres, road- and bridge-building and maintenance of equipment and the camp; but these were peacetime duties and after a while he had grown weary of them and yearned for the excitement of war that he had experienced, only too briefly, in his first couple of months in Thracia. But war never came, just its pale reflection in the form of endless parades and drills.

For entertainment he had been subjected to more dinners than was good for his waistline at the palace with Queen Tryphaena and various local or visiting Roman dignitaries. His attempts to elicit news of Rome from either the Queen or her guests had yielded only vague and unopinionated information – even this far from Rome, people were reluctant to speak their minds, suggesting that the atmosphere in the city was tense. Sejanus was still Praetorian Prefect and very much in favour with Tiberius, who remained isolated on Capreae. How Antonia, his patron, was faring in her political struggle with Sejanus to preserve the legitimate government in Rome remained a mystery. Marooned for so long in this backwater, only nominally a part of the empire, Vespasian was feeling like a forgotten piece on the edge of the gaming board. He longed to return to Rome where perhaps he could once again be of service to Antonia and further his career through her patronage. He could do nothing here but stagnate.

His long sojourn in Thracia did have one inevitable consequence: his Greek, the lingua franca of the East, was now fluent. He had also mastered the local Thracian tongue well enough, but that had been a necessity rather than a pleasure. Hunting had been the only activity that had provided any satisfaction, exercise or excitement; but this morning that too had been an anti-climax.

Vespasian shot at the prone form of the stag in irritation; the arrow passed through its neck and skewered it to the forest floor. He immediately chided himself for acting out of pique and failing to show due respect for the creature that had so bravely tried to evade him for the last hour. He pushed his way through the undergrowth and, after muttering a perfunctory prayer of thanks to Diana, goddess of hunting, over the dead animal he took out his knife and began to eviscerate the still warm body. He consoled himself with the thought that his four years in the army were over; March was coming to an end and the sea lanes were reopening after winter, his replacement would arrive soon. Soon he would be going back to Rome with the prospect of advancement, a junior magistrate's post, one of the Vigintiviri and also, as importantly, the prospect of seeing Caenis, Antonia's secretary. She flickered before his eyes as he worked his blade in and out of the stag's belly; her delicate, moist lips, her sparkling blue eyes so full of love and grief as she had said goodbye to him; her lithe body, naked before him in the dim light of a single oil lamp on the one and only night that they had slept together. He wanted to hold her again, to smell and taste her, to have her for his own; but how could that be? She was still a slave and, according to the law, could not be manumitted until she was at least thirty. He worked his blade harder and faster as he contemplated the futility of the situation. Even if she were freed he could never marry her as he had dreamed of doing with the naivety of a sixteen-year-old; someone of his position, with his ambition, could never take a freedwoman as a wife. He could, however, keep her as his mistress, but then how would that be for the woman whom he would take as his wife? She would just have to live with it, he decided as he pulled the last scrapings of offal from the carcass.

'I could have put a dozen arrows in you in the time that I've been sitting here.'

Vespasian started and spun round, cutting his thumb on the knife in the process. Magnus sat on a horse, twenty paces away, grinning as he levelled his hunting bow at him.

'Hades, you gave me a fright,' Vespasian exclaimed, shaking his injured hand.

'You'd have had more of a fright if I'd been a Thracian rebel and shot this arrow up your arse, sir.'

'Yes, well, you're not and you didn't,' Vespasian said, calming down slightly and sucking the mixture of his and the stag's blood from his thumb. 'Why were you creeping up on me anyway?'

'I weren't creeping sir, I rode and I was making as much noise as a century of new recruits saying goodbye to their mothers.' Magnus lowered the bow. 'You were just too lost in your own world to notice, and, if I may point out the obvious, sir, that's how you get to be dead.'

'Yes, I know, it was stupid of me, but I've got a lot on my mind, Magnus,' Vespasian admitted, rising to his feet.

'Well, you're going to have a lot more on your mind very soon.'

'How so?'

'You've got a visitor: your brother arrived at the garrison late this morning.'

'What?'

'You heard.'

'What's Sabinus doing here?'

'Now how would I know that? But I would hazard a guess that he ain't come all this way just for a nice brotherly chat. He told me to come and find you as quickly as possible so let's get going. Where's your horse?'

*

By the time they had found Vespasian's hunting slaves and strapped his kill on to his horse it was well into the afternoon. The thickly overcast sky had brought an early dusk to the forest floor and they were forced to lead their horses for fear of them stumbling in the fading light. Vespasian walked next to Magnus, contemplating what could have brought his brother hundreds of miles to talk to him, and started to assume the worst. His father had written to him two years earlier with the expected news of his beloved grandmother Tertulla's death, and he still felt a pang of grief every time he thought of her drinking from her cherished silver cup.

'One of our parents must have died,' he mused, trying not to hope that it was not his father. 'Did he seem upset to you, Magnus?'

'Quite the opposite, sir, he was anxious to see you as soon as possible; if he had bad news he wouldn't have been in such a rush to talk to you, in fact he seemed very disappointed when I told him that you weren't there.'

'Well, that's a first.' Vespasian smiled wryly; he and Sabinus had never got on as children and he had been subjected to years of brutality by his brother that had only stopped when Vespasian was eleven years old and Sabinus had joined the legions. Although the tension between them had eased since Sabinus' return from the army, Vespasian could never imagine his brother being disappointed not to see him.

'I'll know what it is soon enough, I suppose,' Vespasian said, looking around and adjusting the hunting bow slung over his shoulder to ease the chafing of the string. 'Come on, let's ride, the trees have thinned out.' He moved to mount up. 'There's enough light for—' A brief hiss and a heavy thwack cut him off; two arrows appeared simultaneously in his horse's jaw, just where his head had been an instant earlier. The animal reared up, whinnying piercingly, knocking Vespasian to the ground; another shaft slammed into its shoulder quickly followed by one into its exposed chest, felling it.

'Juno's crack, what the . . .' Magnus flung himself in top of Vespasian as his own mount bolted. 'Quick, the other side of your horse, jump.'

They leapt over the prostrate animal and crouched behind its back as two more arrows thumped into its belly; it raised its head and screeched, its hooves thrashing at the air as it tried but failed to get up. The two hunting slaves sprinted to join them behind the nearest available cover; with a sharp cry one spun like a top, his billowing cloak wrapping itself around his body as he twisted to the ground with an arrow protruding from a blood-spurting eye socket. His companion flung himself through the air and landed next to Vespasian and Magnus as another shot punched into the still writhing horse, causing it to spasm violently and then lie still.

'What the fuck do we do now?' Magnus hissed as two more shafts fizzed just over their cover to land quivering in the ground five paces behind them. No more came.

'It appears to be me that they're interested in,' Vespasian whispered. 'All the shots were aimed at me until I got behind cover; then they went for the slaves.' He looked at his two companions, pulled out his knife and began sawing on the leather straps that secured his stag to his dead mount. 'There only seems to be two of them, I suggest that I make a run for it in one direction and you two go the other way; with luck they'll go for me and you'll be able to get round behind them. What's your name?' he asked the hunting slave, a middle-aged man with curly jet-black hair and a Greek sigma branded on his forehead.

'Artebudz, master,' the slave replied.

'Well, Artebudz, have you ever killed a man?' The straps parted and the stag slithered to the ground. Another two arrows thumped into the horse.

'In my youth, master; before I was enslaved.'

'Kill one of the bastards out there today and you'll be a slave no more, I'll see to that.'

The slave nodded; a look of hope and determination crossed his face as he eased his hunting bow from its holder hanging from his belt. Vespasian patted him on the arm and then, grabbing the stag's forelegs, slid the creature over his back.

'On the count of three I'll lift the stag; as soon as they hit it run whilst they reload, all right?' His companions agreed. Vespasian tucked his right knee under his stomach ready to push off. 'Let's do it then – one, two, three!'

He raised the stag so that it emerged over the withers of the dead horse, immediately he felt the violent impact of two arrows striking the carcass almost simultaneously; he pushed down on his right leg heaving himself and the dead weight of the stag up and forward and, with a monumental effort, accelerated into a sprint towards a thick-trunked oak tree twenty paces away. Two fierce blows from behind made him stumble, but he kept his footing and felt no pain; the arrows had hit the stag that shielded his back. With cold air rasping at his throat from the intense exertion he reached the tree and dodged behind it to the vibrating report of two more shots burying themselves in its trunk.

Vespasian leaned his head back against the soft moss growing on the bark and sucked in lungfuls of winter air; the stag's head lolled on his shoulder like a new-found, drunken acquaintance expressing eternal friendship. He cautiously peered round towards the dead horse and the trees beyond; there was no sign of Magnus or Artebudz. He held his breath and listened; nothing moved. Realising that he had to keep the attackers occupied as his two comrades worked their way around into a favourable position, he eased the stag down, unslung his bow and notched an arrow. He dropped to his knees whilst working out, from the trajectory of the previous shots, the direction in which to aim. Satisfied with his estimation he took a deep breath and swung his bow around the trunk releasing his shot a moment before a single arrow passed a hand's breadth above his head. Vespasian smiled; they had split up, that would make matters a lot easier. Ten paces to his left was a fallen hulk of an oak, high enough to provide adequate cover. He notched another arrow; then, holding it securely across the bow grip with his left hand and lifting the stag with the right, he rose slowly to his feet keeping his back pressed against the tree.

A sharply curtailed cry came from the direction in which he had been aiming; then a shout.

'One left!'

It was Magnus. He knew that he could not now risk another wild shot for fear of hitting his friend. As their positions were known he had nothing to lose by shouting. 'Are they Romans or Thracians?'

'Neither, I've never seen one of these savages before; he's wearing fucking trousers,' Magnus replied.

'Let's hope they don't speak Latin then. Can you see the dead horse?'

'Just, it's about fifty paces ahead of me; you sound like you're to the left of it.'

'Careful then, you must be close to the other one. I'll make a move, he might show himself; keep down, I'll shoot at head height. Artebudz, watch out for any movement.'

Vespasian steeled himself for another quick burst of energy. He pushed the stag to his right, heard the sharp hiss and thud of another hit to the carcass, then leapt left towards the fallen tree, drawing and releasing his shot in one swift movement. He rolled head over heels through the undergrowth and made cover as an arrow embedded itself, juddering, in the trunk. An instant later came the faint but unmistakable sound of sudden and violent exhalation; someone had been hit.

'I got him, masters,' Artebudz shouted, his voice raised an octave in his excitement.

'Is he dead?' Magnus called.

There was a slight pause.

'He is now.'

'Thank fuck for that.'

Vespasian found Magnus and Artebudz standing over one of the bowmen's corpses.

Magnus wrinkled his nose as he approached. 'I can't believe we didn't smell them before they saw us, I've never smelt a savage as strong; they must have kept downwind of us.'

It was indeed a pungent aroma: a heady cocktail of all the major human male excretions, secretions and discharges that had been allowed to fester for years within clothes of semi-cured animal hide, which had probably never been removed since they were first donned; it was crowned with the acid stench of very old and ingrained horse sweat.

'What is he?' Vespasian asked recoiling, unable to believe his nose.

'No idea. Artebudz, have you ever seen one of these?'

'No master; but his beard's ginger and his cap seems to be Thracian in style.'

Vespasian studied the man's clothing; his cap was definitely Thracian in appearance, a leather skull-cap with long cheek flaps and neck protection, similar to those of the northern tribes in Moesia, as opposed the fox-fur hats of the southern tribes in Thracia itself. But this had crude depictions of horses embroidered in it with dyed twine and the cheek straps were tied under the chin. Apart from knee-length boots, the rest of his attire was definitely not Thracian: hide trousers, well worn on the inside thighs, suggesting a long time spent in the saddle, and a thigh-length leather top-coat worn over an undyed woollen tunic.

'Scythian perhaps,' Magnus ventured, picking up and examining the dead man's composite horn and wood bow.

'No, we've got one of them at home, they're darker and they've got strange eyes; this man looks normal. Well, we can't worry about it now, I need to get back to see my brother; we'll send Artebudz back with some slaves to pick them and our dead hunting slave up tomorrow.'

Artebudz grinned, enjoying the implication that he would soon be free.

Vespasian turned away. 'Let's find the horses.'

It was dark by the time they reached the permanent garrison camp just outside the gates of Philippopolis. Vespasian dismissed Artebudz back to the royal stables with a warning to say nothing of the day's events until he had spoken to the Queen, whose property he was. Returning the centurion of the watch's salute at the Praetorian Gate, he and Magnus rode as quickly as possible, without causing alarm, down the Via Praetoria, between the low brick-built barrack huts towards his more comfortable residence on the junction with Via Principalis. Such was his anxiety that he barely noticed the ill feeling and restlessness with which over a thousand soldiers were taking their evening meal washed down with the generous garrison wine ration that was supplemented with stronger stuff that they had bought locally. His thoughts were alternating between the reason for his brother's journey, how he would react to seeing him again after four years and why two outlandish-looking men had tried to kill him that afternoon.

'The lads seem tense this evening.' Magnus broke into his train of thought.

'What?'

'I've seen it before, sir, it can happen quite quickly; after a long time farting about doing a lot of bugger all on regular basis with nothing to show for it, the lads start to get edgy, and wonder what the fuck they're doing here and how much longer they're going to be stuck in this arsehole of a place. They're legionaries and they haven't had a decent fight for over three years, whereas the boys that went back to Moesia are getting plenty of action if half the rumours are true.'

Vespasian glanced around at the men sitting around braziers and saw more than a few of them glaring at him with resentful, sullen eyes over the top of their wine-filled cups. One or two of them even held his look, a minor act of insubordination that he would normally have dealt with then and there had he not been so preoccupied.

'I'll speak to Centurion Caelus in the morning and find out what's going on,' he said wearily, knowing full well that it was Caelus' duty to come to him and report any bad feeling amongst the two cohorts that he commanded. It was just another example of how Caelus sought to subtly undermine his authority.

Vespasian dismounted outside his quarters; it was the same construction as that of the men's but slightly larger and he was not obliged to share the two rooms inside with seven others.

'I'll get the horses stabled,' Magnus offered, taking the reins from him.

'Thank you, I'll see you later.' Vespasian took a deep breath and walked through the door.

'So, little brother, you're back from skulking about in the woods,' drawled the familiar voice with no trace of affection or even friendship. Sabinus was sprawled out on the dining couch; he had evidently made use of the officers' bath house as there was no sign of the dust and grime of travel about his appearance, and he was wearing a crisp, white, Equestrian toga over a clean tunic.

'I may be your younger brother but I ceased to be little when I joined the Eagles,' Vespasian snapped. 'And, furthermore, I do not, and never did, skulk.'

Sabinus raised himself to his feet; his dark eyes glinted in the dim light of a couple of oil lamps as they glared mockingly at his brother. 'Playing the big soldier are we? Next you'll be telling me that you don't fuck mules any more.'

'Look Sabinus, if you've come all this way to have a fight let's have it right now and then you can piss off back home again, otherwise try to remain civil and tell me what you've got to say.' Vespasian squared up to his brother, his fists clenched by his side. Sabinus smiled thinly at him. Vespasian noticed that he had put on a bit of weight – four years out of the army and living the good life in Rome had left its mark.

'Fair enough, little brother,' Sabinus said, sitting down on a camp stool, 'but old habits die hard. I'm not here to fight; I'm here on the Lady Antonia's business. Aren't you going to offer me a drink?'

'If you've finished insulting me, then yes.' Vespasian crossed to the far end of the room and took a pitcher from a cheaply constructed wooden chest standing next to the door leading through to the bedroom. He mixed a couple of cups of the rough, local wine with water and handed one to his brother. 'How are our parents?'

'They're both well, I have letters for you from them.'

'Letters?' Vespasian's eyes lit up.

'Yes. I've got one from Caenis too, you can read it later; but first you should clean up and get changed, we have to deliver a letter from Antonia to Queen Tryphaena. We've got a job to do and we need her help.'

'What sort of job?'

'One that will make rescuing Caenis seem like a pleasant stroll through the Gardens of Lucullus. Do you know a Thracian tribe called the Getae?'

'Never heard of them.'

'Well, I don't know much about them either except that they live outside the Empire across the Danuvius. They generally keep themselves busy fighting the tribes to their north but recently they've taken to crossing the river and raiding Moesia. The raids have been getting larger and more frequent in the last year or so and the Fifth Macedonica and the Fourth Scythica have been struggling to repel them; the Emperor has become concerned enough about the situation to reinstate Poppaeus Sabinus as Governor.'

'What are we supposed to do about it?' Vespasian asked, not liking the idea of going anywhere near Poppaeus again, knowing, as he did, that he was an ally of Sejanus.

'Antonia doesn't want us to do anything about the raids, they're no concern of hers; but what does interest her is a piece of intelligence that one of her agents in Moesia sent a few months back.'

'She's got agents in Moesia?'

'She's got agents everywhere. Anyway, this one reported the presence in the last three or four of the raids of someone with whom the good lady is keen to have a nice little chat with back in Rome.'

'And we've been asked to go and fetch him for her.'

Sabinus grinned. 'How did you guess?'

Vespasian had a sinking feeling in the pit of his belly. 'Who?' he asked, already suspecting the answer.

'Sejanus' go-between; the Thracian chief priest, Rhoteces.'

CHAPTER II

QUEEN TRYPHAENA PLACED Antonia's letter down on the polished oak table and looked at the two brothers; Vespasian, like Sabinus, wore a toga as it was a private meeting. They were sitting in her sumptuous, warmly lit study, part of her suite of private rooms deep within the palace complex and far away from the flapping ears of the numerous palace functionaries and slaves that infested the formal areas. Here only her secretary and body slave could come and go as they pleased; even her son, King Rhoemetalces, had to wait outside whilst one of the four sentries that constantly guarded the suite's only access sought permission granting him an audience. Because of his close ties with Antonia, Vespasian always found himself quickly welcomed into Tryphaena's presence.

'So my kinswoman has located the priest that would kill my son and me and rule Thracia in the gods' name,' she said, flicking her sharp, blue eyes between the brothers. 'And she requests that I help you capture him by providing men; which I am happy to do, but of how much use they will be against the Getae I don't know.'

'What do you mean, domina?' Vespasian asked, leaning forward on his lavishly cushioned chair in an attempt to get out of the way of the wafts of pungent incense emanating from a brazier close behind him.

'My people are mainly foot soldiers; only the moderately wealthy can afford horses so we have relatively few cavalry. The Getae however live on the grasslands to the north of the Danuvius where horses are plentiful; they fight almost exclusively on horseback; our cavalry would be no match for them and our infantry would never catch them. I could even, as the highest-ranking Roman citizen in Thracia and Rome's puppet ruler, order you to take the two cohorts stationed here but they would also be ineffective against such a mobile force; remember Carrhae, gentlemen?'

'Then we have to wait for them to come to us,' Sabinus said, recalling the strategy that had been employed to defeat the Numidian rebels when he had served with the VIIII Hispana in Africa. 'We go north and speak to Pomponius Labeo and find out where they've been raiding, then work out a likely target and wait for them to attack it; with luck the priest will be with them as he has been for the last few raids.'

Vespasian cast a scathing, sidelong glance at his brother. 'That seems a bit hit or miss.'

'You got any better ideas, little brother?' Sabinus retorted. 'Send them an invitation to the games and then back to yours for dinner after, I suppose?'

'Your brother is right Vespasian,' the Queen cut in before the argument got out of hand. 'It may take time but eventually you will get close to them, and then you will have to see what opportunities Fortuna presents you with.'

'I'm sorry, domina.' Vespasian felt chastened; his brother was right no matter how much it irked him. He quickly put his feelings to one side and expanded on Sabinus' idea. 'We will need men but not many; this would be better done with a half-dozen picked fighters. Stealth is the key if we can't match them in open battle.'

'Well done, little brother, you're catching on.'

'If stealth is the key, gentlemen, then may I suggest that harmony should be the watchword?'

The brothers looked at each other and with a slight nod of their heads called a silent truce.

'Good,' Tryphaena continued, 'that's agreed then. I shall get the captain of my guard to provide you with six of my best men, skilled in all weaponry, especially the bow as you will be up against the best archers that you have ever encountered.'

'But you said they were mainly cavalry,' Vespasian pointed out. 'Thracians don't use horse-archers.'

'This tribe does; they've taken on quite a few of the customs of their northern neighbours, the Sarmatians and the Scythians; they even wear trousers.'

Vespasian's eyes widened at the implication. 'Trousers? I think that I may have met a couple of them today.'

Tryphaena looked amused. 'Impossible, we've had no contact with the Getae since Rome took Moesia as a province over fifty years ago.'

Vespasian quickly related the events of the afternoon, taking care to emphasise Artebudz's role and the promise that he had made to him. When he had finished the Queen sat in silence for a while thinking.

'From your description of them they certainly seem to be Getic,' she affirmed. 'You're convinced that they were targeting you?'

'Without a doubt.'

'Then it would seem that our friend Rhoteces has not forgiven you for preventing him from killing my son and has sent some assassins after you as revenge.'

'Why's he waited nearly four years?'

'Once he fled to the Getae it would have taken him time to ingratiate himself with the tribal leaders; they don't have the same customs as we do and they'd have viewed him with deep suspicion.'

'So, assuming that he eventually persuaded the tribal leaders to send assassins, how did they know what my brother looks like?' Sabinus asked.

'I don't have the answer to that; but what I do know is that Rhoteces is a fanatic and he sees people who thwart his plans as corpses that have to be stepped over; so it won't end until one of you is dead, which will make your trip back to Rome with him very interesting indeed. But first you must capture him. You should leave tomorrow; the snow in the Haemus Mountains is receding and the Succi pass into Moesia has reopened. I will have your men outside the Roman camp at noon and I'll send a message to your commanding officer Prefect Paetus telling him that you will not be coming back.'

'We have every intention of coming back, domina,' Vespasian insisted.

'Yes I'm sure you have, but not through here. I cannot risk having that man in my kingdom again; many of my subjects see him as a hero who could save them from growing Roman encroachment into our affairs. If his presence in Thracia became known and I was seen to be helping you get him to Rome then we would have a very combustive situation which would have only one outcome: Rome would annex us after a lot of killing.'

'So what should we do with him?' Vespasian asked.

'Head for Tomi on the Euxine Sea; I will have my personal quinquireme waiting for you in the port from the beginning of May; its crew are completely loyal to me. They will have orders to stay there until you arrive and will take you directly to Ostia. I think that a month at sea with the priest chained in the hold will be far preferable to two months travelling overland having to watch him day and night, don't you, gentlemen?'

'You are very generous, domina,' Sabinus said, starting to feel a little easier about the mission now that the return trip would involve no more than a month of vomiting.

'I am generous, but am I generous enough to free my most expensive hunting slave, I wonder?' She smiled at Vespasian who reddened, realising that he had been free with someone else's property without knowing its value.

'I'll pay you for your loss, domina.'

'I doubt that you could afford Artebudz; he is worth a small fortune. Not only is he a most talented tracker but he's also the finest shot with a bow that I have ever seen, and it is because of that I will free him; but on the condition that he comes with you. Now, before I start to give away the rest of my kingdom tell me, Sabinus, how is Antonia's campaign against Sejanus proceeding? She only makes oblique references to it in her letters for fear of them being intercepted.'

Sabinus grimaced and shifted uncomfortably in his seat. 'Not well, domina. Sejanus has strengthened his position with the Emperor; he is now almost the only person with any access to him on Capreae. He has managed to convince Tiberius that it's his family that are plotting against him and not Sejanus himself. Just before I left Antonia's eldest grandson Nero Germanicus and his mother Agrippina were arrested and tried for treason on Sejanus' orders; she's been imprisoned on the island of Pandateria and he's been sent to the island of Pontiae. Antonia is now worried that her other two grandsons and prospective heirs to the Purple, Drusus and Caligula, will soon follow their mother and older brother. Sejanus is being very careful, just picking off his targets slowly and methodically.'

The Queen nodded her head whilst digesting the news. 'That's logical; for Sejanus to succeed he'll have to eliminate all of Tiberius' potential heirs who would be too old to warrant a regent; that surely is his route to power: to be made regent of a young emperor who would then tragically die leaving the Senate little alternative but to proclaim him Emperor or risk another period of civil war.'

Vespasian felt unease at the thought of his friend Caligula being the subject of Sejanus' machinations. 'What about Sejanus' letters to Poppaeus proving that they were in league? Even though they were destroyed, has she been able to use the threat that she might be in possession of them to coerce Poppaeus into changing his allegiances?'

Sabinus looked downcast. 'I'm afraid not. Poppaeus was worried for a while and I think he would have come around, but he called her bluff and asked her to produce them, which of course she couldn't. Then Asinius' surviving lictors disappeared and the truth about his death must have been tortured out of them because Poppaeus wrote to her saying that he knew for certain that she didn't have anything on him.'

Tryphaena thought for a moment and then shook her head. 'So Asinius died for nothing then; well, we must be sure that his death doesn't go unavenged.' She rose to her feet to indicate that the audience was at an end. 'Go now, my prayers will go with you.'

The brothers stood. 'Thank you, domina,' they said in unison.

'And I thank you, because if you succeed you will rid me of my greatest enemy as well as helping my kinswoman safeguard our family's position in Rome.' She embraced them in turn. 'Good luck, gentlemen. Get that priest to Antonia so that she can use him to bring down Sejanus.'

Vespasian's mind was racing as he walked with Sabinus through the dim, high-ceilinged corridors of the palace; their footsteps echoed off the marble walls. The prospect of action and relief from the ennui that plagued him was indeed welcome. He also relished the chance to avenge the death of Asinius, to whom he owed his position as a military tribune, by bringing to Rome the one man who could link the silver used to finance the Thracian rebellion to Sejanus' freedman Hasdro. Whether it would be enough to damn Sejanus in the Emperor's eyes he did not know, but if Antonia had requested it he felt sure that it would be worth the effort and risk. But how long would it take? He had been living in anticipation of going back to Rome and Caenis next month, but now he had to go in completely the opposite direction to find and capture a man whose whereabouts were, to say the least, obscure.

'Bugger it, I thought I'd be going home soon,' he muttered.

'You're going home tomorrow little brother,' Sabinus laughed. 'It's just that we're taking the long way.'

Vespasian did not share the joke. 'Yes, but this could take us half a year.'

'It had better not, I need to be in Rome for the elections; Antonia's managed to secure the Emperor's permission for me to be included on the list of prospective quaestors. With her backing I have a very good chance of being elected, especially as now the electorate is only the senate and not the tribal assembly.'

'Well, good for you,' Vespasian said gruffly; he found it hard to enthuse about his brothers successes.

'Thank you for that warm, fraternal speech of congratulations, little brother.'

'Stop calling me that.'

'Bollocks to you.'

'Sir, sir!' It was Magnus waiting at the palace entrance; two well-built, armoured palace guards blocked his path with spears.

'Magnus, what is it?'

'Bastards wouldn't let me in,' he replied, eyeing the two ginger-bearded guards.

'Careful Roman,' the larger of the two growled, he was at least a head taller than Magnus. 'Rome does not rule here.'

'Go piss in your mother's mouth, fox-fucker.'

The huge Thracian slammed the shaft of his spear towards Magnus' face; he ducked under it, hooked his right leg behind the guard's left and pulled, sending him crashing on to his arse.

'That's enough!' Vespasian leapt between them, pushing Magnus away from his adversary. 'Back off, Magnus.' He turned to the guard. 'We leave it there, I apologise on this man's behalf.'

Sabinus moved in front of the second guard who had raised his spear at Vespasian. The prostrate guard glanced quickly between the two brothers, gave Magnus a venomous look and slowly nodded; he knew better than to tangle with two Romans who had the look of men of authority.

Vespasian led Magnus away downhill across the torch-lit square in front of the palace. 'That was fucking stupid; you don't go around picking fights with palace guards.'

Magnus was unrepentant. 'Well, they should have let me through; it was urgent. Paetus sent me to get you as quickly as possible; it's getting a bit out of control at the camp.'

As they passed through the ancient gates of Philippopolis shouts and jeers could be clearly heard emanating from the Roman camp a half-mile away. Breaking into a run they covered the distance across the rough ground as quickly as was possible in the dim light of a half-moon. Magnus had been unable to tell the brothers the reason for the disturbance; all he knew was that there had been some fighting and then Paetus had received an angry deputation from the men. He now wanted to consult with Vespasian, as the tribune of the two cohorts of the IIII Scythica, before he replied.

There were no legionary guards at the Praetorian Gate, just the centurion of the watch who looked grimly at Vespasian as they approached.

'I don't know what's got into them, sir,' he said, saluting. 'It's been brewing all day since we found the bodies.'

'What bodies, Albinus?' Vespasian asked returning the salute.

'Three of our lads were found this morning in the woods, sir; they'd been missing for a couple of days. They were nastily cut up, been worked over with knives so I'm told; didn't see them myself though. Two of them are dead and the survivor's in a pretty bad way.'

'Thank you, centurion,' Vespasian said, passing through the gate on to the Via Praetoria, followed by Sabinus and Magnus.

The camp was speckled with large and small groups of legionaries arguing amongst themselves either in the pools of flickering torchlight or in the shadows between the barrack huts. Here and there fights had broken out which the hard-pressed centurions, aided by their seconds-in-command, the *optiones,* were having trouble stopping, but they seemed to still retain their authority and received no counter-blows as they waded into the knots of fighting legionaries, breaking them up with sharp cracks from their vine canes.

'At least discipline hasn't totally broken down,' Vespasian observed as he watched a centurion violently haul a grizzled-looking veteran off his bloodied younger opponent. The older man went to strike the centurion but then lowered his fist as he realised that there were no mitigating circumstances for striking a senior officer: the punishment was death.

'It's a fucking shambles,' Sabinus said derisively. 'What do you call good discipline in the Fourth Scythica if this isn't a total breakdown? This would have been a cause for decimation in the Ninth Hispana.'

Vespasian was not about to get into an argument about the relative merits of his and Sabinus' old legion. 'Shut it, Sabinus; if there is one thing that I need to do now it is to look dignified. I must find Paetus, you go with Magnus and wait in my quarters; this is a military matter and doesn't involve you.' He adjusted his toga over his left arm, crooked before him, and, with his head held high, started to walk slowly down the Via Praetoria, disdaining the chaos all around him. As he passed the various groups, the shouting and fighting gradually ceased as the legionaries noticed their tribune, haughty as a magistrate back in Rome, resolutely refusing to acknowledge them. The innate respect that they held for the authority of those of higher birth brought them back to their senses and they disengaged from their arguments and confrontations and began to follow Vespasian, in silence, towards the Principia at the centre of the camp.

Once there, the crowd that was already gathered outside parted for him and he ascended the few steps and passed between the columns that supported the portico. The two centurions guarding the garrison's headquarters from the angry mob snapped to attention with a jangling of phalerae and presented immaculate salutes. Vespasian responded then entered the building without looking back at the hundreds of men now congregated outside.

Publius Junius Caesennius Paetus rose from his chair behind the large desk at the far end of the room. 'Ah, tribune, good of you to come,' he exclaimed, beautifully enunciating each syllable with his clipped aristocratic tone. 'I do hope I didn't interrupt your evening with the Queen; your man said that you and your brother were visiting her.'

'No, sir, we met Magnus on our way out,' Vespasian replied, walking the twenty or so paces to the desk in the sputtering light of flaming sconces.

'Oh, good, good. I'm looking forward to meeting your brother, he served with the Ninth Hispana in Africa during the rebellion, I believe? My cousin was there as a tribune with the Third Augusta at the time; they had a tricky time of it. Perhaps you will both dine with me tomorrow?' Paetus said, sitting back down and gesturing to the chair on the other side of the desk. 'Please, make yourself comfortable, Vespasian.'

'Thank you, Paetus,' Vespasian said, following his superior's lead and dropping out of military formality.

'We've a bit of a delicate situation on our hands at the moment: the men aren't happy, they started fighting amongst themselves this evening, then later I had a deputation from them.

It is, as you know, their right to bring their grievances to their commanding officer.'

'Indeed. I noticed some discontent amongst them when I came back from hunting earlier,' Vespasian replied, trying to keep the provincial burr of his Sabine country accent to a minimum, as he always did when talking with this cultured patrician. 'What are their complaints?'

'Well the crux of the matter is that they're bored, but we all knew that. Hades, we're all bored, I'm bored witless stuck in this poxy place; but they at least get their annual leave, whereas the likes of you and I are here for the duration. I haven't seen my little Lucius since he was five, he's almost ten now. Nor have I been to the theatre or seen a wild beast hunt for over four years, and I love a good wild beast hunt as you know.'

'Yes, but boredom is no excuse for what was going on out there.'

'No, no, of course not; the ring leaders will have to be flogged then transferred to another cohort, and I'm afraid we've got to execute a couple of the chaps tomorrow morning for striking superior officers; they're in the guardhouse at the moment feeling pretty stupid, I should imagine. There's no need for that sort of behaviour.

'The trouble is that this morning we found three men who'd been tortured rather savagely; one's still alive, he's in the hospital, the doctor says he may live, though I don't think that I'd want to if I were him, but that's by the by. There were two other bodies found, incidentally, a couple of messengers; they looked to be imperial couriers but there was nothing on them to identify them so we'll never know. Anyway a lot the men want their revenge; you know, go and torch a few villages, lop off some limbs and rape any female under the age of sixty. I explained to them that that sort of thing is just not on any more since we put down the rebellion and most of them took the point. But then a few hotheads started going around saying that it wasn't fair that they were stuck here and their mates in the other eight cohorts are up in Moesia having a fine old time of it fighting off the incursions from the other side of the river.'

'I can see their point, but what can we do about it?'

'Ah, well, that was what the deputation was about. They want me to write to Governor Pomponius Labeo and ask him to rotate them back to Moesia and send another two cohorts to replace them. I have to say that I think it's not such a bad idea. I wanted to run it past you, as their tribune, before I spoke to them again; which I must do soon as they are still arguing amongst themselves. There's a hard core that won't take no for an answer and want to take matters into their own hands.'

'It is a good idea. The men are losing their sharpness after so much inactivity, so from a military point of view it makes sense; but the trouble is that my brother tells me that Poppaeus Sabinus is back in charge in Moesia, Pomponius is now just the legate of the Fourth Scythica again.'

Paetus screwed his face up; he and Poppaeus had never got on. 'Well, I'll write to Poppaeus then, the oily little new man.' Paetus looked at Vespasian apologetically. 'Sorry, dear chap, no offence meant.'

Vespasian smiled at him; although Paetus came from a very old and noble family of Etruscan origin that boasted many consuls, he had always treated Vespasian as an equal, at least in military terms. 'None taken, Paetus.'

'Quite; but it occurs to me that my relationship with Poppaeus won't make him keen to grant my request whereas if you write to Pomponius as a tribune of the Fourth Scythica, making a request of his legate, then it would be a purely internal matter within the legion and therefore nothing to do with Poppaeus.'

Vespasian realised that he should not keep his superior in the dark about his plans any longer. 'I can do better that that, Paetus, I can appeal to him in person on the men's behalf.'

'No need to go that far, my dear fellow.'

'I was going to wait until the Queen sent you a message making it official before I told you, but I've been asked to do something for her.' He told Paetus as much as he could without mentioning Antonia's name or whom he was searching for.

When he had finished Paetus leant forward on the desk and contemplated him, resting his steepled hands against his lips.

'There's more to this than you've told me,' he said after a while. 'Your brother arrives from Rome; you both rush off to see the Queen and then suddenly have to go to Moesia with a small party of the Queen's guard to intercept a Getic raiding party for reasons that you say you can't divulge and then you won't be coming back here. That's about the size of it, isn't it, Vespasian?'

'Yes,' Vespasian admitted, feeling that the whole affair must sound very suspicious.

'Well, I am no fool; I come from a family that has played politics for centuries and I'll fill in a couple of gaps for you, if I may. Firstly, Tryphaena is Marcus Antonius' great-granddaughter, and he, coincidentally, was also the father of Antonia, who was an ally of the late Consul Asinius, to whom you owe your posting, and whom you rushed off to see as soon as he arrived in Poppaeus' camp. You have never told me what you discussed with him and I have never asked you, but perhaps that is irrelevant as Asinius left very soon after and then died of fever on his way to his province, or so we are led to believe.' Paetus spread his hands and gave an incredulous look. 'However, the day Asinius left I found Poppaeus' secretary Kratos, some of Asinius' lictors, a few Praetorian guardsmen and another person, who seemed to have mislaid his head, all dead in the very tent that Asinius had been using; and then you went missing for two days and didn't return until Poppaeus had left for Rome.'

Vespasian shifted uncomfortably in his seat. He could see that Paetus was putting the pieces together, but as much as he liked and respected him he had no idea of where his political sympathies lay; to open up to him could be very dangerous indeed. Paetus sensed his unease, smiled and pressed on.

'Now, you weren't the only person who wasn't there; there was a particularly unpleasant weasely faced priest who was never seen again after that day, if I remember rightly.' Paetus paused and leant forward over the desk, looking directly into Vespasian's dark eyes. 'Now, if I told you that I know that the decapitated body in the tent was Sejanus' freedman Hasdro, whom I recognised from Rome, and if I also told you that I know that he and Poppaeus had dealings with the priest because I saw them together; and if I further told you that I know that Antonia is no friend to Sejanus, would you then like me to make an educated guess as to what you are involved in?'

'I think that it would be better not to, Paetus, for both our sakes,' Vespasian replied carefully. 'The facts as you've laid them out are correct, but I wouldn't like to be put into the position of having to, perhaps untruthfully, deny the accuracy of any possible conclusion that you may draw from them.'

Paetus nodded slowly. 'I see, well, perhaps it would be best if I keep my thoughts to myself. I will say one thing, though: if your brother has come here to see Tryphaena on Antonia's business and if that business has anything to do with the facts that I have just presented you with, I would be happy to aid you in any way I can because it would be furthering the interests of my family.'

'If those things were all true then I would gladly accept your help, Paetus,' Vespasian said, feeling mightily relieved.

'Good, well, that's as clear as it can be then.' Paetus clapped his hands and then rubbed them together. 'We will use this disturbance in the camp as a cover for you going north: we'll tell the men that you are going to appeal to Pomponius on their behalf and take the ringleaders to him for transfer. I'll provide you with a *turma* of my auxiliary cavalry to escort you over the Succi pass into Moesia.'

'Why do I need a cover story and an escort?' Vespasian asked, thinking that this was over-complicating matters.

'The cover story is because not all of our centurions think the way that, perhaps, we do. I know for a fact that certain people in Rome suspect either you or me of killing Hasdro and Kratos; you, because you disappeared for a while straight afterwards and me because I didn't report the killings.'

'Who knew that you knew about them?'

'Our very own centurion Caelus saw me come out of the tent and, as you may or may not know, he is Poppaeus' man through and through.'

'Ah!'

'Ah indeed. And I suspect that it is no coincidence that he is our senior centurion set here to watch over us and report our doings back to Poppaeus and his friend. If he reported that I let you go to Moesia with some of Tryphaena's soldiers it would look as if I was actively working against them and that is something that I wish to avoid, especially if you're successful and take back to Rome what I suspect. And you need an escort because I know for a fact that your life is in danger.'

Vespasian started. 'How did you know? Two men tried to kill me this afternoon, but the only people I've told are my brother and the Queen.'

'Two, eh?'

'Yes and they're both dead.'

'Well, I think you should come and talk to the poor chap in the hospital, but first let's address the men.'

Vespasian and Paetus stepped out of the Principia into the torch-washed camp. All the men of the two cohorts and the auxiliary ala were there waiting upon their commanders' decision; their steaming breath rose above them in the cold night air. An expectant hush fell over the crowd as Paetus, standing on top of the steps, opened his arms to them in a rhetorical gesture signifying unity.

'Men of the Thracian garrison,' he called in loud, high voice, pitched so that it carried to the rear ranks. 'You have come to me with a just grievance. It is shameful that we cannot avenge our comrades here in Thracia. However, I have consulted with your tribune and he has offered to personally ride to the legion's headquarters and put your case to the legate himself; he will beg the legate to relieve you so that you can have your vengeance in Moesia.'

A massive cheer went up.

'However,' Paetus continued over the noise, 'there have been acts of insubordination that cannot go unpunished for the good of morale. The two men guilty of striking senior officers will be executed in the morning.' The cheering petered out. 'It cannot be otherwise. And furthermore you will hand over the ringleaders for punishment; each will receive two dozen stokes of the cane and then, as it would be impossible for them to remain here with the taint of insubordination hanging over them, they will accompany the tribune to the legion's headquarters where they will be transferred to another cohort. This is the price you must pay for threatening mutiny and not first bringing your grievance to me in a dignified manner befitting soldiers of Rome. Rome will not tolerate rebelliousness in the ranks of her legions. If you do not accept these terms then you will have to kill me and your tribune and then you will be hunted men for the rest of your short lives. Raise your right hands if you agree.'

The legionaries fell to muttering amongst themselves; here and there a voice was raised but there was nothing like the tension that Vespasian had witnessed earlier. Gradually hands started to go up until eventually every man held his right hand aloft.

Paetus nodded. 'Very well, now give up your ringleaders. In a spirit of reconciliation, if they come forward on their own free will I will reduce the number of strokes to one dozen.'

At this there was some movement within the crowd and three men stepped forward. Amongst them Vespasian recognised the grizzled veteran he had seen earlier restraining himself from striking the centurion. The man brought himself to attention and addressed Paetus.

'Legionary Varinus of the second century, fifth cohort, begs permission to make a statement, sir.'

'Carry on, legionary,' Paetus replied.

'We three are the mess-mates of the two men in the guard-house and the three men found today. We take full responsibility for the disturbance which we started out of our natural desire to avenge our comrades and gladly submit ourselves to punishment. We would ask one thing: clemency for our two mates under sentence of death, sir.'

'That is impossible, Varinus. Both men hit an officer; they must die.'

From the faces of the legionaries Vespasian could see that if this sentence was carried out it would leave a residue of discontent amongst the men. He leant over to Paetus and whispered urgently in his ear. Paetus' face lit up; he too wanted a way out of this impasse. He nodded at Vespasian who turned and addressed the crowd.

'Prefect Paetus agrees with me that as it was dark when these offences took place there may be a case of mistaken identity; it may be that just one man committed both offences. Seeing as we cannot be sure which man is guilty they should draw lots: the loser will be executed, the winner will receive the same punishment as the rest of the ringleaders. There will be no further negotiation on this matter.'

Varinus and his two mates snapped a salute.

'Centurion Caelus,' Paetus called, 'have them taken away; punishment will be tomorrow at the second hour. Dismiss the men.'

A square-jawed centurion in his mid-thirties stepped forward, resplendent in his traverse white horsehair plumed helmet and numerous phalerae that glinted in the torchlight.

'Sir, before the men are dismissed I wish to make a suggestion.'

Paetus rolled his eyes, he was beginning to think that this meeting would never end, but he was obliged to hear what his senior centurion and acting prefect of the camp had to say. 'Yes, centurion.'

Caelus turned his cold, suspicious eyes on Vespasian. 'I applaud the tribune's offer to intercede on the men's behalf with the legate; however, I think that weight would be added to that appeal if a member of the centurionate were with him.' There was a murmur of agreement from the crowd. 'And it would be appropriate if, as the most senior in the garrison, I were that centurion.'

The murmur turned to cheers then to chants of 'Caelus'. Paetus turned to Vespasian and smiled apologetically. 'I'm sorry, old chap, we've been outmanoeuvred, it appears that you have an unwelcome guest in your party,' he said quietly, then he raised his voice: 'I agree; the centurion will accompany your tribune.' With that he turned and walked down the side steps of the Principia towards the hospital. As Vespasian followed he glanced at Caelus, who gave him a thin smile filled with latent animosity.

*

'It would seem that the centurion means to keep an eye on you,' Paetus observed as they walked across the dimly lit parade ground behind the Principia towards the hospital situated on the other side.

'Yes, something has made him suspicious,' Vespasian replied, 'but it's pointless worrying about it now, I'm stuck with him. The more pressing questions are how I'm going to explain the presence of six of the Queen's men in the expedition and how I'm going to give Caelus the slip once I've spoken to Pomponius.'

'The answer to the first is easy, you just say that they are carrying a message from Tryphaena to Pomponius and are taking advantage of your numbers for protection on the journey. The answer to the second is a little trickier.' Paetus looked meaningfully at Vespasian.

'I'll have to kill him?'

'In all probability, yes; unless of course you want Poppaeus to know where you're going and what you're doing.' Paetus passed through the hospital door; Vespasian followed, realising that he was right.

Inside the smell of rotting flesh and stale blood assailed their nostrils. Paetus called to a slave mopping down the floor. 'Go and fetch the doctor.' The slave bowed briefly then scuttled off.

The doctor arrived without much delay. 'Good evening, sir, how can I be of service?' His accent showed that he was Greek, as were most army doctors in the East.

'Take us to see the man brought in this afternoon, Hesiod.'

'He is sleeping, sir.'

'Well, wake him up then; we need to speak with him.'

Grudgingly the doctor nodded and, picking up an oil lamp, led them off. They passed through a ward of twenty beds, most of them occupied, and on through a door at the end into a dark corridor with three doors down one side. The smell was more intense here. The doctor paused at the first door. 'The putrefaction of the flesh has grown worse since you last saw him, sir. I now don't think that he will live.'

'I don't think he wants to anyway,' Paetus said, following the doctor through the door.

Vespasian almost gagged as he entered; the sickly-sweet, cloying smell of decaying flesh was overpowering. The doctor raised his lamp and Vespasian could see why the man would have no further interest in life. His nose and ears had been severed, the wounds covered by a blood-spotted bandage wrapped around his face. The palms of his hands were likewise bandaged, but just the palms, his fingers and thumbs were all missing and, judging by the bloody dressing on his groin, they were not the only appendages that he had lost. He woke as the light fell on his face and looked up at the visitors with desperate pleading eyes.

'Help me die, sir,' he croaked. 'I cannot hold a sword with these hands.'

Paetus looked at the doctor who shrugged. 'Very well, legionary,' he said, 'but first I want you to tell the tribune what you told me earlier.'

The legionary looked at Vespasian with sorrowful eyes; he couldn't have been more than eighteen. 'They were waiting for us in the woods, sir.' His words came slowly with shallow breaths. 'We killed two of them before we were overpowered. They looked like Thracians, but their language was different to what they speak here and they wore trousers.' His voice grew thinner as he spoke; the doctor held a cup of water to his mouth and he drank greedily. 'They started with Postumus first, they bound his mouth to stop him screaming and then went to work on him with their knives – slowly; he'd been badly wounded in the ambush and so didn't last long. One of them spoke Greek and told us that was what would happen to us if we didn't co-operate. My mate told them to go fuck themselves; that pissed them off and they cut him up worse than Postumus. I was terri-fied by this time, sir, and after they cut me a few times I said that I would help them. I'm sorry.'

'What did they want?' Vespasian asked.

'They wanted me to identify you when you came out of the camp, sir. We waited for a couple of days, and then you came out this morning with two slaves to go hunting. I'm sorry to say that

I was relieved, I thought that they would leave me alone. But they called me a coward for betraying my people and two of them did this to me while the other two followed you.'

'There were four?' Vespasian glanced over to Paetus who raised his eyebrows.

'Yes, sir. Now finish it.'

Paetus drew his sword. 'What's your name, legionary?'

'Decimus Falens, sir.'

He placed the tip of the sword under his lower left rib. 'Leave this life in peace, Decimus Falens, you will be remembered.' He cupped the man's head in his left hand and thrust his sword up under his ribcage and into his heart. Falens spasmed violently, his eyes bulging with pain, then, as the life fled out of him, he looked at Paetus with relief.

CHAPTER III

THE MEN OF the second and fifth cohorts of the IIII Scythica snapped to attention in front of a wooden block and four seven-foot-high posts. The high-pitched call of the signal horn, the *bucina*, echoed around the parade ground. Vespasian stood next to Paetus on a dais, surveying, with tired eyes, the rigid lines of legionaries. He had not slept well; his mind had raced all night. After leaving the hospital he had joined Sabinus and Magnus in his quarters and told them what had transpired during the evening. Paetus' offer of a turma of thirty cavalry to escort them to Pomponius' camp had cheered them slightly but neither had been pleased with the prospect of having Poppaeus' man accompany them or by the fact that there were two more Getae out there with their bows aimed at them. Their complaints, however, fell on deaf ears as Vespasian turned his attention to the letters that Sabinus had brought. The two from his parents contained nothing more than news of the estates from his father and a stream of advice from his mother, but Caenis' words of love and longing made his heart leap.

The horn rang out again, bringing Vespasian back to the business of the morning. Five men were led out of the guardhouse next to the hospital, and paraded before the cohorts; they were halted by their guards in front of the posts and the block. They wore only their sandals and their russet tunics, humiliatingly unbelted, like a woman's.

'Centurion Caelus,' Paetus called out, 'prepare the prisoners for punishment.'

'Prisoners, attention!' Caelus barked. The men jerked rigid. 'Prisoners to draw lots, step forward.'

Two of the five stepped out of the line. Caelus raised his fist; it held two straws. 'Whoever draws the short straw will be seen as being guilty of striking both officers and will receive sentence from the garrison commander, the drawer of the long straw will receive a dozen strokes of the cane with the others. Now choose.'

The two hapless men, both in their early twenties, looked at each other and swallowed hard. Together they reached forward and plucked a straw each from Caelus' hand. Vespasian could easily tell the loser, his head dropped and his shoulders sagged, whereas the other man stood bolt upright, his chest heaving as he hyperventilated with relief. No one has ever been so pleased to receive a beating before, Vespasian mused to himself.

'Prefect Paetus,' Caelus shouted, 'this man is guilty. What is your sentence?'

'Death,' Paetus replied simply.

The speed at which the sentence was carried out surprised Vespasian. The man was brought forward to the block and made to kneel in front of it with his hands resting on it. He voluntarily bowed his head and then tensed his arms against the block, knowing that to get a quick, clean death he needed to hold his body firm. One of the guards stepped up next to him, his sword already drawn, and with a quick, vigorous downwards blow struck off the man's head. His body fell forward and slumped over the block, spewing forth a powerful fountain of blood.

The men of the second and fifth cohorts stood in silence, eyes fixed on their dead comrade as his head was quickly collected and carried away along with his body.

'Prisoners to the posts,' Caelus barked again, tapping his vine cane against his legs. The four remaining men stepped up to the posts and held their hands together above their heads; they had witnessed many a beating and knew the drill. Guards secured their wrists with the leather straps and then tore the tunics from their backs, leaving them in only their loincloths. Brandishing thick vine canes, the mark of their rank, Caelus and three of his brother centurions took positions to the left of each of the men.

'One dozen stokes on my mark,' Caelus shouted. 'One!'

In unison the four sturdy canes thumped down across the

men's shoulders, causing them to tense every muscle in their bodies and exhale with loud grunts.

'Two!'

Again the canes flashed through the air, this time hitting just below the welts made by the first contacts. Vespasian could see that these centurions knew their business as they worked each stroke lower so as not to hit the same place each time and risk breaking bones; the object was to punish, not to incapacitate; had the offence required that, the whip would have been used.

By the eighth stroke blood was beginning to run down three of the men's arms from where the leather straps had eaten into the flesh around their wrists. Only Varinus had managed to avoid this. Vespasian realised that he must be an old hand at being beaten and had learnt not to pull down with his arms at each stroke. He wondered idly if the veteran had passed on this tip to his younger mates; if he had they clearly were not able to show the same self-control as he and were suffering more than necessary because of it.

'Ten!'

The four canes cracked on to the men's buttocks with such force that one, Caelus', snapped in two; the broken end flew through the air and hit the officers' dais with a loud report.

'Get me another,' Caelus roared.

In the ensuing short hiatus Paetus leant over to Vespasian and whispered with a wry grin, 'He should be careful how he asks for a new cane, don't you think?'

Vespasian smiled at the allusion to the centurion Lucilius, known to his men as 'Bring me another' because of the amount of canes he had broken over their backs; he had been one of the first officers murdered when the Pannonian legions mutinied on Tiberius' ascension.

The final two strokes were administered and the men cut down. To Vespasian's relief, all were able to walk away; he would have hated to have been obliged to delay his departure whilst waiting for one or more of them to recuperate; but the centurions had done their job with such expertise that all four of them would be able to ride, if somewhat painfully, in the afternoon.

'Legionaries, punishment is over,' Paetus called out. 'In future bring your grievances directly to me without threatening the discipline of the garrison first. Centurion Caelus, dismiss the men.' He turned and stepped down from the dais. Vespasian followed.

'Well, I'm glad that's over,' Paetus said as they walked towards the Principia. 'I don't mind having to execute men, but when it's due to their frustration at being unable to avenge their mates it leaves a bad taste in the mouth; thank you for seeing a face-saving way of sparing one. I thought the others took their beatings well. Mention that to Pomponius, will you, old chap; they seem to be close comrades and he will split them up, I'm sure, but if he knows that they've taken their punishment like soldiers he might put them in different *contubernia* in the same century.'

'I will, sir,' Vespasian replied, 'when I find him. Do we know where the Fourth Scythica is at the moment?'

'I was sending my despatches to Oescus on the Danuvius before the snows closed the pass. Tinos, the decurion of your escorting turma, has been there a few times; he knows the way.'

'Well, we'll go there first; if they're not there then someone will know where they've headed. Thank you for your help, Paetus.'

'Don't mention it, I'm doing it because I believe that what Antonia has asked of you will be in my family's and Rome's best interests; I hope that I'm not mistaken.'

'You're not; if I'm successful it will be to the benefit of all the families in Rome who have an interest in preserving legitimate government.'

'Let's hope so, eh? I'll say goodbye, then,' Paetus said, clasping Vespasian's forearm. 'I'll have your things sent with mine when I return home in a couple of months, once my replacement arrives. Good luck, see you in Rome.' He turned and walked briskly up the steps of the Principia.

Vespasian called, 'I'm sorry that my brother and I are unable to join you for dinner this evening – a prior engagement, I'm afraid.'

'My dining facilities are far superior at home, we'll have dinner there,' Paetus said as he disappeared into the building, leaving Vespasian wondering whether he had a friend in Paetus or just an ally of convenience.

At noon Vespasian, Sabinus and Magnus rode out of the camp to rendezvous with Queen Tryphaena's men. The three hills of the ancient city of Philippopolis loomed in front of them under a rain-laden sky as they approached the group waiting on their horses a few hundred paces from the gates.

Magnus let out a groan. 'I could have had money on it; the one fucking Thracian that I've had a fight with all year is coming with us.'

In amongst the group, next to Artebudz, Vespasian could see the two palace guards from the previous evening; the huge one glared malevolently at Magnus and then whispered something to his mate, who grinned and nodded in agreement.

'That'll teach you to be more polite to the locals,' Vespasian chuckled, 'especially the big, hairy-arsed ones.'

'You had better pray to whichever god you hold dearest that he doesn't decide to make you his vixen,' Sabinus advised.

'Very amusing,' Magnus snapped.

'Yes, I thought so too,' Vespasian said, pulling his horse up in front of the Thracians. He studied them for a short while. Next to the two guards were three other Thracians sporting thick black beards; they all wore the fox-fur caps favoured by the southern tribes and heavy cloaks against the chill, late-winter air. Each man had a short, recurved wood and horn bow in a holder attached to his saddle next to a full quiver of arrows. Swords hung from their belts and, protruding over their shoulders, Vespasian saw the handles of their lethal curved swords called *rhomphaiai* resting in scabbards strapped to their backs.

Artebudz pushed his horse forward and bowed his head. 'Thank you for gaining me my freedom, master.'

'You deserved it but I'm not your master; you will address me as sir, and that goes for all of you.' Vespasian looked at each man in turn. 'I am Tribune Vespasian; your Queen has seconded you to me and that means that you are under military discipline, is that clear?' The men nodded their agreement. 'Good. I take it that you all speak Greek?' Again the men nodded. 'We will be travelling north to Moesia with some auxiliary cavalry and a few legionaries. You are not to talk to them; as far as they're concerned you are on the Queen's business. Once there we will be looking for the chief priest Rhoteces; I intend to capture him and take him to Tomi and from there take him in a ship back to Rome. Do any of you have a problem with that?'

The huge ginger-bearded guard spat on the ground. 'Fucking priest,' he growled.

The other Thracians also spat and murmured oaths to the same effect.

'Well, that's something that we can all agree on,' Magnus said in a conciliatory manner.

The huge guard glared at him. 'I'm not finished with you, Roman; *that's* something that we can both agree on.'

'Enough!' Vespasian shouted. 'There will be no fighting amongst ourselves; any arguments that you may have you leave here.' He glowered at the guard. 'What's your name, soldier?'

'Sitalces,' he replied gruffly.

'Sitalces, sir!' Vespasian barked.

'Sitalces, sir.'

'That's better. Now, Sitalces, if we are to get out of this alive we need to work as a unit and little squabbles aren't going to make that easier. Yes, Magnus may have dropped you on your arse yesterday but I will not have a small incident like that threaten our unity, so live with it, is that understood?'

Sitalces looked from Vespasian to Magnus and scratched his thick, ginger beard. 'Yes, sir, I will live with it,' he said finally. 'Until this is over,' he added.

'Good.' Vespasian left it there knowing that that was the best that he would get out of the man; to push him any further would make him lose face in front of his mates. 'Wait here whilst we collect our escort.' Vespasian pulled his horse around and the three Romans galloped back to the camp.

'You're going to have to look out for your new friend, Magnus,' Vespasian said as they slowed to go through the gates.

'Don't worry, sir, I've dropped bigger ones than him,' Magnus replied cheerfully. 'You could always send him back, though.'

'I thought about that but the others may resent it, and besides, he looks like he'd be useful in a close fight.'

'So long as he stays on his feet,' Sabinus added with a laugh.

They arrived at the horse-lines to find their escort saddled up and mounting. A tall officer in his mid-thirties with a thin, suntanned face and short curly black hair walked up to them as they approached.

'Decurion Tinos of the auxiliary Illyrian cavalry reporting, sir,' he said, saluting Vespasian. His accent showed that Latin was not his first language.

'Are your men ready to move out, decurion?' Vespasian asked, dismounting.

'Yes, sir.'

'Good; have you seen Centurion Caelus?'

'I'm right here,' a voice came from behind him.

Vespasian spun round to see Caelus marching Varinus and his three mates towards him; all had kit bags over their shoulders.

'Detail, halt!' Caelus barked. The legionaries came to a smart stop. Vespasian noticed a couple of them wince with pain; the three younger ones had the wounds on their wrists bound with clean bandages. 'Take a horse each,' Caelus continued, 'strap on your kit bags and mount up.' The men hurried to do as they were told. In a deliberate slight to Vespasian's authority Caelus turned away to get himself a horse without reporting to the senior officer.

'Centurion!' Vespasian shouted.

Caelus stopped and turned to face him slowly.

'Centurion, come here.' Vespasian pointed to the ground in front of him. Caelus' cold eyes looked around quickly. The men were all busy with their horses but Tinos, Sabinus and Magnus were watching him and he could not afford a display of insubordination in front of witnesses. He sauntered over to Vespasian.

'Report, centurion,' Vespasian said in a quieter tone, fixing Caelus' eyes with a hard stare.

'Centurion Caelus—'

'At attention, centurion.'

Caelus came to reluctant attention, hatred burning in his eyes. 'Centurion Caelus reporting with the four legionaries being transferred away from the garrison.'

'I didn't hear the word "sir" in that sentence.'

'That's because it wasn't there,' Caelus said in a whisper that only Vespasian could hear.

Vespasian brought his face forward close to Caelus' and spoke quietly and quickly. 'Listen to me, centurion, you may have more years of service than me, but I am still the senior officer. If you show me disrespect again I shall have you busted back down to a common legionary. I'm watching you, is that understood?'

Caelus gave a cold smile. 'Oh, I understand all right, it's you that doesn't. You couldn't bust me, I'm protected by people in high places; in fact it's me that's watching you.' He stepped back and saluted as if he had been dismissed. 'Sir!' he bellowed so all could hear as he turned on his heel and marched smartly away, leaving Vespasian fuming and feeling impotent.

'That didn't seem to go too well,' Sabinus observed dryly.

Vespasian turned and glared at his brother with such intensity that Sabinus decided not to pursue any more sarcastic remarks and walked his horse away towards the little column of cavalry that was now almost ready to depart.

'We're going to have to watch Caelus too, sir,' Magnus said as Vespasian remounted. 'If he tries to undermine you in front of the men we could have trouble.'

'I doubt Varinus and his mates bear him any love, they've just felt his cane on their backs. Perhaps you should become matey with them and I'll cultivate Tinos; that way we'll isolate Caelus, then we'll just have to find a way of losing him.'

'I can think of a sure-fire way of losing him,' Magnus said seriously.

'That's what Paetus suggested.'

Magnus raised his eyebrows. 'That's a novelty, a garrison commander suggesting ways of losing a centurion.'

'Well, let's hope that it doesn't come to that,' Vespasian said, kicking his horse forward towards the head of the column. 'I can imagine that Caelus would be a hard man to lose.'

Artebudz and the Thracians joined the rear of the small, double-filed column as it clattered out of the gates at a canter and headed along the newly paved road northwest towards the pass that led into Moesia. Caelus looked back at them suspiciously as they took their place behind the four spare mounts.

'What in Hades are those fox-fuckers doing?' he snarled.

Vespasian knew that the question had been directed at him but did not deign to answer as Caelus, again, had not addressed him as 'sir'.

'Messengers to Moesia from the Queen coming along for the ride,' Tinos replied, having been forewarned by Vespasian of their arrival and seen nothing out of the ordinary in it. 'They often come with us when we go north with despatches; safety in numbers, you see.'

Caelus grunted and let the subject drop. Vespasian smiled inwardly, thanking Paetus for his simple ruse. He turned to Tinos next to him. 'Decurion, send a four-man scouting party a mile ahead on either side of the road and tell them to send a report back every hour.'

The decurion looked at him quizzically, unused to taking such precautions in the now peaceful client kingdom of Thracia.

'Do it,' Vespasian ordered, 'and tell them to keep a sharp lookout.'

'Yes, sir,' Tinos replied, peeling away back down the column to give the orders. A few moments later a *lituus*, a long, straight cavalry horn with an upturned bell end, shrieked a series of high notes and eight troopers galloped past the column and off into the distance towards the looming snow-covered, cloud-ridden massifs of the Haemus to the north and the Rhodope to the west.

Magnus fell back to get himself acquainted with Varinus and his mates whilst Vespasian settled down to the ride, making pleasant conversation with Tinos as the road started to gently climb through familiar rough country. After the first hour of brisk riding two of the scouts returned within moments of each other; both briefly reported nothing moving in the surrounding area before galloping off again to rejoin their respective units. The rain that had been threatening all day finally started to fall lightly; Vespasian pulled his cloak tight around his shoulders and dropped back next to his brother.

'You did well to spot the discrepancy between the amount of silver bullion at the mint and the amount of denarii minted,' he said referring to Sabinus' part in uncovering how Sejanus had utilised Poppaeus' silver to strike the coinage that he had used to encourage the Thracian rebellion. He had been the junior magistrate overseeing the striking of silver and bronze coinage at the time.

Sabinus looked at his brother, surprised; he had never received a compliment from him before, which was not surprising as he had never paid Vespasian one. 'I suppose you want me to compliment you on the thorough way you taught me accountancy,' he replied suspiciously.

'Not necessarily, although you've just implied a compliment by using the word "thorough", so thank you.'

'Hmph, well, thank you too,' Sabinus grunted grudgingly. He turned his head away and hunched his body against the intensifying rain.

They rode on in silence for a while, Vespasian casting the odd sidelong glance at his brother, who resolutely refused to acknowledge him. He smiled to himself, amused by the unintentional compliment that Sabinus had paid him and how it was quite obviously irking him.

'What have you been doing in Rome since you finished your year with the Vigintiviri?' Vespasian eventually asked conversationally.

Sabinus frowned. 'What's it to you?'

'I'm interested; you are my brother, after all.'

'If you must know, little brother, I've been cultivating people to secure me votes in the quaestor elections this year.'

'It can't have been just arse-licking surely?' Vespasian wiped away the drops of rain that dripped from his red-plumed helmet.

'Of course it was; that's how it works, and the bigger the arse the harder I lick it. Your fellow tribune in the Fourth Scythica, Corbulo, for example, he was a quaestor last year and is now in the Senate, his arse has been well and truly licked.'

'You know Corbulo?'

'Don't sound so surprised, it's down to you that his arse was put my way for a good licking.'

'How so?' Vespasian was intrigued.

Sabinus grinned. 'Uncle Gaius knows his father; they were praetors in the same year and didn't tread on each other's toes and so remain on good terms. When Corbulo came home two years ago his father invited Gaius and I to dinner as a thank you from one family to another.'

'What for?'

'Well, little brother, it seems that Corbulo thinks that he's got you to be grateful to for saving his life; something about a strange talisman that you were wearing getting you freed from a Thracian camp just as you were being forced to fight to the death. I didn't quite understand it all, but he seemed convinced that the gods saved you to fulfil your destiny.' Sabinus gave his brother an appraising look, adding, 'Whatever that may be.'

'Well, if he's grateful he never made it obvious to me.'

'That's because he's an arrogant arsehole and would have thought that thanking you would put him in your debt, which it would. His father, on the other hand, has always been a more honourable man and has made it clear that he will do anything to help us because of the a debt of gratitude that he feels his family owes ours. That means he's lobbying for me to become a quaestor and therefore enter the Senate, so you can just imagine how enthusiastically Uncle Gaius and I licked his arse. For once you have been some use to the family, little brother.'

'And you'll be the beneficiary,' Vespasian said with more than a hint of bitterness in his voice.

Sabinus beamed smugly at his brother and nodded. 'As the older brother that is only right and proper, but don't worry, it's not just me who'll benefit; Corbulo also told us about a conversation that he had when he got back to Moesia with a centurion named Faustus whom I believe was with you that day in the Thracian camp.'

'What about?'

Sabinus looked over his shoulder to where Caelus was to make sure that he was out of earshot. 'About Poppaeus,' he said lowering his voice.

'Ah, I see. I had to confide in Faustus in order to get help. I knew that he wouldn't be at all happy to find out that Poppaeus had tried to kill us and the whole relief column for his and Sejanus' political ends; so he told Corbulo?'

'Yes, and Corbulo and his father told us, not knowing that we already knew because Tryphaena and Rhoemetalces had written to Antonia.'

'So?'

'Don't be so obtuse, little brother; they want revenge on Poppaeus and, because your life had also been threatened by his schemes, assumed, correctly, that we would also be looking for revenge. They were offering an alliance of families; so we took them to see Antonia, and Corbulo agreed to come with us when we take the priest to Tiberius. He'll testify before him that Poppaeus wanted the discovery of the Thracian's chest of denarii kept secret when he should have reported it to the Emperor and the Senate.'

Vespasian looked aghast at his brother. 'What? We're to take Rhoteces to Capreae? You never said anything about that to me.'

'Well, someone's got to do it, the Emperor's only going to believe the priest if he's submitted to torture in front of him; and you will have to give your evidence along with Corbulo. Anyway, what difference would it have made if you had known, you'd still be here, wouldn't you?'

Vespasian nodded slowly. He had not guessed that the priest would have to go before the most powerful man in the world, but his brother was right, it would not have changed his mind even if he had; he would still do it.

The rain had become a steady downpour, obscuring the mountain ranges to the left and right. A solitary scout appeared out of the torrent from the west. Vespasian pushed his horse forward to come level with Tinos so that he could hear the man's report, which was again happily negative. As the scout headed off again Vespasian turned his eyes to the north; there was no sign of the other scout. They travelled on another half-mile and still no one had come to report from the north. A sense of foreboding fell over Vespasian. He glanced over to Tinos, who shrugged, sharing his unease. A guttural shout came from up ahead. Tinos raised his hand and halted the column. The shapes of four approaching horses, just visible two hundred paces away through the rain, caused them both to relax momentarily. They kicked their mounts forward towards the returning scouts, but upon drawing closer it became apparent that only one of the horses' riders was upright in the saddle; the other three lay across their mounts, the arrows protruding from them told, only too vividly, of what had happened. Vespasian looked at the surviving scout; watered-down blood dripped off his face and covered his tunic, the broken stub of an arrow shaft jutted out of his right shoulder; he stared back at Vespasian with a terror bordering on madness in his eyes.

'Where did this happen?' Vespasian asked urgently.

The man rolled his maddened eyes and pushed his head forward making a hideous gurgling sound, a parody of speech. A welter of blood spewed from his mouth; his tongue had been cut out.

CHAPTER IIII

THE RAIN HAD not let up for two days and nights and had now turned into a thick, slushy sleet. The column had started to ascend the winding road that led up to the Succi Pass over a thousand feet above them. The men's morale was not good; apart from being soaked and chilled to the bone the spectre of unseen killers lurking close by unsettled them as much as had the mutilation of their comrade. The scout had been able to tell them very little as he could not write; however, he could nod and was able to confirm, before he died from blood loss, that there had been only two attackers, they had both been mounted and that they had indeed been wearing trousers. Vespasian had recalled the other scouts, deciding that it was pointless risking any more men to locate an enemy that could so easily kill twice their number from a distance. He had thought about sending out his Thracians but their lives were more valuable to him than those of the Illyrian auxiliaries – whom he wished were horse-archers to match these ethereal hunters, even though to his way of thinking that method of fighting seemed dishonourable. He reasoned, however, that if the Getae were still tracking the column they would no doubt show themselves sooner or later and then safety would lie in speed of reaction and in numbers; but it was nonetheless a humiliation that just two men could strike such fear into a column of over forty.

As they climbed higher the sleet thickened into snow and the column was forced to slow to a walk to protect their horses from laming themselves on unseen rocks beneath the rapidly thickening white carpet. Vespasian brushed away the snow that had settled uncomfortably in his lap and turned to Magnus, who rode, head bowed, next to him and asked: 'How have you been getting on with our four legionaries?'

'They're a good bunch of lads. It turns out that Lucius – the one who drew the long straw and is fucking lucky to be here and knows it's down to you that he is – well, he used to be a stable lad for the Greens back in Rome before he signed up. He still has a lot of contacts with them and has promised me some introductions when he gets back to Rome, could be very useful for tips and suchlike before the race days, then I can get advance bets down at better odds than you get at the track.'

Vespasian smiled despite the pain it caused his cracked and chapped lips. 'He sounds like a useful friend to have,' he replied with more than a hint of sarcasm, 'if you're intent on wasting your money gambling.'

'Yeah, well, you wouldn't understand, would you? I don't think that I've ever seen the inside of your purse. Anyway, suffice it to say that he knows that he owes you, as do Varinus and the two other lads, Arruns and Mettius. None of them bear any love for Caelus, so if it comes to a confrontation they'll be with you.'

'That's good to know, although our friend seems to be keeping himself to himself.'

Magnus looked back to Caelus, who was shrouded in his cloak and hunched over his horse. 'Perhaps the weather has taken the fight out of the centurion.'

'I doubt it, but for the moment it's certainly taken the centurion out of the fight.'

By the time they had reached the entrance to the pass the snow was falling thick and fast. Their misery was compounded by a howling northwesterly gale that was funnelled down its length creating blizzard conditions. Vespasian paused the column and leant across to Tinos beside him. 'What do you think, decurion?' he shouted, trying to make himself heard above the roaring wind. 'Do we pull back and find some shelter in the lee of the mountains and wait for it to die down, or should we press on?'

'This could carry on for a couple of hours or a couple of days,' Tinos shouted back. His eyelashes and nostrils were covered with small icicles. 'If we wait we could get snowed in and in all likelihood be frozen to death; we either go all the way back down or we have to press on. The pass is only five miles long; with luck we could make it through in less than two hours.'

Vespasian cupped his purpled hands to his mouth and blew into them as he looked ahead into the teeth of the blizzard; it was almost a total white-out, but he knew that the pass was straight and never more than thirty paces wide so they would not get lost. He made his decision. Tinos was right; it was just a question of keeping going. 'We go on,' he ordered. Tinos nodded and moved off.

Vespasian urged his reluctant horse follow with a couple of sharp kicks. Its ears flattened back in displeasure but after a few more kicks it begrudgingly consented to move forward.

After a few hundred paces of unremitting freezing torture he became aware of a rider trying to catch up with him. He turned in the saddle; it was Caelus.

'This is madness,' the snow-covered centurion shouted. 'We should turn back now.'

'You can if you want to, centurion, but we're going on.'

Caelus had managed to draw level. 'Why? What's the hurry? We could get back to the camp and try again when the snow stops and the pass is clear.'

'The pass might not reopen again for days, maybe even a month,' Vespasian bellowed, pushing his horse on through the driving snow. 'We have to take this chance to get through.'

'The men's request to Pomponius can wait another month; why are you risking all these lives for such a small thing?'

Vespasian realised that he had no logical answer that would satisfy Caelus; he could only resort to rank and bluster. 'You will stop questioning my orders and motives, centurion, or by the gods below I will see you busted, whoever may be protecting you.'

Caelus glared at him, full of suspicion. 'Don't give me that shit.' His hand went for his sword. 'Just what are you up to, Vespasian?'

'I wouldn't do that if I was you, Caelus,' Magnus yelled from behind Caelus, pressing the freezing flat of his sword against the centurion's thigh. 'There's nothing to hold me back if you draw that sword; I ain't under military discipline.'

Caelus spun round to face him. 'Then you keep out of this, civilian, this is a military matter.'

'It may well be, but I've still got my sword on your thigh, and if it were to slip and I cut your leg open, you know, just at the place where the blood always squirts out thick and fast, then at this temperature you'd be dead before we could get you to a surgeon.'

'Are you threatening me?'

'No, just like you weren't threatening the tribune.'

Caelus pushed his half-drawn weapon back into its scabbard and turned back to Vespasian. 'I shall be making a report about your recklessness to Poppaeus if and when we get to Moesia,' he spat as he pulled his mount away.

'I'm sure you will, centurion,' Vespasian called after him, 'no doubt the first of many, but it's the legate of our legion, Pomponius, you should report to, unless of course you have other allegiances.' Whether Caelus heard him or not as he retook his place in the column, Vespasian did not know or care; he cursed himself for making it so obvious to Caelus that he had an ulterior motive.

'When I saw him come up to you I thought I'd better come and keep an eye on him,' Magnus shouted against the wind, sheathing his sword.

'I had the situation under control,' Vespasian yelled angrily.

'Well, I won't bother next time if you think that a centurion drawing a sword on a tribune is a situation in control.'

Vespasian turned away, furious with himself and regretting taking his frustration out on his friend. Gritting his teeth and squinting his eyes against the biting wind, he concentrated on keeping his horse moving forward. The snow was now well above the fetlocks and approaching the animals' knees; they were all starting to struggle in the worsening conditions. Vespasian pushed his horse up next to Tinos.

'How far do you reckon we've gone?' he shouted, his voice now barely audible in what had become a gale.

'About a mile I'd guess.'

'With four miles to go and the snow getting deeper all the time I'm beginning to have serious doubts about making it through.'

'One thing's for certain: if the snow gets too far above the horses' knees we'll be forced to dismount and lead them whichever way we go.' Tinos jerked savagely and then looked down in surprise at the arrow embedded in his chest. Blood began to seep from the corners of his mouth and nostrils; he slid to the ground.

Vespasian spun his horse around. 'Get back; ambush!' he bellowed, sensing rather than seeing or hearing another arrow pass a hand's breadth to the left of him. Magnus and Sabinus needed no urging to turn, having been close enough to see Tinos fall but behind them the column was in chaos. Caelus, the four legionaries and the first of the Illyrians had obeyed the order to turn but were being prevented from falling back by a press of horsemen pushing forward from the rear out of the cloud of snow.

'Turn around, spread out and go back,' Vespasian cried as he tried to force his horse through the confusion. An arrow hammered into a legionary propelling him forward off his horse, which reared up on its hind legs, terrified by the escalating panic; its forelegs thrashed in front of it knocking an auxiliary trooper senseless. Vespasian could see that they were getting nowhere; the rear of the column was still pushing forward. He pulled out his hunting bow, notched an arrow and looked desperately around above him for the source of the attack; he could see nothing but driving snow. Sitalces appeared through the chaos, bow in hand.

'Why the fuck aren't you turning around?' Vespasian shouted.

'We're being attacked from the rear, sir, I can't see from where; I've lost one of my men already.'

It then became horribly clear to him: they were trapped in a defile by just two unseen archers, and were unable to move quickly enough in either direction to avoid losing a lot of men.

'Dismount and get to the sides of the pass,' he ordered at the top of his voice, leaping to the ground. The command filtered through the disordered column and men jumped from their horses and ran towards the relative shelter of the steep walls of the pass.

Vespasian's back slammed against the bank next to Caelus and the three surviving legionaries in a flurry of snow, his breath steamed from him after the exertion of running through knee-deep drifts.

'I hope you think this is worth it,' the centurion spat, 'we're losing a lot of men because of your impatience.'

'Now is not the time for recriminations, centurion; we need to work together if we're going to get out of this mess.'

'And a right fucking mess it is too.'

Vespasian could not argue, he had led them into this thinking that the Getae would be just as hampered by the conditions as they were; well, they were not and now it was down to him to save as many of the column as possible.

Sabinus, Magnus and a couple of auxiliary troopers joined them as another trooper fell to the ground just short of safety; blood from his skewered neck seeped into the powdery snow turning it bright red. Judging by the direction of the shot Vespasian could tell that it came from almost directly above him.

'They have to be fucking close to be able to pick targets through this blizzard, so if they can see us why can't we see them?' Magnus puffed trying to regain his breath.

'I saw these conditions sometimes when I was serving in Pannonia,' Sabinus replied, as Sitalces, Artebudz and the surviving Thracians came running in, using their terrified horses as cover. 'It's a lot easier seeing down into a snowstorm than up or through it, there's less glare and the snow doesn't get in your eyes as much.'

'Then we have to somehow get above them,' Vespasian reasoned. 'Sitalces, you and your men get your bows. From which side did the shots that hit the rear of the column come?'

'From the other side, sir,' Sitalces replied, attaching his quiver to his belt as his men did the same and removed their sleek recurved bows from the cases on their saddles.

'Bugger it, the bastards have thought this through. We'll have to split up. Sabinus, I'll take Artebudz, Sitalces and Magnus and deal with the man on the other side, you take the other three Thracians and get the bastard above us.'

Caelus looked at Vespasian quizzically; he started to say something but thought better of it.

Sabinus grinned. 'All right, little brother, it's going to be a race, is it?'

'Think of it in whatever terms you like, Sabinus, but we need to do it quickly before we're snowed in; we'll meet back here and I can assure you that there'll be no prizes for being last.' Vespasian allowed himself a grim smile at his brother before turning to Caelus. 'You take the legionaries and go forward; find those bastards' horses and bring them back here. They must be further up the pass somewhere as we didn't pass them and they can't have taken them up above with them, it's too steep.'

Caelus did not argue and started to lead his men forward, hugging the bank. The two auxiliary troopers looked at Vespasian expectantly waiting for their orders.

'You two, find as many of your comrades as you can, then send out parties to round up our horses.' Vespasian gestured to the group of horses that was milling aimlessly around what had been the killing ground. 'Don't worry about those, you'll get shot. They're not going anywhere, just the ones that have run off forward or back, understand?'

The two Illyrians saluted and started to make their way forward.

Vespasian turned in the opposite direction. 'Come on, let's get this done.'

It was easier making their way back down the pass with the wind and snow howling in from behind them but their lower limbs were starting to suffer; although they were all wearing woollen socks with their sandals and had smeared a liberal amount of pork grease over their legs that morning before making the ascent to the pass, their feet were achingly cold. After a couple of hundred trudging paces, accompanied by the fear of an arrow thudding in from the opposite bank, they passed the last dead horse, just visible as a dark form through the snow; Vespasian judged that they had gone far enough to outflank the rear man. They left the semi-protection of the bank and made the crossing to the far side in an undignified manner: taking long strides and pulling their feet up as high as possible in order to move as quickly as they could over the deep powder-snow; now fearful all the time of an arrow from either direction. After a short search they found an area of the bank less steep than the rest and climbable.

'I'll go up first,' Vespasian said.

Artebudz stepped forward. 'Sir, I come from the mountains in the province of Noricum. I know about climbing and hunting in mountains, I should lead.'

Mightily relieved, Vespasian acquiesced. 'Good man; we need to get up high enough so we can't see the pass, then we'll know that we're above him and we'll start to work our way back at different levels in pairs.'

Vespasian followed Artebudz up the treacherous incline. His teeth were chattering and his fingers numb; he was finding it very difficult to keep up with the nimble ex-slave as he expertly negotiated his way from one foothold to the next. As they climbed the wind grew stronger and buffeted him, tugging at his cloak, which billowed out like a loose sail, pulling him to his right and threatening to unbalance him. He gritted his teeth and forced the stiff muscles in his arms and legs to keep working as they pulled and pushed his body ever higher. Occasionally he risked a downward glance, past Magnus and Sitalces, but although the opposite bank was soon obscured the track down the middle of the pass stayed visible for what felt like an age; Sabinus had been right, it was easier to look down through a snowstorm. As he climbed, he marvelled at the skill of the Getic archers being able to hit targets below them with such a strong crosswind. Then he realised that it had been the crosswind that had saved him; the first arrow had been meant for him, not Tinos. He muttered a prayer of thanks to Fortuna for her continued protection.

After they had ascended a hundred feet or so the pass eventually disappeared into the white-out and Vespasian called a halt. 'Right, that's enough,' he wheezed as he sucked in the razor-sharp, frozen air that his body craved after so much effort. 'Artebudz and I will go up a little further and then start working our way back. Magnus, you and Sitalces stay on this level and keep slightly behind us.'

Magnus looked less than pleased to be left alone with the huge Thracian on a slippery steep slope. Sitalces picked up on it and grinned maliciously at him. 'Don't worry, Roman, you're safe until this is over; besides, I might need you to grab on to if I fall.'

'I won't be able to help you if you do.' Magnus smiled back innocently. 'I've seen how quickly and heavily you go down.'

Sitalces grunted, trying not to enjoy the banter.

'I can see that you'll be best of friends by the time we're finished,' Vespasian observed, getting up stiffly. 'Now let's get going before our balls freeze off.'

With a monumental effort he followed Artebudz up another fifteen feet and then they started to make their way stealthily towards the ambush point. Artebudz held his bow ready drawn, continually pointing it in different directions as he traversed the sharp incline; his natural agility and obvious familiarity with hunting in mountainous terrain enabled him to keep his footing without the use of his hands; Vespasian, who was not so sure-footed, used his right hand to steady himself whilst holding his undrawn bow with a ready notched arrow in his left. He looked down behind him and could see that Magnus and Sitalces were having just as much difficulty negotiating the traverse.

After they had gone about fifty stumbling paces the wind suddenly started to drop and the snow became less horizontal; visibility began to clear so that the opposite slope and the dead bodies down in the pass soon became discernible. After a few more paces Artebudz stopped abruptly, squatted down on to his haunches and pointed to his nose.

'I can smell him,' he whispered excitedly. 'He must be directly upwind.'

Vespasian signalled Magnus and Sitalces to halt and get down, and then sniffed the calmer air; he suddenly caught an unmistakable whiff of the same heady stench that had emanated from the dead Geta in the forest. 'How far away?'

Artebudz pointed directly ahead. 'What's that there, about thirty paces away?'

Vespasian followed the line of Artebudz's finger; at first he could see nothing through the now gently falling snowflakes, then he noticed a small movement as if the settled snow itself had twitched. After a few more moments he could make out, next to a large boulder five paces across embedded in the hillside, a smaller hump, about the size of a man, comprised of two different shades and textures of white, one of snow and the other, slightly darker, of white dyed wool.

Vespasian nodded at Artebudz; they took aim and released. The arrows flew directly at the centre of the hump and disappeared right through, dislodging most of the snow that had collected on it and exposing it as a makeshift shelter made of a white woollen blanket draped over an upright pole.

'Shit!' Vespasian spat; then, in a moment of clarity, he realised that they had just announced their presence to the unseen danger that must be lurking behind the boulder. 'Down!' he roared hitting the ground as the Getic archer, in a blur of motion, appeared over the boulder and released an arrow that disappeared into the snow just where Vespasian had stood an instant earlier.

Caught on the open slope with no cover Vespasian knew there was only one course of action. 'Keep your bow aimed at where he appeared and cover me,' he whispered to Artebudz. 'I'm going forward.' Leaving his bow on the ground, he eased his gladius from its scabbard and, signalling to Magnus and Sitalces to skirt around below the boulder, started to make his way, at a crawl, towards it.

By the time he was halfway his clothes were soaked with freezing slush and his bronze breastplate felt like a huge lump of ice sucking what little warmth remained in him out through his chest. Vespasian was close enough now not to be seen by the archer unless the man stood up, exposing himself to Artebudz's bow and certain death; so he risked a slouched run for the last fifteen paces. He reached the boulder as a double twang of bowstrings told of another exchange of fire between Artebudz and their quarry. Magnus and Sitalces were ten paces below and almost level with him, they drew their bows and slowly crept forward to try for a clear shot behind the boulder. The wind had now completely stopped and the hillside had descended into the eerie silence that accompanies gently falling snow. The stench of the Geta was overpowering. Vespasian held his breath and started to inch his way silently downhill around the huge rock. At the point of rounding the boulder he paused, mentally preparing himself for close combat. He tightened his grip around his sword hilt and nodded to Magnus and Sitalces; they leapt forward, releasing two quickly aimed shots before throwing themselves down into the snow. An instant later the Getic archer's bowstring thrummed in reply; Vespasian hurtled around the corner and pounced on the man just as he was pulling another arrow from his quiver. With no time to go for his dagger the Geta thrust the barbed tip of the arrow at Vespasian's chest. It connected with his breastplate and, as Vespasian pushed himself forward so that his weight forced his sword up under the archer's ribs, the arrow slid off the metal and embedded itself in his left shoulder. A violent shiver of pain rushed through Vespasian's body as the razor-sharp arrowhead struck bone but he pressed home his attack, driving his sword on up and into his opponent's heart, which exploded with a rush of hot blood over his sword arm. The archer let off a gurgling scream, his rank breath clouding Vespasian's senses as they fell, coupled by iron, to the ground.

'Are you all right, sir?' Magnus puffed as he and Sitalces pulled Vespasian off the dead Getic warrior.

'Apart from this thing in my shoulder, yes, I think so,' Vespasian replied as Artebudz joined them. He examined the arrow and then gave it a sharp tug. It came out easily, but not without pain; the bone in his shoulder had prevented it from burying itself deep enough for the barb to have become entangled in flesh.

Blood seeped gently from the wound. Artebudz took a handful of snow. 'Hold that there until we get back down and I can dress it properly,' he said, pressing it on the opening. Vespasian did as he was told and for the first time that day felt comforted by the snow as it took the heat out of the wound and gradually numbed the area, easing the pain. He looked down at the stinking, dead man at his feet. His sea-grey eyes stared sightlessly up at the falling snow; snowflakes settled on his eyelashes; his lips, just visible through a long and bushy black beard, had already started to turn blue. Over his clothes he wore a white blanket, now stained with blood, with a hole cut in the middle for his head; the circular waste material had been stitched on to his cap, camouflaging him almost completely.

'Very clever,' Vespasian said admiringly. 'No wonder we couldn't see them. Let's get back and see how Sabinus has done.' With his toe he lifted the blanket and flicked it back over the man's face. As he turned to leave, something poking out from beneath the blanket caught Vespasian's eye. He knelt down and pushed the blanket further back. Beneath was a cylindrical red-leather case about a foot long.

'What the fuck's he doing with this?' Vespasian exclaimed, picking the tube up.

'That's a military despatches case, isn't it?' Magnus said, equally surprised. 'What good would it be to these savages? They can't read.'

'Neither can you.'

'Fair point.'

'It must be from the couriers that were intercepted; Paetus told me about them, poor buggers. We'll look at it later. Let's go.' He slipped the case under his belt and started to make the steep, snow-ridden descent.

The snow had completely stopped and the clouds were breaking up by the time they got back to the rendezvous point. The surviving Illyrian troopers had finished rounding up the horses and Caelus and the three legionaries were already back with the Getae's mounts: squat, hardy-looking beasts with thick, rough coats.

Artebudz set about cleaning and dressing Vespasian's wound. He had just finished binding it with a bandage when Sabinus and the other Thracians came in.

'All done?' Vespasian asked his brother through chattering teeth; the adrenalin-fuelled heat of close combat had worn off and they were all now freezing again, despite the sun breaking through.

'Yes, just; but as I always say, just is good enough. Tricky bastard though, he very nearly had Bryzos here,' Sabinus replied, pointing to Sitalces' ginger-bearded mate, who grinned viciously.

'Drenis and Ziles need a bit of target practice,' Bryzos said. His two dark-haired compatriots looked suitably sheepish. 'Only one of them managed to hit the bastard before I took him from behind; he was barely wounded and he fought like a lion. I got the stinking heathen, though.' He lifted a bloody scalp that hung from his belt.

'Heathen?' Vespasian looked at Bryzos quizzically. 'I thought all the Thracian tribes had the same gods.'

'Not the Getae,' Bryzos replied, spitting on the ground. 'They rejected all our gods except one, Zalmoxis. The fools, how can there be just one god?'

'What's your chief priest doing with them, then?'

'We don't know or care,' Sitalces said, also spitting on the ground, 'but the fact that he is makes him an apostate in our eyes and so we no longer fear him.'

Vespasian nodded and gave orders to strap the dead, seven in all, on to the spare mounts; they would cremate them when they got down from the pass. As he mounted his horse he felt relieved of one of his concerns: he had been secretly worried that when it came to the final reckoning Rhoteces would put the fear of the gods into the Thracians and they would prevent him from being captured. From what Vespasian knew of the Thracian gods they were a pretty grisly lot and not to be crossed.

The column moved out and, with the ever-brightening conditions, began to make good headway along the pass as it cut straight through the snow-covered mountains, which were now bathing majestically in dazzling, clear sunlight under an azure sky.

As they approached the far end Vespasian, riding between Magnus and Sabinus, remembered the despatch case and pulled it from his belt.

'What's that?' Sabinus asked.

'I don't know, we found it on the archer,' Vespasian replied, slipping off the lid and shaking it upside down; a scroll fell into his lap. He picked it up and looked at the seal. 'Tiberius Claudius Nero Germanicus,' he read out loud. 'Shit, that's Antonia's son.'

'And an idiot from all accounts, or at least he pretends to be,' Sabinus informed him, 'but the consensus of opinion is that you have to be an idiot in the first place to be able to play the idiot; at least that's what Antonia says.'

'Who's he writing to?' Magnus asked, leaning over to look at the seal.

Sabinus looked at Vespasian. 'There's only one way to find out, are you up to opening private letters from a member of the imperial family, little brother?'

Vespasian contemplated that for a moment. 'If we don't open it we won't know who to deliver it to.' He broke the seal, then scanned the scroll and whistled softly.

'Well?' Magnus asked.

'It's to Poppaeus, and it's not signed by Claudius but by someone called Boter, and apart from the greeting and the signature it seems to be all in a code of some sort.'

'Now that is interesting,' Sabinus mused. 'Boter is one of Claudius' freedmen; I've not met him, but Pallas knows him. A few years back he got Claudius' first wife pregnant. Surprisingly, Claudius didn't do anything to Boter at the time, but now I think I can see why: with that sort of hold over the man Claudius can use him to do his dirty work, then if it goes wrong he can distance himself from it by saying that he's been set up by a resentful member of his household. Boter goes down and Claudius has his revenge and is in the clear at the same time. Very crafty.'

'Do you think that he could be going behind Claudius' back?' Magnus asked.

'He could be; Pallas says that he's very ambitious.' Sabinus stopped and thought for a few moments. 'No, he wouldn't have used Claudius' seal if he was; this letter must have been written with Claudius' knowledge. However, as it isn't signed by Claudius but bears his seal it's at the same time both authentic and deniable. Perhaps he really isn't the idiot that everyone takes him for. I think we had better hang on to this and show it to Antonia when we get back; Pallas will probably be able to break the code.'

'Why he should be writing to Poppaeus in code unless he's working in league with him and Sejanus?' Vespasian asked, replacing the scroll in its case. They had reached the end of the pass and started their descent; far into the distance, below them and the snow-line, stretched the heavily wooded, rolling hills of Moesia.

'That is a real possibility; as the nephew of the Emperor and the brother of Germanicus, Tiberius' original heir according to the terms of the deal that he did with Augustus, Claudius is technically very well placed to inherit the Purple, especially if Sejanus helps him.'

'Why would he do that?'

'Because he probably thinks that Claudius is a weak fool whom he can control, which he already seems to be doing.'

'How?'

'Well, after she bore him Boter's daughter Claudius divorced his first wife, Plautia Urgulanilla, for adultery. Then two years ago Tiberius insisted, no doubt on Sejanus' advice, that he get married again, this time to a woman called Aelia Paetina.'

Vespasian frowned; he didn't know the name. 'So?'

'So nobody thought much of it at the time because Claudius is considered such a booby. But Aelia's parents had died when she was very young and she was brought up by her maternal uncle, Lucius Seius Strabo.'

Vespasian's eyes widened in disbelief. 'Shit, not Sejanus' father?'

'Yes, little brother, Sejanus' father, which makes Aelia Sejanus' adoptive sister and Sejanus Claudius' brother-in-law and therefore, should Claudius become Emperor, a legitimate heir.'

PART II

MOESIA, APRIL AD 30

CHAPTER V

'THANK YOU FOR your reports, gentlemen,' Pomponius
Labeo said, eyeing Vespasian and Caelus with a look of
mild amusement on his jowly face. 'I've given some thought to
your request and I will grant it. As soon as the siege of the castle
at Sagadava has been brought to a successful conclusion I will
send the third and eighth cohorts to relieve the Thracian
garrison.'

Vespasian and Caelus snapped a salute in grateful acknowledgement of their commanding officer's decision. They were
closeted in Pomponius' study in the newly constructed fortress
of Durostorum on the banks of the Danuvius, which had only
recently been occupied by a small detachment of the IIII Scythia.
The main building work having been finished towards the end of
the previous year, the room still smelt of newly waxed wooden
floorboards and freshly whitewashed walls. The sounds of
hundreds of slaves working on the final stages of the construction and the shouts of their overseers floated through the
unshuttered window.

'I can only assume,' Pomponius went on, resting his pudgy
arms on the desk and leaning towards them, 'that the marked
difference in your accounts of your journey here is down to a
personal animosity that in my opinion did not unnecessarily put
the men's lives in danger and therefore, in view of Tribune
Vespasian's imminent recall to Rome, I am willing to overlook it.'

Vespasian breathed a sigh of relief; during the twenty days
that it had taken them to find Pomponius, having been told by
the garrison commander at Oescus that the IIII Scythia was
campaigning against a Getic raiding party of at least three thousand men that had been ravaging the east of Moesia, he had fully

expected to be seriously reprimanded for his impetuousness in taking the column through the Succi Pass in a blizzard. In an effort to protect himself, when he made his verbal report to Pomponius, which, owing to his rank, he had been able to do before Caelus, he had taken care not to mention Caelus' insistence that they should turn back, stressing instead the supposed urgency of placing the garrison's request before Pomponius. He had also augmented that urgency with an exaggerated assessment of the men's dissatisfaction, which he knew would reflect badly on Caelus, as their senior centurion and therefore responsible for their discipline, for allowing things to get that far, and well on Paetus and himself for quelling a potential mutiny.

'Permission to speak, legate,' Caelus barked.

'You will remain silent, centurion,' Pomponius snapped, causing his jowls to quiver. 'You had your say when you made your report to me upon your arrival this morning. The matter is closed. On your way back to Thracia you will take the three legionaries that Paetus has sent for transfer to the siege lines at Sagadava where you will hand them over to Primus Pilus Faustus; they wanted to avenge their comrades, well, they'll have plenty of opportunities to do so in the first century of the first cohort when they storm the castle. My secretary has their transfer orders as well as some despatches for Paetus; pick them up on your way out. You're to leave immediately; understood, centurion?'

'Yes, sir!'

'Good. Take the Illyrian auxiliaries with you and get them back to Thracia as soon as possible. Dismissed.'

Caelus saluted, turned smartly on his heel and marched out of the room, burning with ill-concealed rage.

As the door closed behind him Pomponius smiled grimly. 'He was always Poppaeus' sneak and he'll have a lot to say to him when he gets to Sagadava.'

'Poppaeus is at Sagadava?' Vespasian blurted out, forgetting that he was still at attention and therefore should not speak unless he was addressed directly.

Pomponius overlooked the offence. 'At ease, tribune, sit down. Yes, he arrived four days ago, the slippery little bastard. I spent the last two months chasing the Getae around eastern Moesia and I finally managed to corner them at Sagadava, whilst they were waiting for their transports to ship them back across the river. Then, three days ago, as soon as the siege lines were completed and it was obvious the horse-fuckers were going nowhere without a fight, he turns up with four cohorts of the Fifth Macedonica aboard two squadrons of the Danuvius fleet, takes overall command and orders me straight back here to sit and wait whilst, again, he grabs all the glory. He even had the temerity to accuse me of failing in my duty to Rome for not stopping the Getae's raids, as if it were that easy against an enemy that can move thirty or forty miles a day as opposed to our fifteen, if we're lucky. Pluto's balls, we need more cavalry in this province.' Pomponius slumped back in his chair and wiped the beads of sweat from his brow that, despite the cool temperature in the room, had accumulated there.

Vespasian shifted uneasily in his seat, wondering how he was going to find out whether Rhoteces was with the besieged raiding party and, if he was, how they were going to get through the Roman lines, into the castle, apprehend him and then get him back out without it coming to the attention of Poppaeus. 'Why have the Getae started raiding the province so often?' he asked. 'It's not as if there's a lot to plunder here and if they carry on it will surely just provoke the Emperor into extending the Empire over the river.'

Pomponius looked up from the self-pitying reverie into which he had sunk. 'What? Oh, I know; strategically it's pure madness on their part. But it seems that their king, Cotiso, who's the grandson of the king of the same name that we defeated over fifty years ago, has been encouraged to exact revenge for that humiliation to his people.'

'By whom?'

'That disgusting priest that had the ear of Poppaeus; you might have seen him when he led Dinas' people down to surrender – you were there, weren't you?'

'Yes, I was,' Vespasian replied, trying to keep his voice neutral. 'So he's been with the Getae ever since the revolt was put down?'

'I don't know if he went to them immediately but he's certainly been with them for the last year or so; he's been seen with them during some of their raids.'

'Was he spotted on this one?' Vespasian asked innocently.

Pomponius was about to answer, but then stopped himself and peered at his young tribune with his piggy eyes. 'Ah, I see,' he said slowly. 'Your brother's with you, isn't he?'

Vespasian's pulse quickened. 'Yes, sir.'

'Yet he doesn't hold a military commission at the moment, does he?'

'No, he's a civilian.'

'Has he recently arrived from Rome?'

Vespasian knew that it was pointless denying it. 'Yes, sir, at the end of March.'

Pomponius nodded thoughtfully and raised himself to his feet. Vespasian stood immediately.

'I have other business to attend to now, tribune,' Pomponius said, indicating that the interview was over, 'but I would be pleased if you and your brother would dine with me this evening.'

'I think you'll find this dish to be particularly fine,' Pomponius enthused as a huge platter of river perch, topped with a thick brown sauce, was placed upon the table. 'This is my cook's speciality, his honeyed-wine and plum sauce is second to none and he understands exactly how to poach a fish so that the flesh peels perfectly off the bones. He's a marvel; I bought him twelve years ago and, like a good wine, he gets even better as the years pass.' To emphasise the point he took long draught of the excellent wine, belched, and then set his cup down whilst greedily eyeing the beautifully presented dish.

Vespasian glanced across the table to Sabinus, who was showing no sign of fatigue, and then smiled politely at his host. 'It does look most appetising, Pomponius,' he managed to say, half-truthfully.

It would indeed have looked most appetising if it had been the second or third course; however, it was the eighth. Vespasian had assumed, judging by the girth of his host, that the dinner would be an arduous affair, and not for the faint-hearted, so he had paced himself over the first four courses, thinking that the pastries and fruit would surely come soon after; but he had been sadly mistaken. He had since been obliged to contend with a roast suckling goat, a plate of various game birds and a haunch of venison, all swathed in sundry rich sauces. It would be the height of impoliteness to refuse a portion of any of the courses set before him even though the words full, replete, stuffed and bloated were echoing around his head. His only respite had come from emulating Pomponius' habit of breaking wind freely from both ends – a practice that he did not normally approve of at the dinner table. However, by the sixth course he had put his scruples to one side and had since, on numerous occasions, followed his host's lead and eased his straining innards. Feeling very envious of Magnus, whom they had left carousing with Artebudz and the Thracians and an inordinate amount of wine, he uncomfortably adjusted his position on the couch as Sabinus helped himself to an unnecessarily large portion of perch and spooned a copious amount of sauce over it.

'Tuck in, little brother,' he said with a malicious glint in his eye. 'Our host has saved his best dish for last. We should do it justice.' He popped a large, dripping hunk of fish into his mouth and started to chew whilst making appreciative sounds.

'You are mistaken, Sabinus,' Pomponius corrected him as he enthusiastically pulled the dish towards him and took an even larger portion. 'It would surely be a mistake to save the best for last, we would be too full to enjoy it properly; I believe we've still got a couple more courses to come, and then of course the honeyed dormice just to fill in the corners before the sweet pastries.'

Sabinus blanched at the news; Vespasian felt sick. He braced himself and then manfully spooned the smallest piece of perch that good manners dictated on to his plate and then made a show of eating with gusto whilst discreetly dropping as much as he could on the napkin spread before him on the couch.

'Poppaeus may travel with all the trappings that his new money can buy,' Pomponius said, returning to his favourite subject of the evening, 'a marble-floored tent, mobile frescoes, gaudy pieces of furniture and too many horses, but his lack of breeding prevents him from understanding the finer points of life.' He began to mop up the excess sauce on his plate with a large hunk of bread. 'Believe me, gentlemen, I know, I've had the misfortune to dine with him many times and, if it'd been down to me, I would've had his cook whipped for the paltry fare that he served up. Almost as bad as common legionary rations – it's no wonder the general's so small.' He enjoyed his own witticism so much that he almost choked as he drained his wine cup. 'On those pitiful occasions I always make sure that my cook has a proper meal waiting for me upon my return,' he carried on, wiping away the wine that had come up through his nose. 'It's only the thought of that that gets me through his frugal little dinner parties.' He held his cup out to be refilled by a waiting slave, adding, 'And his wine, of course. I'll give the man his due: he does serve a decent wine.'

'As do you, Pomponius,' Sabinus said, raising his cup, pleased that he had managed to get a word in. 'Where does it come from?'

'From my estates in Aventicum in the south of Germania Superior,' Pomponius replied, taking another mighty slug. He looked wistfully at the brothers. 'It's a beautiful place, on the shore of Lake Murten in the tribal lands of the Helvetii. My grandfather, Titus Pomponius Atticus, bought a lot of land around there whilst he was extending our banking business into the province.'

Vespasian tried to look interested as Pomponius went on about his family's business venture, bemoaning the fact that his lack of financial acumen meant that under his tenure it was beginning to fail and he was thinking of selling it. Another course came and went, followed by yet another, and he began to wish that he could call for the vomit bowl, another practice that he disapproved of but of which he would have happily taken advantage had Pomponius had not already made his views clear on the subject: a waste of good food.

At last his plate, with a half-eaten dormouse on it, was taken away, the pastries and fruit were laid out, two full jugs of barely watered wine were placed on the table and Pomponius dismissed the slaves.

'So, gentlemen, to the matter in hand,' Pomponius said as the last slave closed the door and they were left alone in the large, unadorned room, which had only just begun to take on an intimate air with the setting of the sun and the lighting of oil lamps and braziers. 'I'd be very interested to know, Vespasian, why you led our conversation this afternoon so quickly, and with some degree of skill, to the subject of Rhoteces? I may be a plain soldier and administrator with no political aptitude and pickled in my own wine but I can tell when a man asks me three questions in quick succession to which he knows the answers and then asks a fourth to which he doesn't, but desperately wants to.'

Vespasian found himself cornered. To deny that he had been trying to wheedle out information from Pomponius concerning the whereabouts of Rhoteces would be to insult his host's intelligence; to confirm it would only leave him open to a series of questions as to why he, as a mere military tribune, wished to know whether the priest was with the Getic raiding party. Making a mental note to be more subtle in his questioning in future, he glanced over to Sabinus, who shrugged unhelpfully.

'You're going to have to be quicker than that when you find yourself in a tight spot, Vespasian,' Pomponius remarked sternly. 'The very fact that you paused for so long and looked to your brother for advice tells me that that you want to find this priest but you don't want to tell me why.'

'Yes, sir,' Vespasian replied.

'This is a private dinner not the parade ground, there's no need to call me "sir",' Pomponius snapped. 'Why do you want to find this priest?'

'We've been asked to take him to Rome.' Vespasian felt his over-full belly starting to churn.

'By whom?' Pomponius' eyes had lost all sense of joviality and now bored into Vespasian's with an intensity that made him suddenly afraid.

'I can't tell you that, Pomponius,' he answered with an edge of adrenalin-fuelled steel in his voice. He could sense Sabinus tensing on the other side of the table, preparing himself to pounce on Pomponius.

'You will tell me, tribune, or by the gods I will forget the fact that I owe you my life, which was the only thing that prevented me from upholding Caelus' complaints about your leadership this morning, and reverse that decision and have you sent back to Rome in disgrace.'

'Then that is what you must do, legate, for I cannot tell you.'

Pomponius looked for a moment as though he might explode, then he controlled himself. 'Very well, tribune, so be it.'

'May I ask a question, Pomponius?' Sabinus said quickly.

'If it helps us out of this impasse.'

'My brother rightly won't tell you who has asked us to take this man back to Rome, but equally would you wish to tell us why you're so keen to know?'

Pomponius did not need to think about it. 'No.'

'Because you're aware that what this man knows is important to two opposing factions within Rome and neither of us can be sure, as yet, who the other one is working for?'

'I think that sums it up.'

'So you have an interest in a certain party getting hold of the priest before he falls into the hands of someone else, or is eliminated?'

Pomponius laughed. 'You must think that I was born yesterday if you believed for one moment that I would answer that question. We both know that only one party would be happy to see Rhoteces dead.'

'Yes, but we've already told you that we want to take him to Rome, and that means keeping him alive.'

'So you say, but what if I was to want him dead?'

Sabinus swiftly slipped his hand under his tunic, pulled out a knife and advanced on Pomponius. 'Then I would have to kill you, which I might do anyway just to be on the safe side.' Pomponius heaved himself to his feet and stood his ground.

'Sabinus, stop,' Vespasian shouted. 'You've heard him this evening – you know how he despises Poppaeus. He wouldn't be working to further his interests.'

Pomponius smiled. 'Young man, you do have a lot to learn; despising someone is no reason not to work with them if your interests coincide. I know that you hate him too, otherwise you wouldn't have told me that he stole my victory when we defeated the Thracian revolt, but that's almost four years ago and your allegiances may well have changed. However, by appealing to your brother in my defence just now has proved to me that we are on the same side; unless you are a very good actor, which I don't think you are . . . yet. So I will trust you, despite the fact that you've pulled a knife on me in my own dining room, Sabinus, which I consider to be the height of ill manners. The priest is in Sagadava.'

Sabinus kept his knife raised. 'How can we trust you?'

Pomponius looked him in the eye. 'Because I was the person who told Antonia, whom I assume sent you to find him, that Rhoteces was with the Getae.'

'You're Antonia's agent in Moesia?' Vespasian sounded incredulous.

'Don't be absurd, I'm nobody's agent, I told her because I know that our interests do coincide. You told me after the battle, Vespasian, how Sejanus and Poppaeus had used Rhoteces as a go-between, so when he turned up again last year I passed on the information anonymously to Antonia assuming – correctly because she sent you to get him – that he would be of use to her. I know that she is working to bring down Sejanus and if she is successful then with luck Poppaeus will go down with him and I shall have revenge for his theft of my rightful victory.'

'How did you know that Antonia is working against Sejanus?'

'Sit down both of you and refill your cups, and mine as well whilst you're about it, and I'll explain.'

The brothers did as they were told and soon felt much calmer for the strong wine. Pomponius drained his cup in one gulp and held it out for more; Vespasian obliged him.

'Thank you,' Pomponius said, reclining back down on his couch. 'I'll be brief. When the Thracians threatened to revolt six years ago I was in Rome. I had just been appointed legate of the Fourth Scythica and was about to leave for Moesia. Asinius approached me to act as his eyes and ears in Moesia and Thracia. He took me into his confidence and told me that he was working with Antonia against the rising threat of Sejanus. Because of the large amount of Roman money found in Tacfarinas' possession, after the Numidian revolt had been suppressed, Antonia and Asinius had begun to suspect that fomenting rebellions in the provinces was part of Sejanus' wider strategy to destabilise the Empire as he secured his position with the Emperor. They suspected that the threatened revolt in Thracia was a part of this strategy. At this point they didn't suspect Poppaeus of being involved as he had been out of Rome since he'd been appointed Governor of both Moesia and Macedonia ten years earlier and had had no known contact with Sejanus; also because he is considered respectable but with no striking abilities – a threat to nobody. However, they had no reason to trust him either, so they needed their own man on the spot.'

'Why did he trust you enough to tell you all this?' Vespasian asked.

'Because we're kinsmen. His mother, Vipsania Agrippina, is my father's niece.'

'And she was Tiberius's first wife and the mother of his late son Drusus who Antonia believes was murdered by her daughter Livilla, Sejanus' mistress,' Sabinus said, understanding the connection.

'Exactly. So we both had a kinsman to avenge and an Emperor, to whom we are both connected to by marriage, to defend. So I seemed like a safe bet to him – but I refused.'

'Why?'

Pomponius smiled at the look of outraged disbelief on Vespasian's face. 'Because my judgement is no longer clouded by the enthusiasm and idealism of youth, as yours evidently still is, by the look on your face. Sejanus had just blocked me from becoming Consul in order to put one of his men forward; he had given me the Fourth Scythica as a sop, and I knew that his eyes were on me and probably still are. I would have been a liability to Asinius and Antonia and, more importantly, I intend to die in my bed, unlike most of the people who come to Sejanus' notice.'

'So why the change of heart?' Vespasian asked with more than a trace of scorn.

Pomponius regarded him levelly. 'You will speak civilly to me in my dining room, young man, and refrain from judging me by your own rather impetuous and naive standards.'

Vespasian reddened, embarrassed as much by Pomponius' assessment of him as he was by the realisation that he was right. 'Forgive me, Pomponius; that was crass of me.'

Pomponius inclined his head. 'To answer your question: my time here is up; in a month or so I'll return to my estates in Aventicum to lie low and drink my wine until the political turmoil in Rome resolves itself one way or the other. So I decided to risk passing Antonia a piece of information that would hurt Poppaeus, in the hope that she would use it.'

'Why didn't you try to capture Rhoteces when he first reappeared and have him sent to her?'

'I have been trying to get my hands on that priest for over a year now and just when I had him cornered, and was trying to think of a way to extract him, Poppaeus turns up. Sejanus must have heard that Rhoteces had resurfaced and persuaded the Emperor to reinstate Poppaeus as Governor, using the increased raids over the river and my seeming inability to deal with them as a valid excuse. So Poppaeus has taken command at Sagadava because he knows that Rhoteces is there and he means to make certain that he never comes out. You need to ensure that he does.'

The brothers looked at each other as Pomponius drained his cup and, with slight nods of their heads, silently agreed to trust him.

'How do you recommend we do that, Pomponius?' Sabinus asked. 'You said that you were working on a plan.'

'I said that I was trying to think of a way to get him out,' Pomponius corrected him. 'I hadn't completely formulated a plan. It's going to be difficult. There are nearly three thousand of the bastards crammed together in the fortress and the fortifications next to it; I imagine that there is barely room to move, although they have left most of their horses out in the open.'

'And if we did manage to get in we'd be very conspicuous,' Vespasian added, not liking the scenario one bit.

'Unless we disguise ourselves as Getae,' Sabinus pointed out.

'Exactly,' Pomponius agreed, 'that was what I had been thinking of, but I didn't have the men to do it; there're no Thracians that I would trust with such a delicate task and we Romans wouldn't be able to pass ourselves off as Getae, even if we were wearing their festering trousers.'

'We've brought five of Queen Tryphaena's men with us, they'll be able to if they have the clothes,' Vespasian said. 'Sabinus, Magnus and I will just have to make the best of it and try to blend in with them.'

Pomponius looked at him and raised his eyebrows. 'That's very risky. Why don't you just send the Thracians in by themselves?'

'Because it will take at least two of them to carry the priest out, which would leave only three men to defend them; if one or two get killed then it would be all over. We need to go too to lower the odds.'

Sabinus grunted. 'I've a nasty feeling that my brother's right, Pomponius. So how do we get in and out?'

'Well, first you've got to get the clothes, that should be easy enough as there is a compound full of prisoners in the Roman camp; Centurion Faustus, whom you know, Vespasian, and we both trust, will be able to help you. As to getting in, that's much harder; there are only three ways that I can see and the best one, in my opinion, is through a little sewage drain in the north wall facing the river; you could reach it by boat which would mean that you wouldn't have to go through the siege lines as they only extend as far as the river on either side of the fortress.'

Sabinus turned up his nose. 'I really don't like the idea of wading through Getic shit. What are the other two ways?'

'Through the main gate in the west wall, or scale the walls themselves, neither of which you'll be able to do without someone noticing.'

'We could just wait until Poppaeus storms the fortress and try and grab Rhoteces in the chaos of the attack,' Vespasian suggested.

'You could, but if I were Poppaeus I would have a crack squad of legionaries charged with eliminating him and you would find yourselves fighting Romans as well as Getae.'

'It looks like we're going to be in the shit, then,' Vespasian observed. 'Don't worry, Sabinus, you won't be able to smell it over the stench of your clothes.'

Sabinus allowed himself a wry smile. 'Very funny, little brother. What about getting away, Pomponius?'

'By boat again; get Faustus to have your horses and things waiting a mile or so downstream and you'll be away before Poppaeus even knows you were there. The only thing you'll have to worry about is not bumping into the Danuvius fleet, which is stationed in the river to prevent the Getae's transports from rescuing them.'

Vespasian resigned himself to the inevitable. 'Well, I suppose it's a plan of sorts, and seeing as it's the only one we have it will have to do. The only alternative is to walk away and let the priest die in Sagadava.'

'That sounds like an appealing option,' Sabinus observed, 'and a lot less hassle.'

'In the short term, yes,' Pomponius said, 'but in the long term if Sejanus isn't removed everyone suspected of opposing him will find themselves and their families faced with options a great deal less appealing. So I suggest that you go and get a decent night's sleep, gentlemen, because you've got a day and a half's hard ride ahead of you followed by a long and dangerous night's work as soon as you get there.'

'We should do it the night that we arrive?' Vespasian exclaimed. 'Surely we should make a reconnaissance of the place and finalise the plan?'

'I'm afraid you don't have the time. When I left, Poppaeus boasted to me that every Getic warrior would be dead by the end of this month. If he's going to keep that promise I imagine that he's going to attack on the second to last night of the month and that is only three days away.'

CHAPTER VI

A THICK CLOUD OF grey smoke hung over the ancient fortress of Sagadava. At first Vespasian and his companions were worried that Poppaeus had already made his attack and they had arrived too late, but as they drew closer it became apparent that the smoke was the issue of the Roman fires and mobile forges crammed into their siege lines surrounding the beleaguered Getae. Although the scale of the siege was nothing compared to the huge, four-mile-long fortification that Poppaeus had built to pen in the Thracian rebels four years previously, it was still an impressive sight, even from a distance.

The fortress had been constructed with great slabs of brown stone almost four hundred years earlier by the Getic king Cothelas, a vassal of Philip II of Macedonia, to protect his western border from attack by river. It was set on the spine of a sharp ridge at its junction with the equally steep slope that ran parallel to the river 150 paces from its bank. Another ridge thrusting inland, two hundred paces to the west, not only made attack from that direction extremely hazardous but also funnelled a frontal assault from the south into a flat killing ground before the main gate in the west wall at its junction with the south wall; it was a formidable refuge. Great walls, three hundred paces square and twenty feet high, surrounded an inner keep on the northeast corner, which towered over the river. In its heyday catapults would have been mounted on its wide, flat roof that would have been able to sink enemy shipping without receiving any return fire; but now the roof was empty, the catapults having rotted away long ago, as the Getae's power to the south of the Danuvius faded after the Gallic invasion and they withdrew across the river, making way for more primitive tribes without the technology to repair them. When the Romans, under the general Marcus Crassus, grandson of the triumvir of the same name, had conquered Moesia in the early years of Augustus' reign they had found the fortress in a dilapidated state and had easily overcome the remnants of the Saci tribe sheltering within it. They made a few repairs to its fortifications but, because its strategic significance had been overshadowed by the great Lysimachid fortress at Axiopolis a few miles downstream, they had since garrisoned it only with a nominal force of low-grade auxiliaries who had been no match for the Getic horde that had descended upon them.

Vespasian and his comrades paused a mile from the Roman lines on the crest of a hill, stripped of trees by the besieging army to build the siege wall, and looked down upon the bustling hive of activity that was a siege in progress. A two-mile-long horse-shoe-shaped wooden wall, with each end abutting the river, enclosed the castle and a fortified settlement that had grown up next to it, in the lee of the other ridge to its west; between these hundreds of horses milled aimlessly.

Three gates had been built into the siege wall, close together, at its central point; behind each stood a massive, newly constructed, wheeled siege tower, thirty feet wide at their base, tapering to ten feet at their summit. Each had a long ramp attached to their top levels; the ramps had been hauled vertical by pulley systems in readiness for the slow, manhandled journey across no-man's-land which would end with them crashing down upon the walls of their objective and disgorging hundreds of assault troops from the bellies of the towers.

Behind the Roman lines, set back just far enough to be able to shoot over the wall when the order to attack came, dozens of stone-throwing onagers and bolt-shooting ballistae were being assembled. They, along with the Cretan auxiliary archers advancing with the towers, would provide the covering fire, peppering the walls of the fortress – just within range over four hundred paces away – with lethal missiles in an effort to prevent the Getic bowmen from causing too many Roman casualties.

In amongst all the siege apparatus scurried thousands of legionaries working as carpenters on the towers, as navvies levelling the ground for the artillery pieces, as smiths in the mobile forges, hammering out iron bolts to feed the hungry ballistae, or as masons chipping away at chunks of rock, rounding them off so that they would fit snugly into the slings of the onagers. The sound of their ceaseless labour blended with the shouts of their officers in a cacophony so loud that it was plainly audible from where Vespasian and his group sat on their horses.

'Ain't that just typical of the army,' Magnus said with a wry grin. 'They've got the whole of Moesia to run about in but they decide to cram as many people as possible into one small corner.'

'But I don't think that they'll be here that much longer,' Sabinus observed. 'To my eye they look to be almost ready. Pomponius' guess was right, they'll be going in tomorrow.'

'We'd better get on with it, then,' Vespasian said, kicking his horse forward. 'We need to find Faustus in amongst all that.'

Faustus was easier to find than expected. The first cohort was stationed at the middle gate, putting the finishing touches to the huge siege tower parked a few paces behind it. The din of scores of legionaries working wood with hammers, saws and chisels, constructing the staircases and staging platforms in the bowels of the tower, was intense but not quite loud enough to drown a familiar voice.

'It just has to be fit for purpose, not a fucking work of art; you're not going to live in it with your sweethearts, no, you lucky sods are going to fight from it. Now get a move on. If the Fifth Macedonica finish their tower before we do I'll lose ten denarii to their primus pilus and I'll be forced to send every tenth one of you back home to your mothers without any balls.'

The noise of construction intensified as Faustus stepped out of one of the tower's entrances, brushing sawdust off his shoulder.

'Centurion Faustus,' Vespasian called as he dismounted.

Faustus looked up and immediately snapped a rigid salute. 'Tribune Vespasian,' he said, grinning all over his face, 'and

Magnus, you old dog, have you come to join our little war? Thracia must be very boring if you've been forced to travel all this way to see a bit of action.'

'Thracia is indeed boring,' Vespasian replied, clasping the centurion's heavily muscled forearm, 'but we haven't come to help you enjoy your war, we've got a little battle of our own to fight before you go killing every Geta that you can find. This is my brother Sabinus and this' – he indicated Artebudz and the Thracians – 'is our army.'

'Ah, now let me guess, you're on the hunt for that weasel-faced priest. I won't ask why but I assume that you want to find him before Poppaeus does; in which case you'll have to get him tonight as it's an open secret here that we attack tomorrow night.'

'Very astute, Faustus. Now we need your help to get some Getic clothes and a boat.'

Faustus looked hesitant. 'Poppaeus has started to make things very difficult for me since his return; I can turn a blind eye to what you're up to but as to—'

He was interrupted by a shout from the centurion of the century stationed on the walkway along the wall. 'Incoming! About five hundred of them. Get down, lads. *Pila* ready.'

His men up on the walkway immediately crouched down, hefting their spears into a throwing position.

'Shields,' Faustus shouted, 'then get yourselves under the wall.'

All around the legionaries dropped their tools, grabbed their shields and ran for safety in the lee of the wall.

'Get your men and horses to the wall, sir, you'll be safe enough there. The stinking horse-botherers do this once an hour or so, trying to set fire to one of the towers; it seems that it's our turn again, although I wish they'd pick on the Fifth Macedonica more often as I'm desperate to win a bet.'

Shrill, ululating war cries filled the air and the sound of hundreds of hooves pounding the earth drew closer as Vespasian and his comrades reached the wall. Moments later came the sharp hiss of multitudes of flaming arrows streaking over it, leaving trails of thin smoke in their wake; they thumped into the tower with a seemingly never-ending staccato beat. The sudden impact caused a lot of the burning rags attached to the arrows to come off and fall, like flaming rain, to the ground, but more than a few remained intact and the tower started to burn in dozens of places.

A century waiting with a pump and water-filled buckets beneath the tower reacted immediately to douse the flames on the lower parts of the tower; but further up, out of reach of their efforts, the fire started to spread as another huge volley of fire arrows careered in, augmenting the damage already done.

'Get that fucking pump working properly, you come-stains; that fire is not sacred to Mithras, it's the sort that needs to be put out,' Faustus hollered, waving his vine cane threateningly at the group of legionaries desperately pushing and pulling the see-saw pump handle up and down in an effort to get the device up to a high enough pressure to reach the top of the tower. The threat of their primus pilus bearing down on them in all his wrath worked wonders for the pumping legionaries and the stream of water from the nozzle of the hose, held by two men, burst into a jet that reached up to the flames beyond the range of their bucket-wielding comrades.

A new threat came flying over the wall; the Getae had got close enough to hurl the resin-soaked torches some of their number carried to light their comrades' arrows. Dozens thundered on to the tower, scraping flaming resin down its side that carried on burning despite the water being flung at it. The fire-fighters renewed their efforts as, from above, Vespasian heard the centurion shout the order to release pila at the now in-range Getae. The war cries from the other side of the wall turned into screams as eighty pila slammed into what Vespasian imagined would be by now a tightly bunched body of cavalry. A scream from above him caused him to look up as a legionary came tumbling, head first, off the walkway to fall at his feet. Even if the arrow embedded in his jaw had not killed him, the fall on to his head certainly had; his necked lolled at an unnatural angle, indicating a severe break. Young but lifeless eyes stared up at Vespasian; the lad could not have been more than seventeen.

'Poor bugger,' Magnus said from beside him. 'He just learnt the hard way that you don't stick around to see whether you've hit anything once you've chucked your *pilum*.'

Vespasian nodded in rueful agreement as another volley of pila was ordered above. This time the Getae were ready for it and another couple of legionaries, with arrows protruding from their necks or faces, crashed to the ground accompanied by a roar of triumph from the other side of the wall.

'That's it, they're going,' the centurion above shouted.

'And about fucking time too. Artillery!' Faustus roared.

The crews of the ballistae and onagers stationed with the first cohort rushed out from the wall and began to frantically load their weapons.

'Two hundred paces; two fifty,' the centurion on the wall called down. He was waiting for the enemy to be far enough away for the missiles not to overshoot them because of the trajectory they needed to use to clear the wall. 'Now!' he yelled, flinging himself down so as not to have his head taken off.

Fifteen assorted artillery pieces released simultaneously with a loud rasp of metal grating on wood followed by sharp cracks from the wooden arms of the machines slamming into the restraining beams as they released their projectiles.

Faustus came strolling up to Vespasian as the volley flew over the wall. 'We hardly ever hit any of them with the artillery, I just consider it to be good manners to send a few bolts and rocks after them as they go,' he said grinning, 'and besides, it's good fun.'

'And good practice for the crews,' Sabinus observed. 'They had their weapons loaded very quickly. I'm impressed.'

'Well, don't tell them, it'll go to their heads and they'll slow down.'

'I won't, my brother in light.'

Faustus raised his eyebrows. 'So you heard my slightly profane reference to our Lord Mithras, brother? I'm sure he will forgive it, but, to make certain he does I will do my utmost to help a fellow believer. A boat and clothes you say; not a problem.'

Faustus turned his attention to his men. 'What are you all looking at, you idle buggers?' he bellowed. 'Haven't you ever seen a steaming siege tower before? Get back to work, the lot of you; the Fifth Macedonica didn't stop in all the time we were under attack so jump to it and clear those bodies up.'

The reaction was instantaneous; shields and buckets were downed and the men returned to their tasks. Once he was satisfied that all was proceeding as quickly as possible he returned to Vespasian and his comrades. 'Well, gentlemen, the Getae have solved the clothes problem. Rather than me having to get eight of the prisoners and executing them, there are probably dozens of already dead ones just beyond the gate. We'll go and take a look when it gets dark, but first let's find you a boat.'

'From what I know of this sewage drain,' Centurion Faustus said, pointing to a crude diagram of the fortress lit by a single oil lamp, 'it's just to the west of the keep, which means that it will open up into the main courtyard.'

'Shit, that isn't going to be very private,' Magnus exclaimed. 'It'll be packed with Getae.'

'Yes, two thousand or so, the rest are in the fortified settlement,' Faustus replied. 'However, if you go in the dead of night there's a good chance that they'll be asleep.'

'A good chance you say, but not definite?' Vespasian asked, scratching his crotch, which had been playing havoc with him since donning Getic clothes.

Faustus shrugged. 'Who's to say what these fuckers get up to at night, they do keep a few horses in the fortress. Anyway, if you get in, the priest will probably be found in the keep itself. According to the few auxiliaries who managed to escape when the fortress was overrun, the most comfortable rooms are halfway up, on the third floor; I would guess that the Getic commanders will commandeer them.'

'This is getting silly,' Sabinus observed. 'Even if we do manage to tiptoe past all these sleeping savages, make it up three flights of stairs and find Rhoteces, we're bound to make some noise getting hold of him. So how do we get back down and out again through all that lot? Not even the Lord Mithras could spirit us past them.'

'You don't go back down, but you will need our Lord Mithras' help.' Faustus grinned. 'I'll give you some rope and you can leave through the windows, it's fifty feet down straight on to the river-bank. I'll lend you two or three of my lads to stay in the boat and they can pick you up as you come out.'

Vespasian nodded. 'I suppose that give us the best chance of escape, but, no offence, Faustus, I would prefer if you would give me the three lads who were transferred from the Thracian garrison to man the boat; one owes me his life, they'll have more reason than most to hang around when it starts to get dangerous.'

With a shrug Faustus acquiesced. They were hunched around a table in a small, ill-lit hut built up against the siege wall, which Faustus used as the headquarters for the first cohort. The air inside was barely breathable owing to the stench of the disguises they had ripped from the dead Getae three hours before.

Vespasian looked at Sabinus and Magnus, who nodded reluctantly, then around at Sitalces and the rest of the Thracians crowded behind him, peering at the map. 'Well, Sitalces, what do you think?' he asked the huge Thracian.

'We have a saying in Thracian: "A faint-heart never fucked a pig."'

Vespasian joined in the general laugher. 'I'll remember that one. Well, gentlemen, we've got a Titan of a pig in front of us, let's give it a fucking that it won't forget.'

'What do you think the chances of success are when you storm the place tomorrow?' Vespasian asked Faustus as they wove their way through the crowded siege lines towards the river. They had drawn some questioning looks from the legionaries still at work in the torchlight, but the sight of their primus pilus and an escort of a heavily armed *contubernium* – a unit of eight men – led the soldiers to the assumption that it was a group of Getic deserters being taken for questioning. They had removed their weapons which, along with their regular clothes, Vespasian's uniform, a couple of crowbars and the ropes, were in a hand-cart being pulled by Varinus and his two mates Lucius and Arruns.

'It'll be a hard slog but we'll get there. The key to it is timing. We need to contain the thousand or so enemy in the fortified village so that they don't take the towers in the rear in the half-hour that it will take to push them to the walls, or, once we're there, burst through the siege lines and escape whilst we're busy trying to get over the fortress's walls. That'll be the job for the seventh, eighth, ninth and tenth cohorts, whilst we and the sixth take one tower, the third and fourth take another and two cohorts of the Fifth Macedonica take the third, leaving their other two cohorts to guard the gates. I'll give Poppaeus his due, he does think things through and he knows how to conduct a siege, which is more than can be said for some of the twats that I've served under.'

'What time is the attack set for?' Sabinus asked.

Before Faustus could reply a horribly familiar voice interrupted. 'Faustus, where the fuck did you find these savages?' Centurion Caelus loomed out of the darkness accompanied by two torch-bearing legionaries. 'If you're taking them to the general for questioning then you're going the wrong way.'

'Piss off, Caelus, and mind your own business,' Faustus growled. Vespasian and Sabinus lowered their heads in an attempt to hide their shaven un-Getic faces; Magnus retreated behind Sitalces.

'Prisoners are the general's business, and I make the general's business my business,' Caelus replied, taking a torch from one of his legionaries and thrusting it towards Vespasian. 'They don't seem too keen to be seen, do they?'

'Keep back,' Faustus warned as he tried to step between Vespasian and Caelus, but Caelus was quicker and he grabbed Vespasian's chin and forced his head up.

'Well, what have we here?' he drawled, staring coldly into Vespasian's eyes. 'A tribune disguised as a Getic warrior.' He looked around at the rest of the party and recognised Sitalces and the other Thracians. 'All of you dressed the same . . . not really messengers from the Queen, eh? Spies, more like.' He turned back to Vespasian. 'I knew you were up to something with these hairy bastards back up in the pass when you gave them orders. You hadn't spoken to them once on the journey yet you knew

Sitalces' and Artebudz's names. Now I understand why you put all our lives in danger, you're on a secret mission for someone that couldn't wait. The general will be very interested, I'm sure, when I tell him what's going on.'

'Centurion, you will do no such thing,' Vespasian ordered futilely. 'Faustus, grab him!'

Caelus jumped to his right, away from Faustus as the primus pilus made a lunge for him, and swung his torch round, narrowly missing Faustus' face, causing him to back off. Then, with a sneer, he sidestepped between his two accompanying legionaries and sprinted off into the night.

'You two get back to your century,' Faustus ordered Caelus' two legionaries, 'and don't say a word about this to anyone unless you want to spend the rest of your service on latrine duty and having the skin whipped off your backs at regular intervals.'

The two men, looking suitably terrified at the very real threat, nodded quickly, saluted their primus pilus and beat a hasty retreat.

'Bugger it,' Vespasian snapped, 'he's going to cause us a shit-load of trouble.'

'Yeah, but what can Poppaeus do? He might guess that we're going to try and enter the fortress but he doesn't know how, and by the time Caelus reaches the camp we'll be getting in the boat,' Magnus pointed out.

'You're right, I suppose; we'd best get a move on.'

Vespasian scrambled down the steep riverbank towards the eight-oared, flat-bottomed oak boat, twenty paces long and three across at its widest point. It was moored on a jetty amongst the reeds at the bottom of the bank and guarded by two of Faustus' men. It was mainly used for transporting supplies to and from the ships stationed out in the river; their stern- and bow-lamps could be seen, bobbing lethargically in the oil-dark night, sending sparkling ruby reflections in thin, rippling lines across the gently flowing water.

'Get the gear stowed as fast as you can, Varinus,' Vespasian ordered as the three legionaries brought the hand-cart down the slope accompanied by much swearing.

'I'll have some men waiting a couple of miles or so downriver from our camp, with your horses and one for the priest,' Faustus informed them as they started to clamber into the boat. 'They'll have torches so you can see them. From there Tomi is one day's hard ride; you will need to follow the river until the old fortress at Axiopolis where it bends sharply to the north, leave it there and head towards the coast just south of east.'

'Thank you, my brother,' Sabinus said, taking Faustus' hand in a strange grasp. 'May our Lord keep you in his light.'

'And you also, brother,' Faustus responded as Sabinus turned to go.

'Live through tomorrow night,' Vespasian said, clasping the centurion's forearm.

Faustus smiled. 'Oh, don't worry about me; it'll take a lot more than a pack of horse-fucking savages to send me to the warmth of Mithras' light.'

'I'm sure it will.' Vespasian turned to get into the boat. As he took his place in the stern next to Sabinus at the steering-oar a series of bucina calls broke out from the Roman siege lines above them.

'Shit!' Faustus exclaimed.

'That's "all cohorts to stand to arms". What is it, do you think?' Vespasian asked.

'Well, either the Getae are attacking the whole wall instead of one section, which is unlikely and we would have heard their heathen war cries by now, or Poppaeus has just brought forward the assault to tonight, If he has he's mad, it'll go off half-arsed and will be an almighty fuck-up.'

'Shit,' Sabinus spat, 'he's guessed what we're doing from what Caelus has told him and he means to beat us to the priest.'

'I'd better go,' Faustus called back to them, as he scrambled back up the bank followed by his men. 'If it is the assault I'll still make sure that your horses are waiting for you. Poppaeus has just helped you unwittingly; if we are attacking now, the Getae will be manning the walls and the courtyard should be clear.'

'Yes, but every one of the buggers will now be wide awake,' Magnus grumbled, 'and where will the priest be?'

'I can't imagine that slippery little shit defending the walls if he's got a nice warm room to hide in,' Vespasian said, grabbing the steering-oar. 'Cast off, Varinus.'

'Aye aye, trierarchus,' the grizzled veteran called back with a grin as he loosed the mooring rope and pushed his oar against the jetty. Vespasian frowned at this over-familiarity but knew better than to reprimand a man to whom he was shortly going to entrust his life for a bit of harmless banter.

The boat eased out into the flow of the river and began to glide downstream towards the fortress half a mile away. Although all the oars were manned Vespasian did not order the men to start pulling; the current was doing the work for them and the efforts of eight untrained scullers would, in all likelihood, have hindered rather than helped their progress. The half-moon was obscured by a thick layer of cloud and, even though they were only ten paces or so out into the river, it was almost completely dark now that they were away from the torch-lit Roman lines. On shore, to their right, the high-pitched blare of bucinae gave way to the deep bass rumblings of *cornua*, horns used by the army to give battle signals, their deeper tones being more easily heard over the sharp clash of weapons and the shouts and screams of men in combat.

'That'll be the attack starting,' Vespasian whispered to his brother beside him. 'The bastard brought it forward and a lot more of the lads will die because of the chaos.'

'When *cornua* blow, blood will flow,' Sabinus said, quoting an old legionary truism.

Vespasian peered towards the shore trying to get some measure, from the noise, of what was going on. He could make out a soft, orange glow that silhouetted the riverbank and guessed that it was the torches in the fortified settlement a hundred paces inland. 'Faustus said it will take half an hour to roll the towers forward but they wouldn't start until that village was secured.'

'Assuming they stick to the original plan, which at the moment they most certainly aren't,' Sabinus pointed out. 'Anyway, it's pointless worrying about it, it's out of our hands;

we've got to concentrate on our own problems, the first of which is where are we going to land.'

Vespasian nodded and turned his attention to keeping the boat going in a straight line. He felt a knot begin to develop in his belly and realised that the wound he had received in the Succi Pass was the first time he'd had blood drawn in combat and, although only small, it had made him far more aware of his own mortality; if he had not been wearing a breastplate he would in all probability have been killed. He was not wearing a breastplate now and he was feeling decidedly vulnerable. Images from his childhood working on the family estates flicked through his mind and for a few moments he longed to be safely home, where the most he had to fear was a kick from a belligerent mule. He banished the thought, knowing it was futile; he had made his choices and they had led him far from home to this boat. All he could do now was steel himself to face the oncoming danger and override the fear of death by trying to concentrate on the practicalities of the task in hand.

Looking ahead, he saw that a few small points of light from the fortress keep's windows were now visible; they were getting close. When they were about level with the centre of the fortress he started to ease the boat towards the shore in an effort to find, in the deep gloom, a spot where the reed beds thinned out and he could get the boat adjacent to the bank. The wall, 150 paces away, appeared as a long slab of intense darkness haloed by a thin light from the few torches burning within the courtyard. At its extreme left the keep towered over them, its shape only definable by hints of torchlight that rose from the courtyard reaching partway up the inner wall and the odd glimmer of light from open windows in the outer wall that fell to the riverbank.

In the distance the rumblings of the cornua continued.

Eventually the boat hit the solid earth of the bank. Varinus secured the mooring rope to the base of a scraggy bush as Vespasian and his party scrambled out on to dry land. Lucius and Arruns passed them the crowbars and ropes and their Getic weaponry: bows, quivers of arrows, sleek knives and the long-handled axes, with six-inch blades and spikes on their reverse, which the tribe favoured for fighting hand to hand on horseback. Sitalces and his Thracians had also brought their rhomphaiai, which they strapped to their backs. Artebudz and Sabinus each slung a thick coil of rope over their shoulders.

'Hide the boat amongst the reeds, Varinus,' Vespasian whispered, attaching a quiver to his belt. 'We'll come back to this spot as quick as we can.'

'Right you are, sir, good luck.'

Vespasian grunted something unintelligible, turned and led his men off, crouching low as he cautiously made his way up the bank. As he neared the summit the sound of movement close by, dead ahead, caused him to stop suddenly.

'What is it?' Sabinus hissed next to him.

'Something's moving at the top of the bank,' Vespasian replied, pulling an arrow from his quiver and straining his eyes to peer through the gloom; as they adjusted he began to make out two or three shapes, then a few more, on the ridge of the bank. He notched the arrow; behind him he sensed his comrades doing the same. One of the shapes moved fractionally. Vespasian did not dare to breathe; then he heard a soft, flaccid-lipped exhalation followed by a snort and a couple of hard stamps on the grass-covered ground.

'It's just horses, lots of them,' he whispered, lowering his bow and breathing a sigh of relief. He moved on cautiously up the hill. The others followed.

The tightness in his stomach that had been growing since they had got in the boat was now excruciating and, despite the chill of the night, he had begun to sweat with fear. It was a fool's mission that they had embarked on and he began to resent the ease with which Antonia, from the safety of her sumptuous villa back in Rome, could expect him and his brother to accomplish it. Then he remembered his grandmother's words of warning: do not get involved with the schemes of the powerful because they use people of his class to do their dirty work and then tend to dispose of them once they knew too much and were of no further use.

'Having second thoughts about this, sir?' Magnus asked, as if reading his mind as they crested the bank and paused; ahead of them the forms of countless horses at rest fell away into the darkness.

'What makes you ask that?'

'Well, stands to reason, don't it? Here we are about to take on thousands of savages who anyone in their right mind would steer well clear of, in order to get a disgusting little man whom, having made his acquaintance once, no one with any sense would ever want to meet again; and all for what, I ask you?'

Vespasian smiled in the darkness. 'Well, I suppose we're doing it for Rome.'

'Rome, my arse! You may be doing it for Rome but I'm doing it because you're doing it and I'm obliged to go with you because of the debt that I owe your uncle; that's why I was wondering whether, by any luck, you'd come to your senses and were having second thoughts.'

'Are you two going to sit and chat all night?' Sabinus hissed from the gloom.

'That sounds like a much better option to me,' Magnus muttered, only half to himself.

Buoyed by the fact that his friend was evidently as scared as he was, and surprisingly reassured by the presence of his brother, Vespasian pulled himself together. Remembering Sitalces' Thracian adage with a half-smile, he led the group, zigzagging carefully, through the hundreds of resting Getic horses that, recognising the smell of their Getic clothes, parted slightly for them and, with the occasional whicker or snort, let them pass.

It took a while to cover the hundred paces over the rough ground through this living obstacle to the steep slope below the fortress. As they reached the foot of the slope, they could hear, from above them, shouts and the sound of hundreds of feet running.

'Sounds like they're all awake now,' Magnus complained.

'But they're up on the walls,' Vespasian said, feeling that they might have a chance after all. 'Let's find this sewer outlet.'

They made their way up the slope to the base of the wall and began to follow it towards the keep.

They smelt the sewer long before they saw it. Nearly four

hundred years' worth of sewage had poured out of it, creating a reeking, septic marsh below its discharge point.

Eventually they heard the trickle of flowing liquid and they stopped by a circular grill, three feet in diameter, emitting an even worse stink than the marsh.

'Pluto's unwashed arse, that smells even worse than these clothes,' Magnus gasped; he had just about got used to the stench of his disguise.

'A good choice of expletive, my friend,' Vespasian observed. 'I think it is Pluto's unwashed arse and we're just about to climb up it.'

'Imagine how we'll smell when we get out the other end,' Sabinus said, trying not to retch.

'Sitalces, Ziles, bring the crowbars over here and get this thing off,' Vespasian ordered, realising that there was no point in delaying the inevitable.

Seemingly impervious to the reek, Sitalces and Ziles placed their crowbars under the lip of the grill. With a couple of powerful wrenches it came loose from the wall and Drenis and Bryzos pulled it free.

'Let's get this over with,' Vespasian muttered, drawing a deep breath and forcing himself inside the pitch-black tunnel.

There was only enough space to crawl and for the first time since he had put on the oddly unfamiliar and constricting trousers he felt thankful for them; they protected his knees from the centuries of shit that coated the tunnel floor. But his hands had no such protection and squelched through the slimy effluence clinging to the rim as he eased his way up the dark, narrow passage.

After what seemed like an age of breathing in the noxious gas produced by decomposing faeces, but was in fact only the time it took to cover fifteen gruelling feet, Vespasian heard harsh voices ahead and could make out a faint flicker of orange light at the end of the tunnel. Torn between his desire to get out into the open air quickly and his fear that the exit was guarded, he kept going at the same pace: as fast as was possible. Upon drawing closer to the end, he realised that the light was not coming directly into the tunnel but was in fact reflecting off a wall a few feet from its opening. He forced himself to slow down and came to a halt three feet from the exit; he felt Sabinus bump into his hindquarters, then the added pressure of the man behind pushing him forward and so on down the line, as they all came to an unexpected, concertinaed halt in the bowels of the sewer.

Vespasian craned his neck forward in an attempt to see out of the tunnel and over the wall beyond; he was rewarded by the sight of two very hairy Getic arses in action, their owners talking vigorously as they perched on top of the wall, which was one of three that surrounded the sewer's exit, forming an open and well-used latrine. Another arse appeared over one of the side walls as the first two came to their noisy finale and were withdrawn, to be replaced, almost instantaneously, by two more.

'What the fuck's going on? Why have we stopped?' Sabinus hissed from behind.

'Not surprisingly we've come out in their latrine and a few of them are taking the opportunity to have a last shit.'

'Oh, for fuck's sake, how long are they going to be?'

'How should I know?' Vespasian whispered, craning his neck again. 'There're now five of them up there at the moment; two of them seem to be quite scared,' he added with a grin.

A few moments later the unmistakable sound of a bollocking being administered along with a couple of cuffs around the ears caused the arses, two of which were still in full flow, to hasten away. Vespasian counted to one hundred and, when no more appeared, deemed it safe to move forward and out of the sewer. Despite squatting calf-deep in fresh turds he felt like a new man as he sucked in the comparatively fresh air above the open latrine and wiped the shit from his hands on to his trousers. It had fallen unnaturally quiet. He edged closer to the front wall, peeked over and found, to his surprise, that he was surrounded by horses; they had been corralled in the northeast corner of the courtyard to keep them as far away as possible from the gate and out of the way of the main fighting. They were all displaying an understandable reluctance to get too close to the latrine. Looking beyond the horses, as the others started to emerge from the sewer, he could see that the south and west walls were crammed with Getae, two or three deep, almost shoulder to shoulder, bows at the ready, staring out towards the Roman lines with the still silence of men watching their fate coming inexorably towards them.

Sabinus joined him. 'That's a bit of luck,' he whispered as he took in the situation.

'I've never heard someone standing knee-deep in shit consider themselves lucky,' Vespasian observed, 'but yes, it is. Let's go.' He looked around at the others to make sure that they were all present and then started to creep over the wall.

A deep cornu signal rumbled through the air.

'Shit,' Sabinus hissed pulling him back, 'that's "artillery open fire". Get down.'

All eight of them squatted behind the wall. The distant hiss of many approaching fast-moving projectiles suddenly filled the air; it quickly intensified before exploding into a series of shattering impacts as rock and iron missiles crashed into the fortress; some punching men, sometimes whole but more often in pieces, back off the walls, others striking stone, in a shower of sparks, and sending a deluge of sharp chippings cascading down to hit the ground, kicking up puffs of dust. Above the screaming, the Getic chieftains roared a series of orders. The defenders raised their bows and began to release volley after volley into the night sky at a speed that astounded Vespasian.

'Shit, if they're firing back it must mean that the towers are getting close,' Sabinus exclaimed, pulling his axe from his belt. 'Stop gazing around, little brother, we don't have much time.' He leapt out of the latrine and ran towards the keep, twenty paces away to the left, hugging the wall, not because he was worried about stealth any longer, as the defenders were by now far too busy to notice, but in an attempt to keep clear of the now panicking horses. Vespasian and the others followed him as a huge storm of arrows flooded in from the advancing Romans and rained down on to the walls and into the courtyard, felling dozens of men and a score of their already terrified mounts. This was too much for the beasts and they surged towards the crude fencing that corralled them in and broke through with ease to go bucking and rearing around the corpse-strewn courtyard.

Vespasian, axe in hand, caught up with his brother at the door to the keep. He was burning with shame at Sabinus' rebuke because it had been the truth, he had hesitated and now Sabinus had taken charge.

'On the count of three, little brother,' Sabinus said, putting his shoulder to the locked door. 'Three!'

They rammed their bodies in unison against the solid oak.

It held.

'Shit! Sitalces, Ziles,' Sabinus yelled above the din, 'where're those crowbars? Fast as you like, lads, there'll be another artillery volley pretty soon, those crews were quick.'

Sitalces and Ziles ran straight up to the door and quickly jammed their bars between it and the frame. But not quickly enough; another series of crashing impacts caused them all to duck involuntarily as the second artillery volley smashed in. Two onager stones hit the keep wall a few feet above the door, shattering on impact in a myriad of sparks. Large fragments of stone ricocheted down over them, striking their crouched backs and the ground around like sharp, heavy rain, leaving them bruised but uninjured.

Sitalces was the first to recover; he hurled his huge body on to the end of a crowbar; with a splintering crack the door came loose but not open. Ziles rejammed his bar into the widened gap, Sitalces swept his rhomphaia from the sheath on his back, nodded at him and they forced their combined weight on to the two crowbars. This time the door flew back and the huge Thracian went tumbling through, his momentum sending him crashing to the ground. Ziles leapt in after him and jerked immediately back through the air, as if punched by a Titan, with a half-dozen arrows in his chest. Before the dead Thracian had even hit the ground Vespasian hurled himself through the opening, darting to the left as a mighty roar came from within. He arrived in time to see Sitalces, in the torchlight, leaping through the air, sweeping his rhomphaia two-handed from above his right shoulder, towards a line of six Getae who were struggling, under the pressure, to reload quickly. A flaming flash of iron arced into them, severing two heads and half an arm in a welter of blood and speed. As the huge Thracian crashed into the right of the Getic line Vespasian flung himself, bellowing, towards the left-hand Geta, who had dropped his bow and was drawing a long-bladed knife; an arrow from the door felled the man next to him. The knife coursed through the air at chest height towards Vespasian, who had the presence of mind to duck as he noticed the deft flick of his opponent's hand. It skimmed over his head, which, an instant later, pounded into the solar plexus of the man, thumping the air from his lungs and him to the ground with Vespasian on top of him. With an animal howl Vespasian heaved himself to his knees, raised his axe and swiped it down repeatedly on to the choking Geta's face, cracking it open in an eruption of bone, blood and teeth, then mashing it to a pulp with his frenzied attack. A strong grip caught his wrist and he swivelled round to see Magnus straining to hold his arm back.

'I think you'll find he's dead now, sir,' he said through gritted teeth. 'In fact they all are.'

Vespasian blinked a few times and began to relax; the whole room came into focus for the first time since he had charged. The six Getae lay dead, in various states of dismemberment, and Sitalces, Bryzos and Drenis were busy trying to wedge the battered door shut whilst Artebudz and Sabinus were covering the narrow, stone staircase leading to the next floor. He started to breathe deeply to bring himself back from the primeval part of his nature to which, he was now realising, his fear of death had taken him.

'You've got to watch that, sir,' Magnus said in a hushed voice, pulling him to his feet. 'They only die once and you can easily get killed yourself as you're trying to kill them a second, third or, in your case, a sixth time.'

'Thank you, Magnus, I'll try to remember that,' Vespasian replied, slightly more curtly than he intended. 'Sorry, I was shit scared,' he added by way of an apology. He noticed a blood-stained rhomphaia in his friend's hand.

Magnus caught his look. 'I borrowed it from Ziles, he won't be needing it no more. It's a lovely weapon, much nicer to fight with than against, especially if it's wielded by the likes of Sitalces, if you take my meaning?'

Vespasian certainly did.

Another crashing volley of artillery projectiles battering the keep's wall brought him back to the matter in hand. He joined Sabinus at the bottom of the steps.

'Any noise from up there?' he whispered, just audible above the shrieks and shouts of the Getae on the walls.

'Nothing,' his brother replied.

Sitalces rushed over from the door. 'That's the best that we can do, but it won't last long.'

'Best get going, then,' Sabinus said, taking one of the brightly burning torches from the wall. 'Bring the other torches; we'll leave it dark down here. Artebudz, with me.' He began to swiftly climb the stairs with Artebudz, bow drawn, next to him. The noise from outside remained at a steady level and easily masked their light footsteps.

Vespasian grabbed a torch and, with Magnus at his side, followed. His heart was beating fast; he was still afraid but his fear of death had been overshadowed by another, stronger, more positive emotion: the will and desire to survive. He felt much calmer now and also grateful to his brother for taking the lead when his own actions, as he was well aware, had been found wanting.

A creak of a wooden floorboard told Vespasian that his brother had reached the first floor. Sabinus and Artebuduz moved cautiously ahead; Vespasian followed. They were in a storeroom that extended the full length and breadth of the keep. It was windowless as it was still below the height of the fortress' walls. In the middle of the room was a sturdy-looking wooden staircase leading up to the next level. Dotted around in the gloom were piles of grain sacks, stacks of amphorae and water barrels. Hanging on the walls were what Vespasian first took to be dead bodies but on closer inspection turned out to be deer and sheep carcasses.

'Looks like we've found the Getae's dinner,' Sabinus observed. 'Quick, lads, pile a load of those sacks around the staircase and see what's in those amphorae. Let's hope it's oil, fire will be our friend.'

It was the work of moments. As they finished by pouring the contents of the amphorae, which had indeed proved to be oil, over the pile of sacks, the level of noise from outside suddenly changed; the shouting grew louder and mixed in with it now was the unmistakable clash of weapons.

'That's our boys on the wall, we've really got to hurry,' Sabinus said, giving his torch to Drenis and grabbing an unopened amphora. 'Take an amphora if you can, lads, we may need fire upstairs. Drenis, wait until we're all on the next floor and then set light to the sacks.' He dashed up the stairs with Vespasian pursuing, hot on his heels.

They burst on to the second floor; again it was a single large room, but with a staircase at the far end, and with windows that looked out only over the river, not the courtyard. Piles of bedding scattered around the floor indicated that it had been used as a dormitory for those of the Getae important enough not to sleep outside. Sabinus and Vespasian ran towards the next staircase; four arrows smacked into the floorboards just before them, bringing them to a sudden, almost overbalancing, halt. They pulled back immediately as Magnus, carrying two amphorae, and the rest of their comrades cleared the second staircase.

'There's a reception committee on the next floor. Artebudz, Sitalces and Bryzos: pump some arrows up those stairs,' Sabinus ordered. 'Vespasian, we'll follow.'

As Artebudz, Sitalces and Bryzos slowly moved forward, shooting alternately so there was always an arrow fizzing up the stairs, Sabinus followed with his amphora of oil and Vespasian with his torch. Drenis came crashing up the stairs behind, the smell of burning travelling in his wake.

Ten feet from the stairs, Sabinus sprang forward and hurled his amphora up them; it disappeared with a crash on to the next floor. Vespasian paused as a few more arrows were pumped up the stairs, then he ran forward and hurled his torch after them. The intense heat of the torch caused the oil to ignite almost instantaneously; the fire soon engulfed the third-floor landing and drips of burning oil flowed, like flaming tears, down between the gaps in the stairs.

'Artebudz, Bryzos, bows first; Magnus, Sitalces and Drenis after us,' Sabinus shouted, drawing his axe; they all nodded. Sabinus turned to Vespasian and grinned. 'This is more fun than arse-licking back in Rome but it's going to hurt, little brother. Go!'

Artebudz and Bryzos hurtled up the stairs and disappeared into the inferno, with Vespasian and Sabinus speeding after them as gushes of liquid splattered down on to the burning oil, evaporating immediately into a thick, foul-smelling steam. This, along with the flames, blinded Vespasian for a few steps but his vision returned as he emerged through the fire and on to the landing at the far end of a long corridor running back along the width of the keep to another set of stairs. It was punctuated with four, evenly spaced doors on either side. He spun round to his left, Sabinus to his right, both taking care not to slip on the burning oil, as an arrow bisected them and slammed into the wall beyond. Feeling grateful to his trousers for protecting his legs from burns, Vespasian looked up to see, by the light of the flames, Bryzos and Artebudz both releasing arrows at two Getae, one about to shoot, one reloading, halfway down the corridor; two more lay dead at his feet, slop-buckets at their sides. Both arrows punched into the shooting man, hurling him to the ground as his shot thwacked harmlessly into the wooden ceiling. Vespasian and Sabinus charged forward as the second Geta fired; Artebudz recoiled on to his back with an arrow in his chest as they surged past him. With no time to reload the Geta turned, pelted down the corridor and leapt up the staircase, disappearing with a sharp cry and a well-aimed arrow from Bryzos through his calf.

The corridor was clear but was now starting to fill with smoke as the oil burned off, leaving the wooden floor and stairs aflame through which Magnus, Sitalces and Drenis appeared, smouldering and singed. From outside the sound of fighting had grown closer.

'Sounds like our boys are pushing them off the walls,' Sabinus shouted. 'Bryzos, cover that far staircase with oil. If anyone tries to come down torch it.'

Magnus handed Bryzos his amphorae and Drenis gave him his torch and he hurried off to obey his instructions.

'Right, let's get searching these rooms,' Sabinus continued, 'and Sitalces, get that rope from Artebudz.'

'It's all right, I can carry it,' Artebudz said, raising himself painfully to a sitting position. 'I don't seem to be dead, just a bit bruised.' He pulled at the arrow, which was embedded in the coil of rope; that and the thickness of the Getic topcoat had saved his life.

'Well, you're a lucky bugger,' Sabinus said. 'You and Sitalces come with me: we'll do the right-hand rooms. Vespasian, you take Magnus and Drenis down the courtyard side. We'll do it alternately so we don't get caught in any crossfire. Get moving.'

The heat from the fire was intensifying as Vespasian kicked the door nearest to it open and pulled himself back quickly behind the wall, out of shot. No arrows hissed out, but a huge draught of air from an open window was sucked in to feed the oxygen-craving fire, which started to burn with renewed vigour. Drenis twisted into the room, bow at the ready.

'Clear!' he shouted a beat later. They moved on to the next door. Behind them Sabinus' group crashed open their first door.

By the time both groups had got to their last doors the smoke, gradually filling the corridor, was forcing them to stoop in order to breathe with relative ease. Heat from the fire on the floors below was rising through the floorboards.

'Rhoteces had better be in one of these,' Vespasian said to Magnus as he braced himself to kick it open, 'I don't fancy going up another level.'

A cry from Bryzos stopped him mid-kick. Vespasian spun round to see the ginger-haired Thracian, feathered with arrows, drop his torch and fall at the foot of the stairs, from the top of which appeared the feet and legs of a charging posse of Getae. Sitalces, Drenis and Artebudz immediately started pumping arrows into the attackers, sending the foremost tumbling and slithering down the oil-slick stairs. With a desperate last burst of energy the dying Thracian reached for the torch and with the tips of his fingers flicked it towards him. Vespasian and his comrades watched it roll with a slow inevitablity, into the pool of oil; the burning pitch caused it to fizzle and smoke, then, reaching its flashpoint, it burst into flames, engulfing Bryzos and the dead Getae piled around him; his screams grew with the intensity on the fire. Unable to get through the conflagration the surviving Getae withdrew, trapped on the floor above.

With the smell of burning human flesh assaulting his nostrils and Bryzos' dying screams reverberating around his head, Vespasian kicked open his final door. Again Drenis wheeled in and again the room was clear. Vespasian rushed over to the window and risked a quick look out. Files of legionaries were spewing on to the south and west walls from the left- and right-hand siege towers. The central one, nearest the gate, was on fire; men, some burning, some not, were hurling themselves out of the inferno. Something had gone badly wrong. However, down in the courtyard the Getae were being split up and becoming encircled in small groups, as fresh legionaries poured down the steps from the wall to bolster their comrades already embroiled in savage, hand-to-hand combat. Directly underneath him a couple of contubernia broke down the keep's door; flames gushed out and they immediately withdrew towards the fortress gate, led by the easily distinguishable figure of Caelus.

Knowing in his gut that Caelus was coming for them, Vespasian ran back towards the corridor as Sabinus kicked open the final door; two arrows whistled out, narrowly missing Vespasian as he cleared the doorway. Artebudz and Sitalces jumped from their places either side of the door and returned fire, bringing down the two Getae inside.

Sabinus rushed in. 'Fuck!' he shouted. 'He's gone.'

Vespasian ran in and joined his brother by the window. A taut, vibrating rope, attached to a ceiling beam, led out of it. The brothers stuck their heads out of the window; ten feet below them was a Getic warrior and beneath him, twenty feet from the ground and just visible in the orange ambient light cast by the burning siege tower, was the recognisable figure of Rhoteces.

'Quick, pull,' Vespasian shouted, grabbing the rope. Magnus and Sitalces joined the brothers heaving on the rope. After a couple of sharp tugs the Getic warrior appeared, wide-eyed with fear, at the window. Artebudz sent an arrow into his open mouth and he fell with a shriek. The rope went suddenly slack and they all fell back into the room.

'The bastard's jumped,' Vespasian bellowed as he picked himself up and darted to the window. He grabbed the rope and without pausing leapt through the opening and started to slide down.

Vespasian descended quickly; the rope burned his hands, but the thick trousers protected his legs. As he passed the second-floor window he caught a blast of heat from the fire now raging within. From below came the sound of whinnying and neighing; the fire and noise had spooked the Getae's horses and they were surging, like an undulating black cloud, east, along the flat ground between the river bank and the slope leading up to the fortress walls.

Vespasian hit the ground; Sabinus arrived an instant later. The horses continued to thunder past just below them.

'Rhoteces couldn't have got through this lot,' Sabinus shouted to his brother as Magnus and then Sitalces joined them. 'He must have gone along the walls, but which way?'

'Away from the horses,' Vespasian replied. 'Once they've passed he'll cross behind them and head for the river; it's his only chance of escape.' He darted along the wall, against the tide of the horses, as Artebudz and Drenis made it to the ground. Above them flames burst out of the keep's windows.

The din of the battle raging in the courtyard, on the other side of the wall, intensified as they left the lee of the keep. They crossed the path of the sewer outlet as the rear of the stampede passed them by. To their right they could see the dark shapes of scores of dead horses who had floundered in the foul-smelling sewage marsh to be trampled over by their fellows.

There was no sign of the priest.

'We'll skirt around the marsh to the riverbank and then work our way upstream,' Vespasian shouted as he raced right, down the slope.

They were halfway across the flat ground to the riverbank when a shout caused Vespasian to pause.

'There they are, lads; up and at 'em.' Caelus and the sixteen men that he had used to try and break into the keep had rounded the west wall, a hundred paces away, and were sprinting down the slope towards them, silhouetted by the siege tower burning like a huge beacon.

'Shoot on the run,' Vespasian ordered, unslinging his bow and notching an arrow. They each had time to release three or four shots apiece before they came to the steep bank leading down to the river. The resulting fire brought down none of Caelus' men but forced them to raise their shields and slow down to a trot so as to keep them level and firm. Vespasian and his comrades turned and pumped volley after volley at them but they came on, flamelight flickering off their helmets and shield rims, impervious, behind their shield wall, to the arrows loosed at them, until they were almost within *pilum* range.

'That's it,' Sabinus growled, 'we've got to get out of here.'

'You're right, brother,' Vespasian agreed, 'back to the—' He was cut off before he could complete the order.

'Men of the fourth century, third cohort, Fourth Scythia, I command you to halt!'

The powerful and unmistakable voice of their primus pilus, bellowing from behind, brought the line to a sudden stop thirty paces from Vespasian.

Caelus spun round.

'About turn!' Faustus yelled.

With the discipline honed from years of obeying orders unconditionally they turned their backs on their supposed Getic enemies and faced Faustus, who came running out of the shadows. With a roar Caelus threw himself at him, sword pulled back for a deadly thrust to the groin. At the very last moment Faustus deftly stepped to his left and, as Caelus overbalanced past him, brought the hilt of his gladius crashing down on the back of his neck, sending him sprawling, semi-conscious, to the ground. Faustus quickly relieved him of his weapon and turned to address the bemused legionaries.

'This piece of filth was using you to sabotage a Roman mission,' he bawled at them. 'Those men are ours; they had no choice but to fire at you. Tribune Vespasian, bring your men forward.'

Vespasian led his comrades up to the legionaries and pulled off his Getic cap.

'When I saw Caelus leading his men back through the gate I knew he'd be after you so I legged it over here,' Faustus told him as the legionaries recognised Vespasian and started to mutter amongst themselves.

'Thank you, my friend,' Vespasian replied, 'I'm afraid we missed the priest though, he'll be well away by now.'

'Well, we've all had a bad night then; the attack was a fucking shambles. We didn't seal off the village properly and almost a thousand of the Getae broke out and torched our tower as it reached the fortress walls, killing a lot of my lads, before forcing their way out through the gates in the siege-wall. But at least we've dealt with the rest of them, the fortress is ours.'

'Come on, little brother, we'd best be going,' Sabinus said. 'There's still an outside chance of catching Rhoteces if he's taken a boat downriver.'

Vespasian sighed. He was exhausted, but knew that even if there was just the smallest of hopes they should try. 'What are you going to do with him?' he asked quietly, looking down at Caelus, who was just starting to come round.

'Well, I couldn't kill him in front of the men,' Faustus replied in a low voice, kneeling down over Caelus. 'One of them would talk and Poppaeus would have me for murder, so I'll take him back to the fight and finish him off there.'

A quick series of shrill whinnies caused them both to turn. The air filled with the rumble of hooves.

'Shit! The horses are coming back,' Vespasian cried.

'Form a wedge, shields both sides,' Sabinus yelled. 'Pila to the front!'

The confused legionaries, aware that there was a danger fast approaching but unaware of its nature, quickly ordered themselves around their erstwhile opponents into a pilum-bristling V-formation as the first of the horses appeared out of the night, surging towards them.

In the confusion Caelus took his chance; he whipped his *pugio* from its sheath and rammed it into the side of Faustus' neck; as the blood spurted from the jugular vein he leapt to his feet and pelted towards the fort. Vespasian made to run after him but one glance left, towards the dark tide of terrified beasts now only feet away, checked him. He let the doomed centurion go and instead knelt by Faustus, desperately trying to stem the gushing stream of blood.

The stampede reached the wedge.

An instant before contact the leading horses, perhaps sensing more than seeing the solid-looking, spike-ridden obstacle in front of them, veered right and left to avoid it; the rest followed their lead and the stampede flowed around the wedge like a river streaming around an island. From the relative safety of the interior Vespasian, hands pressed to Faustus' neck, glanced back to see Caelus flick a terrified look over his shoulder and put on another turn of speed before disappearing, with a curtailed shriek, under the torrent of hooves.

The legionaries stood firm as the stampede washed around them; the ground shook with such force they were obliged to loosen the tension in their knees to soak up the shock waves pulsing up through the earth. The cries and the hoofbeats of the maddened, wild-eyed, foaming beasts enveloping them were deafening as they passed not an arm's length from the shields; some animal instinct kept them just clear of the pilum points.

Finally the tip of the wedge appeared through the tail of the stampede and the last horses passed either side to be sucked together again, sealing the rend in the herd as if it had never existed.

They were clear.

It was a while before anyone moved.

'Fuck me! I think I shat myself,' Magnus said eventually in a hoarse whisper, 'not that you'd be able to tell over the smell of these trousers. How's Faustus?'

Vespasian looked down at Faustus who smiled weakly. 'I told you the horse-fuckers wouldn't get me,' he whispered. 'My Lord awaits me.'

His eyes glazed over and he was gone. Vespasian closed them with the palm of his blood-soaked hand and stood up. 'Take Centurion Faustus back to the camp with honour,' he ordered the legionaries, 'and scrape up that lump of shit as you go,' he added pointing to the battered and raw body of his friend's murderer lying in a mangled heap a few paces away.

The dazed legionaries gave a few ragged salutes and lifted their primus pilus on to their shoulders. Sabinus touched Faustus' chest and muttered a few unintelligible words over him, and then, without a word, they walked slowly away.

As he watched his friend being borne away Vespasian's eyes were drawn to the fortress walls. They were now clear of Getae. Small squads of legionaries sauntered along them with the nonchalance of soldiers who have survived the rigours of battle and have nothing now to fear. A small, solitary figure appeared and looked out towards the river; his high-plumed helmet and crimson cloak glowed in the firelight. Vespasian knew that it was Poppaeus; the general raised his gladius and shook it at them. Whether he could see them or not Vespasian did not know or care.

'Let's go,' he said to nobody in particular, and started to trudge towards the river.

It took a while to find the place where they had left Varinus and his mates in the boat.

'Varinus,' Vespasian called softly.

The prow of the boat appeared out of the reeds with Lucius and Arruns rowing; Varinus steered it to the bank.

'We might have what you've been looking for, sirs,' Varinus said with a grin as Vespasian and Sabinus stepped aboard.

'What?' Sabinus asked absently.

'Well, we was watching the keep and then after a while we saw fires in the windows. Then suddenly a rope came out of a window and two men climbed out, then one was hauled back in but the other one jumped; then you all came sliding down. So I decided to modify my orders slightly and Lucius and me, we crept ashore; it weren't long before we caught him about to get into a little boat hidden just downstream.'

Vespasian was suddenly alert again. 'Did you kill him?'

'Well, I figured that if you'd gone to all that effort to find him I should leave that pleasure to you.' Varinus replied, flicking back a piece of waxed material at his feet. Under it, bound hand and foot, eyes brimming with hatred, lay the priest, Rhoteces.

'You!' he spat when he recognised Vespasian. 'You should be dead. I sent men to do the gods' work and kill you,' he snarled, baring his sharply filed front teeth.

Vespasian crashed his fist into the priest's face. 'That's for all the lads that you managed to kill instead.' He pulled back his arm and punched the stunned Rhoteces again. 'And that's for Decimus Falens.'

Vespasian felt a restraining hand clasp his wrist as he went for another blow.

'I think that it would be a pity to beat him to death, sir,' Magnus whispered in his ear, 'especially after all the trouble we've been to.'

'You're right,' Vespasian replied, taking a rapid series of shallow breaths. He jerked his arm free, looked down at the unconscious body of Rhoteces and spat in his bloodied face. 'But I do loathe the little shit.'

CHAPTER VII

THE SMALL BOAT slid with the current and the help of a light, westerly breeze down the Danuvius; past the siege wall, past the main Roman camp just beyond that and headed towards the faint pre-dawn glow in the eastern sky. Lucius and Arruns rowed steadily with Varinus at the steering-oar keeping a course as close to the shore as possible so as to avoid the attentions of the Danuvius fleet, bobbing to the left of them, faint shadows in the gloom. Vespasian and his comrades were too tired to do anything but sit and stare at nothing.

The memory of Faustus, Bryzos and Ziles hung over them all.

Rhoteces, now gagged as well as bound, lay in a heap in the bilge. He had come round earlier but Magnus had knocked him unconscious again when his struggling and grunting had become too tiresome to tolerate. Water slopped around him.

After a while a small, yellowish point of light on the shoreline in the distance caught their attention.

'That should be Faustus' men with our horses,' Vespasian said, rousing himself from semi-slumber. 'Make directly for them, Varinus.'

'Aye, aye, trierarchus!'

Vespasian rolled his eyes and, again, let the insubordination pass; Varinus had done more for their cause that night by his self-initiated modification of his orders than he would, as a mere legionary mule, ever realise.

Faustus' men had had the sense to wait by a length of river-bank that was low and clear of reeds. The boat glided towards them and gently came to rest tucked up against the bank. The first birds of the morning had started to sing in anticipation of a new day as the early rays from the sun, still buried beyond the horizon, struck the highermost clouds with dashes of soft crimson and indigo.

'Optio Melitus reporting, sir, with your horses, on Primus Pilus Faustus' orders.' The smart young optio snapped a salute, blanching somewhat at the smell of the Getic clothes, as Vespasian disembarked first, followed by Sabinus and the others.

'Thank you, optio,' Vespasian said, returning the salute wearily. 'You and your men have done well,' he added, nodding to the two legionaries standing to attention behind Melitus. 'I'm sorry to say that Faustus is dead, so be careful when you go back to the camp; there may be some, er . . . repercussions.'

'Faustus is dead?' Melitus exclaimed. 'That is shit news; Centurion Viridio will be primus now and he's a savage bastard, not just a bastard like Faustus was.'

Varinus and his mates offloaded the gear and the recumbent priest as the exhausted party stripped off their filthy disguises and took an icy bath in the river, rubbing each other down vigorously in an attempt to eradicate all vestiges of the Getic stench. They were only partially successful.

Eventually, dressed in their own clothes and feeling refreshed by the cold water and the bread, sausage and cheese that Melitus had brought for them, along with two skins of fairly decent wine, they strapped Rhoteces over a horse and their provisions on to the two that had been brought for Bryzos and Ziles and prepared to leave.

'Cheers, lads,' Magnus called to Varinus and his mates as they got back in the boat, 'and I'll see you in Rome, Lucius, and we'll visit the Greens' stables.'

Lucius grinned. 'We've both got to get back there first,' he called back whilst steadying the boat for Melitus and his two men to get in. 'But if Fortuna smiles on us and we do, then she will surely smile on us and the Greens at the circus.'

They cast off and, spinning the boat around, began to pull upstream. The westerly breeze had stiffened but they were soon lost in the shadowy half-light.

Vespasian kicked his horse forward and they set off at a trot, east, along the river. Magnus rode next to him, leading the priest's horse.

'A decent bunch of lads, as I said, sir,' he observed, after a time of companionable silence.

'It depends on how you define decent,' Vespasian replied, 'but yes, they suited our purpose very well and if it were down to me I would make Varinus an optio for the initiative that he showed last night.'

'Be a waste of time that, sir; he's tried it twice and it didn't suit him, if you take my meaning?'

'You mean he didn't suit it?'

'Well, yeah, I suppose you could look at it that way; the army did, that's for sure.'

'I'm sure they did,' Vespasian replied, laughing for the first time in what felt like ages as the sun crested the horizon, splashing fresh, warm light over his face. 'Anyway, let's hope your mate Lucius makes it home, then you can have a lovely day together talking fluent chariot or whatever the official language of the track is.'

Magnus frowned. 'Now you're taking the piss, sir. Your trouble is you'll never understand how an insider like Lucius is worth cultivating over a period of time, worth doing favours for; keep him happy and he'll keep the tips flowing.' He looked back over his shoulder towards the boat conveying his potential gold-mine of information away and turned back abruptly. 'Shit! Sir, look behind us!'

Vespasian turned in his saddle; his face dropped. Less than a mile behind them eight biremes and two triremes of the river fleet were, under full oars and sail, heading towards them, bene-fiting greatly from the freshening breeze. With the golden rays of the morning sun adding lustre to their sleek wooden hulls and an amber sheen to their white sails they would have been a beautiful sight had they not been so threatening. The shrill whistles of the stroke-masters' flutes keeping time could just be heard floating across the water.

'Sabinus, look,' Vespasian shouted.

His brother turned. 'Shit! Poppaeus has sent a squadron after us; that bastard never gives up. All right, we won't wait for the bend; we'll head away from the river now.'

'I don't think that that's an option,' Sitalces piped up, pointing at a dust cloud three or four miles to the south.

'Roman?' Vespasian asked.

'No, a legionary cavalry detachment would never make that amount of dust, there's never more than a hundred and twenty of them,' Sitalces replied. 'There's got to be at least five or six times that number under that cloud. They're the ones that got away last night; they're Getae.'

'They can't be after us, they've no idea that we're here,' Magnus pointed out.

'Whether they have or haven't, they're heading this way, my friend,' Sitalces replied, 'and I don't fancy our chances if they come across us.'

'We'll have to outrun them along the river,' Vespasian shouted and urged his horse into a gallop.

The jolting and bumping of the rough ride brought Rhoteces back to consciousness and his struggling and muffled protestations could be heard over the hoofbeats.

In less than a third of a mile the country started to become rougher and the horses were forced to slow to a canter; even at that speed they were pulling away from the Roman squadron, but the Getic dust cloud was gaining on them. They crested a hill and the great Lysimachid fortress of Axiopolis came into view two miles away.

'That's where the river bends to the north,' Vespasian called across to Sabinus as they sped down the slope. 'I don't fancy taking the priest in there; Poppaeus doesn't know for certain that we've got him, but he's bound to have agents within the garrison who'll put him right. What do you think we should do?'

'Skirt around it and carry on in a straight line,' Sabinus called back, 'that way we'll lose the fleet and only have the Getae to worry about.'

'Oh, that's all right then,' Magnus said.

A dull thump and then whinny from Rhoteces' horse as it

reared up brought them all to a skidding halt. The priest had managed to undo the rope that bound his wrists to his ankles under the horse and was now hopping, feet still tied together, in the opposite direction.

'The little sod,' Magnus exclaimed, leaping off his horse. He raced back and jumped on Rhoteces, slamming him to the ground and dealing him a crashing right hook. The priest went limp, blood oozed out from under the gag and another bruised swelling appeared on his left cheek.

Sitalces ran back to help Magnus lift the unconscious prisoner back on to his horse, which refused to stand still and danced this way and that, snorting and shaking its head. They struggled to secure the rope under the beast's belly.

'Hurry up!' Sabinus urged. 'The squadron's gaining on us.'

From across the water the flute whistles had quickened. In an effort to catch their quarry before the river took them away all ten ships had accelerated to ramming speed, which they could maintain for only a few hundred strokes before the rowers were blown. They were now under a half-mile away. Vespasian could see their ballistae crews loading their weapons, which would very soon be in range.

To the south the Getic horde was now visible under its dust cloud as a dark stain on the ground.

'Done,' Magnus shouted eventually as he and Sitalces finally pulled the knot tight and headed back towards their horses.

Two plumes of water burst from the river, just five paces short of the bank, covering them all in a fine spray.

'Fuck, we're in range!' Sabinus yelled, turning to go. Another stone whistled just over their heads causing Magnus to look up; he instantly jumped on Sitalces, pushing the huge Thracian over; a rock slammed into the ground that he had been standing on an instant before and went bouncing off, narrowly missing the provisions horse that Artebudz was leading.

'I'd forgotten how easily you went down, my friend,' Magnus quipped as he hauled himself to his feet.

'I suppose you think that makes us even, Roman,' Sitalces grinned, 'but I'd say that's two falls I owe you for.'

They raced for their mounts as the others began to pull away. As Magnus flung his leg over his horse's back it let out a shrill cry and buckled underneath him. Its hindquarters were a mash of torn flesh and splintered bone. A bloodied rock, twice the size of a man's fist, rolled on the ground.

'Take this one,' Artebudz called back, offering Magnus the lead of the provisions horse. Another plume of water burst from the river. Magnus did not need a second invitation; pulling the priest's horse behind him, he sprinted forward and threw himself over the fresh mount, kicked it into action and accelerated after his comrades, leaving his wounded horse thrashing and screeching, helpless behind him.

Vespasian looked over his shoulder to make sure his friend was following; another two shots slammed into the ground, kicking up tufts of grass and showers of earth as Magnus wove between them. Spray from a series of eruptions close to the bank filled the air with a fine mist, soaking their hair and clothes and producing small rainbows that arched in front of them as they pressed their mounts forward at full gallop.

The shots started to fall short as the ships' exhausted rowers, freemen with rights, not slaves to be whipped to the point of death, slowed their stroke, unable to sustain for a moment longer the relentless beat of ramming speed without fouling their oars. Vespasian eased his horse back into a canter, which they maintained for a further mile. The river had begun its turn northwards and they left its bank so as to pass to the south of Axiopolis. To their right the Getae were just over a mile away.

'They've changed direction,' Sitalces called out over the hoof-beats.

'What?' Vespasian shouted.

'The Getae, they've changed direction; they've veered to their left,' Sitalces called back. 'They seem to be heading for the curve in the river, they'll pass behind us.'

'That's the first good news I've heard today,' Magnus said, trying to ease a particularly lumpy bag of salted pork out from under his bruised backside.

They had reached the apex of the curve. Looking north, up the river, Vespasian gasped as he understood the reason for the Getae's change of course. The river, over five hundred paces wide at this point, was flecked with scores of coloured sails. The Getic fleet had left the safety of its home ports to the north of Scythia Minor, as yet unconquered by the legions of Rome, and had sailed south in an attempt to rescue the stranded raiding party.

'Shit, our boys in the squadron can't see them, they're hidden by the bend,' Vespasian exclaimed as they all slowed to take in the magnificent sight.

'What do you mean, "our boys"?' Magnus grumbled. 'The bastards were shooting at us just now.'

'There's fuck-all that we can do about it,' Sabinus said. 'If we try to warn the squadron they'll just start shooting at us again, so let the navy-boys sort out their own problems.' Sabinus, like most Romans who had served in the legions, had nothing but contempt for the navy, which they considered a poor relation to the army.

'I suppose you're right,' Vespasian agreed. 'Let's get out of here whilst we still can.'

They passed to the south of Axiopolis, heading southeast, and started to climb the ridge of hills that forced the Danuvius north, away from its easterly route. At the summit they paused and looked back, with a bird's-eye view, on the events unfolding below.

The Getic war band had arrived at the river's edge and had opened fire on the surprised Roman squadron. Patches of river were obscured by fast-moving clouds – volleys of Getic arrows – which swarmed on to the decks of the Roman ships, felling artillerymen and marines as well as causing havoc amongst the unprotected rowers in the biremes. Despite their losses they returned fire, still oblivious to the presence of the Getic fleet half a mile from them around the bend in the river. Vespasian watched as scores of horsemen were felled by the lethal ballista shots; but they kept pumping volley after volley of arrows into the three closest ships, which were now unable to manoeuvre owing to severe casualties amongst the rowers. Disembodied shouts and screams floated up on the wind that was gradually gaining in strength. The two triremes and the five remaining biremes turned to face the Getae cavalry on the shore and, firing as they went, rowed to the rescue of the stricken ships, leaving them broadside on to the leading triremes of the Getic fleet as they rounded the bend. On sighting the Romans they accelerated to attack-speed, their whistled beats cutting through the air. The ballistae on the walls of Axiopolis opened fire at them as they passed beneath it; white explosions peppered the water around the fleet but they came on undeterred at the Romans who, caught between manoeuvres, failed to turn to face them.

The flutes' whistles accelerated into the almost constant screech of ramming speed and the lead Getic ships surged forward into the Roman squadron. Two caught a trireme broadside, crashing into it fore and aft, whilst another shipped its larboard oars as it skimmed up the side of a bireme, breaking its oars like twigs and catapulting rowers out of their seats, their backs broken and the skulls smashed. The sounds of cracking wood drowned the flutes as the two Getic vessels reversed stroke in order to wrench themselves free of the crippled Roman ship. The second wave of the Getic fleet crunched into the hapless squadron and Vespasian turned his horse.

'I think I've seen enough of that to know I wouldn't want to be involved in a sea battle,' he said, shaking his head.

'There'll be some good lads crossing the Styx today,' Magnus muttered as he followed, pulling the priest's horse after him, 'and all because Poppaeus wants to silence one man.'

'Or, conversely, because we want to keep him alive,' Sabinus pointed out. 'I wouldn't worry about it though, the timing of a man's death is down to the will of Mithras and there's bugger all to do about it.'

Not wanting to get into a theological debate with his brother, Vespasian kicked his horse into a canter and started to make his way down the hill to the plain that rolled all the way to the Euxine Sea and the port of Tomi.

Vespasian and his comrades were chilled to the bone by the time they reached the town gates, two hours after dusk. The wind had strengthened to gale force, dispersing the clouds, and the temperature had plummeted under the clear, starry sky. The sight of a military tribune's uniform was enough to persuade the surly gatekeepers to open up after curfew and they passed through into a wide thoroughfare, dimly lit by the moon, which led directly to the port, the town's main reason for its existence. The buildings on either side were mean and shabby and the whole town had an air of neglect about it; it had seen better days.

'What a miserable shit-hole,' Magnus opined as a few ragged beggars peered at them out of a gloomy side street.

'That's why it's used as a place of exile,' Sabinus said. 'The poet Publius Ovidius Naso lived out the last years of his life here, the poor bastard.'

'It once was a great Odrysian port,' Sitalces said mournfully, 'until you Romans conquered the northern part of Thracia and turned it into the province of Moesia; then it went into decline as you have no need for a port here and we now use the ports in what's left of our kingdom.'

'How do the inhabitants survive then?' Artebudz asked.

'They still do some trade with the Bosporan kingdom in the north and the kingdom of Colchis in the east, but that's about it; so it's mainly fishing and piracy, not that they'd admit to the last, of course.'

'I thought that Pompey Magnus cleared the seas of pirates,' Vespasian pointed out. 'Not the Euxine,' Drenis said, spitting on the ground. 'He only cared about protecting your precious trade and grain routes in your sea. A lot of the pirate crews just moved north to the Euxine.'

'There're still some in the Mare Aegeum,' Sabinus informed them. 'There're plenty of places to hide amongst all those islands. On the way here my ship was chased by pirates as we sailed around the southern tip of Achaea; if it hadn't been for some fine archery they'd have got us, but they lost their enthusiasm after we brought ten or twelve of them down including the captain, a nasty-looking, ginger-haired brute; he could have been one of your lot, Sitalces. Mind you, not all pirates are bad; the Cilician pirates brought the Lord Mithras to the Empire about the time of the Spartacus slave revolt.'

'Who'd have thought it, Mithraic pirates.' Vespasian laughed. 'I suppose they make light of heavy weather.'

'Don't laugh, little brother,' Sabinus cut in seriously. 'The Lord Mithras shines his light on all men equally, good or bad, believers or not; he makes no judgement because he died to redeem us and was resurrected after three days to show us that death can be beaten.'

'I didn't notice Faustus beating it,' Magnus observed.

Sabinus glared at Magnus. 'Death is not just physical.'

Vespasian stopped short of making a flippant remark as he saw the depth of conviction on his brother's face.

'That looks to be our ship,' Sitalces said, defusing the tension. The Thracian royal standard flapped in the wind on the mast of a huge, bulky, moon-lit quinquireme, rocking at its mooring on a swell that was substantial, even within the harbour.

Relieved that the theological discussion had been curtailed, they hastened along the deserted quay to the quinquireme's guarded gangway.

'Sitalces, you big old bugger,' the guard captain called as they approached, 'we didn't expect you to be on time; not that we're going anywhere in this weather.'

'I'd have thought that the trierarchus would be the best judge of that, Gaidres,' Sitalces replied, dismounting and slapping the guard on the shoulder. 'What makes a foot-slogger like you think you're qualified to make such a nautical judgement?'

'I'm not a foot-slogger any more, I'm a marine and well qualified to make nautical judgements; I base them upon the amount of praying the old man's doing, which is a lot since this wind got up,' Gaidres said with a grin. 'Come on board and hear it for yourselves. Tie the horses up, I'll have someone feed them; we can see to them in the morning.'

'This weather will deteriorate,' Trierarchus Rhaskos said, looking up past the mast to the night sky that had started to fill with scudding clouds. 'This wind is forewarning us of Zbelthurdos' wrath. He is coming; he rides to hurl his lightning-bolts at us and soon we'll hear the thunder of his great horse's hooves and the howling of his faithful hound.'

'Do you mean there's going to be a storm?' Vespasian asked testily. How much talk of gods did a man have to endure in one evening?

'Yes, when Zbelthurdos is angry a storm usually follows,' Rhaskos replied, scratching his woolly grey beard, which, set under his short-cropped, grey hair, gave Vespasian the curious impression that his head was on upside down. 'We must placate him. I shall prepare a sacrifice; one of your horses should do the trick.'

'You are not sacrificing our horses to your gods,' Sabinus stated categorically. 'They—'

'They're army property,' Vespasian put in quickly before his brother offended anyone by denouncing the Thracian gods in favour of Mithras.

'Mine is the property of the Queen,' Sitalces said. 'I'm sure that she would be pleased to offer it for sacrifice.'

Vespasian was not so sure but knew enough about the consequences of insulting the Thracian gods to keep his doubts to himself. Rhaskos looked pleased. 'Good, that's settled then. You have a prisoner, I believe?' He turned to where Rhoteces lay struggling on the deck between Magnus and Artebudz. 'The Queen asked me to construct a special cell for him; you'll find it on the oar-deck. Gaidres will show you down, he's been assigned with ten of his men to guard the prisoner.'

'Drenis and I will, er . . . sort out the horse,' Sitalces said to Vespasian as he turned to follow Gaidres. He nodded his assent; Sabinus snorted.

They followed Gaidres the fifty paces down the length of the huge ship, Magnus and Artebudz dragging the bound priest between them by his arms. The deck creaked and heaved below their feet and the wind whistled past the vibrating stays supporting the mast. The two brothers were already starting to feel the ill effects of the sea by the time they reached a hatch at the bow of the vessel. A waft of human excrement and urine hit them as they made their way down a ladder on to the oar-deck.

'Smells like we're in the shit again, sir,' Magnus remarked from the top of the ladder as he passed the unwilling Rhoteces down to Artebudz and Sabinus.

Vespasian's eyes adjusted to the dim light of a few weak oil lamps and his mouth dropped open in shock as he made out the forms of scores of rowers asleep over the oars that they were chained to. The Thracians, unlike the Romans, used slaves to power their ships.

'How do you maintain discipline down here?' he asked Gaidres, astounded.

Gaidres shrugged. 'They're all chained hand and foot and can't go anywhere. Besides, they all know that if they make trouble they just go over the side and we replace them with one of the spares we keep down in the bilge.'

'Yes, but if a slave has so little to live for then he has nothing to lose. That's why we use freemen; you can trust them to all pull together and not try and sabotage the ship, because if they stay alive they get citizenship after twenty-six years' service.'

'Look, don't ask me, I'm just a marine; I don't know the whys and wherefores of it all. And don't go feeling sorry for the bastards either, a lot of them are captured pirates getting a taste of what they've meted out to others.'

'I don't,' Vespasian muttered, looking around incredulously. 'I just worry about my safety on a ship powered by slaves who don't care if they live or die.'

'It's no wonder you never became a sea power,' Sabinus observed. 'You must have been too busy worrying about what's going on down with the slaves to be able to concentrate properly on winning a battle.'

'Well, that's how it's always been done and I don't ask questions. Come on, the cell's this way.' Gaidres opened a small door, ducked and stepped through.

Vespasian and Sabinus followed him into a small, dank-smelling cabin. By the faint light of the moon, streaming down through a grating in the deck above, Vespasian could see an iron cage, five feet high, wide and deep.

'Bring him in here, Magnus; Artebudz, get one of those oil lamps,' he said as Gaidres started fumbling with a key.

With the help of the small amount of light provided by the lamp, Gaidres managed to get the key in the lock and the cage door swung open. Inside were a set of manacles and leg-irons attached to the cage by heavy chains.

'I'm going to take the gag off,' Vespasian warned Magnus and Artebudz, who both had a firm grip on the priest. 'Watch out for his teeth, they're nastily sharp.'

As the gag came off a gobbet of phlegm flew into Vespasian's face. He punched Rhoteces in the stomach, causing his head to fall forward; Magnus and Artebudz's firm grip preventing him from doubling up.

'Now listen, you little shit,' Vespasian growled, 'we can do this the easy way and you don't struggle as we chain you up; or the hard way, which will involve you waking up with another crack in your skull.'

Gasping for breath Rhoteces lifted his head, his vicious eyes glaring with hatred; he contorted his weasel face into a snarl, baring his filed, yellow front teeth. His mouth was uneven, unhealed from where Asinius had slit it nearly four years previously.

'It doesn't matter which way we do it, Roman,' he hissed. 'This is futile, none of us will get to Rome; you because you will all die on this voyage, and me because my gods will bring me back alive to Thracia without ever setting foot in that accursed city of yours. This I predict by the will of Zbelthurdos whose anger you have incurred by seizing me. I curse this voyage in his name; this ship will never reach Rome.'

A shrill whinny pierced the air and then was suddenly cut off, followed almost instantaneously by the sound of a heavy body collapsing to the ground.

Rhoteces' snarl turned into a lopsided leer. 'Zbelthurdos has heard the curse. But it'll take a lot more than a horse to expiate the insult to my gods; Roman blood is what will be needed.'

Vespasian slammed his fist into the priest's face, flattening his nose. He slumped, unconscious, between Magnus and Artebudz.

'The hard way it is then,' Vespasian said, walking past Sabinus and out of the cabin.

PART III

THE MARE AEGEUM,
JUNE AD 30

CHAPTER VIII

IT WAS HOT; very, very hot. There was not even the slightest breeze to bring a modicum of relief from the relentless heat as the quinquereme rowed down the eastern coast of the island of Euboia. The sun burned down on to the ship from its midday high, heating the timber deck so that the barefooted crew were unable to walk upon it and were forced to stay under the large awning that had been rigged at the stern of the ship. Not that there was much for them to do; the sails could not be set as there was no wind; nor had there been since they had left Tomi.

For twelve days now the slaves had driven the ship forward, stroke after stroke to the steady beat of a drum – used by the Thracians in preference to the Roman flute – ten hours a day, in the oven-like conditions of the oar-deck; their only respite being two hours in the blackness of the bilge before being rotated back up again to the misery of their mono-purposed existence. Encased in a wooden prison, chained to the oars that gave the only definition to their lives, shitting and pissing in a bucket brought round to where they sat, they existed in a twilight world were the only different sensation during the mind-numbing day was the lick of the whip across their shoulders should their toil be deemed inadequate.

The stench of their living hell wafted up above them to Vespasian and his comrades who sat under the awning. They sweltered in the heat that had plagued them since the storms and rough seas, which had delayed them for almost twenty days in Tomi, had suddenly ceased overnight, after Rhaskos had sacrificed both Drenis' and Artebudz's horses. The following morning the clouds had dissipated, leaving the sun free to burn down on them, intensifying with every mile they travelled further south.

Their routine aboard ship was mind-numbing too, but through boredom rather than repetitive labour; from dawn when they sailed to the tenth hour when they anchored for the night there was absolutely nothing to do other than watch the coastline drift past and make scraps of conversation. Relief from the tedium came in the form of evening hunting expeditions in the game-abundant hills above the coves and inlets that provided their nightly shelter.

Fresh water had become the biggest problem. Although Rhaskos knew the coastline well and always managed to contrive to anchor for the night near a stream, the ship did not carry enough casks to supply the parched slaves with the fuel they needed to maintain their relentless exertions. Despite often stopping during the day to take on new supplies of the precious liquid there was never enough and the slaves had started to weaken. Every day for the last few days two or three, either dead or too frail to be of any further use, had been thrown over the side.

'There goes another unlucky bastard,' Magnus commented as the latest filth-encrusted body was thrown overboard; a weak cry showed that he was not quite dead.

'If we carry on at this rate there'll be none left to make the crossing to Italia,' Vespasian observed, calculating that the more slaves that died the more work surviving ones would be forced to do, thus accelerating the death rate. 'We need a wind.'

'I have never known it to be so calm for so long,' Rhaskos moaned from his position next to the steering-oars. 'I sacrifice every evening to the mother-goddess Bendis but she does not listen to my prayers, even though in the past she has always looked kindly upon me. I'm beginning to worry that this voyage is cursed.'

Magnus raised his eyebrows and looked at Vespasian, who kept his face neutral. None of them had said anything about Rhoteces' curse to anyone. They had all considered it to be the theatrical gesture of a cornered and desperate man and had dismissed it from their thoughts. However, the strange weather conditions since had started the superstitious parts of their minds thinking, and their worries were not helped by the sound of the priest constantly muttering in his cage in a strange language that neither Sitalces nor Drenis could understand. Only Sabinus had seen the positive side of a potential curse upon the voyage when they had discussed the possibility the previous evening: the flat calm had meant that he had kept the contents of his stomach where they were supposed to be rather than spreading them across the length of the Mare Aegeum.

They sank back into the torpor that they had become accustomed to, their minds dulled by the monotonous beat of the stroke-master's drum, and stared blankly at the mountains of Euboia as the ship followed the curve of the island and began to head east towards Cape Caphereas.

A shout from one of the slave-masters appearing out of the hatchway at the bow of the ship brought them out of their slow thoughts.

'Trierarchus, look at this one,' the man shouted, hauling a limp body out of the oar-deck.

The slave-master dragged the body the length of the ship and then turned it over for his trierarchus' inspection.

His face was barely visible beneath the matted, long, black hair and beard but his torso was covered in dark red rashes.

'The gods above,' Rhaskos cried, 'slave fever. How many more are there down there with the symptoms?'

'Three, trierarchus, but they are still able to row.'

'Get them overboard now.'

The slave-master ran off to do as he was ordered whilst two crewmen heaved the infected slave over the side. Moments later shouts erupted from the hatchway and three struggling creatures were hauled out and dragged kicking and screaming to the bow. As they were still very much alive a heavy chain was attached to each of them before they were thrown overboard to disappear into the sea churning beneath the ship's hull.

'That's the final proof of it,' Rhaskos announced. 'We are under a curse and I've no doubt it's because of the priest. We've offended the gods by taking him on board.'

Vespasian moved closer to Magnus and Sabinus. 'I think that we should tell him,' he whispered.

'What's the point?' Sabinus questioned. 'You don't believe all that bollocks, do you?'

Before Vespasian could answer there was a clatter of oars and the ship lurched to the right, knocking the men on each steering-oar to the deck.

'On your feet, steersmen, pull her round,' Rhaskos barked, hauling the men back up to their feet.

Beneath them, on the oar-deck, shouting broke out accompanied by the crack of whips and the rattle of chains.

The slave-master came pelting out of the hatchway and ran the length of the deck to Rhaskos.

'Trierarchus, the slaves have fouled the oars and are refusing to row,' he puffed.

'Well, whip them until they do,' Rhaskos shouted, his voice rising in pitch.

'We are, but it's not doing any good.'

'Then throw a couple of them overboard as a lesson to the rest.'

'That's just the point, sir, they're saying that now that the slave fever has broken out they're all going to get thrown over anyway so what's the point of rowing any more?'

'For the love of the earth mother Bendis, they can't hold us to ransom like that,' Rhaskos roared. 'Get three of the ringleaders and secure one of them in the bilge and take the eyes of the other two out in front of the rest; they'll soon realise that they don't need to see to row.'

'Yes, sir, that's a good idea,' the slave-master said, turning to go.

'And tell them that no one else with slave fever will be thrown overboard, unless they're already dead,' Rhaskos called after him.

'Is that wise?' Sabinus asked. 'Won't it just spread through them all until there's no one left to row?'

'Not in two days it won't,' Rhaskos snapped, 'and that's what we need to get to the oracle of Amphiaraos, at Oropos on the coast of Attica.'

'What's that?' Vespasian asked.

'It's a sanctuary dedicated to healing and foretelling,' Rhaskos replied with awe in his voice. 'I've been there before for healing and to ask about the outcome of a voyage. There I will get guidance on how to counter the curse on this ship and how stop the slave fever, I'm sure of it.'

A series of loud shrieks from below halted the conversation. The stroke-master's drum restarted and the ship got under way.

'Who's this Amphiaraos then?' Magnus asked Rhaskos as they walked up a steep track from their anchorage in the glittering cove below. 'If he's a god I've never heard of him.'

'He's not a god; he's a demi-god, one of the Heroes,' Rhaskos replied, removing his floppy straw hat and rubbing the sweat from his freshly shaven head. 'He was the king of Argos and greatly favoured by the Greek god Zeus, who some say is our Zbelthurdos; he gave him oracular powers. He was persuaded to take part in a raid against Thebes led by Polynices, one of the sons of Oedipus, in an attempt to wrest the kingdom from his brother, Eteocles, who had gone back on his word and refused to share the crown with him after their father had killed himself. Amphiaraos went despite the fact that he foresaw his own death. During the battle, when Periclymenus, the son of Poseidon, tried to kill him, Zeus threw his thunderbolt and the earth opened up, swallowing Amphiaraos and his chariot, saving him from a mortal death so that he would be forever able to use the power that Zeus had given him.'

'How's telling the future going to remove this curse?' Vespasian asked.

'So you agree that there is a curse?' Rhaskos replied.

Vespasian glanced at Sabinus beside him, who shrugged. 'It can't do any harm telling him now if he wants to believe all that bollocks.'

'Tell me what?'

'Rhoteces did pronounce a curse on the voyage when we brought him on board,' Vespasian admitted.

'Why in the name of all the gods didn't you tell me?' Rhaskos exclaimed indignantly. 'I could have got a priest to come and counter it when we were at Tomi.'

'Because it's rubbish, that's why,' Sabinus replied forcefully.

'Rubbish! Have you not noticed all the misfortune that has happened to us on the voyage? That's the proof that it's not rubbish.'

'We weren't the only ones to be affected,' Vespasian pointed out. 'Every ship in the Euxine was affected by those storms and every ship in the Aegeum is affected by this calm. What makes you think that the weather is directed solely at us?'

'Because we're carrying a priest; he has great influence with the gods and can call on their help.'

'Well, I have some sway with my god, Mithras, and so far his influence has been the most powerful,' Sabinus said. 'Before we left Tomi I prayed to him and he answered; he's kept the sea calm for me and I haven't been sick once.'

'Believe what you like,' Rhaskos said dismissively, 'but if you heard that priest utter a curse I can promise you that we are cursed, and I intend to put an end to it.'

'Well, it can't do any harm, can it?' Magnus said, looking from one to the other, clearly confused by the argument. 'I mean, if there is a curse we'll get rid of it and if there isn't we'll just have to do some more praying or whatever.'

'If you start praying for wind and I'm sick all the way back to Ostia I shall personally see to it that you are cursed by every god that you hold sacred,' Sabinus warned as the track entered a resin-scented cedar wood.

After a couple of miles of steady uphill walking in the pleasant shade of the sweet-smelling trees the wood suddenly ended and they found themselves in a ravine between two steep hills. Before them, on the west bank, was the sanctuary of Amphiaraos. It was a long thin complex overlooked by a theatre cut into the hillside above. There was a soporific quality about the atmosphere; the few people that Vespasian could see were either walking very slowly or lying in the shade of a colonnaded, covered walkway leading away from the temple just ahead of him. The only sounds were the ubiquitous cicadas and the mournful bleating of a dozen rams in a pen just behind the temple. The rich smell of cooking mutton filled the air.

'There doesn't seem to be a lot happening,' Vespasian said, suppressing a yawn.

'That's because the Hero speaks to the supplicants in their dreams,' Rhaskos replied. 'You make your sacrifice of a ram, ask your questions of the priests and then you go to sleep on the ram's fleece and wait for the reply.'

'You mean to say that the priests do nothing,' Sabinus scoffed.

'They're the conduit, they eat a part of the sacrifice and in doing so they transmit the question or request for healing through to the Hero.'

'Oh, so they do do something, they eat mutton all day.' Sabinus laughed. 'Nice work if you can get it.'

Rhaskos scowled at Sabinus. 'This is a very old and sacred place; you didn't have to come but now that you're here, respect other people's beliefs. Now I'm going to buy a ram and make the sacrifice; you can join me if you wish.'

The ram was, of course, hideously over-priced, the shepherd being well aware that he could charge what he wanted to supplicants who had made the mistake of arriving without their own. After much haggling and a few barely veiled threats from Magnus concerning the shepherd's wellbeing after dark, they made the purchase and entered the temple.

A huge, marble statue of Amphiaraos, reaching almost to the ceiling, dominated the cool interior. Seven flaming sconces were set in a line along its base; beneath each one sat a well-fed priest. In front of the statue stood a hearth filled with red-hot charcoal covered by a grill; next to it was a blood-stained altar upon which lay a knife. Hanging on all the walls were innumerable fleeces from past sacrifices.

'Come forward, supplicants,' the oldest priest said, rising from the central chair as they entered. 'My name is Antenor, chief priest of Amphiaraos. What is yours?'

Rhaskos led the ram to the altar and bowed his head. 'Rhaskos.'

'Tell us, Rhaskos, what you wish to know of Amphiaraos and what healing you require of him.'

'I have had a curse put upon my ship in the name of Zbelthurdos. I wish to know how to preserve my crew so that we may complete our voyage and I look for healing for my galley slaves who suffer from fever.'

'We will make these requests. Make your sacrifice, Rhaskos.'

Rhaskos turned to Vespasian, Sabinus and Magnus and indicated that they should help him lift the ram on to the altar. As they came forward Vespasian noticed Antenor staring intently, first at him and then at Sabinus.

'Who are these men, Rhaskos?'

'They're passengers aboard my ship; they are here to witness the power of the Hero, not to make sacrifices themselves.'

'You two are brothers?'

'Yes, we are,' Sabinus replied dismissively, unimpressed by the old priest's perception; even the most cursory glance at them would discern a sibling likeness.

'From where did you sail?'

'From Tomi in the Euxine Sea,' Vespasian replied, gripping the ram's horns as it was lifted, unwillingly, on to the altar.

'And you are sailing west?' Antenor asked, stepping forward to the altar staring all the time at the two brothers.

'To Ostia, yes,' Vespasian confirmed as he and Sabinus fought against the growing urgency of the ram's struggling.

The priest nodded, as if satisfied by what he had heard, and then turned his attention back to Rhaskos. 'In the name of truth and healing accept this ram, mighty Amphiaraos.'

Rhaskos picked up the sacrificial knife and flashed it across the ram's throat. Blood splattered on to the altar. The ram's eyes rolled in their sockets and its back legs kicked violently as it tried to resist death. Gradually the kicking died down and it sank to its knees; then it collapsed into the pool of its own blood, which soaked up into its fleece.

The other six priests came forward, each brandishing knives, and began to skin the victim.

After a while of hacking and sawing the blood-matted fleece came off intact. Antenor nodded his approval and turned the red-raw carcass on to its back. He took the sacrificial knife from Rhaskos and slit open the skinned ram's belly. With a couple of sharp cuts he removed the liver and placed it on the altar's edge.

Again he nodded his approval – the auspices evidently were good – before something caught his eye and he turned the liver over, picked it up, looked closely at it and then glanced at Vespasian and Sabinus.

'Stay a while,' he said to the brothers, putting the liver back down. He turned to Rhaskos. 'Now sleep, Rhaskos, whilst we eat a part of your sacrifice. Amphiaraos' reply will come in your dream; take care to mark it well.'

Rhaskos bowed and, taking the fleece, turned to leave as the six priests set about the carcass with their knives, jointing it and throwing pieces of meat on to the grill. Fat sizzled and spat as it dripped on to the charcoal.

'What I have to say is for you two alone,' Antenor said once Rhaskos had left.

Vespasian looked at Magnus, who smiled. 'I can take a hint, sir; I'll see you outside.'

As Magnus' footsteps echoed down the temple the old priest walked around the altar and took the brothers by the chin, one in each hand, and closed his eyes. Vespasian glanced sideways at Sabinus, who looked as nonplussed as he himself was feeling.

Eventually the priest let them go and opened his eyes. 'It is as I thought when I first saw you,' he asserted, 'and the liver confirmed it.'

'Confirmed what?' Sabinus asked rubbing his chin.

'For centuries we have been waiting to deliver a prophecy to two brothers who sail north to west on a cursed ship and come before the Hero as witnesses, not supplicants. I am satisfied that you are those brothers.' He turned to the priests gathered around the cooking mutton. 'Leto, fetch the scroll.'

A younger priest scurried off to the temple's recesses and returned momentarily with a box. Antenor lifted the lid and brought out a parchment scroll of great antiquity.

'This is a record of the prophecies of Amphiaraos,' he said, unrolling the scroll. 'Each one has a description of the person or persons to whom it must be delivered. Only the chief priest may read the scroll so that its contents will not be revealed by the loose tongues of the young.'

Behind him his colleagues had started to return to their seats, each chewing on a hunk of mutton.

'Through the ages all but seven of the prophecies have been read,' Antenor continued. 'If you both choose to hear it I will read the one pertaining to you.'

Ever since overhearing, at the age of fifteen, his parents discussing the omens that surrounded his birth and the favourable prophecy attached to them Vespasian had been intrigued to know its exact content. He looked at Sabinus, whom he knew had, aged almost five, been present when that prophecy had been made but had been bound by an oath never to reveal it. Their father, Titus, had made the two brothers swear a further oath, a greater oath, before all the gods, including Mithras – the only god that Sabinus truly revered – that would enable him to tell Vespasian the contents of the prophecy at some time in the future; perhaps that time was now.

'I'm willing to hear it,' he said. 'What about you, Sabinus?'

Sabinus looked reluctant. 'It can be dangerous to know too much of the future.'

'I didn't think you gave much credence to the mysteries of the old gods now that you're happily bathing in Mithras' light,' Vespasian said – unable to keep the sarcasm out of his voice – 'so how can you fear something that you no longer believe in?'

'I don't deny the existence of the old gods, little brother; I just deny their supremacy over my lord, Mithras. Prophecies made before his coming may well have substance and should be treated with caution; I prefer not to hear it.'

Vespasian snorted in exasperation. 'All right, if you don't want to hear it then that's fine. Just read to me, Antenor.'

'I can only read it to both of you together or not at all,' the old priest replied.

'Then it's not at all,' Sabinus said, turning to leave.

'Sabinus!' Vespasian shouted, his voice so commanding that it stopped his brother in his tracks. 'I need to hear it. You will do this for me.'

'Why should I, little brother?' Sabinus shouted back, spinning around to face Vespasian.

'Because I have as much right to hear it as you have to refuse, but if it is not read out we will never know which one of us was right. So if you walk away now I swear to you, Sabinus, that all the wrongs you have done to me throughout our lives will seem as nothing to the wrong that you do me today, and I will hold a grudge in my heart against you until my grave.'

The fire in Vespasian's eyes caused Sabinus to pause and think for a moment. Vespasian could see that he was wrestling with an inner turmoil. He was not just resisting out of pigheadedness; he was genuinely afraid.

'What are you scared of, Sabinus?' Vespasian demanded.

Sabinus glared at his brother. 'Of being left behind.'

'By whom? Me?'

'I'm the elder brother.'

'Age has nothing to do with this, Sabinus, nor does our individual ambition. It's our duty to raise our family's *dignitas* within Rome and in that we're both equal. Whatever is in this prophesy is for both of us and we should listen to it for the sake of the house of Flavius.'

'As you wish, Vespasian,' Sabinus said eventually. 'Let's hope that I'm wrong and it's just a load of meaningless twaddle.'

'Thank you, brother.'

'If you have decided then I will read it out to both of you,' Antenor said placidly. Behind him the other priests sat expectantly on their chairs, gnawing on bones.

'Yes, Antenor,' Vespasian said.

Sabinus grunted his assent.

Antenor lifted the scroll and read out loud:

'Two tyrants fall quickly, close trailed by another,
In the East the King hears the truth from a brother.
With his gift the lion's steps through sand he should follow,
So to gain from the fourth the West on the morrow.'

Vespasian frowned and looked at Antenor. 'So what does it mean?'

'That I can't tell you.' The old priest rolled up the scroll and placed it back into its box. 'We do not interpret these things, we are—'

'Just conduits?' Sabinus chipped in.

Antenor smiled benevolently at him. 'Precisely. Now, if you'll excuse me I have done my duty by you and must return to Rhaskos. I have his mutton to eat.'

'Thank you,' Vespasian said, turning to go.

Sabinus nodded his head and followed. 'For the first time I'm happy to concede that you were right, Vespasian, there was nothing to fear in that prophecy, it did no harm to hear it and it made an old lunatic very happy because he now thinks that he's done his duty by his god or whatever Amphiaraos is.'

'I was hoping that you might be able to add something to it, Sabinus.'

'Like what?'

'The prophecy at my birth. I know that you know about it.'

'Then you will know that I'm forbidden to speak of it.'

'Not if you go by Father's oath.'

'But that is relevant only if one of us is unable to aid the other because of a previous oath and I don't see you in need of help at the moment.'

'There must be something that you can tell me.'

'Look, I was very young, my memory of it is hazy; what I can tell you is that there was no prophecy as such, it was just the auspices that caused a fuss.'

'What were they?'

'I can't tell you any more, I'm sworn against it. Anyway, I was four; I barely remember them and I didn't understand them – just as I didn't understand the prophecy that you were so keen to hear just now. None of these things ever makes sense unless you look back with hindsight, and what good are they then, eh?'

'But surely that defeats their point; they're not hindsight, they're foresight so you've got to work out how to interpret them,' Vespasian said as they walked out into the burning midday sun. 'The only part that seemed to have any relevance to us was "the truth from a brother". Would you tell me the truth if I was an eastern king?'

'I certainly wouldn't just tell you what you wanted to hear, if that's what you mean. Anyway, I don't see either of us becoming eastern kings; and as for all those tyrants, who are they?'

'Perhaps Sejanus does succeed in becoming Emperor and the other three are his successors.'

'Then what relevance would the prophecy have to us in those circumstances? We'd be as dead as these,' Sabinus said, pointing to the long row of statues that lined the path to the colonnaded walkway.

'Well, I'm glad to have heard it even though it does seem to make no sense,' Vespasian muttered.

'What was that all about then?' Magnus asked from the shade of the colonnade.

'Nothing, it seems,' Sabinus replied.

'Where's Rhaskos?' Vespasian asked.

Magnus grinned and pointed to the sleeping form further along the colonnade. 'Gone to receive a message.'

Sabinus looked up – and then stared in disbelief. A huge ginger-haired brute of a man, with a missing left eye, was walking towards them.

'What's wrong?' Vespasian asked, 'you look like you've seen a ghost.'

Sabinus turned away as the man passed and waited until he was out of earshot.

'That's exactly what I have seen.'

'What are you talking about?' Vespasian asked, thinking that his brother was rambling.

'That man,' Sabinus replied pointing at the receding figure, heading out of the complex towards the coast. 'Remember I told you about the pirate attack on my way here?'

Vespasian and Magnus both nodded.

'Well, he was the trierarchus. He should be dead; the ships were only thirty paces apart, I saw him get an arrow deep in his left eye.'

Magnus was unimpressed. 'You must've been mistaken. Perhaps he had a brother.'

Sabinus shook his head. 'No, that was him, all right; you saw how his left eye was missing?'

'He must have survived then,' Vespasian said, 'and his crew brought him here for healing.'

'It couldn't have been far, I suppose,' Sabinus conceded, 'no more than a few days. But even if he did survive the journey I saw enough of those wounds in Africa to know that there is no way that he could have been healed.'

'Perhaps there is more to this place than we thought,' Magnus said with a trace of reverence in his voice.

'More than meets the eye, you mean?' Vespasian quipped.

'Don't laugh, Vespasian,' Sabinus said quietly. 'If they can heal a man who should be dead then there must be real power here, a power older than Mithras, and it should be taken seriously.'

CHAPTER VIIII

B Y THE TIME they got back to the ship it was early evening and too late to sail. Rhaskos had slept most of the afternoon away but had not looked at all refreshed upon waking. He had refused to tell them what reply he had received from Amphiaraos; all he would say was that he had been spoken to in his dream by the Hero and that he was now contemplating the meaning of the message. Whereas that morning they would all have found some amusement in the situation, now even Sabinus was taking Rhaskos seriously; not because they believed in the curse but because they were curious to see if the slave fever would disappear through Amphiaraos' intervention.

After a mild night lying on the open deck beneath a swathe of stars, thickened by the early setting of the moon, Vespasian awoke to a turquoise dawn sky feeling refreshed. He had been lulled asleep by the gentle sound of water lapping against the hull but now this had been replaced by a more strident sound: waves breaking on the rocky cove. He felt the ship swaying beneath him and sat up immediately; a cool breeze blew in his face.

All around him the ship was coming to life. Half of the forty-man crew were bending the main- and foresails on to their respective yards, then furling them ready to be hauled up the masts, whilst the rest were preparing to weigh the fore and aft anchors. Rhaskos moved around the deck like an excited hound, barking at everyone and baring his teeth and growling at the slightest error or sign of slacking, such was his anxiety to be under way as fast as possible.

'What do you make of that, sir?' Magnus asked, giving Vespasian a thick cut of cold pork and a cup of well-watered wine. 'A fucking wind, eh, who'd have thought it? What a weird place.'

'That was some strange stuff we saw yesterday,' Vespasian agreed, biting off a hunk of pork. 'Where's Sabinus?'

'Ah well, he's a bit too busy to be joining us for breakfast, if you take my meaning,' Magnus replied, pointing towards the bow.

Vespasian turned to see his brother leaning over the side, convulsing violently.

A series of loud orders from Rhaskos through a speaking-trumpet caused the fore-anchor detail to start to heave on their cable. As the anchor – a small boulder – cleared the water the stroke-master began his monotonous beat and the slaves started to back oars. The ship eased gently away from the cove then, as the aft-anchor cable tautened, began to swing round. The huge quinquereme came parallel to the shore and Rhaskos shouted through his trumpet again. The aft-anchor detail heaved hard on their cable and the anchor lifted from the seabed; below on the oar-deck the slaves, as one man, reversed stroke and the ship started to glide forward. Once the aft anchor had been secured on deck another series of shouts caused the mainsail hands to start hauling on a halyard, raising the yard aloft. When it was in position six men clambered up the rope ladder on the mast and made their way, three on either side, along the footropes of the yard. At another signal from Rhaskos they released the brails, unfurling the sail that flapped in the wind until its sheets were tallied. The wind snapped the sail taut, the drumbeat from the oar-deck accelerated and Vespasian felt the ship lurch forward.

'Thanks to our Mother Bendis for this wind,' Rhaskos called to the sky as the crew went forward to deal with the foresail.

'Shouldn't it be Amphiaraos you should be thanking?' Vespasian asked, walking over to him at his position between the steering-oars.

'No, this is Bendis' work,' Rhaskos replied with a grin and shouted another series of orders through his trumpet.

The yard was hauled up the forward-raked foremast and soon the foresail was set and the ship put on another turn of speed.'What makes you so sure that it wasn't Amphiaraos?'

Vespasian continued when Rhaskos' attention was again free from nautical matters.

'Because the dream that he sent me was so fanciful I can't understand it and so I haven't done what he suggested.'

'You still believe that the ship is cursed then?'

'Without a doubt.'

'So why have we got a wind?'

The old trierarchus smiled; there was a self-satisfied glint in his eye. 'Because whilst I was communing with the Hero yesterday, as insurance I had my crew sacrifice the third ring-leader to Bendis, under the mast. They cut his body in two and placed a half on either side of the ship then walked between it with the sails to purify them and themselves. The Macedonians do the same sort of thing with a dog but we find a human much more potent.'

Vespasian raised his eyebrows slightly; Rhaskos' religious fervour had ceased to amaze him. 'Well, it seems to have worked,' he conceded, 'but what about the slave fever, has that gone?'

'No, we're still cursed in that respect; over a quarter of them are suffering from it now.'

'So why don't you do whatever Amphiaraos told you in your dream?'

Rhaskos shook his head mournfully. 'Because it seems so ridiculous, and it would be suicide.'

'Suicide?'

'Yes. Perhaps I should have more faith in the Hero but I just can't bring myself to do what he suggested.' He looked at Vespasian apologetically. 'I dreamt that I took a slave by the hand and in return for his oar I gave him a sword.'

The breeze and the stroke-master's beat remained steady; the day wore on. The extreme heat had diminished with the arrival of the wind and conditions on deck were much improved. On the oar-deck, however, the fever was spreading gradually and the slave-master had been forced to abandon the lowest level of thirty oars on each side, operated by single slaves, leaving just the middle and top rows working, both operated by pairs of slaves.

The resulting loss of speed irked Rhaskos, who kept up a constant stream of entreaties to his various gods.

Keeping a mile or so out to sea, the ship slid past the bay of Marathon and on down the Attic coast. After two days they crossed the Saronic Gulf to the Peloponnese, weaving through the numerous trading vessels making their way to and from the port of Piraeus in one of the busiest shipping lanes in the world.

Early in the morning on the fifth day they approached the strait between the southern tip of the Peloponnese and the island of Cythera. Vespasian and Magnus were leaning on the bow-rail watching the dry coastline pass by, so clear through the pure air that, even at a distance, individual trees could be picked out on its hills. Sabinus joined them, looking pale and none too steady on his feet although he had not been sick for a couple of days now.

'We'll be making the crossing to Italia soon,' Vespasian said, idly turning his attention to a couple of distant trading ships some three miles ahead. 'What happens when we get to Ostia?'

'We've got to get the priest to Antonia,' Sabinus replied weakly, leaning against the rail, 'and then we wait.'

'For what?' Magnus asked.

'For Macro to tell us how and when to get Rhoteces to Capreae.'

Magnus looked alarmed. 'Hold on a moment, there're two things in that sentence that I don't like the sound of: Macro and Capreae. Why's this the first that I've heard mention of them?'

'Yes, Sabinus,' Vespasian said, equally as alarmed, 'why haven't you told me about Macro's involvement before?'

'Oh, so he's told you about taking Rhoteces to Capreae then, but you just didn't bother to mention it to me, did you?' Magnus sounded aggrieved.

'That's because you don't have to come.'

'Are you going?'

'Yes.'

'Well then, so am I. And what's Macro got to do with this?'

'Antonia's using him as our route to Tiberius,' Sabinus replied. 'In return she'll commend his loyalty to the Emperor and recommend that he uses him to replace Sejanus. It's an alliance of convenience.'

'Well, it don't sound too convenient to me,' Magnus grumbled. 'The last time we saw Macro he was trying to prevent us getting out of Rome; I tried to take his head off and he left a dagger in Vespasian's leg.'

'Magnus is right, Sabinus; and he would have got a good look at us both.'

'Yes, and I don't suppose he'll be too pleased when he gets a good look at the two of us again, if you take my meaning.'

'Well, I doubt that Antonia's going to change her plans just because you've had a difference of opinion with Macro,' Sabinus said dismissively. 'Anyway, he's working with us now so I'm sure that he'll be happy to put the past behind him – if you ask him nicely and give him his dagger back, that is,' he added with a thin smile.

'Very funny, Sabinus,' Vespasian snapped, 'but I don't intend to get that close to him.'

'You might not have a choice,' Magnus said darkly and stomped off to the other end of the ship to where Sitalces was sitting with Artebudz and Drenis under the awning.

Vespasian swallowed hard; he did not fancy coming face to face with Macro but it seemed that it was going to be unavoidable. Contemplating the problem, he turned his attention back to the two distant ships and watched with interest how they were forced to tack with the wind, zigzagging to negotiate the narrow strait between the island and mainland. Even at its reduced speed the quinquereme was slowly overhauling them as it made the passage on a straight course, under oars.

'Do you have any more surprises in store for me, Sabinus?' Vespasian asked after a while. 'It would be nice to know now whilst there's still time to think about them.'

'I've always told you whatever you needed to know at the time,' Sabinus replied testily.

'No you haven't, you've only told me what you thought I needed to know. If we're to work together effectively we need to share everything because it's impossible to make the right decisions without all the information. You weren't aware that I had come across Macro so you didn't think it important to tell me that his interests and ours are now aligned.'

'You should've told me that you'd come across him in the first place.'

'He was trying to arrest me on the Aemilian Bridge four years ago; the way I saw it he was just another Praetorian doing his duty. I would have mentioned it if I'd known that he's now changed sides.'

'So I've told you now; what difference does it make?' Sabinus snapped, hating being lectured to by his younger brother.

Vespasian fought to retain his temper. 'The very fact that Macro has got to where he is in the Praetorian Guard shows that he is a man of ruthless ambition and not one to let bygones be bygones. He will have his revenge on me if he sees and recognises me, there's no doubt about it. The question is whether his desire for revenge will interfere with whatever plan we put into place to get Rhoteces in front of the Emperor.'

'He would be a fool if it did.'

'You might think so, but pride is blind. I left him sprawling in an undignified heap in the dust; he may well think that the slight to his dignitas is too much to bear and use the opportunity to stick a knife between my ribs, just to make himself feel better, even if it jeopardises everything else.'

Having met the man Sabinus could see that his brother's hunch might not be so far from the truth. 'You could be right, I suppose,' he conceded. 'We'll just have to try and keep you away from him.'

'How will that be possible?'

'We'll see, but I'm sorry that I didn't tell you about him before, Vespasian.'

'So, any more surprises then, Sabinus?'

A shout from the forward watch, just next to them, cut short any reply.

'Trierarchus! Dead ahead.'

Vespasian looked up. A trireme had appeared from behind the headland at the tip of Cythera and was speeding towards the two traders, now no more than a mile away.

Rhaskos came running forward for a closer look.

'Oh, Bendis help me,' he wailed. 'Pirates, and we don't have the men to fight them off. We are truly cursed.'

'The sun's low behind us. We must be in its glare on the water – they haven't seen us yet,' Vespasian observed. 'Let's just leave them alone. They'll be more than happy with what's on board those two traders.'

'We could try to sail past,' Rhaskos replied, 'but that will only arouse their interest. They'd expect a ship of this size to try and intervene; if we don't they'll assume that we're either under-manned or carrying someone or something too precious to warrant risking. Either way they'll come after us.'

'What about turning and running?' Sabinus suggested.

'That will definitely tell them that we're scared and with so many of the slaves too ill to row they'd catch us in a couple of hours. The only thing to do is to call their bluff. I'll have Gaidres and his men arm the crew and we'll sail straight for them as if we're going to ram them and pray to every god that you can think of that they run.'

'How many bows do you have?' Sabinus asked, thinking of his only previous encounter with pirates.

'More than we have crew,' Rhaskos replied as he ran back to give the order to Gaidres to break out the ship's weaponry.

Up ahead the trireme had reached the first of the traders. Vespasian watched as grappling hooks flew over the little ship's stern and it was hauled into a deadly embrace. A stream of men flooded from the pirate galley on to their prey. By now they were close enough to hear the screams of the defenders float across the water as they were cut down within the close confines of their small, nautical world. The second trader sailed on.

By the time the first trader was taken the quinquereme's crew and Gaidres with his men had assembled on deck. Each was armed with a bow and – much to Vespasian's unwarranted surprise, since they were Thracians – a rhomphaia strapped on their backs.

Rhaskos shouted an order and the stroke-master accelerated the beat to attack speed. From below the sound of whips cracking over the backs of the labouring slaves intensified as they were goaded into the more rapid rhythm.

The quinquereme surged forward, its huge ram cutting through the swell, churning the water beneath its bow into white foam. It powered towards the pirate trireme, which had now spotted them and was in the process of hurriedly disengaging from its newly acquired prize. The skeleton crew left aboard the trader cast off the grappling hooks and the trireme, with surprising speed, executed a 180-degree turn, bringing it round to face the quinquereme. They were not going to run.

Gaidres immediately started to organise the crew into small units, each commanded by one of his marines, and positioned them around the ship ready to pump volleys of arrows into the pirate's crowded deck. A couple of deck-hands were circulating with skins of water. Magnus pushed through the milling crewmen with Sitalces, Artebudz and Drenis in tow.

'Looks like they mean to take us head to head,' he observed calmly, handing a bow and quiver each to Vespasian and Sabinus; he then adjusted the rhomphaia he had taken from the dead Ziles, which hung down his back, and took his place at the rail.

Sabinus notched an arrow and smiled grimly, all traces of seasickness having disappeared beneath the rush of adrenalin. 'A few good volleys should see off this rabble before they get anywhere near us,' he said with confidence as the quinquereme passed the headland at the northern tip of Cythera.

The ships were now less than a half-mile apart. Vespasian's mouth dried as the distance between them lessened with every beat of the stroke-master's drum. He reached for his sword hilt and pulled on it slightly, checking that the weapon was loose in its scabbard, and then drew an arrow from his quiver. All around him men were going through their various personal rituals before combat; there was a tense silence on deck broken only by the rhythmic drumbeat and irregular whip-cracks from below.

At two hundred paces the pirates let off an ill-disciplined volley that fell short, bringing a half-hearted cheer from the

Thracian crew. Gaidres shouted encouragingly in Thracian and they cheered again, this time with more conviction.

As the quinquereme's bow was raised by the swell a second long-range volley found its mark but the shots were spent and most bounced off the hull. Of those that reached the deck only a few retained enough velocity to pierce the planking. One crewman went down with an arrow dangling from his shoulder; it was soon extracted and he took his place again, bleeding lightly, back in the line.

Gaidres shouted in Thracian and the crew raised their bows and took aim. Vespasian, Sabinus and Magnus followed suit and waited for the order to release. Gaidres lifted his arm in the air and paused, judging the rise and fall of the trireme's bow.

At a distance of ninety paces his arm flashed down.

Over fifty arrows tore towards the pirate ship. The volley hit as its bow slipped down a trough exposing more of its deck and the hundred or so men within, felling almost a dozen of them as they let fly a ragged reply.

The drumbeat quickened and the quinquereme lurched forward into ramming speed.

Vespasian quickly reloaded and waited for the order to shoot, confident, as were the rest of the cheering crew, of Gaidres' ability to judge the moment correctly.

Gaidres' arm flashed down again and they released another perfectly timed volley.

The celebratory cheering as they reloaded was cut short by a cry from the larboard watch. The cheers turned into a collective groan. Vespasian looked over his left shoulder to see another ship emerge from under the lee of the headland, a mile behind them, and head straight towards them.

They were trapped.

'There's fuck all that we can do about them at the moment,' Sabinus shouted, having seen the threat. 'Let's deal with these bastards first.'

The trireme was now less than thirty paces away. Gaidres' arm came down again but he mistimed it; most of their third volley slammed into the pirate's hull, causing little damage.

At a shouted order from Rhaskos the Thracian crew grabbed the side of the ship.

'That was brace for impact,' Vespasian shouted at Magnus and Sabinus.

'Thanks, sir,' Magnus shouted back gripping the rail; he had never really got the hang of Thracian.

Vespasian tensed his body against his arms and spread his feet, one in front of the other as the two ships hurtled towards each other.

At what seemed to be the very last moment the trireme veered to its left and shipped its starboard oars.

Vespasian heard Rhaskos scream an order and felt the ship reel to the right in an attempt to prevent the trireme raking its starboard oars. The pirate trierarchus was ready for this and, as the heavier quinquereme's bow came round, he shipped his larboard oars and, with a sharp push on the steering-oars, brought his smaller, more manoeuvrable ship back into its original course to grate down its opponent's larboard side, disgorging a close-range volley followed by a boarding party as it went by.

Whether Rhaskos' last order included anything about shipping oars, Vespasian could not tell, but, if it had, it came too late. The pirate trireme crashed into the quinquereme's larboard oars, cracking the thick wooden shafts like twigs, with sudden, explosive reports that belied the ease with which they snapped. The ships shuddered violently with each impact, throwing defenders and attackers alike to the deck. The slaves below shrieked in tormented agony as their oar-handles, to which they were manacled, were punched back, crunching into their faces or throats or shattering their ribcages and hurling them, bodily, off their soiled benches only to be abruptly restrained by their leg-irons, fastened to the deck. As the momentum of the trireme pushed the stumps of their oars ever back those slaves who had the misfortune not to be killed outright suffered the added torture of being stretched between their shackles until the sinews in their wrists could take it no more; hands ripped off under the intense pressure, flying through the air like macabre missiles to land with sickening thuds around the deck, causing the rising hysteria of the unharmed slaves on the opposite side to overflow into outright panic.

They ceased to row.

Without the purchase of the starboard oars the quinquereme started to spin, pulling it away from its tormentor which carried on in a straight line, its bow clearing the oars as it came level with the mast and leaving the thirty-man boarding party temporarily stranded. The violent shuddering ended and the deck became stable.

As if upon a given signal everyone got to their feet as one, each man knowing that an instant's delay could spell death. Too close for archery, the two sides hurled themselves at each other. Vespasian leapt forward, drawing his sword as rhomphaiai hissed from their scabbards all around him; he threw himself at the shield of the nearest opponent. With no shield of his own, his left shoulder cracked into the leather-covered, wooden *hoplon*, knocking its wielder back a pace. A flash of iron through the air as the pirate brought his weapon down in an overarm cut caused Vespasian to parry his sword above his head, meeting his assailant's wrist. His sword juddered and blood spurted on to his tunic as the pirate retracted his arm with a scream, leaving his hand, still grasping the sword, to clump to the deck. A quick jab to the throat put paid to the howling man; swiftly Vespasian grabbed his shield, squatted, and glanced around. To his right Sabinus and Artebudz were both grappling hand to hand in desperate wrestling matches. To his left Magnus and Sitalces were scything their way, with Gaidres, his marines and the rest of the crew, through the outnumbered and disorganised boarding party, like harvesters in a wheat field. More used to attacking ships in the southern Aegeum, where the defenders fought with swords (if at all), the pirates were buckling under the vicious assault of so many long, slicing blades, wielded two-handed, out of reach of the thrusts and cuts of their shorter weapons. Without the discipline to form a military shield wall, they let the Thracians in amongst them and they paid with their limbs and heads that now littered the blood-soaked deck.

Advancing steadily to his right, Vespasian thrust the point of his sword down through the eye of Sabinus' opponent and then squared up to a young, desperate-looking man pointing a shaking sword nervously before him as he took a step back, on to the rail. A head spun through the air between them, spewing gore that flecked the young pirate's face. Vespasian pounced forward; with a yelp the man threw himself overboard. Vespasian laughed.

'What the fuck are you finding so funny?' Sabinus growled from behind him.

Vespasian spun round to see his brother, spattered in blood, looking incredulously at him. All around the pirates, and a few Thracians, lay dead. The fighting was over.

'I just met someone who would rather drown than die with some degree of honour,' he replied through his mirth. 'Although why that's funny I don't know,' he added, getting himself under control.

A screamed order from Rhaskos abruptly ended the conversation. The brothers looked up. A hundred paces away the trireme had unshipped its oars and was turning back to face them, but, more worryingly, the second ship was now just half a mile away and approaching fast. As they watched it they heard the unmistakable sound of the drumbeat changing to ramming speed.

Vespasian looked over the rail. Below him, over half the oars were missing; those still in place hung limply in the water. It was obvious, even to his nautically untrained eye, that it would be some time before the ship would be able to manoeuvre. They were helpless and would be rammed and then boarded by both triremes and, without the manpower to repel two crews; Vespasian knew that they would perish.

'Sabinus,' he called, running towards Rhaskos at the stern, 'take Magnus and get Rhoteces out of his cage.'

He wove his way up the chaotic deck, through crew throwing copses and limbs overboard whilst others were being marshalled by Gaidres into groups ready to repel boarders at either end of the ship. He found Rhaskos in a heated debate with the slave-master.

'Rhaskos,' Vespasian shouted, cutting short the argument, 'we need more men.'

Rhaskos looked at him as if he were an idiot. 'And just where are we going to find them in the middle of the sea?'

'There're over two hundred below.'

'They're slaves, we need them to row.'

'But they're not rowing now and we haven't got the time to run; we're going to die, as will they when the ship goes down. This is what your dream was about, you have to free them all and arm them; our cause is now theirs if they want to live.'

Rhaskos looked towards the triremes; their proximity made the decision easy. 'You're right; if they fight for us we may just beat off both attacks. Get Gaidres to bring all the spare weapons to the hatchway.' He looked at the slave-master, who was standing dumbfounded, evidently worried about the vengeance that over two hundred armed slaves might wreak on him and his mates. Reading the man's mind, Rhaskos said: 'We'll worry about what happens afterwards if there is an afterwards. Get the keys and unlock them all. I'll come down and speak to them.'

Vespasian raced off to find Gaidres as a volley from the nearest trireme hailed down upon the deck, reducing the defenders' numbers by a precious few more.

'Fighting alongside slaves,' Gaidres said grimly, having been told the plan, 'that's novel. Let's hope they fight with us and not against us.'

'There's only one way to find out,' Vespasian said, making for the hatchway down to the oar-deck. A violent shudder ran through the whole ship, knocking him to the deck just short of the hatch. The first trireme had rammed them but fortunately had been unable to build up sufficient momentum for its bronze-headed ram to pierce the hull timbers. The second trireme definitely had and was now only three hundred paces away. Vespasian dropped his shield and scrambled down the ladder on to the oar-deck.

Rhaskos was addressing the slaves. 'You have a choice: drown at your oars as the ship goes down or fight with us as free men, to live or die as the gods will. And remember, the pirates will chain you to your oars again if they prevail, but if we beat them off you will still be free, and I will have the Queen confirm that freedom when we return to Thracia. What's it to be?'

Vespasian opened the door to the small forward cabin. Inside Magnus was unlocking the priest's foot-irons whilst Sabinus restrained him.

'Get a move on, boys,' Vespasian urged.

'What the fuck's going on?' Magnus asked, fumbling in his haste with Rhoteces' chains.

'We're enlisting a small army,' Vespasian replied as a large cheer went up from the slaves.

'Unchain them,' Rhaskos shouted above the din.

The slave-master and his mates started working up the benches, quickly turning keys for the eager ex-slaves to cast off their shackles.

'I pray to Amphiaraos that he has shown me the right thing to do and I haven't misread his message,' Rhaskos said to Vespasian, brushing past him to make his way back on deck with cheering ex-slaves following in his wake.

'What did he mean by that?' Sabinus asked as he and Magnus hauled the still manacled and muttering Rhoteces through the cabin door.

Before Vespasian could reply a deafening crack reverberated around the oar-deck; the ship lurched to starboard, throwing everyone into the air. Sharp splinters of wood exploded all around and a bronze-headed ram burst through the hull, accompanied by the roar of gushing water and headed straight for Vespasian. It came to a sudden halt a hand's breadth from where he lay with another booming thud as the attacking ship's bow powered into the quinquereme's hull. Screams of anguish filled the air. The ship rolled again, lifting the ram, which tore at the fissure, cracking through the planking with a series of ear-splitting reports. Water surged in under high pressure. As the ship rolled back the ram came thumping down on to the deck, splitting it open and crashing through, down into the bilge to crush to a pulp a handful of sick slaves unfortunate enough to be in its path. With another creaking roll the ship settled, bringing the ram back up to the oar-deck where it stayed, rocking menacingly, like a wild beast preparing to pounce, just in front of Vespasian's face.

'Bacchus' bell end,' he croaked, staring in wide-eyed horror at the ram's bronze head; on it was engraved in Greek: 'Greetings to Poseidon'. A piece of mangled slave plopped back down into the bilge.

Magnus recovered first. 'Come on, sir,' he shouted, pulling Vespasian up out of the churning water. Ex-slaves dashed past, jumping over the unsteady ram and pounding up the ladder away from the terror of the quickly flooding oar-deck. The slave-masters hurriedly unlocked the remaining rowers and joined the rush to escape. Those too maimed to walk were left behind calling pitifully for aid as the water level rose. Fingers appeared through the gratings to the bilge, but they remained locked and the ram blocked any hope of exit through the smashed deck.

Magnus pushed his way to the foot of the ladder; Sabinus dragged Rhoteces, who was gibbering with fear, behind him. Vespasian followed, his senses gradually returning, and clambered up on to the main deck.

Vespasian picked up his shield, drew his sword and looked around; it was a fearsome sight. Ahead of him pirates hurled themselves from the bow of the second trireme, still embedded in the quinquereme's hull, and on to the deck. They crashed into the wild mêlée that was being fed all the time by the arrival of newly armed ex-slaves who, with the pent-up rage of years of servitude freshly released, fought like feral beasts, uncaring of their own safety as they once again experienced the exhilaration of free will. The years spent chained to their oars, incarcerated in that dark dungeon, faded in an instant as they used their powerful limbs to maim and kill, their rotten teeth bared beneath long, matted beards, screaming, almost with joy, like furies.

Seeing that the pirates were being slowly pushed back at the bow Vespasian ran up the deck to where the other trireme had fastened itself, broadside on, with grappling hooks to the Thracian ship. Here the wider front meant that more of the attackers had been able to board and the fighting was less one-sided. Having seen what happens when you let rhomphaia-wielding Thracians get in amongst you the pirates had formed a shield wall. Crouching low behind their shields, ducking beneath the deadly sweeps of the rhomphaiai, they took slow, steady paces forward and were pushing back the crew and marines, who were having difficulty holding their ground. On the flank of the fight closest to him, next to the rail, Vespasian spotted Sabinus and Magnus, both with shields captured in the last fight, standing shoulder to shoulder pushing back at the pirates' wall; Sabinus mechanically worked his blade whilst Magnus attempted to wield his rhomphaia one-handed. Vespasian rushed to join them, taking care not to slip on the blood that flowed freely on the deck, and pushed in between his brother and the rail; he held his shield firmly in front of him and began jab and thrust.

As the pirate line steadily advanced more of their mates were able to board behind, broadening it, until all sixty of the remaining crew were aboard, adding extra weight to the scrum and putting increasing pressure on the Thracians whose line was becoming thinner as it extended. A couple of the boarders had had their legs swept from under them and lay screaming on the deck, blood spurting from their freshly carved stumps, but other-wise their line remained intact.

'This is no fucking good,' Sabinus wheezed as he was forced to take another step back and almost losing his balance as the ship listed suddenly to its bow, 'we're sinking. We need to take their ship, not the other way round.'

'We'll wheel them so their backs are towards the other fight,' Vespasian grunted as he stabbed again only to connect with a wooden shield. 'Then the slaves could take them from behind.'

'Or the pirates will just swarm all over the deck.'

'Not if we co-ordinate it and do it very swiftly. Listen out for my shout then quickly give ground.'

Sabinus nodded; Vespasian disengaged and rushed around the rear of the mêlée. He found Gaidres with Sitalces and Drenis hacking down on the tightly packed shield wall with brutal swipes of their rhomphaiai but doing little to stop its slow advance.

'Gaidres, with me,' he shouted. 'Sitalces, keep the left of the line firm when the right falls back.'

The huge Thracian shouted his acknowledgement and continued to beat ferociously down on the shield in front of him.

With Gaidres closely following, Vespasian ran, downhill, to the mêlée at the bow. Bodies littered the deck. The ex-slaves' furious onslaught had driven the pirates back, with heavy losses on both sides, on to their ship. Here they were fighting desperately to prevent their wild, long-haired opponents from boarding them, whilst the trireme's rowers backed oars in an effort to extricate the ram from the quinquereme's hull.

'Gaidres, I need at least fifty of our rowers to follow me; can you control them?'

'I'll try,' the marine replied, looking nervously at the frenzied horde.

A high-pitched, teeth-chilling, rasping grate of wood scraping wood cut in above the screams and clash of weapons and the deck listed ominously; the trireme had released itself. With the support of the ram gone the quinquereme's bow sagged lower into the water.

'Hurry, Gaidres,' Vespasian urged, 'we don't have long.'

With a grimace Gaidres waded into the baying mob, shouting for order. Those ex-slaves armed with bows had begun a frantic exchange of fire with the crew on the retreating trireme. Men from both sides plunged howling into the churning water clutching at shafts embedded in their dying bodies.

Gaidres soon managed to get most of the ex-slaves into some sort of order and ready to charge. Checking that they would not be threatened from behind Vespasian looked over to the retreating trireme, now thirty paces away. For a brief instant he made eye contact with a familiar figure standing in the prow: the wounded pirate trierarchus from the sanctuary. His one eye blazed with fury and he hurled a stream of oaths at Vespasian before ducking down under the rail in the face of another volley from the bow-armed ex-slaves.

Thrusting the shock of the coincidence to one side, Vespasian bellowed at the top of his voice: 'Sabinus, now!'

At the other end of the ship Sabinus heard his brother's call and he and Magnus pulled back immediately, taking the Thracians to their left with them. Sitalces held his position in the centre and the line pivoted on him. The pirates surged forward, not sensing the trap as Vespasian and Gaidres charged up the sloping deck with more than a hundred matted-haired, shrieking savages behind them.

With their blood-lust far from sated they crashed into the pirates' backs, ripping them open in a deluge of blood and offal with a savagery that shocked Vespasian, even as he killed. The joy of once again feeling alive was magnified for the ex-slaves as they took life after life in a killing spree almost as brutal as their existence had been for the past few years.

Caught between the torrent of rage behind them and the flashing, two-handed swipes of rhomphaiai to their front the pirates knew that they were doomed and, expecting no quarter, resolved to sell their lives dearly. They fought with an intensity that matched their foes for the last few moments of their lives as their numbers were quickly whittled down and their line thinned.

Vespasian plunged his sword into another exposed back and twisted his wrist sharply, left then right; the man screamed, throwing his head back which, with a sudden jolt and a flash of iron, toppled from his shoulders. Blood spurted from the gaping neck as the man's heart pumped on, spraying over Vespasian. The body collapsed and the red rain cleared leaving Vespasian staring at Sitalces, eyes aflame, teeth bared, swinging his rhomphaia back towards him. With an instinctive jerk, Vespasian pulled his shield up in front of his face and the blade slammed into its rim in a cloud of sparks.

'Sitalces, stop!' he yelled, lowering his shield.

Sitalces paused and peered at Vespasian, then grinned apologetically. In that instant a blood-covered ex-slave leapt at him with a howl and drove a knife into the huge Thracian's throat.

'Nooooo!' Vespasian shouted as Sitalces collapsed with the maddened savage stabbing repeatedly at his throat. Vespasian grabbed the man's tangled hair and hauled him off. He twisted round, screaming unintelligibly, and thrust his knife towards Vespasian's thigh; a blade arced down and took his arm off at the elbow and then swiped up to sever his head.

'You filthy little cunt,' Magnus raged, slashing his rhomphaia back down, unnecessarily ripping open the corpse's belly.

All along the line similar scenes were playing out as the ex-slaves came through the last of the pirates and face to face with the Thracians. Warning shouts ripped through the air as the two sides collided. Although heavily outnumbered, with the longer reach of their weapons and better discipline, the Thracians managed to hold their allies off, but not before the slave-master and one of his mates had been set upon and hideously cut up. The perpetrators were summarily despatched by a hiss of rhomphiaia blades, which seemed to bring the rest out of their frenzy and the two groups lowered their weapons and stared at each other with wary distrust, breathing heavily.

An eerie silence fell over the ship.

Vespasian glanced behind him; the bow of the ship was now almost completely submerged; the quinquereme was afloat still solely because the pirate ship, now devoid of its fighting crew, was fastened to it by four straining ropes. The second trireme was now speeding towards its sister ship in an attempt to board it and prevent the Thracians from taking it as a prize.

'Transfer to the trireme,' Vespasian yelled, 'and prepare to repel boarders.'

The shout suddenly brought home the precariousness of their situation to the exhausted men and the two groups silently and mutually called a truce and then quickly set about abandoning ship.

'Archers with me,' Sabinus shouted, leaping over the rail and on to the trireme whose bow was slowly being forced down by the weight of the sinking quinquereme. 'We'll hold them off as long as possible.'

Fifty or so bow-armed crew and ex-slaves followed him.

'We take all our wounded with us, even the ex-slaves,' Gaidres called out so that all could hear. 'How's the big man?'

Magnus knelt down by Sitalces and checked for signs of life. There were none. 'He's dead,' he said blankly.

'I'll get his body on to the trireme; the Queen will want him buried with honour. Drenis!'

'Where's Rhoteces?' Vespasian asked.

'I left him with Artebudz at the stern,' Magnus replied, watching Gaidres and Drenis bearing Sitalces away through the remaining crew and ex-slaves who were busily checking the fallen for those still alive.

'I'll get him; you go and get our stuff, especially that scroll.'

Magnus did not react.

'Come on, otherwise we'll all be joining him.'

With a start Magnus snapped out of his reverie and dashed off to retrieve their belongings from the small cabin in the stern of the stricken ship.

Bodies floated all around in the gently swelling sea; the waterline had reached the mast, down which a crewman was climbing, having saved the Thracian royal standard. Vespasian found Artebudz in amongst the chaos, hauling a screaming Rhoteces by his manacles towards the trireme. Arrows started to fly overhead as an archery duel with the second pirate ship flared up.

The quinquereme pitched suddenly. Gaidres had cut the forward rope to ease the pressure on the trireme, which was so low in the water now that its lower oar-ports were only a hand's breadth above the surface.

'Hurry, Artebudz,' Vespasian called, steadying his balance as the ship settled.

'He doesn't want to go, sir,' Artebudz said, pulling the struggling priest another couple of paces across the now severely lilting deck.

'Come on, you little shit,' Vespasian said, grabbing him by the tunic. 'What's the matter? Don't you want to leave your precious cursed ship?'

'My gods will pluck me away only if I remain on a Thracian ship,' Rhoteces screeched; religious fervour burned in his bloodshot eyes. 'The other pirate vessel will kill you all but I will be saved if I remain here.'

'Don't be stupid.' Vespasian laughed as they reached the

crowded rail. 'If you weren't so valuable to me I'd enjoy leaving you here and watching you being disappointed.'

'I told you this ship would never reach Rome.'

'That wasn't too difficult to predict,' Vespasian said with a malicious grin, hefting the priest over the rail. 'Rome's not a seaport; it was never going there, it was going to Ostia, so bollocks to you and your predictions.'

He and Artebudz threw the priest on to the trireme where he landed with a loud thump and a yelp. Artebudz followed him over and dragged him away.

Gaidres cut the sternmost rope and the quinquereme lurched again; bodies started to slither down the deck. 'For the love of Bendis, hurry,' he screamed, 'I can't hold her much longer.'

Desperate cries issued from the slaves manacled to the trireme's oars as they watched the water rise ever closer to the oar-ports.

Arrows hissed through the air, the archery duel intensifying with the arrival of more and more Thracians and their unlikely allies forcing the pirate ship to lay off.

The last of the crew were leaping across as Magnus came scrambling up to Vespasian with their bags and they jumped on to the trireme. Rhaskos was the last man over the rail, clutching a strongbox and his speaking-trumpet. Gaidres and Drenis cut the final two ropes. The trireme immediately surged upwards, almost clearing the surface, and then fell back down with a jolt and a loud splash. Every one of the two hundred and more men on deck sprawled on to the deck. The pirates took good advantage of the temporary lack of return fire and many did not get back up again.

Vespasian pulled himself back on to his feet; the roar of rushing wind caused him to turn. Just behind him the quinquereme's stern flicked upright, towering almost seventy feet above the waves, cracking the mast in two under the intolerable pressure and catapulting dead bodies through the air to land with a quick succession of splashes, like a handful of shingle cast at the sea. Foul air billowed from the oar-ports as churning water surged up through its belly; it started to slide under. Its timbers creaked and groaned in anguished cries as the once proud ship was sucked down into the depths of Poseidon's dark kingdom to the accompaniment of cheering from its ex-oarsmen.

With a final explosion of water, which rocked the trireme, it was gone. The archery battle, which had tailed off as both crews had stopped to watch the awe-inspiring death agonies of the huge ship, resumed again with vigour as Sabinus screamed at his men for a faster rate of volleys. The pirate ship started to back its oars to escape the relentless hail of arrows. After a couple more volleys Sabinus called a halt. The two ships lay a hundred paces apart; too close together for them to be able to build up enough momentum to do much damage to each other's oars, let alone crack open a hull, and too far apart to threaten each other with archery. They were in a stalemate.

The air became still.

As it stood, with more than 250 men on the Thracian deck, many of them bow-armed, they could not be taken by a boarding party but equally they would not have enough provisions to get to Ostia. It was obvious to Vespasian that they had to attempt to take the pirate, either to capture the ship outright or to, at least, take off its victuals before it sank. They needed to move forward, yet they were still stationary, their oars limp in the water.

He ran back to the stern where Rhaskos had taken up his position. 'Why aren't we moving, Rhaskos?'

'We're in trouble again, my friend, may the gods preserve us,' the trierarchus replied, raising his palms to the sky. 'The pirate slave-masters killed more than a hundred of the rowers at their oars before our men could get to them, so we can't manoeuvre. And when the pirates realise that they'll pull back until they've got enough sea-room to get up the speed to ram us.'

'Then we need some of our rowers to take the dead ones' places – and fast.'

'Yes, but now they're free how will they take rowing again, especially shoulder to shoulder with slaves?'

'We free the slaves; I would have done so anyway as a lot of them will have been taken from Roman ships. Talk to our rowers and send a hundred down to me.'

Calling Gaidres to follow him, Vespasian made his way down on to the oar-deck. It was a scene of carnage. Corpses lay slumped over oars, despatched by vicious thrusts through their backs and chests. The survivors were sitting, hollow-eyed with fear, staring vacantly at four Thracian marines who were unshackling the dead bodies and slithering them out of the oar-ports.

'Release the slaves first, then get rid of the bodies,' Vespasian ordered the Thracians. They looked at him, puzzled.

'You heard him; do it now!' Gaidres shouted.

The Thracians shrugged and carried out their orders.

'You will stay in your seats,' Vespasian shouted so that all of the slaves could hear. 'We need you to row, but now you will row as free men. If you refuse, we will all die. Are there any Roman citizens here?'

Over twenty men raised their manacled hands.

'You're excused rowing, go up on deck and find a weapon each.'

There was a growl of protest from the rest.

'Silence!' Vespasian roared. 'A citizen of Rome does not bend his back to an oar. You, however, do not have the protection of citizenship so you will row. If we survive, we're going to Ostia where you may leave the ship or, if you prefer, you can return east with it; it's down to you.'

There was a muttering of assent.

The Thracian stroke-master clambered down the ladder from the main deck followed by the rowers. He looked at Vespasian, who nodded at him to take his place behind the round ox-skin drum.

With a real sense of urgency the oar-deck was cleared of bodies and the replacement rowers took their positions. Vespasian and Gaidres hurried back up on to the deck.

The mournful cries of gulls, attracted by the flotsam and jetsam of the sunken ship, filled the air as they circled overhead and dived on edible morsels that littered the sea.

'Looks like they've had enough, sir,' Magnus said, pointing to the pirate ship; it had turned and was now a quarter of a mile away, rowing quickly west.

'Let's hope so,' Vespasian replied dubiously. 'Rhaskos, the oar-deck's ready. What do you think we should do?'

'Pray to the gods.'

'And then what?' Vespasian exploded, storming up to the old trierarchus, 'go to sleep and hope for another helpful dream? Be practical, man! Do we try and take the pirate and get his supplies? Or do we make a run for it and worry about what everyone's going to eat later? You're the trierarchus, you decide what we humans on this ship should do right now.'

The vehemence of his outburst caused Rhaskos to blink his eyes quickly and then look around. 'They're not running,' he said lucidly, 'it's as I said: they're preparing to ram us because they think that we're still crippled. We need to sail west anyway so we should go straight at them, then they can choose: fight or run.' He picked up his speaking-trumpet. 'Attack speed,' he shouted down to the stroke-master, who reacted immediately. The steady booming started; slow at first, as the ship got under way, then quickly accelerating as the oarsmen, now free and with a real stake in the survival of the ship, willingly put their backs into the matter at hand.

The pirate ship made a hurried turn as their trierarchus saw that the Thracian ship was no longer disabled but was under full oars and coming straight towards him.

'He's mad if he thinks he can retake this ship,' Magnus said, coming up to Vespasian and Rhaskos, who were watching the distance start to close between the two ships.

'He's not mad, he's angry. He's lost one of his ships but he's not lost his judgement; he won't board us, he'll try to sink us,' Vespasian replied, loosening his gladius in its sheath for the second time that day. 'There's no way that he can win but it is still possible that we can both lose.'

'Archers ready,' Sabinus shouted, running to the bow.

Despite losing a hundred or so rowers to the oar-deck there were still over a hundred men on deck.

The Thracian ship shifted course slightly to the left.

'What are you doing, Rhaskos?' Vespasian shouted.

'What I'm good at,' Rhaskos replied, his eyes fixed firmly on the oncoming vessel. 'You just worry about your job and let me concentrate on mine.'

The pirate changed direction to match. At a distance of two hundred paces apart Rhaskos veered back on to the original course; the pirate followed suit. Now they were not quite head on, leaving the pirate with a choice: to go for an oar-rake or come round more to his left and try to ram at a slight angle. With the ships a hundred paces apart he chose to ram.

'Ramming speed!' Rhaskos shouted through his trumpet. As the stroke accelerated he veered away from the pirate, to the right, leaving the Thracian ship broadside on to their attackers but now rowing fast enough to pass them.

'Release!' Sabinus shouted. Scores of arrows shot away towards the pirate ship, now less than fifty paces away; they peppered its hull and deck bringing down half a dozen more of its crew. After the first volley the Thracians kept up a constant stream of fire, forcing the pirate crew to take shelter behind the rail.

Vespasian could see the huge pirate trierarchus by the steering-oars, impervious to the rain of arrows, screaming at his men to return vollies as he tried to bring his ship back on to an interception course. But it was too late; with the ships just thirty paces apart Rhaskos ordered another turn away to the right and the pirate was now directly behind them, chasing. A smattering of arrows fell on the tightly packed Thracian deck; a few screams from the wounded rose up above the pounding of the stroke-master's drum and straining grunts of the 180 willing oarsmen below. The archers continued their relentless barrage.

Vespasian pushed his way through to Rhaskos. The old trier-archus was grinning broadly. 'How about that?' he shouted. 'I out-steered him without a single prayer; may the gods forgive me.'

'Why did you pass him?' Vespasian asked. 'I thought that we were going to try and take him.'

'Because, my young friend, when he came about and headed straight for us I realised that you were wrong. He had lost his reason; he was prepared to lose his ship just to destroy us, out of spite. It was madness and I never like to fight a madman; who knows what they will do next?'

Vespasian looked over Rhaskos' shoulder to the chasing pirate. 'What do *we* do next? He's gaining on us.'

'We keep running, we can keep at ramming-speed for longer than he can,' Rhaskos replied with a wink. 'Gaidres, send the spare rowers down in batches of twelve to relieve the others, two sets of oars at a time starting from the bow.'

Gaidres acknowledged the trierarchus and started to round up the rowers without bows.

Vespasian joined Sabinus, who was now at the stern rail. The pirate was less than twenty paces behind them and gaining slowly as the slaves on its oar-deck were whipped mercilessly to squeeze every last drop of energy from them. The swell made accurate shooting between the ships almost impossible and the pirate trierarchus still stood at the steering-oars, shouting for all he was worth, despite Sabinus' repeated attempts to shoot him down.

'That man's got a charmed life,' he muttered, notching another arrow and taking careful aim. Again the shot went wide. 'He's got balls just standing there, I'll give him that.'

Gradually the relieving of the blown rowers began to reap benefits as fresh limbs pulled on straining oars. Even the Roman citizens had volunteered for duty, realising that the privileges of citizenship did not extend to the dead. The Thracian ship was beginning to pull away when the first few oars on the pirate fouled as the exhausted slaves collapsed and it started to lose way. The pirate trierarchus pulled his ship off to the south, towards Cythera, and roared his defiance until a volley of arrows sent him ducking under the rail.

'Cruise speed,' Rhaskos shouted.

The drumbeat slowed gradually as did the ship.

'My thanks to Amphiaraos for showing me the way,' Rhaskos called to the sky. 'I will sacrifice another ram when we reach Ostia.'

'If we get there,' Vespasian said. 'How are we going to feed all these people?'

'The gods will provide. I have no doubt of it as they showed us how to escape the pirates.'

'They didn't show us how to defeat the pirates,' Sabinus scoffed. 'Wasn't your dream about how to preserve the crew and get rid of the slave fever?'

Rhaskos looked pleased with himself. 'Yes, but you can't deny that releasing the slaves did preserve the crew against the pirate attack. As to stopping the sickness spreading through the slaves, I gave orders that only the ones without the fever should be released; the ill ones down in the bilge all drowned on the ship. We are free of the fever now and should be able to complete our voyage.'

Vespasian could see the truth of it: the oracle had indeed shown Rhaskos the answer to his question. He walked to the rail and, whilst enjoying the calming effects of a cool breeze and a warm sun on his skin, contemplated everything he had seen and heard at the sanctuary of Amphiaraos.

'It seems that the sanctuary was quite a powerful place, Sabinus,' he said quietly to his brother a short while later as they watched the pirate and the captured trader disappear to the south, past Cythera. 'What do you make of the prophecy now?'

'I don't know,' his brother replied. 'But one thing's for sure, I will never forget it.'

'Neither will I,' Vespasian agreed as their ship left the strait of Cythera and entered the Ionian Sea, heading on towards Ostia.

PART IIII

ROME, JULY AD 30

CHAPTER X

AN INTENSE PROFUSION of contrary smells assaulted Vespasian's olfactory senses as the trireme docked against one of the many wooden jetties in the port of Ostia: the ravenous mouth of the city of Rome. The fresh, salt tang of sea air clashed with the muddy reek of the Tiber as it disgorged the filth of the city, just twenty miles upstream, into the Tyrrhenian Sea. The decay of decomposing animal carcasses bobbing between the ships and wharves conflicted with the mouth-watering aromas of grilling pork, chicken and sausages that wafted across from the smoking charcoal braziers of quayside traders, eager to sell fresh meat to stale-bread-weary sailors. Sacks of pungent spices – cinnamon, cloves, saffron – from India and beyond, were offloaded by Syrian trading ships next to vessels from Africa and Lusitania disgorging their cargoes of high-smelling garum sauce, made from the fermented intestines of fish. Unsubtly perfumed whores solicited unwashed seamen; garlic-breathed dock-workers took orders from lavender-scented merchants; sweat-foamed horses and mules pulled cartloads of sweet, dried apricots, figs, dates and raisins. Rotting fish, baking bread, sweating slaves, resinated wine, stale urine, dried herbs, high meat, hemp rope, ships' bilges and warm wood: the combinations made Vespasian's head spin as he watched the Thracian crew secure the ship and lower the gangplank to the constant shouted entreaties of Rhaskos.

'At times I thought that we'd never make back, sir,' Magnus said, joining him at the rail, 'but that is definitely Ostia.'

'Having never been here, I'll just have to take your word for it,' Vespasian replied, smiling at his friend and sharing his relief at finally getting home.

It had not been a straightforward journey, purely for the foreseen logistical problems of feeding so many men. The provisions that they found in the hold had only been sufficient for a few days and, although Rhaskos had been able to buy, with the gold in his strongbox, sacks of hardtack, chickpeas and dried pork at ports along the way they had been forced to stop for two or three days at a time to hunt sufficient game to keep the 350 or so men onboard from going too hungry. Their voyage, therefore, had taken almost thirty days from Cythera, much longer than intended but it had, at least, been without incident.

With the ship finally secured Rhaskos came pushing through the crowded deck. 'So, my young friend, here's where we say goodbye,' the old trierarchus said, sweating profusely from the exertion of so much shouting at his crew. 'Although how I shall get home I don't know, as I've used up all the gold that the Queen gave me for the return trip.'

'I'm sure that the gods will provide,' Vespasian replied, instantly regretting his flippancy.

Thankfully it was lost on Rhaskos, who just nodded his head sagely. 'Yes, you're right; I'm sure they will.'

There was a stirring on the quayside and raucous shouting; a group of twenty armed men were shoving their way towards the bottom of the gangway. Although they were not in uniform they certainly had a military look; each was armed with a gladius. However, more worryingly, because of the fine quality of their tunics and the smartness of their appearance they had more than a whiff of the Praetorian Guard about them.

Thoughts of betrayal flooded into Vespasian's mind and he glanced nervously at Magnus and Sabinus, who had joined him having heard the disturbance.

The soldiers reached the bottom of the gangway and their leader, a tall, wiry, auburn-haired man with a pinched face and pasty skin, motioned them to stop. From within their midst appeared a smartly dressed, bearded Greek.

'Welcome home, masters,' Pallas said, making his way up the steep ramp.

'Pallas!' Vespasian was astonished to see Antonia's steward. 'How did you know when we would arrive?'

'I didn't,' Pallas replied, bowing low. 'I have been waiting here for ten days now, ever since a messenger from Queen Tryphaena arrived, overland, telling the Lady Antonia that you had left Tomi towards the end of May. She sent me here to escort you and our mutual friend back to Rome.'

'And I suppose that is our escort,' Sabinus observed, looking suspiciously at the phalanx of men on the quay.

'Yes, master. I will explain later, when there are fewer people listening.' Pallas indicated the mass of crew and ex-slaves that had crowded around to see what was going on.

'I look forward to it,' Sabinus said uneasily.

'Get back to work, all of you,' Rhaskos suddenly shouted at his milling crew, 'there's nothing to see here.'

'Ah, you must be the noble trierarchus,' Pallas crooned, bowing towards Rhaskos as the crew started to thin out.

'Rhaskos, sir,' Rhaskos stammered, unused to being addressed in those terms.

'Please, master, do not address me as "sir", I am but a mere slave.'

Vespasian and Sabinus both smiled; there was nothing 'mere' about Pallas whatsoever.

Rhaskos looked confused. 'I'm sorry, er . . .'

'Please do not apologise to me. My name is Pallas, master.'

'Pallas,' Rhaskos spluttered, 'indeed. Thank—'

Pallas raised an eyebrow; Rhaskos halted mid-flow. 'The Lady Antonia wishes me to inform you, Trierachus Rhaskos, that you are to revictual your ship totally at her expense; I have delivered her promissory note to the port aedile guaranteeing full payment for anything that you require.'

'May the gods be praised.' Rhaskos raised his palms and faced to the sky. 'Please give my thanks to the Lady, sir . . . er . . . Pallas. I am in her debt.' He bowed, then, realising his mistake, quickly stopped himself and beat a hasty retreat, calling out his thanks for his good fortune to every god that he could think of, which were many.

Vespasian was sure that Pallas had been amused by the

conversation but was unable to confirm it as the steward's face remained, as always, absolutely neutral.

'We should go, masters,' Pallas said with just the faintest trace of urgency in his voice. 'We will need to ride fast if we are to get to Rome before dusk.'

In less than an hour they were on the move. Having said their goodbyes to Rhaskos, Drenis and Gaidres, they transferred Rhoteces, hissing and hooded, to a covered wagon that waited for them, along with their horses, a short distance from the crowded harbour. Artebudz, who was on his way north to his mountainous home in the province of Noricum, had come with them and he and Magnus rode in the wagon, guarding the priest.

'They are Praetorians, as you suspected, masters,' Pallas informed Vespasian and Sabinus as they rode through the gates of Ostia at a quick trot. 'However, they're Praetorian Cavalry; their decurion, Marcus Arrecinus Clemens—'

'Clemens?' Vespasian interrupted. 'I've heard that name before; he was with Macro and Hasdro when they were following me up the Via Aurelia. Macro sent Clemens north with half of his cavalry to block the road, whilst he took the rest to look for me in Cosa.'

'Yes, he is loyal to our new friend, Macro,' Pallas confirmed. 'He also happens to be a client of my mistress's son Claudius.'

'How did that come about?' Vespasian was intrigued.

'I believe he is a man who enjoys gambling at the circus on the team with the longest odds.'

'There's a difference between betting on an outsider as compared with a no-hoper,' Sabinus pointed out.

'I wouldn't say that Claudius is a no-hoper,' Pallus replied with a slight rise of his eyebrows. 'His mother would, as would the Emperor and Sejanus, but that's why he is still in the race. He may seem stupid because he stutters, drools and limps, because he has a tendency to say the most inappropriate things in public and makes pathetic jokes under the misapprehension that he's one of the finest wits of our age; but underneath he's an ambitious, power-hungry viper and not to be trusted. He's also very intelligent, if somewhat chaotic, and has written extensively on a wide variety of subjects. Some of his work is, I'm told, quite edifying.'

Vespasian was intrigued. 'Would you bet on him, Pallas?'

Pallas looked at Vespasian shrewdly. 'The disadvantage about gambling at the circus is that you can only place a bet before the race starts; to my mind that is the worst time to put your money down. I prefer to lay a bet after the final turn when you have a much clearer idea as to who will be the eventual winner. That system has two advantages: you are more likely to win and you'll have been parted from your money for a shorter time.'

'So Clemens has got a long wait before he sees any return to his outlay, then?' Sabinus chuckled.

'Perhaps, but like any sensible long-odds gambler he has hedged his bet with a little flutter on Caligula; he escorts him when he goes out at night incognito, gets him out of any embarrassing scrapes that he may fall into and clears up his mess – which is sometimes considerable.'

'I'm sure it is,' Vespasian agreed, thinking of his friend's voracious sexual appetite. 'So Clemens is one to watch, is he?'

'Oh yes, and I'm sure that he will make himself very useful to you both.'

'What makes you think that?' Sabinus asked.

'Because you are in the Lady Antonia's favour and he is a kinsman of yours. A very distant one, but nevertheless the link is there. Your father's mother and Clemens' grandmother shared the same grandfather and I'm sure that he will make much of it.'

'He doesn't look much like a kinsman of ours,' Sabinus observed, eyeing with suspicion the thin-faced decurion riding just ahead of them. 'He's an ugly bugger, that's for sure.'

'I tend to find it best not to judge people on their looks, master,' Pallas said, bringing the subject to a close.

Vespasian rode on in silence. The tingle of anticipation that had been growing in his stomach since they had sighted the Italian coast was now a churning and he was finding it increasingly hard to concentrate on anything other than Caenis. After more than four years he would see her again tonight; at least he hoped that he would. Surely she would be with Antonia? But would he get to talk with her, a chance to be alone with her, to touch and hold her? None of these questions could he answer; he would just have to wait and see – and the knowledge that he was not in control of the situation was driving him to distraction. He tried to put his mind to other matters – his parents, the estates, his uncle Gaius, the island of Capreae whose rocky coastline they had sailed past the previous day – but it would not settle. It just kept on coming back to the most urgent subject: Caenis. He felt blood rushing to his groin as the image of her stepping out of her tunic in the lamplight flitted across his inner eye and he was forced to make an adjustment to his dress.

'Thinking about your romantic reunion with the mules at home, brother?' Sabinus drawled, noticing his unfortunate predicament.

'Piss off, Sabinus,' Vespasian snapped, hugely embarrassed in more ways than one.

'I asked Clemens to send a rider ahead to warn my mistress that we would arrive this evening,' Pallas said, picking up on the problem and guessing its cause. 'I'm sure there will be a dinner awaiting you and I will make sure that every member of the household fulfils their normal roles.'

Happy in the knowledge that he would at least see Caenis that evening, Vespasian smiled awkwardly at Pallas, whose expression, as ever, remained neutral, as if he had said nothing at all of import. Sabinus gave a wry chuckle.

It was almost dusk as the column clattered up the Palatine Hill. The culture shock that Vespasian had felt at being back in a city so packed with people was wearing off as the crowds thinned out and the houses grew, quite literally, more palatial.

Antonia's seal had been sufficient to get them and the wagon through the Porta Ostiensis without any questions from the Urban Cohort soldiers on guard – wheeled vehicles not normally being allowed in the city during the day. It had then taken them almost a half-hour to fight their way through the crowds of the Aventine, around the Circus Maximus and finally to the foot of the Palatine. But now their journey was over.

Clemens thumped on the gate to the stable yard at the rear of Antonia's villa; it opened after a short delay.

'We're being observed,' Pallas remarked as they rode into the yard.

Vespasian glanced back up the street to see a couple of figures lurking in the shadows of a cypress tree overhanging a wall, fifty paces away. 'Sejanus' men?' he asked.

'More than likely,' Pallas said, dismounting, 'but they won't be able to tell him any more than that a group of men arrived escorting a carriage.'

'Welcome, gentleman,' came a strong, familiar, female voice. Antonia descended the steps from the main house and walked elegantly towards Vespasian and Sabinus. Although in her mid-sixties she was still beautiful in a way that could not just be ascribed to expensive beauty treatments and the best coiffure and gowns that money could buy. She smiled radiantly at the brothers. 'I cannot begin to express my gratitude at what you have achieved for our cause.' She took Sabinus' hand and pressed it warmly. He bowed his head and muttered something inaudible.

Antonia turned to Vespasian and took his hand in both of hers. 'I see that four years in the army has been the making of you, Vespasian,' she said, lowering her voice so that only he could hear. 'You look to be a man in perfect physical condition; I hope that your mind has grown in conjunction with your body because in the next few months it will be politics that'll be our main concern, not fighting.'

Vespasian reddened slightly. That so powerful a woman should come out to greet them rather than awaiting them in the cool of her study was humbling, and a great honour. 'I hope that I'll be up to the tasks ahead, domina,' he managed to say, bracing himself to once again be swept into the sea of political intrigue in which he knew the highest strata of Roman society wallowed.

He was saved from any more searching questions by the arrival of Magnus and Artebudz dragging the cringing Rhoteces from the carriage. They threw him to the ground in front of Antonia.

'So this is the creature that's forced us to go to so much effort bringing him to Rome.' She looked with distaste at the filthy priest who, shaking with fear, tried to touch her feet in supplication. Magnus kicked his manacled hands away.

'Thank you, Magnus.'

'My pleasure, domina,' Magnus said with a grin. 'He's had the fight taken out of him since we landed at Ostia; he'd always thought that his gods would prevent him being brought to Rome but now he's here he's been muttering nonstop about them deserting him. Mind you, with one look at him, who would blame them, if you take . . .' Magnus ground to a halt, realising that he was far too lowly to be expressing his unsolicited opinions to Antonia, no matter what his previous relationship with her may have been.

Antonia cast him a mildly disapproving look, which to Vespasian's eye had the hint of desire in it. He could not help but wonder again what form their couplings must have taken having been indiscreetly told by Caligula that Antonia had indulged her passion for boxers fresh from a fight; Magnus had fought in front of her more that a few times.

Magnus bowed. 'Forgive me, domina,' he said contritely.

Vespasian suppressed a smile; one question had been answered: his friend had not been the dominant partner.

'Pallas, secure the prisoner away,' Antonia ordered, getting back to the matter in hand. 'Feed him just enough to keep up his strength but no more; we don't want him thinking that he's a guest.'

Pallas bowed to his mistress and with Artebudz's help hauled the writhing priest away.

'Now, gentlemen,' Antonia said, wrinkling her nose and turning back to Vespasian and Sabinus, 'I think that, for all our sakes, you should avail yourselves of my bath house before we dine. I will see you later when you are refreshed. Magnus, you may join them. Show them the way.'

A short while later the three of them were sitting, sweating profusely, in the small, brightly lit, white marble-walled *caldarium*. Male slaves were rubbing sweet-perfumed oil into their skin and then scraping it off with strigils, slowly removing the ingrained grime of travel.

Neither Vespasian nor Sabinus had bothered to ask Magnus how he had come to be so familiar with the whereabouts of Antonia's bath house; his embarrassed countenance and inability to look either of them in the eye as he led them unerringly through the maze of corridors were sufficient enough to gain all the amusement they needed from the situation.

Travel weariness had caught up with them in the baking temperature of the caldarium and they eased into a delightful semi-consciousness as their bodies were expertly cleansed.

A booming voice from the doorway abruptly brought them back from the somnolent world into which they had slipped.

'My dear boys, how lovely to have you back.'

Gaius Vespasius Pollo, their uncle, burst into the room completely naked. His bulbous body wobbled furiously as he waddled the short distance across the mosaic floor. Vespasian and Sabinus stood up and were subjected to his all-enveloping, enthusiastic embraces. Magnus, much to his relief, had to endure no more than a hearty grasp of his forearm.

'Antonia told me that I would find you here,' Gaius exclaimed, slapping an arm around each of the brothers' shoulders and sitting them back down on the hot stone bench. 'My, my, you look well, Vespasian, what a fine figure the army has given you; much like my own in my younger, more vigorous days. And you, Magnus, how I've missed your services these past four years – which reminds me: Antonia asked me to send you to her, she wished to see you before she had dinner; she didn't say why.'

Magnus grimaced. 'I suppose I'd better be going then,' he mumbled, picking up his linen towel and making as dignified an exit as possible.

As the door closed behind Magnus the brothers burst out laughing.

Gaius looked at them, bemused. 'What's so amusing, dear boys?'

Vespasian managed to get his mirth under control and indicated subtly to the slaves hovering around them. 'We'll fill you in later, Uncle; in the meantime tell us your news.'

Gaius was delighted to ramble on for a good while about his

recent achievements, which if not inconsiderable were at least inconsequential.

By the time he had finished they had moved into the *tepidarium*. Vespasian lay face down on a pleasantly warm leather couch having just enjoyed a good, almost violent, pummelling at the expert hands of one of Antonia's masseurs. He was vaguely aware of Sabinus and Gaius leaving and being told that he would be called shortly before dinner was served as he fell into a blissful sleep.

Oil being drizzled on to his back and then two thumbs gently working the muscles around his shoulder blades caused him to stir and grunt with pleasure. He lay still with his eyes shut as he submitted himself to the soothing massage, which was far more tranquil than the kneading and pounding that he had received earlier. The hands worked their way down his spine, easing the muscles and drawing from him long groans of relaxed contentment. As they passed the small of his back they moved on to his buttocks and caressed them with a tenderness that was unusual in a massage. He half opened one eye; his heart leapt.

'Caenis!' he exclaimed, turning and sitting up all in one swift motion.

'Shh, my love,' she softly said, pressing a slender forefinger to his mouth, 'lie back down and let me finish. It has been such a long time that words may fail us whereas caresses will tell you all you need to know about how I feel; how I will always feel.'

Vespasian gazed at her, his heart thumping within him. There she stood, the woman he had dreamt of for so long, naked; her tender, ivory skin glowed in the soft lamplight that caused her thick black hair to shine with a reddish sheen as it fell in ringlets to her slender shoulders. She smiled at him and shook her head slowly as if unable to believe the reality that her eyes, wide and blue and glistening with unformed tears of joy, were showing her.

Vespasian grasped her hands, linking his fingers through hers, whilst forcing himself not to squeeze too hard and cause her pain. 'Caenis, I can't tell you how much I've dreamt of this moment, how much I've ...'

'Quiet, my love,' she said, pulling her hands from his and resting them on his shoulders. 'I can't tell you either; that's why we shouldn't rely on words.' She pushed him gently down on to his back. 'Lie still and let me finish massaging you, I'm getting to know your body again.' She bent over him and kissed him full on the lips; he savoured the touch and the taste of her. As their tongues found each other she lifted herself on to the bench and straddled his waist. Pulling away from the kiss she started to rub his broad shoulders, then worked her way down over the well-formed muscles of his chest; all the while gazing at him with love and disbelief. Vespasian gazed back with equal emotions as she continued the massage on to the happiest of endings.

Vespasian found dinner that evening a very pleasant affair, augmented, as it was, by the frisson of stolen glances with a radiant Caenis as she served her mistress. He spent the evening with a smile on his face as he tucked in, with the gusto of a sexually satisfied man, to the various courses laid in front of him. The food, as expected, had been of the highest quality, as had the wine, and the conversation far more convivial and relaxed than the last time Vespasian had dined with Antonia in the same room. Four years of dining with Queen Tryphaena and her high-ranking Roman guests had taught him the art of dinner-table conversation; it was an art in which he feared he would never excel, because of his rural upbringing, but he had, at least, gained a sufficient proficiency in it for the dining table no longer to seem daunting. He was able to relax and contribute to the conversation, not because he felt that he ought to, and hence come out with the first thoughts that entered his head, but because he had something relevant and interesting to say. The presence of Gaius Caligula made for a welcome reunion, adding to Vespasian's general sense of well-being. His young friend was in fine spirits despite – or perhaps, because of – his mother's and eldest brother's banishments the previous year. His other brother, Drusus, had recently joined them in exile in Sejanus' bid to neutralise all Tiberius' potential heirs one by one.

To Vespasian's surprise, apart from himself, Caligula, Sabinus and Gaius, Clemens had also been invited and had proved to be very good company; he had a pithy wit and the ability to lead the conversation without seeming to dominate it. He also managed to flirt with Antonia without being inappropriate or too earnest, so that his compliments were taken not seriously but as homage paid to a beautiful woman by a young man many years her junior.

Over the course of the evening Vespasian came to understand that Clemens was actually there in an official capacity: he was Caligula's gaoler. Since Drusus' arrest Tiberius had ordered Caligula to be kept under constant guard, poisoned as he was by Sejanus' constant whisperings in his ear concerning the loyalty of his immediate family. Macro, who still enjoyed Sejanus' trust, had managed to appoint Clemens to guard him and therein lay their hope, as Antonia explained once the slaves had been dismissed and Pallas had taken up his place by the door.

'My information from Macro, a strange but necessary bedfellow as you will all no doubt agree, is that the Emperor does not intend to harm my young Gaius,' she said, looking affectionately at her grandson reclining on the couch beside her and ruffling his hair.

'Do stop doing that, Grandmother,' Caligula protested with a mock-grimace. 'When I become Emperor my first decree will be to forbid the ruffling of a man's hair by any woman that he hasn't paid for.'

'In which case I would give the Lady Antonia a talent of silver just to ruffle my hair,' Clemens shouted through the good-humoured laughter.

'Very gallant, my dear Clemens,' Antonia replied. She was glowing, though not, Vespasian suspected, solely from the compliment or the effect of the wine. 'However, that would only be possible if my grandson survives to take what is rightfully his. As I was saying, Tiberius does not intend to harm my grandson but he does intend to keep him under close observation and the rumour is, according to Macro, that he will invite Gaius to join him on Capreae in the near future. When he does, Macro will ensure that Clemens goes with him as the commander of his guard. With Gaius and Clemens both on the island we will have our chance to smuggle the priest across.'

There was a general murmur of agreement that was broken by one voice of dissension.

'Domina,' Sabinus said carefully, 'I don't mean to cause offence, but how do we know that we can trust Clemens? He is, after all, Macro's man.'

Clemens was about to answer the charge himself when Antonia raised her hand. 'I think that your uncle had best explain that, Sabinus.'

'My pleasure, domina,' Gaius said, a little too loudly; he had been thoroughly enjoying Antonia's wine. 'Apart from the normal inducements – money, favour and promotion to Praetorian tribune when Macro is made the prefect – there is only one thing that can guarantee loyalty and that is family.'

'I know that he's a kinsman of ours from our father's side,' Sabinus said dismissively, 'but so distant as to not make much of a difference. Please don't take offence, Clemens, I just need to be sure.'

'None taken, cousin,' Clemens replied cheerfully, taking a sip of wine. 'I totally understand your concerns. That's why I made the offer.'

'What offer?'

'Allow me?' Gaius cut in slightly more abruptly than necessary. Clemens raised his cup and nodded graciously.

'The problem is that he doesn't have close enough family ties,' Gaius continued, 'wouldn't you agree, Sabinus?'

'Yes, I would.'

'So we need to make those ties closer, wouldn't you say?'

'Yes, but how?'

'By your marrying Arrecina Clementina, his only sister.'

Sabinus' mouth opened and closed as he struggled to say something. 'I've got no wish to be married yet,' he eventually managed to splutter. Vespasian stifled a snigger.

'My dear boy, don't be so silly; every man wants to get married,' Gaius laughed. 'With a few exceptions, of course,' he added, holding his hand to his ample chest. 'Besides, it's perfect because firstly: it's a marriage within the larger family. Secondly: she is of equestrian rank. Thirdly: it secures us an important ally. And finally: your parents are very keen on the idea; in fact your father wrote to tell me that it was now his wish that you marry her and he has given me permission to negotiate the terms on his behalf as he cannot come himself to Rome.'

Sabinus swallowed; he knew what that meant.

'As for me,' Clemens chipped in, 'it would be an honour to have my sister marry someone with such good prospects, provided we succeed with our plan, of course; and if we don't we'll in all probability be dead so it won't matter. As for my sister, she'll do what I say as our father is dead and she is mine to dispose of as I please; and it pleases me to give her to you.'

'I am very honoured,' Sabinus said evenly, not forgetting his manners and not wishing to offend Clemens by making light of his very generous offer.

'You'll be more than honoured when you see her, Sabinus,' Antonia said huskily, 'she's beautiful.'

Sabinus glanced at Clemens whose narrow face and pallid skin did not inspire him with any confidence in the veracity of that assertion.

'Pallas, show the lady in,' Antonia ordered.

Pallas bowed and slipped out of the door.

'I hope you don't mind, Sabinus,' Antonia said, smiling, 'but I took the liberty of sending my litter for Clementina whilst we were eating. She is fully aware that she has come to meet her future husband.'

Vespasian was enjoying watching the net tighten around his brother whilst at the same time being relieved that it was not he in that predicament. For the first time in his life he was glad of being the younger sibling.

The door opened and Pallas ushered in a young girl, no more than fifteen years of age; she was clad in a saffron *stola* with a turquoise *palla* draped around her. She stood before the company, lifted the palla from her hair and then slowly raised her head.

Vespasian had to suppress a gasp.

Sabinus jumped to his feet and recoiled back.

Antonia had not exaggerated: she was beautiful. Her eyes were the green of a newly sprouted leaf in spring and her lips and hair were the colour of that same leaf in autumn. Like her brother she had pale skin but, whereas his was pallid, hers glowed with a soft sheen that spoke of tender nights full of warm caresses. Like her brother she had a thin face but, whereas his was pinched, hers was delicate and fine boned with a slender nose and a full mouth that demanded to be kissed.

'Titus Flavius Sabinus,' Clemens said, walking over to her and taking her hand. 'May I present my sister: Arrecina Clementina.'

'Lady, I am honoured,' Sabinus almost whispered.

'It is you that do me honour, sir.' Clementina's voice was soft and melodious. She reached into the folds of her palla and brought out a small ivory statuette. Placing it in Sabinus' hand, she lowered her head and waited for the gift, and therefore her, to be accepted. He lifted it and smiled as he recognised the carving: Mithras slaughtering a bull.

'Thank you, Clementina, I accept this gift in token of our forthcoming marriage,' he said, all doubts evaporated.

'I look forward to learning about your god,' Clemintina said sweetly, meeting his eyes.

'I'm sorry that I have nothing for you,' he replied, quickly changing the subject, Mithraism not being at all inclusive of women, 'but I have been taken slightly by surprise.'

Vespasian swallowed a laugh; it was one of the biggest understatements that he had ever heard.

'But a happy surprise, I hope,' Clemens said to cover any embarrassment. 'I will escort you home, sister. Senator Pollo, I shall come to your house tomorrow to discuss the dowry and the terms and time of the marriage.'

'It will be my pleasure, Clemens,' Gaius replied.

Clemens took his future brother-in-law by the forearm. 'I shall be delighted to have you for a brother, Sabinus.' Sabinus mumbled something positive, unable to take his eyes off his future wife.

'Domina, thank you for the evening,' Clemens said, bowing his head to Antonia. 'Gentlemen, I wish you all goodnight.'

With that he led his sister from the room; Pallas followed, to see them to the litter. Sabinus stood motionless, staring at the closed door. Gaius and Antonia shared a smile as Caligula and Vespasian looked at each other incredulously.

Caligula was the first to recover. 'Jupiter's balls, why haven't I had—'

'Gaius, my dear,' Antonia cut in sharply, ruffling his hair again, 'none of your smut.'

Caligula excused himself from the table soon after, muttering something about a headache. Judging by the speed with which he left the room Vespasian had no doubt that the ache was in another part of his anatomy and he was off to ease it with one, or maybe a few, of his grandmother's many house slaves.

Since Clemens' departure with his sister, the talk had been of Sabinus' good fortune in having such a beautiful young bride. Sabinus himself was drinking deeply at each toast and had started to slur his words. Vespasian knew that he should bring up the subject of the scroll found on the dead Geta before his brother passed into oblivion brought on by a surfeit of antici-pated matrimonial bliss. He had an instinct that as few people as possible should know its contents; with Caligula now otherwise engaged the time seemed right.

'Domina,' he said as they lowered their cups from yet another toast to the newly engaged couple, 'there's a matter that I think I should bring to your attention, sooner rather than later.'

'By all means,' Antonia replied, her voice steady, having drunk very little and then only of well-watered wine.

He turned to Pallas, who had returned to his position by the door. 'Pallas, would you call for Magnus to bring the scroll? He'll know what you mean.'

'Yes, master.' Pallas slipped out briefly to send the message and then resumed his place.

Whilst they awaited Magnus' arrival Vespasian recounted the circumstances in which they had found the scroll and what it contained; then Sabinus, who seemed to have sobered up slightly, explained his theory as to how Claudius might be using Boter as an expendable shield.

When they had finished Antonia shook her head. 'That sounds far too subtle for my son; he's never been anything other than an idiot.'

Vespasian cast a sidelong glance at Pallas who, despite what he had said on the subject earlier that day, showed no sign of disagreeing with his mistress. He did think, however, that he saw the faintest flicker of interest in the steward's eyes.

'With respect, domina,' Gaius said, 'you look down on Claudius because compared with his late elder brother, the great Germanicus, he is physically such a disappointment to you; but it may be that underneath that crude exterior some of your brains and subtlety may still exist.'

Antonia scowled. 'Brains and subtlety in that runt? Never! He's probably just writing to Poppaeus to ask him if he can borrow some obscure books from his library and it amuses his childish sense of intrigue to have it written in code.'

'But a code needs the recipient to have the key,' Vespasian pointed out. 'It would seem a bit extreme to go to all that effort just to talk about books, however obscure.'

'Well, we'll find out soon enough,' Antonia said as a scratching came from the other side of the door.

Pallas let in a rather florid-looking Magnus. He had evidently been partaking rather too liberally of Antonia's wine after his exertions earlier on that evening, Vespasian mused with a slight grin.

'Good evening, domina, gentlemen,' Magnus mumbled from the doorway, unable to meet anyone's eye.

'Thank you, Magnus,' Antonia said. 'Leave the scroll with Pallas. Your party will be staying here for the night; Pallas will send someone to show you to a room later. That'll be all – for now.'

Magnus nodded wearily and left.

Antonia looked at Pallas. 'Do you think that you could break this code?'

'I would hope so, domina,' Pallas replied, perusing the scroll. 'I'm well acquainted with another of your son's freedmen, his secretary, Narcissus, a man of far greater intelligence than this Boter; we've had numerous conversations about codes and ciphers and have shared ideas on how best to construct them. I'm sure that if the code was written by Boter then it would be one that he got from Narcissus. Give me a little time and I'll be able to find the key. I need something to write with – please excuse me, I won't be long.' He slipped quietly out of the room.

As they waited for Pallas, making small talk, Vespasian felt a thrill of excitement as he contemplated the possibility of a whole night with Caenis. It was more than he had expected and he felt sure that Antonia had done it purposefully, even if it did appear that she had an ulterior motive; but then a woman in her position could always get what she wanted without having to worry about the happiness of the likes of him, let alone one of her slaves. She must indeed be very fond of Caenis.

A couple of cups of wine later Pallas returned brandishing a wax tablet. 'It's done, domina,' he announced. 'It's a substitution cipher such as Caesar used, but with a rolling shift, based on the number twelve. So the first letter you shift by one, so A becomes B; then the second by two, so A becomes C; the third by three and so on up to twelve. Then you start again but this time you shift the next letter by two, the next by four, then six, eight, ten, twelve. Then you continue with the next letter shifted by three, then six, nine, twelve. Then you do fours, then sixes and then twelve itself, after which you start again with one and so on. Very simple really.'

'Very good, Pallas.' Antonia looked as baffled as everyone else around the table. 'So what does it say?'

Pallas cleared his throat and began to read aloud.

'"I send my greetings" etc., etc.; then:

'As you are aware, my master has an agreement with your mutual friend that he will support my master as and when the time comes. However, my master now feels that once he has achieved his aim that friend will move to eliminate him and take his place through a familial right. In order to counter this, my master proposes to free himself immediately he has gained his rightful position and thereby cut the tie to the friend and therefore any legitimate rights he may have. In place of what he loses my master would take what is dearest to you, bonding himself with you, in order to still be able to expect your support, with its full force, at the appropriate time. He realises that certain arrangements would need to be made in advance and suggests that you make them sooner rather than later. He would have you know that he has made similar, though not, of course, the same arrangements with other people of your calibre and would hope that you would see the sense in joining his cause, rather than opposing it, as he would value your and your family's support highly in the endeavour that he feels is nearing fruition. He awaits your reply.'

There was a stunned silence in the room; all the men turned towards Antonia. The expected explosion did not come; instead she just nodded her head slowly as she digested the barely veiled meaning of the letter.

'It seems that you may be right after all, Gaius,' she said eventually. 'Claudius the booby isn't quite as stupid as I thought; he's hidden it well.'

'That's why he's still here, domina,' Gaius replied quietly, knowing all too well the fragility of Antonia's temper when it came to discussing her two surviving children. 'We need to work out what this means for us. I assume the mutual friend is Sejanus; so it seems that he has already got his support to succeed Tiberius.'

'What a fool I've been,' Antonia whispered, gazing into the middle distance. 'When Tiberius suggested that Claudius marry Aelia Paetina I jumped at it, thinking that he was using Claudius to give something to Sejanus that he had always wanted: a connection to the imperial house, without giving him anything of value because his sister was marrying someone who could not possibly aspire to anything. How wrong I was. Sejanus is going to make Claudius Emperor, then depose him and take over as his legitimate brother-in-law; he'll then secure his position by marrying my daughter Livilla. Claudius recognises this threat and is preparing very sensible precautions: divorcing Aelia Paetina once her brother, Sejanus, has made him Emperor and she is of no more use, thereby taking away Sejanus' claim to legitimacy. Then he's going to marry Poppaeus' daughter Poppaea Sabina, thus ensuring her father's support for her new husband with his full force of the Moesian legions and all his auxiliary cohorts. She'll have to divorce her husband, Titus Ollius, with whom she's just had a daughter, another Poppaea Sabina; that must be the arrangement Claudius wants Poppaeus to make. Well, that's no great hardship, he's nobody, and Poppaeus won't be able to resist the chance of his daughter becoming Empress. The other people of influence he's approached must be the Governors of provinces with legions close to Rome: Pannonia, Africa and on the Rhine. He'll try to make himself unassailable and one of his first victims will be my little Gaius. I will not let this happen.'

'It won't happen, domina,' Vespasian said with some confidence, 'because you're ensuring that Sejanus will fall. Without Sejanus surely Claudius is impotent?'

'Not necessarily; if he has ambitions to be Emperor, however ludicrous that may seem, then he won't let a setback like losing an untrustworthy ally stop him. He'll resort to another strategy, the only possible alternative in the absence of anyone willing to aid him: murder. If he really is as ruthless and cunning as that letter indicates then his obvious course of action would be to clear the way to the Purple by removing all potential rivals; and again my Gaius will be one of his victims. Claudius has to be stopped but, short of killing my own son, I can't as yet see how.'

Pallas cleared his throat quietly in the corner.

Antonia smiled. 'You no doubt have a suggestion, Pallas.'

'Never, domina; but perhaps I may be permitted to make some observations?'

'I never tire of your observations.'

'You are most gracious, domina,' the steward said smoothly,

stepping forward into the room. 'There're a few things that occur to me. Firstly: the letter states that Poppaeus is aware of the arrangement between Claudius and Sejanus; therefore, at least the three of them, but probably more, must have met to discuss the deal whilst Poppaeus was recently in Rome.'

'So who else was there?' Gaius asked.

'The people of "calibre", as my mistress suggested, the other Governors or their representatives. At that meeting they would have pledged the support of their legions; you'll notice that it says: "*still* be able to expect your support".'

'So what has he offered them to keep them on his side?' Vespasian mused.

'That brings me on to my second point: Claudius must assume that Poppaeus has just as much interest in his becoming Emperor as he has in Sejanus deposing him – he is close to both of them and would gain by whoever wore the Purple – otherwise he wouldn't have made as big an offer as to make Poppaea Empress. He must believe that this will tip the balance in his favour otherwise he would not be making him party to his thwarting of Sejanus' ambitions.'

Vespasian smiled as he saw the major flaw in the plan. 'But he can't offer as high an incentive to the others, so one or two of them are bound to be disappointed and may decide to throw in their lot with Sejanus, in which case Claudius' scheme is bound to be revealed.'

'Exactly; so Claudius seeks to counter that by a threat, which he must have made in various forms in the other letters he wrote; he gives Poppaeus a clear choice: with him or against him, no middle ground. He then, in the same sentence, goes on to mention his family; in other words: Poppaea is either Empress or dead.'

'And if, by some chance, he was to become Emperor,' Sabinus said slowly, 'and he went through with that threat against Poppaeus or any of the other Governors who stood against him, they would be obliged to take revenge, for the sake of their dignitas, and—'

Antonia cut in and finished his sentence: 'We would be

plunged back into civil wars as destructive as those in my father's time.'

'But I don't believe it would get that far,' Pallas continued, 'because, as Vespasian has pointed out, Sejanus is bound to hear of Claudius' plan from one of the Governors who's not been offered enough; in fact he probably already knows about it, as this letter was found four months ago and it's reasonable to assume from the wording that the other letters were sent at the same time.'

'And because Poppaeus never received this letter he won't have had the opportunity to betray Claudius to Sejanus,' Gaius said with a grin, 'which will leave Sejanus thinking that Poppaeus is now working against him.'

'So Sejanus must now think that his plan to gain the Purple through my son won't work because he'll have at least the Moesian legions against him and probably a lot more,' Antonia concluded with genuine concern in her voice. 'So Claudius is now a liability that needs to be got rid of. In trying to be too clever my son has set himself up to be murdered. The idiot almost deserves it but I couldn't bear to lose another son, however stupid or badly advised.'

'Which brings me to my final point, domina: this letter was not written by his secretary, my good acquaintance Narcissus, which, in the normal course of events it would have been; which leads me to believe that Narcissus doesn't know about the deal with Sejanus or, if he does, has sensibly advised against it and Claudius is now going behind his back.'

'Why would he worry about his freedman's opinion?' Sabinus asked. 'Surely a freedman's duty is to do what his patron tells him?'

'Claudius' household is run by his freedmen, all of whom hate each other and vie with each other for influence over their patron. Because Claudius is weak he tends to take the advice of whoever is the most forceful, which means he often finds himself vacillating between two contrary courses of action. However, as Claudius' secretary, Narcissus has control of all his finances; Claudius is in awe of him and can do nothing without him, so he tends to keep his more scurrilous plans from him for fear of being cut off from his money.'

'That's outrageous!' Antonia exploded. 'How dare some jumped-up freed clerk hold such power over a member of my family, however stupid he may be?'

'May I speak frankly, domina?' Pallas asked, bowing his head and looking his most subservient.

'If you're going to tell me more things about my idiotic son that I've overlooked, I think that you had better.'

'Yes, domina. Your son, in many ways, appears to be an idiot: he drools and stutters, he cannot organise his own affairs and is very easily influenced as he's unable to tell the difference between good advice and bad. However, he has an over-inflated opinion of himself, is ruthlessly ambitious and harbours a deep resentment towards his family for all the slights that he believes that he has suffered at their hands. He has never held any offices or priesthoods nor is he even a member of the senate and consequently feels overlooked and undervalued and is determined to redress that. Narcissus has always tried to keep Claudius' desire for revenge in check; he knows that his patron could never become Emperor at present because there far more suitable candidates within the imperial family.'

'You say "at present"?'

'Narcissus is not without his ambitions for his patron and therefore himself, domina, but if he were to find out that Claudius is making a bid for the Purple now I'm sure that he would put a stop to it – especially as it seems that the advice Claudius is following is Boter's, who has been out of favour since that unfortunate incident a few years back.'

'Unfortunate? Pah! He cuckolded my son and made him more of a laughing stock than he normally is and my son did nothing about it.'

'Well, perhaps he is now; your son didn't sign the letter, so he can deny it if Boter's advice fails, which I think we're all agreed that it will. He'll make Boter the scapegoat, an eventuality that Narcissus would be very keen to see come about, leaving him free to then carry on with whatever plans he has for his patron.'

'You mean following the strategy that I explained earlier and trying to whittle down the suitable candidates that stand in his patron's way?'

'I don't think that he feels that he needs to do that, domina, as, at the moment, Sejanus seems to be doing it for him. Narcissus takes the long view; for the present his strategy is to keep his Claudius unnoticed and therefore safe.'

Antonia gave a half-smile and nodded in agreement. 'As ever, your observations have been most enlightening, Pallas, thank you. Send this Narcissus a message; I think that we should talk to him first thing in the morning, and then afterwards I'll deal with my son.'

CHAPTER XI

VESPASIAN WOKE THE following morning as a trail of soft kisses worked their way down his chest towards his belly. He opened his eyes; the room was still dark and a gentle breeze blew through the open window beyond which the sky heralded the coming day with a faint, pre-dawn glow. The kisses worked their way across his belly; with a sigh, Vespasian closed his eyes again and lay back in bliss.

'That's my master attended to,' Caenis whispered a while later as she lay her head back on his shoulder, 'now I have to go and attend to my mistress.'

'I hope that she doesn't require you to be so considerate,' Vespasian murmured, gently kissing her soft, sweet-smelling hair.

Caenis giggled. 'I have to do anything and everything that she asks,' she teased, her smiling features now visible as the first rays of dawn light flooded through the window.

Vespasian felt his heart flutter and smiled down at her. 'So do I, it seems; in a way we're both her slaves.'

'But you don't have to pare her toenails or pluck her eyebrows.'

'True, but then you don't have to drag unpleasant priests back from Moesia and then take them to the Emperor on Capreae.'

'Yes,' Caenis said, giving him a worried look. 'My mistress is very concerned about that at the moment.'

'Why? She didn't mention any worries yesterday evening.'

'That's because she's not sure whether they have any substance.'

'What do you mean?'

'My love, you must swear that if she talks to you about them you'll feign ignorance. I'm trusted by her and I wouldn't want her to think that I've betrayed her trust, which I do only for my love for you, because if her suspicions are correct, you could be in danger.'

'You don't need me to swear, you must know that I'd never do or say anything that would in any way compromise you with Antonia.'

Caenis leant up and kissed Vespasian on the lips. 'I know,' she whispered softly. She laid her head back on his chest. 'When my mistress wishes to communicate with Macro she sends Clemens and when Macro wants to relay something to her he uses another of his men, Satrius Secundus, who's based with him in the Praetorian camp. They're always verbal messages, for obvious reasons, but I know the content because she dictates them to me after, along with the replies, for her records. Now, Secundus' wife, Albucilla, is a notorious slut, something that he actively encourages in the hopes of advancing his position – provided her affairs are with men, or sometimes women, of influence. My mistress found out a few days ago, from a spy that she recently managed to place in her daughter Livilla's household, that last month Albucilla began an affair with not only Livilla but also Sejanus; when he's in Rome the three of them share a bed.'

'And so Antonia suspects that Secundus has encouraged this in order to gain favour with Sejanus; in which case she must be worried that he's probably betrayed all her correspondence with Macro and therefore Macro's involvement with her. Has Antonia told Macro of her suspicions?'

'Yes, she sent Clemens to him as soon as she found out; Macro replied that he would stop using Secundus as his messenger. He's also threatened Secundus and Albucilla with a very unpleasant death if he suspects that he's been betrayed. Secundus has sworn that he hasn't said anything to Sejanus and to show his good faith has started providing Macro with any interesting bits of pillow-talk that his wife picks up in that crowded bed. So Macro is now happy with the arrangement.'

'Well then, what's the problem?'

'Yesterday Clemens saw two of Sejanus' men at Ostia taking a great interest in your arrival; and two more watched you arrive here.'

'Yes, I saw the last two. So Secundus may have double-crossed Macro after all?'

'That's the strange thing; if Secundus has betrayed Macro then surely Sejanus would have done something about him by now, but he's done nothing. Macro is still in command of the Guard in Rome and Sejanus continues to go between Tiberius and the Senate.'

'Perhaps he's just waiting for the right excuse.'

Caenis kissed him and slipped out of the bed. 'What more of an excuse does he need?' she asked dipping her hands into a bowl of water set out on the chest and splashing her face. 'He knows that my mistress is trying to bring him down, that's no secret. So if he's found out that Macro is communicating regularly with her then he would assume that he's part of her plot and would surely want to remove him as quickly as possible.'

'Could he know about the priest?' he asked as Caenis rubbed herself dry with a linen towel.

'She's sure Sejanus doesn't know the details of the plot or the time scale because we checked the records and Secundus never carried any message that mentioned the priest or getting him to Capreae. The most recent one he carried was just after Queen Tryphaena's letter arrived saying that you'd be arriving soon. Secundus came with the news from Macro that Caligula was to be called to Capreae and my mistress told him to tell Macro that what they were waiting for was arriving any day now.'

'No mention of Ostia?' Vespasian asked, regretfully watching Caenis slip on her tunic.

'No; yet his men were there.'

'He probably always has men watching the docks.'

Caenis sat down on the bed and started to strap on her sandals. 'Yes, but according to Clemens these men were very high up in Sejanus' staff and based at Capreae, not the normal sort of people he would use for hanging around the port watching who gets off what ship. This is what's puzzling my mistress; how did Sejanus know of your arrival in time to send two of his most trusted allies to Ostia if Secundus hasn't betrayed her and Macro to him?'

'It's possible that Secundus told Sejanus Antonia's message without mentioning that it was meant for Macro. He could have said that he got the information from one of Clemens' men. That way he thinks that he can claim loyalty to whoever wins the struggle between Macro and Sejanus.'

'Perhaps you're right,' Caenis said, leaning over and kissing him. 'But however Sejanus found out it doesn't change the fact that his spies have seen you and Sabinus get off a ship with a prisoner and bring him here. They then would have seen Senator Pollo arrive, so it won't be long before Sejanus knows your name. I must go, my love; I'll mention your theory to my mistress, pretending that it's mine, of course.' She smiled and stroked his cheek, then lifted the amulet hanging around his neck that she had given him as a parting gift over four years ago.

'You've kept it safe.'

'It kept me safe; it saved my life.'

'I knew it would.'

Vespasian stared at her incredulously. 'How?'

'I don't know, but I knew that I should give it to you.'

He told Caenis the story of how the amulet had saved him from the Caenii tribe in Thracia and how their chief, Coronus, believed that she was the granddaughter of his enslaved sister.

When he had finished she took the amulet in her hand and gazed at it. 'After my mother died I used to lie awake at night holding this; it used to make me feel close to her, almost a part of her. I also felt as if it connected me with a larger family in a way that I couldn't understand but it was a comforting feeling. Now I know why. It's a powerful thing; it saved your life and found my family.'

'Take it back, my love,' Vespasian said, lifting the leather thong over his head, 'I've no further need for it. It's given me life; what more can it do?'

She took it from him. 'Thank you,' she whispered. She kissed him and then padded softly out of the room.

*

Antonia called for Vespasian, Sabinus and their uncle at the second hour of the day. Pallas ushered them into the lavishly furnished formal reception room where she sat on a plump divan in front of a low, pink-marble table. At a right angle to her left, a corpulent, fair-skinned Greek with oiled black hair and beard perched uncomfortably on a wooden chair. He wore a citizens' toga over a pale-blue linen tunic. Despite the inequality of seating arrangements the Greek managed to keep an air of dignity about his posture as if it were beneath him to notice such an obvious slight.

As he crossed the mosaic floor Vespasian glanced at the curtain behind which he and his brother had hidden with Caligula four years ago and wondered if his young friend was eavesdropping there even now. Antonia caught his look and smiled. 'I've had a lock put on the door to that room now, so little Gaius has to find other places hide in.'

Disconcerted by Antonia's ability to read his thoughts, however trivial, Vespasian took the seat that Pallas proffered to Antonia's right. Sabinus and Gaius sat opposite her.

'Gentlemen, this is the freedman Narcissus, my son's secretary,' Antonia said by way of introduction.

Regardless of his lower status Narcissus made no attempt to get up but waved a stubby hand, heavy with bejewelled rings, imperiously at each of the brothers and Gaius as Antonia named them, without meeting their eyes, as if he was welcoming them to his court. His strongly scented pomade hung heavily in the air. Vespasian and Sabinus nodded briefly in reply.

There was a brief interruption as cups of pomegranate juice were served to each of them by a couple of young, male slaves. As they left Caenis appeared with writing materials and settled at a table just behind Antonia. Pallas stood next to her.

'Would you mind if my secretary minutes this conversation?' Antonia asked Narcissus in a casual tone. Narcissus half closed his eyes, held out both hands and slowly shrugged his shoulders, as if graciously giving his consent in a matter of little or no importance to him, before picking up his cup and taking a delicate sip.

A flash of anger passed briefly over Antonia's face. Vespasian was amazed by the lack of deference the Greek showed the most powerful woman in Rome. What sort of household did Claudius run if his secretary was free to act like some eastern potentate?

'Thank you for coming at such short notice, my good Narcissus,' Antonia said, her face now a mask of politeness.

'My pleasure, dear lady,' Narcissus replied in a surprisingly high voice whilst dabbing his lips with a silken handkerchief. 'Your note suggested that you wished to consult me on a matter concerning my patron, your son, the noble Claudius. Being his loyal servant and ever mindful of his wellbeing I felt obliged to drop everything and answer your summons.'

'I'll come straight to the point then, as you seem to be such a busy man.' Antonia was evidently anxious to puncture as soon as possible the Greek's air of self-satisfied smugness. 'These gentlemen found a letter written in code by your colleague Boter on behalf of my son and using his seal. Pallas, be so good as to read it for us.'

Vespasian watched Narcissus' face carefully as the letter was read out. He kept his eyes closed; a couple of twitches at the corner of his mouth were the only outward signs of worry as he listened. When he opened his eyes after Pallas had finished there was an unmistakable look of panic in them as he glanced quickly around the table.

'This has been written without my knowledge, domina,' Narcissus asserted, his voice slightly higher than before.

'Pallas guessed as much; he said that you were far too sensible to advise my son to take such a foolish course of action as to intrigue with Sejanus. That's why I thought that I'd speak to you before deciding how to proceed.'

Narcissus gave Pallas a grateful look. 'What do you intend doing with this, domina?' he enquired.

'What do you think I should do?'

Narcissus looked at Antonia hopefully. 'Perhaps you could give it to me?'

'My dear Narcissus, that wouldn't solve the problem as there is already a copy. Since you so kindly agreed to my secretary minuting our meeting she has just written down the contents of the letter word for word. I'll be happy to give you a copy of the minutes but, as I'm sure you'll understand, I must keep the original for my records.'

Vespasian suppressed a smile as Antonia's elegant trap closed around the oily Greek and his shoulders sagged.

'Most noble lady, who else knows of this?'

'Just the people in this room; you were fortunate that Vespasian and Sabinus brought it to me and not to Sejanus or the Emperor, both of whom would have rewarded them handsomely.'

'Indeed, domina, I owe them a debt of gratitude which I can assure you will be repaid if ever I am able,' Narcissus agreed with a genuine note of sincerity. 'However, until that time what would you have me do?'

Antonia smiled, knowing that she now had the Greek in her power. 'Now that, my dear Narcissus, is a very good question. As you are no doubt aware I am working to counter Sejanus' power and this letter would be all I need to show Tiberius to finally convince him that Sejanus is plotting to become Emperor. However, it also implicates my son and although it doesn't mention whether they are planning to wait for Tiberius to die naturally or to hasten the matter along by murder, Tiberius may well choose to believe the latter. In which case Claudius would either be executed and his property seized, and you would become destitute; or Claudius, along with his entire household, would be banished to some rocky island in the middle of nowhere, and you would become irrelevant.'

Narcissus swallowed hard; the options were hardly appealing. 'Illustrious lady, you wouldn't risk the life of your own son to destroy Sejanus, would you?'

Antonia's eyes narrowed. 'Don't tell me what I would or wouldn't do, freedman. To tell you the truth, I'm so angered by Claudius' stupidity that I'm almost minded to throw him to Tiberius' mercy, or lack of it.'

'Please accept my humblest apologies, domina,' Narcissus spluttered, hastily rising to his feet and bowing low.

'Sit down and stop fawning!' Antonia barked.

Narcissus sat back down on his uncomfortable chair as quickly as he had got up; all traces of his imperious dignity had vanished.

'Now, listen well to what I want you to do,' Antonia said in a calmer voice. 'I will not show the letter to the Emperor, even though it would get me what I want at the cost of no more than a useless son. In return for this I require you to go to your patron and persuade him to come to me with the names of all the other "people of calibre" that he wrote to and what their replies were. He should do it today before I change my mind; and make sure that he understands well that if he doesn't I will forget that he's my son.'

'He will be here in a couple of hours, I promise you, domina.'

'Good. The other thing I require you to do is kill Boter; I will not have him leading Claudius on any more ill-conceived attempts to make him Emperor and it is high time that he paid for the shame that he caused my family by cuckolding him.'

'It will be done today, domina,' Narcissus said with a malicious grin. 'He has endangered me and my patron, whom I work hard to protect and keep safe.'

'Not hard enough evidently,' Antonia observed. 'As to your personal plans for Claudius, if you still harbour any thoughts of him becoming Emperor, forget them. I intend to make sure that my grandson Gaius succeeds Tiberius. Unlike his uncle Claudius, he is young and sensible; the people love him because he is Germanicus' son, and he will reign for far longer than Claudius has left to live.'

'I assure you, my noble lady, that my plans for Claudius are only to keep him alive; as to what happens in the future, that is in the hands of the gods.'

'Wrong, it is in my hands; and if I so much as suspect that you're trying to alter my arrangements I'll have you chained up with your testicles stuffed into your empty eye sockets and left to starve to death.'

'That won't be necessary, domina,' Narcissus said, blanching at the image.

'I hope not. You may go.'

'Thank you, domina,' Narcissus said, standing and bowing. He looked over to Vespasian and Sabinus. 'Thank you again, gentlemen, for your discretion in this matter. If there is ever a service I can render you then please don't hesitate to ask. Senator Pollo, goodday.'

Trying to muster as much dignity as possible, he left the room with Pallas in attendance. Caenis followed them out, giving Vespasian a sweet smile as she left.

'I thoroughly enjoyed that, domina,' Gaius boomed once the Greek was out of earshot. 'I don't think that I've ever seen such an odious man so satisfyingly dealt with.'

'Yes, it was enjoyable,' Antonia agreed. 'Well, I only hope that he has the sense to keep Claudius under control; not that he will be in any doubt about the precariousness of his position after I've talked to him later.'

'What'll you do with the names that he gives you, domina?' Vespasian asked.

'They'll be my sport once I've got rid of Sejanus. I'll feed them to Tiberius one by one and enjoy watching him tear them apart.'

With the interview over Antonia dismissed them and a short while later, having retrieved Artebudz and a tired-looking Magnus, they stepped out into the heat of a July morning to walk back to Gaius' house on the Quirinal. Vespasian planned to spend the night there before travelling to Aquae Cutillae to see his parents and spend the time, whilst waiting for Caligula and Clemens to be transferred to Capreae, working on the estate. He was also keen to visit his grand-mother Tertulla's estate at Cosa, which, true to her word, she had left solely to him in her will, much to Sabinus' chagrin.

'So, dear boy, you're planning a farming holiday,' Gaius said, having been acquainted with Vespasian's plans as they walked down to the Via Sacra. 'How quaint!'

'A mule-humping holiday more like,' Sabinus chipped in, unable to resist any opportunity to goad his brother.

'You could come too, Sabinus,' Vespasian said with a grin. 'It always helps to have someone holding the head end, and just think of all that kissing you could get whilst you're at it.'

'A very kind offer, brother, but I'm staying in Rome. I've got a lot to do if I'm to be elected as one of the quaestors for next year; there're a lot of senators' arses to lick. And besides, I'll soon have something much prettier to kiss than even your most favoured mule.'

They turned left on to the Via Sacra heading towards the Forum Romanum. The crowds thickened as they drew nearer to the heart of the city but Magnus cleared a way for them whilst all the time giving Artebudz a guided tour. The mountain-dweller was in awe at the sheer scale of the buildings and the amount of people surrounding them and he gazed around with wide eyes and his mouth open unable to take in anything that Magnus was saying. His only experience of a city had been Philippopolis, which, while it was far older than Rome, was tiny by comparison.

Although Vespasian had been in Rome only briefly, four years earlier, he had become accustomed to its magnitude; he felt very comfortable compared to the ex-slave from Noricum. As they crossed the Forum Romanum with its open-air law courts and bustling street traders selling their goods to the crowds of spectators he felt very much a part of it. The awe that he had felt when he had first seen the scale of Rome from a hill on the Via Salaria, and the excitement that he had experienced as he had entered her for the first time through the Porta Collina, had relaxed into an easy habitude; he had the perception, now he was back, that this was his city. He knew that he would always consider his parents' estate at Aquae Cutillae and Tertulla's estate at Cosa his true homes, but they would be places that he would visit to relax; Rome would be where he would live.

They passed the House of the Vestals, went on past the Curia Hostilia, where the Senate met, then turned right and entered Caesar's Forum. Here the business was not legal but civic; the aediles, the urban praetor and city prefect could be approached and petitioned in the shadow of a huge equestrian statue of the dictator riding Bucephalus, Alexander's horse, as if he still had an influence over the workings of the city.

Passing by the statue they crossed into the Forum of Augustus, which was used as an overflow court from the Forum Romanum; with the recent upsurge in treason trials it too was very busy with lawyers, jurists and spectators, all sweating freely under the hot July sun.

Leaving Augustus' Forum behind them, they started to climb up the Quirinal Hill and felt the air freshen as a light breeze blew down from its summit.

'I'll see you home, gentlemen,' Magnus said, 'and then take Artebudz down to the crossroads tavern. He's going to be staying with me and the lads for a few days before he leaves.'

'Thank you, Magnus,' Gaius replied. 'I expect your crossroads brotherhood has been missing your leadership, there'll be quite a party tonight to welcome you back.'

'Yeah, and I'll be paying. The lads have kept my share of the takings whilst I've been away, so they'll expect me to be generous with the wine and whores.'

'I'm surprised that you can even contemplate having a whore after all the demands made upon your services last night,' Vespasian observed.

Magnus looked embarrassed. 'Very funny, sir. I'll thank you not to mention it again; I'm feeling slightly dirty and used. I'll certainly be having younger flesh tonight; the younger the better.'

'Let's hope they won't be feeling dirty and used in the morning.'

'They'll at least have been paid for what they do; I've always felt that money is a great cleanser.'

Vespasian laughed. 'Well, I'm sure Antonia would be more than happy to give you a good wash when you see her next.'

Their arrival at Gaius' house ended the banter suddenly; the door was open and there was no sign of the ancient doorkeeper.

Gaius ran in.

Pulling his dagger from its sheath, Vespasian leapt after him.

'Get the swords,' Sabinus shouted as he disappeared through the door.

Magnus and Artebudz rummaged about in the kit bags as they followed the brothers inside.

In the atrium Vespasian found Gaius cradling the body of one of his beautiful, fair-haired, German slave boys. The ancient doorkeeper lay in a pool of blood next to him, his throat slit. Two more of Gaius' young slaves lay dead by the pool.

'My dear boy, Arminius, my dear, dear boy,' Gaius wept, stroking the youth's blood-matted hair.

A scream rang out from the direction of the courtyard garden.

'Uncle, whoever's done this is still here,' Vespasian said, taking the proffered sword from Magnus. 'Stay here, we'll get them.'

'And sit and wait while my boys are butchered? Bollocks I will.' With surprising speed he ran to his study, one of the rooms to the left of the atrium, and reappeared a moment later with a sword. 'Magnus and Artebudz, check each of the rooms off the atrium; we don't want anyone behind us. And lock the front door.'

A long wail of agony came from the garden. Gaius looked grimly at the brothers, turned and walked at speed in its direction. The brothers followed at run in order to overtake him.

Vespasian and Sabinus burst through the doors of the *tablinum* into the warmth of the garden. Two men held a struggling youth over the fishpond in the centre whilst a third held a squirming lamprey to his face. The water in the pond heaved with scores of lampreys gorging themselves on another writhing boy; his arms and legs thrashed as the snake-like fish used their teeth to cut through the skin in search of blood. The boy lifted his mouth above the surface to gasp for breath and let out another agonised scream; the twisting lampreys attached to his head and face made him look like Medusa.

The brothers flung themselves towards the three men who promptly dropped their captive into the pond. Before they could retrieve their weapons Vespasian and Sabinus were upon them. With a savage thrust to the belly and then a sharp rip upwards Vespasian disembowelled the first; the second went down to a clean jab to the throat from Sabinus. The third man ran to the other side of the garden.

'I want him alive,' Gaius roared as he pulled the boy from the pond. He had managed to get him out quickly enough for him to have only suffered a few bites; most of the lampreys were busy devouring the body of his now dead companion.

Magnus and Artebudz appeared at the door from the tablinum. 'We found two more of the bastards hiding in the *triclinium*,' Magnus said, 'but they won't be bothering us.'

'Stay there, lads,' Sabinus shouted over the screaming of the gutted man, 'we've got the cunt cornered.'

The third man, realising that he was trapped, weaponless, and could expect no quarter, ran with a roar straight for Magnus. With impeccable timing Magnus slammed his fist into the man's stomach, immediately bringing his knee up into his face as he doubled up and then, as his head ricocheted back with blood spurting from a flattened nose, Magnus cracked his fist down on to the back of his skull. He collapsed into an unconscious heap.

Leaving the rescued boy sitting on the ground, more shocked than damaged, Gaius walked over to the gutted man, who was now moaning as he tried feebly to stuff his colon back in.

'Who sent you?' Gaius asked menacingly.

Knowing that he was going to die, the man shook his head. Gaius reached down and grabbed a handful of intestines and pulled. The scream that the man let out as his innards unravelled was excruciating.

'Who sent you?' Gaius asked again.

Still the man would not say.

'Throw him in the pond. Let's see how he likes being eaten from the inside out,' Gaius ordered.

Vespasian looked at Sabinus, who shrugged. They picked him up by the arms and legs; guts trailed down to the ground like slimy creepers.

'Last chance,' Gaius said. There was no reply; he had passed out.

With a splash, the brothers tossed him in. The water seethed again as the lampreys, maddened by blood, swarmed around him, burying themselves in the gaping wound in his belly.

'Let's see if we have more luck with the other one,' Gaius said, picking up a small fishing net. He dipped it into the writhing pond and scooped out a couple of lampreys. 'Bring him round.'

A couple of slaps to the face brought the third man to his senses, groaning softly.

'Your friend has just met a nasty end,' Gaius informed him, holding the net with its contents in front of his face; the lampreys' circular mouths filled with razor-sharp teeth opened and closed in a vain attempt to suck in water. 'You can either go quickly or painfully, it's down to you.'

The man spat on the ground.

'So be it. Pull him out flat.'

Magnus and Artebudz took his wrists and hands and stretched him out.

With his free hand Gaius lifted the man's tunic and ripped off his loincloth.

'Hold this,' he said, giving the net to Vespasian. He then took a lamprey in one hand and, with the other, pulled back the man's foreskin.

Vespasian closed his eyes. A shriek filled the air. He opened them again and saw exactly what he expected to.

'The next one goes in your eye. Who sent you?' Gaius asked again.

'Livilla,' came the gasped reply.

'Was I the only target?'

'No, there was another group sent elsewhere.' The man screamed again as the thrashing lamprey tightened its grip and sucked harder in a desperate attempt to extract life-giving water from its host.

'How many and where to?

'Ten, but I don't know where. Please, for the love of the gods, finish me.'

'Where?' Gaius took the second lamprey from the net and held it close to the man's right eye.

'All I know is that they were leaving the city by the Porta Collina and heading up the Via Salaria.'

Vespasian looked at Sabinus with horror as it dawned on them both where the killers were headed.

'Thank you,' Gaius said. He picked up his sword and calmly thrust it into the man's mouth.

'Magnus, take Artebudz and get ten of your crossroads brothers and meet us, with horses and swords, outside the Porta Collina at the junction of the Via Salaria and Via Nomentana, in an hour,' Vespasian ordered.

Magnus grinned. 'Well, that's got me out of paying for a party tonight,' he said by way of taking his leave.

'We should just get going with them,' Sabinus said. 'We haven't got time to hang around.'

'We're at least two hours behind them, Sabinus, there's no way we'll overtake them if we can't change horses. We need Clemens with a Praetorian pass so we can use the imperial relay horses; that way we'll have a chance of catching them before they reach our parents.'

CHAPTER XII

'I WILL NOt listen to any more of your pitiful whinging.' Antonia's raised voice thundered out from her formal reception room and echoed around the cavernous atrium where Vespasian and Sabinus waited restlessly for Pallas to find Clemens.

'But M-m-m-mother, I demand the recognition and honour due to a m-m-m-member of the imp-imp . . . imperial family.' The other voice too was raised but had more than a hint of fear in it, which was magnified by the stutter.

'You are in no position to demand anything, you runt. With just one act I could ensure that you are at the very least banished. Now give me that list and be off with you.'

'But, M-m-m-m-m-mother . . .'

'Stop "but M-m-m-mothering" me! Just go; and take my advice, Claudius: divorce that liability of a wife of yours immediately and spend more time with your books and less making a fool of yourself trying to play politics.'

'But . . .'

'Go!'

Vespasian winced at Antonia's screamed dismissal.

A shambling figure appeared in the corridor leading off the atrium and, keeping his head down, lurched, as if his knees were about to give out at any moment, towards the brothers. As Claudius drew close he gave a start and looked up at Vespasian; his eyes were blinking incessantly and a trail of clear mucus ran from his nose and on to his toga.

Vespasian nodded his head; Sabinus followed suit. Claudius stared at them in surprise and managed to get the blinking under control. His grey eyes were calculating and intelligent; they peered at the brothers from a face that would have been hand-some and noble had it not been given a sorrowful air by its downturned mouth and bags under the eyes.

'Bastard families,' he blurted without changing expression, as if he was unaware that he had said anything. He wiped his nose with a fold of his toga, nodded at the brothers and then shambled out.

Antonia came in as soon as Claudius was out of the door.

'What are you two doing back here?' she asked abruptly, her equilibrium having not quite returned after her interview with her son.

'So Sejanus has linked your family with me,' she said after the brothers had told her of the attack on Gaius' house and the men heading towards their parents' estate, 'and is using Livilla to do his dirty work so as not to risk the chance of any of his Praetorians being implicated in the murder of a senator. Where's Gaius now?'

'We brought him here,' Vespasian replied. 'Pallas had one of your house slaves take him to the baths; he's gone to sweat out his anger.'

'Good. He'll have to stay here until I can get him out of Rome. Livilla, that bitch of a daughter of mine, won't give up until she's given her lover what he wants. Why am I cursed with children who work against me?'

Vespasian and Sabinus were spared having to answer by the arrival of Pallas with Clemens.

'Horses are being saddled up in the stable yard for you, masters,' Pallas said, bowing, 'I'll return when they are ready.'

'How many men are we taking?' Clemens asked, having already been informed by Pallas where they were going and what was hoped of him.

'Including us three, fifteen,' Vespasian replied.

'I'm not sure that my pass will give us access to that many horses from the relays.'

'Take this,' Antonia said, slipping her seal ring off her finger and giving it to Vespasian. 'No one will dare argue with the holder of my seal; return it with Clemens. Where are you going to send your parents? It will need to be a long way away to be safe from Sejanus.'

'I've been thinking about that,' Vespasian replied, slipping the ring on his little finger. 'The only person I could trust is Pomponius Labeo; he has estates in Aventicum on the other side of the Alps. He should be there by now.'

Antonia nodded. 'That should be far enough away. What about you two?'

'I'm coming straight back to Rome, domina,' Sabinus said firmly. 'I've got the quaestors' election to consider.'

'I don't think that would be advisable for the moment,' Antonia contended. 'You should stay away until I can find out whether Sejanus was just targeting Gaius and your parents because your mother is his sister, or whether the whole family was to be killed, in which case you won't be safe in Rome. You'll have to leave the election in the hands of Fortuna.'

Sabinus made to protest but stopped himself as he saw the truth of the statement.

'You could both go to my estates in Campania; I need you to be close enough to Rome to be able to come quickly should Macro send me a message stating that everything is ready for the other matter to proceed.'

'Thank you, domina, but I would prefer to go to my estate in Cosa,' Vespasian said. Sabinus gave him a sour look but grunted his assent. 'It's one day's ride from Rome. We should be safe enough there. Magnus knows where it is if you need to find us.'

'Very well,' Antonia agreed as Pallas came hurrying back into the room.

'All is prepared, masters.'

'Thank you, Pallas,' Antonia said looking at the brothers. 'Ride fast, gentlemen. May the gods bring you there in time.'

Night had fallen and they rode as fast as they could – a slow canter – up the Via Salaria by the light of torches held by each man. Vespasian, Sabinus and Clemens had met Artebudz, Magnus and his brothers just before midday. Vespasian had a very brief reunion with the slow but reliable Sextus and the one-handed Marius before they started, hell for leather whilst daylight held, up the Via Salaria. They had changed horses every ten miles at the imperial relays. Antonia's seal had proved invaluable as the relay-keepers were all reluctant to give them fresh horses, saying that they had already exchanged ten horses earlier in the day with a group of men bearing a warrant signed by Sejanus. Not having foreseen that Livilla's men would be using the same form of quick transport as them, they rode on with an increasing sense of desperation. Their only hope lay in flogging their mounts to the limit in the hope that their parents' would-be murderers were taking the journey more leisurely. This seemed to be confirmed as the relay-keepers' estimations of how long before the ten men had passed through lessened gradually.

By the time that the long July day succumbed to night they had covered sixty of the eighty miles to Aquae Cutillae and they reckoned that they were just over an hour behind by the last time they changed horses.

'We'll save time by not changing again,' Vespasian said to Sabinus as he peered ahead into the gloom. 'At this pace these horses will be able to cover the last twenty miles.'

'We need to speed up, brother,' Sabinus replied. 'The bastards ahead of us will be almost there now; they'll have had less of the journey in the dark, so we're falling behind them.'

'They might decide to stop for the night.'

'Bollocks they will; as far as they're concerned they've timed it perfectly, arriving just as everyone's gone to bed.'

'What do you suggest then?'

'You'll laugh at me but I'm going to trust to my Lord Mithras; his light will guide me. You follow on as quickly as you can.'

With that he kicked his mount forward and pulled away. Vespasian raised his eyebrows and then shrugged and followed. Behind him the rest of the party felt obliged to do the same, although all thought it madness to ride so fast at night, even on a straight, well-paved road.

*

The torches had been extinguished and they walked their horses as quickly as possible up the rutted track that led to the Flavian estate. There were no lights burning in the complex and the toenail moon provided only a dim shimmer that vaguely outlined the buildings, now only one hundred paces away.

At Sabinus' reckless pace they had covered the last twenty miles in a little under two hours. The fact that none of the horses had stumbled or thrown their riders was, to Vespasian's mind, nothing short of miraculous, but he hesitated to say as much to Sabinus for fear of another homily on the power of the Lord Mithras.

The absence of light sharpened his other senses and the familiar smells of his childhood greeted him like old friends, one after the other. Sweet warm resin oozing from pine trees; musty earth cooling after a day of baking in the summer sun; freshly cut hay; meadow flowers; faint wood smoke: each one brought back images from the past that he feared was now about to be brutally intruded upon by the present.

'It's quiet,' he whispered to Sabinus and Clemens, who rode either side of him. 'Perhaps it was just a coincidence and they weren't coming here after all?'

'Or we're too late,' his brother replied grimly. They dismounted and tied their exhausted horses to a fig tree; a soft breeze rustled its leaves. In the distance a fox called; another, slightly closer, answered.

Artebudz, Magnus and his crossroads brothers joined them, drawing their short swords. They were fifty paces away from the fifteen-foot-high wall of the stable yard. In the moon's dim light they could just see the gates; they were closed.

'There's no sign of a break-in. Looks like we may be in time,' Sabinus whispered. 'We'll alert the household quietly and stand to to surprise those bastards if they do turn up. Vespasian, take Magnus, Artebudz and five of the brothers and try to wake the gatekeeper. I'll take Clemens and the rest of the brothers around to the front of the main house and wake the doorkeeper. If we're—'

A series of loud shouts split the night; over the roofs along the far end of the stable yard flaming torches cartwheeled through the night air. They were quickly followed by more torches but this time held aloft by silhouetted figures clambering on to the roof. Some jumped down into the yard, others ran at speed along its length and then up on to the roof of the main house. A fire, now burning on its far side, gave an orange definition to its shape.

'Shit!' Sabinus cried. 'Get over the wall with your lads, Vespasian; I'll take mine around the front. No plan, just up and at them.'

Sabinus' group sped away around the side of the house.

'Bring your horses,' Vespasian shouted, unhitching his and leaping on. He galloped the fifty paces to the wall and pulled his mount up sharply next to it. Cries, shouts and the clash of weapons came from within the yard. Vespasian stood up on his horse's back and stretched up; the top of the wall was still two feet from his outstretched hands.

'Magnus, get up here and give me a leg-up.'

'Coming over, sir.' Magnus climbed from his mount on to Vespasian's horse's hindquarters. The horse started to shy.

'Sextus,' Vespasian shouted, 'hold the horse's head whilst Magnus pushes me up.'

'Hold the head whilst Magnus pushes; right you are,' Sextus said, as always slowly digesting his orders.

The horse steadied; Magnus cupped his hands for Vespasian's foot and heaved him up. With a frantic scramble that grazed his knees, Vespasian managed to pull himself on to the roof. He reached back down and grabbed Magnus' proffered arm and with a huge effort hauled him up. Artebudz and the other cross-roads brothers followed their leader's example.

Even though it was less than a hundred heartbeats since the start of the attack the stable yard was now lit by fires burning in the windows of a few of the buildings that looked on to it. Half a dozen bodies lay scattered around. Screams came from the field slaves' barracks as the shackled slaves inside panicked at the smell of smoke and rising heat in their windowless place of confinement; flames were threatening their door. There was no sign of the attackers; the door to the courtyard garden of the main house swung unsteadily on its buckled hinges.

Vespasian dashed along the roof and leapt down into the stable yard as, at the far end, a group of men came running out of the freedmen's lodgings, armed with swords, javelins and bows. Vespasian recognised Pallo, the estate steward, at their head, followed by Baseos the Scythian and the Persian Ataphanes, both bearing their recurved, eastern bows. Unfortunately they did not recognise him; two arrows careered towards him as he hit the ground. He felt a rush of air pass over his head and then a lightning strike of pain in his left shoulder twisted him backwards on to the floor.

'Pallo!' he yelled. 'It's me, Vespasian!'

But too late. Thinking that he was no longer a threat Baseos and Ataphanes had turned their attentions to the crossroads brothers still traversing the roof; two fell into the yard as Ataphanes went down with an arrow from Artebudz in his chest.

'Artebudz, don't shoot!' Vespasian roared again in a monumental effort to make himself heard over the clamour from the field slaves' barracks. 'Pallo, stop! It's me, Vespasian.' He got to his knees and waved his arms; pain from the arrowhead grinding against bone shot through his senses.

This time Pallo recognised his young master, whom he had not seen in over four years, by his voice.

'Stop shooting,' Pallo ordered, running across the yard. His men followed, weapons raised warily. 'Master, is that really you? Why are you attacking your own home?'

'I'm not. There's no time to explain,' he said, wincing as he broke off the shaft of the arrow a thumb's length from the entry point.

Magnus and Artebudz jumped down from the roof followed by Sextus and Marius.

'Follow me into the main house,' Vespasian cried, running through the swinging gate, 'and be careful who you shoot at, Sabinus is coming in through the front.'

The courtyard garden was deserted apart from the body of the slave whose job it had been to sit by the gate all night. From the house came the sound of hand-to-hand fighting. Vespasian pounded around the colonnaded walkway towards the tablinum;

blood oozed from his wound and was now soaking his tunic and his head was feeling light from pain.

Pushing aside the broken tablinum door he hurtled through and on into the atrium. It was a mass of writhing and struggling bodies all locked in bitter close-quarter conflicts: some standing, fighting with swords and knives; some wrestling, rolling around on the floor. At the far end of the room the open door burned like a beacon; by its light he could see, next to his brother and Clemens, fighting with a dagger in each hand, his father, Titus. Blood poured down the side of his face from where his left ear was missing.

With a roar, Vespasian jumped over the dead and blood-soaked body of Varo, the house steward, and flung himself through the chaos and on to the back of his father's adversary. Grabbing him by the hair he swung his sword in a short, sideways arc into the flesh at the top of his right arm and on through the bone, like wire through cheese. The man howled as his severed limb dropped to the floor; a sharp thrust from Titus curtailed the bestial sound and he fell, dead.

Behind Vespasian, Magnus, Sextus and Marius descended on the rear of their crossroads brothers' opponents like furies released from hades. Livilla's men stood no chance as they were hacked and stabbed at from all angles. Artebudz, Pallo, Baseos and the rest of the freedmen stood back, uncertain of friend or foe; but they were not needed. In a few short moments only two of the attackers were left standing, herded into a corner, surrounded and defeated. Both dropped to one knee in token of surrender.

'You come to my house to kill me in front of the death masks of my ancestors and the altar to my family's gods and then expect mercy?' Titus thundered, pushing his way through the surrounding men. In one fluid movement he swiped up a discarded sword and flashed it through the air at neck height, almost taking the first man's head clean off. The body slumped forward, spraying Magnus and his brothers. The second man raised his head. His eyes showed no fear as they stared at Titus from beneath a mono-brow; he nodded and lowered his head to receive the killing blow in the manner of a Roman citizen.

'Don't!' a voice shouted as Titus lifted his sword.

Titus jerked around to see who would prevent him from taking his just vengeance.

Clemens stepped forward.

'Who are you, young man?' Titus enquired, breathing heavily.

'Marcus Arrecinus Clemens, sir,' Clemens replied steadily. 'Your son is to marry my sister.'

'Well, Clemens, if you think that family ties will force me to grant mercy to this man, you are much mistaken.'

Sabinus stepped up to Clemens, outraged. 'Who the fuck do you think you are, coming between coming my father and his rightful justice? Every one of Livilla's men must die,' he shouted, pointing an accusatory finger at the kneeling man.

'Calm, my friend, Livilla's men are all dead,' Clemens said pointing at the captive. 'He's not one of them.'

Sabinus looked carefully at the man whilst slowing his breathing. A memory flashed across his mind and he stared harder at the kneeling man's face. 'Clemens is right, father,' he said, remembering the mono-browed guard in Macro's room the previous year. 'This one's not Livilla's man, he's a Praetorian. That's Satrius Secundus.'

CHAPTER XIII

'I DON'T CARE HOW useful you think he might be; I want him dead.' Vespasia Polla was adamant. Outraged by the murder done in her home and still recovering from the mental exhaustion brought on by accepting that she was going to die, she wanted her revenge. 'If none of you men have the balls to do it then I'll do it myself. Titus, give me your dagger.'

'My dear, if Sabinus and Vespasian say that Secundus should live for political reasons then I'm not about to gainsay them,' Titus said as patiently as he could. Blood still oozed from his wound. 'I would remind you that the last time you got involved in matters that neither you nor I understood, your impetuousness—'

'Impetuousness!' Vespasia snorted.

'Yes, impetuousness, woman,' Titus retorted sharply. 'Your impetuousness caused us to be smuggled out of Rome like thieves in the night, and made me look like a foolish country bumpkin unable to control a wilful wife; a laughing stock in other words. Now enough of your opinions; go and organise whatever slaves we have left to clear up this mess.'

Vespasia looked for a moment as if she would explode. She glanced at Vespasian and Sabinus.

'Mother,' Vespasian said placidly, 'trust us.'

Realising that she was not going to get the better of her menfolk in this argument, she acquiesced, but resolved to some day have her revenge for the time she had spent locked in Titus' study, listening to the savage fighting outside and gazing at the knife that he had given her. One moment she had been peacefully asleep in her bedroom; the next, her husband was dragging her through the atrium. Flames were coming from under the front door and the door to the courtyard garden was being battered down. Titus had hauled her into his study – the only room off the atrium with a lock – and given her his knife with the order to kill herself should the door be broken down. She had been terrified, staring at her reflection in the blade distorted by the strange lettering engraved on it. When Titus and his sons had unlocked the door after the fighting had ended they had found her on her knees holding the knife to her breast ready to fall on it, in the expectation that the defenders were all dead and the attackers had found the key. It was only the quick reactions of her husband in catching her as she fell forward that saved her life.

The men breathed a sigh of relief as she walked, with as much dignity as she could muster, out of the body-strewn atrium.

Titus approached his two sons and put a hand round each of their necks. They were alone. Pallo and Clemens had taken Secundus to be locked up and Magnus and his brothers were helping the rest of the household extinguish the fires. The front door still smouldered but the fire was quenched; smoke drifted through the room.

'Thank you, my sons, thank you,' Titus said, pulling them to him and resting their foreheads on either side of his own.

Vespasian tried to place his left hand on his father's shoulder but winced with pain.

'We need to get that thing out, brother,' Sabinus said surprisingly gently. 'I'll send for Chloe.'

'And Father needs to get his ear sewn back on,' Vespasian replied, trying to make light of Titus' disfiguring wound.

'That ear's long gone, my boy.' Titus gingerly felt the side of his face. 'It was nearly the death of me; I slipped on it during the fight and almost lost my balance. Still, there's one good thing to come out of it: I won't be able to hear your mother's sharp remarks nearly as well!'

The three of them burst out laughing – more in hysteria than amusement. The relief of still being alive, the relief at finding his parents still alive, the relief from the anxiety he had felt all the way up the Via Salaria flooded over Vespasian and he released the tension with a laugh so strong that his chest heaved uncontrollably, pushing at the arrowhead embedded in his shoulder;

the pain and loss of blood suddenly overwhelmed him and he collapsed on to the floor in a faint.

Vespasian opened his eyes and recognised the ceiling of his old room. It was day.

'And about time too!'

Vespasian turned his head to see Magnus sitting on a chair in the corner of the room, polishing his sword.

'What time is it?' Vespasian asked weakly.

'Almost midday, I should think.'

Vespasian put his hand to his shoulder and felt a well-padded dressing tightly bandaged on.

'You didn't make a sound as that old Chloe was cutting it out, sir. Stayed unconscious all the way through you did, even when she cauterised the wound. Remarkable woman. I've never seen an arrow removed so quickly. I'll bet she was quite a looker in her younger days.'

'I'm sure that if you asked her nicely she'd be only too glad to revisit her youth for you. I know how partial you are to the older female form.'

'I'm never going to hear the end of that, am I? Gods below, you fuck one goat and you're branded a goat-fucker for life.'

'At least you earned your reputation justly; I've never touched a mule but Sabinus still mocks me about them. Anyway, how are your lads?'

'Lucio didn't make it, but Chloe reckons that Cassandros may well pull through. The arrow went through the roof of his mouth and out through his cheek, just knocked a few teeth out; that's the luck of the Greeks for you.'

'I wouldn't call that particularly lucky, given that he was shot by someone that he was trying to defend.'

Magnus grunted. 'Well, if you look at it that way I suppose you're right. And it'll be some time before he can chew on a decent Roman sausage again; being Greek, he's partial to sausage, if you take my meaning?'

Vespasian grinned. 'I'm afraid I do. Help me up, Magnus.'

'Is that wise, sir?'

'Are you so enamoured now of Chloe that you think your medical opinion is worth something?'

'No, it's just that I know how weak I feel after every time I get spitted.'

Vespasian raised himself off the bed with an effort; his wound throbbed but stayed closed. 'Well, I've got no choice in the matter; we've got to see to our dead and then leave.'

'What's the rush?' Magnus asked, helping his friend to his feet.

'Livilla will be expecting her men back today,' Vespasian replied as he walked unsteadily over to a basin of water placed on the chest. 'When they don't show by nightfall she'll want to know why; she'll probably send some more up here tomorrow to find out, a lot more. They'll more than likely arrive tomorrow night – I'd say it would be best if we weren't here, wouldn't you?'

'If they find the place deserted they'll burn it to the ground.'

Vespasian splashed handfuls of water over his face. 'Then we'll rebuild it.'

'Where are we going?'

'You and your lads are going to help Clemens take Secundus back to Rome,' Vespasian replied, drying his face. 'I want you to stay there until Antonia sends for you to bring me a message at Cosa.'

Magnus didn't look too pleased. 'If she knows that I'm in Rome she'll be sending for me all the time.'

'Well, that's the perks of the job. I wouldn't mind borrowing a couple of your boys to come to Cosa with Sabinus and me, just for a bit of extra security.'

'Sure, have Sextus and Marius; they know the place. What about your parents, where are they going?'

'They're going north and Artebudz will go with them, it's nearly on his way home and he seems anxious to get back to Noricum as soon as possible.'

'Yes, I know, he's was going on about it for the whole voyage home. He's worried that his father, Brogduos, may already be dead.'

'How long has he been away?'

'Nearly twenty years.'

Titus came in without knocking. The side of his face was

heavily padded; a linen bandage around his head held the dressing in place.

Magnus diplomatically slipped out of the room.

'You're awake, good,' Titus said, smiling. 'How are you feeling, my son?'

'Fine, Father, how about you?'

Titus cocked his head. 'What?'

'Fine, Father, how about . . . Oh, very funny!'

'Your mother didn't think so when I played the joke on her earlier; and she's in a worse mood now that Sabinus has told us that we need to get out of Italia and go and hide in some forsaken place – what's it called again?'

'Aventicum. It's for the best; until things change in Rome, that is.'

'I know, I understand but your mother doesn't. She thinks that because we beat them last night that should be the end of it.'

'Well, she's wrong,' Vespasian asserted, slipping on his tunic.

'I know, but you try telling her that. Sabinus and I have both tried and given up. It was only when I ordered the valuables to be packed on to wagons that she realised she had a choice: stay alone and undefended in an empty house that's liable to another attack, or come with me.'

'What did she choose?'

'I don't know, she's still thinking about it. I gave her my knife back though.'

Vespasian chuckled as he fastened his belt. 'What are you going to do with the livestock?'

'The mules and the sheep are all up on the summer pastures on the north of the estate. Pallo and some of the freedmen are going stay up there with the herdsmen for a while. They'll be safe enough; no one's looking for them. As to the slaves, we'll take the household ones with us.'

'What about the field slaves?'

'They're all dead; burnt last night.'

'Shit, no? All forty of them?' Vespasian looked up incredulously from tying on his sandals.

'Sixty now. We've been expanding whilst you were away. Yes,

I'm afraid so. Still, it's solved the problem of what to do with them.'

'That's a very expensive way of solving a problem. They were worth a lot of money.'

'You don't need to tell me that, I paid for them. But that loss to the family will be more than made up by the dowry that Clemens' sister will bring; I made the arrangements with him this morning. He's going to bring her to Cosa for the marriage within a month; I assume that you're going straight there.'

'Yes, we'll take a couple of Magnus' lads to—'

Sabinus popped his head around the door. 'Father, Vespasian, Ataphanes is dying, he's asking for us.'

The freedmen's lodgings were at the far end of the stable yard where, along with the estate office and the estate steward's quarters, they ran along the whole wall; they had escaped the worse ravages of the fires.

Titus led his sons through the chaos of three wagons being loaded with the family's possessions and on into the freedmen's common mess room, where meals were served and the men drank and played dice in the evenings. At the far end was a long windowless corridor with the doors to the men's individual rooms down the side facing on to the stable yard. Titus made to enter one and then paused; although as the master of the household he had the right to go anywhere he pleased without asking he thought to honour a man who had served him for six years as his slave and a further ten as his freedman: he knocked.

The door opened and Chloe peered out. Surprise that the master should have knocked showed on her wrinkled, sunburnt face, which always reminded Vespasian of a walnut shell.

'Masters, come in,' she wheezed, bowing her head. 'Master Vespasian, it's good to see you conscious. How is the shoulder?'

'It's stiff and it aches but it'll be fine. Thank you for what you did for me last night, Chloe,' Vespasian replied, taking her hand in genuine affection. She had sewn up many cuts and dosed him with all sorts of potions a child, and he had come to think of her as a part of the immediate family.

'You were lucky that it hit nothing vital,' she said, beaming at him. The few teeth that remained to her were yellow or black. 'I was able to clean and cauterise the wound. Not, alas, like poor Ataphanes; the arrow pierced his liver and he bleeds inside. He doesn't have long.'

Vespasian nodded and stepped into the small whitewashed room. To his surprise, Artebudz was standing by the only window; behind him, in the stable yard, the business of loading the wagons continued apace.

Ataphanes lay on a low bed. His once-proud, sculpted Persian features seemed flaccid and grey. His breathing was laborious. He opened his eyes – they had a yellow tinge to them – and he gave a weak smile.

'I am grateful that you have come, masters,' he whispered.

'The master knocked,' Chloe piped up from the door; she was well aware that she was talking out of place but wanted Ataphanes to be aware of the fact.

'Thank you,' he said to Titus, 'you do me honour.'

'No more than you deserve after the long years of service to my family,' Titus replied, taking his hand. He squeezed it gently and then looked quizzically at Artebudz.

'I'm Artebudz, sir. Your son won my freedom for me; I owe your family a debt of gratitude.'

'This is the man that shot me, master,' Ataphanes informed Titus weakly. 'It was a great shot; far better, Ahura Mazda be praised, than mine at Vespasian.' He spluttered a faint laugh; blood appeared on his lips. 'But my squat Scythian friend, Baseos, missed altogether. I have had my last archery competition with him and I won.'

'Though, luckily for me, not with a bull's-eye,' Vespasian said, feeling his shoulder.

Ataphanes nodded and closed his eyes. 'I have two favours to ask of you, masters.'

'Name them,' Titus said.

'First, that you do not cremate my body but rather expose it for the carrion fowl to devour on a tower of silence as is the custom of my people who follow the teachings of the prophet Zoroaster.'

'That will be done.'

'Thank you, master. My second request isn't so easy. I have saved a good deal of money, in gold; it's in a box under my bed, along with a few personal possessions that I want my family to have. I had planned to use it to return to my homeland one day, but now that's not to be. I would ask you to return it to my family with a letter telling them of my life; I've had no time to write one. They can read Greek.'

'Gladly, Ataphanes, but how will we know where to send it?'

'My family are from Ctesiphon; we are spice merchants. Being the youngest of five sons there was no place for me in the business so I was sent to pay my family's feudal dues and serve in the army of our Great King. And here I am and shall remain. My family did a great deal of trade with the Jews of Alexandria; I would have thought that they still do.' Ataphanes paused to catch his breath; his chest heaved irregularly. 'There was one Jewish family in particular – they had received Roman citizenship two generations before from Julius Caesar, the man's name was Gaius Julius Alexander. He would know where to send the money.'

Ataphanes' breathing became increasingly sporadic.

Titus looked down at him, concern in his eyes. 'No one of our class is allowed into Egypt without permission from the Emperor himself. How can we trace that family without going there?'

Ataphanes opened his eyes with a huge effort and whispered: 'Write to the alabarch, he'll know. Farewell, masters.'

He was gone. Artebudz stepped forward and closed his staring eyes.

They stood a moment in silence.

'Get the box, Sabinus,' Titus said after a while. 'I'll have Pallo get some men to deal with the body; we've got our other dead to cremate, the pyres are ready.'

Titus walked out, leaving the brothers looking at each other.

'What's an alabarch?' Sabinus asked.

'Fuck knows. We'll worry about that later. Come on, get the box and then we'll talk with Secundus after the funerals.'

Sabinus bent down and felt around under the bed. He pulled out a plain wooden box, one foot cubed; there was no lock on it, just a catch. He opened the lid. The brothers gasped; it was a quarter full of not just gold coins but also nuggets and jewellery.

'How did he get all this?' Sabinus asked, picking up a handful and letting it drop.

'He saved everything your father ever gave him for his work,' Chloe said. There were tears in her eyes. 'Once a year he would go to Reate and buy gold.'

'But that's more than ten years' worth, surely?' Vespasian exclaimed. 'Father's not that generous.'

'Baseos always gave him most of his money. He said he had no need of it; he had everything that he needed here and if he ever did go back to his home what good would so much money do him in the grasslands of Scythia? He thought it better to give it to his friend, who'd have some use for it.'

Sabinus grunted. 'I suppose that makes some sort of sense,' he said, heaving the heavy box up. 'In future I'll go out of my way to befriend Scythians.'

He walked out. Vespasian followed him, struggling with the concept that someone could have no need or desire for something that had always been very close to his heart: money.

With Titus officiating, the rest of the dead had been cremated on two pyres outside the stable-yard gates: one for the estate's dead and the crossroads brother, Lucio, and one for the others. A coin for the ferryman had been placed in all their mouths, including, much to Vespasia's disgust, Livilla's men's.

Vespasian now stood next to his father by the hastily constructed wooden platform, supported by four eight-foot poles, upon which Ataphanes had been laid. The estate's freedmen and Artebudz were gathered behind them. Baseos, who was weeping freely, held Ataphanes' bow, which he was keeping in memory of his friend. When Vespasian had asked him if he wanted to have any of his money back the old Scythian had said that he could get more food with Ataphanes' bow than he could buy with all his money; he seemed very content with the transaction so Vespasian had let the subject drop.

As no one knew the Zoroastrian funeral rites Sabinus had decided to use the Mithraic, the religions being in some ways related. He said prayers to the sun for the dead man's soul, whilst holding aloft a green ear of wheat. He then sacrificed a young bull and did some strange hand gestures above the fire before throwing the heart into it. It seemed all very weird and foreign, yet at the same time the sacrifice was familiar.

'What was that all about?' Vespanian asked his brother as they walked back through the stable-yard gates. It was the eighth hour of the day; the business of loading was almost complete and the mules were being harnessed to the wagons; Pallo had told them that they would be ready to leave in under an hour.

'If I told you I'd have to kill you and then kill myself,' Sabinus replied without a trace of irony. 'If you want to know you have to be initiated into the lowest grade: the Ravens.'

'How can I know if I want to be initiated if I don't know a thing about the religion?'

'Faith, brother.'

'Faith in what?'

'Faith in the Lord Mithras and the Sun God.'

'And what am I supposed to believe about them?'

'That they will guide your spirit and cleanse your soul in the transition from one life to the next.'

'How?'

'The mysteries are revealed gradually as you are initiated into the different grades.'

'What grade are you?'

'I'm a Soldier, the third grade. It's not until you reach the seventh that all is revealed, then you become known as "Father". But seriously, if you're interested I can arrange for you to be initiated.'

Vespasian found it odd that a religion could be so hierarchical that its secrets were kept by the few from the many, who were required just to have faith and follow blindly. He guessed that it must be something to do with power and control, which was why, he surmised, that it was becoming popular within the army.

'Thanks, but no thanks, Sabinus. I prefer the old gods whom you just have to appease in order to ask practical favours of: like bring me victory or a good harvest or death to an enemy; tangible stuff, not worrying about your spirit or your soul, whatever that may be.'

'The old gods too have their mysteries, which, I'm led to believe, are very similar to those of Mithras.'

'Then why have you chosen to follow this new god?'

'All religions are essentially the same if you delve deeply into them; it's a matter of choosing the one that best expresses the truth to your inner self about life, death and rebirth.'

'Well, I'm very happy just worrying about life; whatever happens after, if indeed anything does happen, can look after itself.'

'As you wish, brother.'

Their theological musings were brought to a close upon finding Clemens, who was remonstrating with a young stable lad about the tightness, or lack of it, of his saddle's girth.

'I'd swear that the little idiot was trying to kill me,' he said indignantly to the brothers, having given the boy a sharp cuff around the ears and sent him to redo his work.

'Where's Secundus, Clemens?' Sabinus asked. 'We want to ask him a few questions before you take him back to Antonia.'

'He's in one of the storerooms. I'll show you, but you'll be lucky to get anything out of him. I've already tried.'

'Perhaps you didn't use the right sort of persuasion,' Vespasian replied as Clemens led them away.

'It seems to us,' Vespasian said reasonably, 'that you have a very clear choice, Secundus: talk to us and you'll receive the Lady Antonia's protection; or say nothing and Antonia will inform Macro that you have betrayed not only her but him, and the unpleasant death that he promised, for both you and your wife, will be forthcoming.'

'You leave Albucilla out of this,' Secundus snarled. His pronounced mono-brow was creased over his narrow, pale-blue eyes. His high cheekbones and square jaw showed signs of bruising.

'I'm afraid that she's very much a part of it,' Vespasian replied smoothly, 'and has been ever since you prostituted her to Livilla and Sejanus.'

'I didn't prostitute her. What she does is of her own volition.'

'So it's of her own volition, is it,' Sabinus drawled, 'that she repeats to you all the interesting snippets of information she could only have learnt whilst being crushed between her two new clients? Who does what to whom, I wonder?'

Secundus leapt from his chair at Sabinus but was immediately restrained by Vespasian and Clemens. A sharp punch to the solar plexus from Sabinus' right fist took the wind out of him and he dropped to the floor.

'Now listen, Secundus,' Vespasian continued reasonably, 'you and your wife have played a dangerous game, which is now over. Antonia can very easily have a nice little maternal chat with her daughter Livilla, even though they loathe each other, and mention a few of the things that Albucilla has passed on to you, which you have, in turn, shared with Macro. Just imagine what Sejanus will do when he finds out that there is a spy in his bed? I don't know about you, but I think I'd prefer to take the unpleasant death that Macro promised rather than the lifetime of agony that Sejanus would doubtless offer you and your dear wife.'

Secundus had regained his breath; he looked up at Vespasian with a mixture of resignation and loathing. 'What do you want and what can you offer me?' he asked.

'That's better; I knew that you'd see sense. I admire ambition in a man but only if it is tempered by some degree of loyalty – something you don't seem to possess at all. I suggest that you acquire some; the Lady Antonia and Macro may well reward you for it by keeping you and Albucilla alive and safe. As to what we want, it's very simple: tell us why you went to Sejanus and what you've told him.'

Secundus struggled to his feet. 'May I sit back down?'

Clemens retrieved the chair for him. Secundus sat down, wiped the sweat from his forehead and rubbed his bruised chest.

'So,' Sabinus said, 'start talking.'

Secundus looked miserably around him. He knew that he had no choice and took a deep breath. 'I've always been loyal to Macro,' he protested, 'but when he started to conspire with Antonia against Sejanus I began to worry that I might have backed the wrong chariot. Sejanus is a formidable enemy and I feared that Macro could well be destroyed by him and that I would go down with him. However, Antonia is not to be underestimated either and if I was seen to be disloyal to Macro and therefore her, I would also suffer if she won the struggle.'

'But you didn't want to risk being on the losing side,' Sabinus said with a thin smile.

Secundus shrugged. 'Well, it's always better not to be. I don't know anyone who'll tell you different because they tend to be dead. Anyway, I told my wife about my concerns and she came up with the idea that she should seduce Livilla and then hopefully Sejanus and in that way it wouldn't matter to us who won the power struggle as we would have a foot in each camp.'

'That's one way of putting it,' Vespasian mused.

Secundus ignored the jibe. 'Once she had managed to inveigle her way into their bed she started passing on bits of information about Antonia that I gave her under the pretence that she'd got them from one of the Praetorians guarding Caligula with whom, she told them, she was also having an affair.'

'Who?' Clemens asked suspiciously.

Secundus looked at him with a sneer. 'You.'

Clemens' fist lashed out. 'You little bastard!'

Secundus ducked and avoided the blow. 'What else could she have said? They wouldn't have believed that she was having an affair with a mere ranker; it had to be the captain of the guard. In that way I could pass on what I found out about Antonia's plans from the messages that I carried between her and Macro without betraying him.'

'So Sejanus doesn't know that Macro is working with Antonia,' Vespasian said, placing a calming hand on Clemens' forearm.

'Of course not. I'm not stupid – if Albucilla told Sejanus that, he'd have Macro murdered and Antonia would guess that it was me that betrayed them. I know what she's like, I wouldn't last a day, however far and fast I tried to run.'

'So what have you passed on to Sejanus?' Sabinus demanded, stepping threateningly close to Secundus.

'Mainly small things, the things that Clemens would know: like the names of people I saw coming in and out whilst I was waiting to see her. The main thing that I passed on was about the arrival of the prisoner. You see, I knew that Antonia was trying to bring a witness to Tiberius to testify against Sejanus because I was there at the meeting with you, Pallas and Macro.'

'Wait a moment,' Vespasian butted in, turning to Sabinus. 'You never told me that you had a meeting with Macro.'

'You never asked,' Sabinus replied dismissively.

'How was I to know to ask you that question? I thought that we agreed to tell each other everything of relevance.'

'Look, it doesn't matter. I accompanied Pallas when he approached Macro on Antonia's behalf. Secundus was there as Macro's bodyguard, and that's how I recognised him last night. Now carry on, Secundus.'

Secundus raised his mono-brow at the brothers. 'When Antonia told me to tell Macro that what she was waiting for would arrive soon I guessed that it was this witness. Albucilla passed that on and Sejanus set a watch on the port and all the gates into the city. Albucilla told me that Sejanus was furious that his men couldn't see the man's face because he was hooded.'

'So Sejanus has no idea who this witness is?' Sabinus pressed.

'No, or where he comes from. I couldn't have Albucilla tell him that he was being fetched from Moesia because why would Clemens be a party to that sort of information? It would have made Sejanus suspicious and he might have got rid of her, in more ways than one. I needed her in that bed because I was getting information that pleased Macro; it was she that found out that Caligula was going to be summoned to Capreae.'

Vespasian admired the man's duplicity, subtlety and nerve. He had indeed played a dangerous game, and had played it well, and would have guaranteed himself being on the winning side whoever won, had he not ended up being captured in the act of murder. 'Why were you sent to kill our parents?' he asked.

'We weren't; our orders were to take your mother to Livilla.'

'What would Livilla want with her?'

'Sejanus desperately wanted to know the identity of this witness and because he couldn't get to Antonia he decided to ask one of her close confederates. Albucilla had mentioned your uncle's name a few times to them and because Senator Pollo has been making a nuisance of himself in the Senate – as Albucilla said Sejanus put it – Sejanus calculated that he may know Antonia's plans in some detail, so he sent some of Livilla's men to his house to fetch him for an interview.'

'Yes, we know. They didn't find him,' Sabinus said bitterly, 'they just killed most of his household.'

Secundus shrugged. 'We were to bring his sister along to help him with his memory. I was asked to come along because none of Livilla's men knew what she looked like; Albucilla suggested I should accompany them because I've seen Senator Pollo a few times and would be able to recognise a family likeness.'

'What about Sabinus and me?' Vespasian asked.

'You haven't been mentioned by name, either in the bed or by Macro,' Secundus replied, looking at the brothers shrewdly. 'However, Albucilla said that two young men whom no one recognised were seen getting off the boat with the prisoner and then going into Antonia's house. Perhaps it would be best if you stayed out of Rome for a while.'

'We've every intention of doing so,' Sabinus assured him.

'So, what are you going to do with me?' Secundus asked.

'Livilla will send men here to find out what happened,' Vespasian said. 'They'll find the place deserted and two funeral pyres; she'll assume that you're in one of them. Clemens will take you to Antonia where you can stay dead for a while whilst she decides what to do with you.'

'What about my wife? Is she going to think that I'm dead?'

'That's down to Antonia to decide; I expect it will all depend on how loyal and useful you prove to be to her.'

'Oh, I can be very useful.'

Vespasian smiled inwardly; he could well believe it. 'Then you may find her grateful.'

'She'll be very grateful.'

'Why?'

'Because I can give her the biggest prize of all. I can give her Sejanus.'

PART V

Cosa to Capreae,
December AD 30–March AD 31

CHAPTER XIIII

'Io, io, io, Saturnalia!' Vespasian and Sabinus cried together as they came through the door of the triclinium at Vespasian's estate at Cosa, bearing dishes of food.

'Io, io, io Saturnalia,' the few freedmen and house slaves that were left on the estate, along with Sextus and Marius, replied boisterously.

They reclined on the three couches around a low table and held their wine cups aloft in a toast to the annual festival of goodwill. All of them had been drinking steadily throughout the afternoon whilst Vespasian, Sabinus and Clementina had, with some help from the kitchen slave, prepared the meal. Vespasian and Sabinus placed the dishes on the table and Clementina did the rounds with the wine jug, replenishing the empty cups that had just been enthusiastically drained.

The room was decorated with the branches of fir trees and brightly berried holly; everyone within it, whether free, freed or slave, was wearing a brimless conical felt hat: the *pileus*, the symbol of manumission. All their tunics were brightly coloured, not the normal white, russet or plain undyed wool, but a dazzling array of clashing colours, worn only at this time during the year: the six-day-long festival of Saturn. This was the climax of the festival; the day when the household was turned upside down and masters waited on slaves and freedmen and they, in return, were allowed to be disrespectful (but not blatantly rude) back.

The diners surveyed the dishes of grilled fish with fennel and whole, roast suckling kid with a plum and caper sauce and made appreciative sounds.

'That looks a lot better than the slop your wizened old grandmother used to turn out after her annual foray into the kitchen;

if she could find it,' Attalus, Tertulla's steward and sparring companion, observed. 'But I don't suppose you spoilt young brats can remember the horrors of the old bat's cooking?'

'And I've no doubt that you let her know your exact feelings each year as she presented it, Attalus,' Vespasian replied, laughing at the description of his grandmother by the one man who had probably loved her more than he.

'On the contrary, boy, as you should remember.' Attalus grinned as he again drained his cup. 'Because I was allowed to be disrespectful to her over the Saturnalia it wasn't nearly so much fun, so I used to be deferential, compliant and meek instead. The perfect slave, in other words. Six days of that used to drive her mad; she could never wait for the festival to be over. I sometimes think that she used to make her "King for the day" feast awful on purpose, just to get me to make a sarcastic remark about it; but I never did, I ate every morsel of the ghastly swill that the daft old cow put in front of me. An act of genius, but then, I was always far more clever than any of your family.' He held his cup in the air and waved it at Clementina. 'Fill this up, wench, to the brim, just like you've been.'

Raucous laughter broke out around the room; Clementina reddened but smiled as she automatically put her hand on her swollen belly, and hurried around the table to serve him.

Sabinus bristled slightly but managed to join in the laughter; the comment had not been malicious and was well within the spirit of the Saturnalia, which he still enjoyed despite his new religion; he now looked on it as a prelude to the solemnity of celebrating the birth of Mithras in a few days' time. 'If you think that those two dishes look edible, Attalus,' he cried, 'just wait until you see the others. I think that even a starving Gallic sailor who'd been at sea for a month would shy at them.'

This brought another round of rowdy laughter; Gauls were not known for their nautical abilities or their culinary skills.

'Clementina, my dear, would you distribute the gifts whilst we fetch the remaining dishes?' Sabinus asked, pointing to a collection of wax candles, earthenware figurines and the pile of new tunics on a table in the corner of the room.

Clementina smiled prettily at her husband. 'My pleasure, Sabinus.'

Sabinus smiled back at his new wife and left the room.

Vespasian followed him out, full of of seasonal wellbeing. He had always loved the Saturnalia; it cheered him up, which was exactly what it had been designed for when it had been first brought in almost 250 years before to bring joy to the Roman people after the disastrous defeat at Lake Trasimene at the hands of Hannibal, where over fifteen thousand Roman sons, brothers and fathers had been killed. It had originally been just a one-day celebration but had grown over the years. Humourists suggested that because the year after Trasimene over fifty thousand Romans were killed at Cannae an extra day was added to cheer people up even more.

Vespasian did not know the truth of the matter but enjoyed the macabre wit. He was pleased to have his spirits lifted; it had been a long and difficult five months at Cosa. He had not been bored – there had been so much to do around the estate, which had fallen slightly into decline in the two and a half years since Tertulla's death. Attalus had done his best to keep it running smoothly since but because in her will she had freed all her slaves the estate was undermanned. Some of the newly freed decided to stay on the estate but most had decided to try their luck in Cosa or even Rome. Attalus had bought a few new slaves but had, rightly, been reluctant to make large purchases without Vespasian's permission. The restocking of the field-slave force had taken up a lot of his time in the first couple of months and then more recently he had been occupied by getting the estate back up to its full capacity before winter slowed down the agricultural life for a few months.

He had busied himself every day from dawn until dusk working hard at what he knew best; the days had not been the problem, it was the evenings. Since Clemens had brought his sister Clementina to Cosa in August for her marriage to Sabinus, Vespasian had been forced to have dinner every evening with two people who had very quickly fallen in love. The truth of the matter was that, for the first time in his life, he was jealous of his brother.

He was jealous of his happiness; he was jealous of his love and how it was returned; he was jealous of him having the woman he loved in his bed every night; he was jealous of everything that Sabinus had because he could not share the same thing with Caenis.

Antonia had once sent Caenis to Cosa, ostensibly with a message saying that Caligula had arrived on Capreae along with Clemens and that she was awaiting news. However, three months on no news had come and Vespasian was starting to fret about his inactivity; his career was not going to progress so far from Rome, however much he enjoyed farming.

Caenis had stayed for four days – and nights – but that had been back in September and he had not seen her since. Four days they had had playing man and wife – sharing a walk in the morning, a couch at dinner, a bed at night. He had been grateful to Sabinus and Clementina for treating her as an equal, despite her slave status, without a hint of condescension; but in some ways that had emphasised the problem: no matter how much anyone pretended, she was still a slave and could only ever hope to be freed, never free.

When Clementina's pregnancy had been confimed at around the time of his birthday in November, his jealousy had become almost impossible to keep hidden; his brother was having a child with a woman that he loved yet he, Vespasian, could never do the same with Caenis because the child would not be a citizen. He could never marry Caenis because of the Augustan law, the Lex Papia Poppaea, which forbade the union between a freedwoman and a senator; if he was to continue to serve Rome he would be elected as a quaestor, at or after the prescribed age of twenty-four, and, because his uncle was of senatorial class, he would automatically gain a seat in the Senate.

It was a situation that he could see no way out of short of giving up his career. Since he had first been overwhelmed by the majesty of Rome as viewed from the hill on the Via Salaria, he knew that was something he would never do. So he had no choice but to keep his feelings locked away and busy himself with the estate until Antonia called upon him and Sabinus to finally complete their mission and take Rhoteces to Tiberius.

This evening, however, he had managed to put all his troubles to one side; it was almost impossible to feel miserable during the Saturnalia, which was exactly what it had been designed for, all those years ago during the dark days of Hannibal's invasion of Italia.

Another chorus of 'Io, io, io, Saturnalia!' greeted Vespasian and Sabinus as they re-entered the triclinium and set down the two final dishes.

'You weren't exaggerating, Sabinus,' Attalus observed, poking his finger into the very sloppy sauce that surrounded an over-cooked brace of rabbits. 'You've surpassed your grandmother; the Gallic sailor would also have to be blind and drunk to eat that.'

'Well, you're already halfway there, Attalus,' Vespasian laughed, picking up a knife from the table and pointing it at the steward's face. 'Would you like me to help you with the other half?'

'You're most kind, but I must decline as I fear that you would regret the offer in the morning when things get back to normal and you need a numerate person with full use of his eyes to correct all the mistakes that you've made in the estate's account books.'

'Io, io, io, Saturnalia!' the assembled company shouted, raising their cups.

With the toast drunk the diners began to tuck into the meal.

'Allow me to serve you, Master Marius,' Sabinus said, noticing that the one-handed crossroads brother was having difficulty carving off a leg of suckling kid.

'Yeah, he needs a hand,' Sextus piped up, pleased with the joke that he had made a hundred times before but never tired of.

'It must be the Saturnalia if you've got your only joke out, brother,' Marius responded with a grin as Sabinus placed the leg on his plate. 'Thank you, Sabinus.'

'No need to thank me, it's good to be able to do something useful seeing as I can't even get myself elected as a quaestor.'

'Io, io, io, Saturnalia!' everyone roared in response to this unusual piece of self-deprecation. Vespasian joined in. He had, at first, been surprised by how well Sabinus had taken his failure in the elections – especially as he, Vespasian, had on more than one occasion mentioned that his friend Paetus, now back in Rome, had come top of the list – but then, observing the regularity with which his brother consoled himself for the defeat in the arms of his new young bride, he began to think that for Sabinus it had come as a relief. There were always next year's elections and in the meantime he was free to enjoy married life rather than be second in command of some far-away province for a year or more, which was bound to be his fate – the plum jobs in the city being reserved for men of Paetus' lineage.

The meal gradually petered out as the diners got more and more drunk; eventually they had all passed out on their couches or under them. The brothers and Clementina left them to their noisy slumber, surrounded by the debris of the meal; the Saturnalia did not extend to the masters clearing and washing up, that was something that the diners would have to do, with raging hangovers, when they returned to their normal roles early the next morning.

Sabinus led Clementina off to their bedroom, his grin assuring Vespasian of the night of consolation ahead of him, leaving Vespasian alone. Since it was still early and he was not yet tired he decided to go to his study and carry on working through the surprising amount of history books and historical documents that his grandmother had left him. As he crossed the atrium a loud knock sounded on the front door. In the absence of the doorkeeper – drunk in a pool of his own vomit on the floor in the triclinium – he opened it himself.

'Good evening, sir, did I miss the party?'

'Magnus!' Vespasian exclaimed, surprised and pleased to see his friend. 'Yes, I'm afraid that you did.'

'That's a shame.' Magnus stepped into the vestibule, shaking off his cloak and handing it to Vespasian with a grin. 'Never mind, it's still Saturnalia so you can make up for it by pouring me a drink once you've hung this up.'

'What are you doing here?'

'I'll have that drink first, boy.'

Vespasian rolled his eyes; perhaps Saturnalia did last just a bit too long.

'Not until March?' Vespasian exclaimed.

'At the very earliest,' Magnus replied.

They were sitting in Vespasian's small but cosy study; a mobile brazier in the corner glowed red, giving out a pleasing amount of heat. A jug of wine and a couple of oil lamps stood on the desk between them.

'What's the delay for?'

Magnus took a gulp of wine, spilling a bit down his tunic, and set his cup down. 'I don't know the exact details, sir, but it's something to do with Satrius Secundus.'

'What's he doing?'

'Well, when we got him back to Antonia he spent an hour closeted with her and Pallas in her study. I was waiting outside because she'd asked me to . . . wait, if you take my meaning?'

Vespasian smirked. 'Yes, I do, you old goat.'

'Well, so when she comes out she looks at me and smiles and says: "I've really got him now."'

'And?'

'That was it. She doesn't talk to me that much, just tells me what to do, you know, orders and such.'

'Yes, I can imagine,' Vespasian replied, trying not to. 'So Secundus has given her something on Sejanus that she believes will really convince the Emperor of his treachery?'

'It looks that way; she was certainly in a very good mood that evening,' Magnus replied, grimacing slightly. 'But I don't know what it is. I tried asking Pallas, but you know what he's like, he wouldn't disclose a confidence even if his own mother was being nailed to a burning cross with a pitch-soaked, wooden stake up—'

'Yes, yes,' Vespasian interrupted, not liking the image even before it was completed. 'What about Caligula?'

'Antonia told me to tell you that he's worked out a way of getting us on to the island.'

'Well, tell me then.'

'I have.'

'No you haven't. What is it?'

'Ah, I don't know that part; she just said to say that he's found a way, she didn't say what it was, she doesn't . . .'

'Talk to you much, I know.'

'No, exactly. Still, you can ask her yourself very soon, if you want.'

'How? I'm going to be staying here until at least March.'

'If you do, you'll be in trouble.'

'What are you talking about now? I thought that it was safer for me to stay out of Rome for the time being.'

'Well, Antonia said to tell you that she thinks that it's safe for you to come back. Sejanus is to be Tiberius' colleague as Consul in the New Year and has been given permission to become betrothed to Livilla.'

Vespasian frowned and took a sip of wine. 'How does that make me safe?'

'Because he's feeling secure, he thinks that he's now untouchable and is pursuing vendettas against people who've crossed him in the past rather than worrying about Antonia's plans for him in the future. He hasn't made any more attempts on your uncle, who's been back in his own house for the last three months. And as you may already know, they left your estate at Aquae Cutillae alone after they found the pyres. Antonia thinks that you and Sabinus are both – how did she put it? – "too small a pair of fish for Sejanus to have noticed".'

'That's very comforting, I'm sure. So why will I be in trouble if I stay here?'

'Because Antonia and Senator Pollo have managed to get you a position.'

'What sort of position?'

'Now that is a silly question,' Magnus said, draining his cup and helping himself to more. 'On the next rung of the ladder, of course; one of the twenty junior magistrates, the Vigintiviri.'

Vespasian's eyes lit up; he had not been expecting to be able to further his career until Antonia had won her struggle with

Sejanus. But now, if she thought that it was safe for him to return to Rome and take another step up the *cursus honorum* he would grab the chance. He would be closer to Caenis and would not have to have his brother's happiness shoved down his throat all the time.

'That's excellent news.'

'Well, yes and no, sir.'

'What do you mean?'

'It's the least popular position.'

'Not working for the aedile in charge of roads?'

'No, I'm afraid not. You're going to be one of the triumviri capitales.'

Vespasian groaned; he knew what that entailed.

'I'm afraid so, sir,' Magnus said sympathetically, 'one of the three men in charge of book-burnings and executions.'

CHAPTER XV

'MY DEAR BOY, you're as white as your toga,' Gaius boomed in alarm as an attractive new doorkeeper let Vespasian in through the front door of his house.

'That's because again today my service to Rome amounted to nothing more than cold-blooded murder,' Vespasian replied, irritably brushing off the attentions of one of Gaius' many new young German slave boys.

'Aenor, bring some wine,' Gaius ordered the young lad, who immediately scuttled off to do his master's bidding. 'Come and sit down, Vespasian.'

'The irony of it all is that for the last three months I've been doing the dirty work for someone whom I'm meant to be helping Antonia try to destroy,' Vespasian said, taking a seat next to the *impluvium* in Gaius' spacious atrium. The fountain's continuous tinkling helped to calm Vespasian as Gaius sat down opposite him and Aenor served them their wine.

'So whom did Sejanus get today?' Gaius asked once the boy had been dismissed with a hearty slap on the arse.

'I forget his name,' Vespasian replied, taking a long slug of wine and savouring its delicate taste with his eyes shut and shaking his head slowly. 'He was an equestrian who had business connections in Egypt; apparently he had defrauded Sejanus' father, Strabo, shortly before he died, whilst he was the prefect of that province.'

'And sixteen years later Sejanus gets his family's revenge.'

'Exactly. On a trumped-up charge of treason. The man wasn't even allowed the citizens' right of decapitation. I've just had to watch the public executioner strangle an innocent Roman citizen. Then, to cap it all, his family weren't allowed to take the body for burial and it's now lying on the Gemonian Stairs for anybody to dishonour as they see fit. It's an absolute disgrace.'

'Calm, my dear boy, there's nothing you can do about it at the moment. Just be thankful that Sejanus is concentrating his energies on the long list of people who've upset his family in the past; although not a day goes by when I don't worry that some snotty-nosed little urban quaestor is going to appear at my door with a summons.'

'I wouldn't call Paetus "snotty-nosed".'

'Well, he's younger than me. Anyway, what was the actual charge?'

'That he'd entered Egypt without the Emperor's permission with the express purpose of defrauding the Emperor's personal representative in that province.'

'Very neat. Had he obtained permission?'

'He swore in court that he had and then the prosecution brought out the list, supplied by guess who, of every equestrian who had applied for permission to visit Egypt in the last twenty years and, would you believe it, his name turned up missing.'

'And that was that?'

'Yes, Uncle, that was that. I had to take him away for immediate execution, no right of appeal, and all his property was forfeited to be split between the crony of Sejanus who'd accused him and the emperor, leaving his family destitute.'

'Try to remember his name, will you, because when the situation changes here it may be possible to redress some of Sejanus' wrongs.'

'How? Sejanus has evidently removed his name from the list.'

'Ah, but that isn't the only list, there's a duplicate in Alexandria – there has to be otherwise the prefect wouldn't know whom to allow in. When Sejanus is no more I'll ask Antonia to write to her friend the alabarch to see—'

'Alabarch?' Vespasian interrupted. 'That's the second time that I've heard that word recently. What is an alabarch?'

'The alabarch of Alexandria is the secular leader of the Jews of that city. He's used by the Emperor to collect taxes, like import duties and such, from the Jewish population. They resent paying them to Rome but don't seem to mind paying them to a fellow Jew, even though the money ends up in the same place.'

'What's Antonia's relationship with him?'

'Not surprisingly she has a massive amount of land in Egypt. The alabarch looks after her interests there and has done since before he was appointed. He's the first alabarch to be a Roman citizen; his grandfather was granted citizenship by Caesar.'

'Gaius Julius Alexander,' Vespasian said slowly, dragging the name from his memory.

'You know him then?'

'No, but Sabinus and I need to find him,' Vespasian replied. He then told his uncle about Ataphanes' last request and the box that lay buried for safekeeping on his estate at Cosa.

'Well, it sounds to me as if one of you boys is going to have to get permission to visit Egypt and take that box to the alabarch.'

'Do you think that Antonia would be able to use her influence with the Emperor and write to him in order to get us that permission?'

'I'm sure that when her mind is free to worry about more mundane things she would be only too pleased to write to him. Talking of letters, I had one from my sister this afternoon. It seems that your father is moving into banking; he's bought Pomponius' banking concession in the lands of the Helvetii off him at a decent price.'

Vespasian raised his eyebrows at the news. 'So it sounds like he means to stay up there then. A Helvetian banker! Who'd have thought that he'd end up doing that?'

Their conversation was interrupted by a knock on the front door. The attractive new doorkeeper jumped up off his stool and peered through the viewing slot. A moment later he pulled the door open and in walked Pallas.

'Good afternoon, masters,' he said, bowing deferentially. He handed his cloak to Aenor who had padded across the room to be of service.

'And greetings to you, Pallas.' Gaius did not get up. However much he liked and respected Antonia's steward, he was still a slave. 'What brings you here?'

'Two things, master: firstly the timing is finally right to take all the evidence that my mistress has collected to the Emperor. Messages have been sent to Sabinus and Corbulo to come to the Lady Antonia's house immediately; she requests Vespasian to join them. Magnus is already there as she seems to like to keep him handy at the moment.' He dipped his hand into a leather documents satchel slung around his neck, pulled out a thick scroll and handed it to Gaius. 'My mistress sent this for your safe-keeping, senator. It's a copy of the letter that she has written Tiberius detailing the conspiracy of Sejanus. She requests that should we be unsuccessful in our mission, and she herself is compromised, that you read it aloud in the Senate, even if it costs you your life.'

Gaius swallowed hard. 'It will be an honour to serve the good lady in such an important way,' he said, taking the scroll and then adding quickly, 'should it become necessary.'

'Master Vespasian, we should go at once. My mistress has made a quiet arrangement with one of your two colleagues to perform your duties whilst you are away; your absence won't be noted.'

'Thank you, Pallas,' Vespasian replied, getting to his feet. 'I'll just lose my toga and get into some travel clothes. I won't be long.'

'But be sure to pack your toga, dear boy,' Gaius called after him.

'Whatever for, Uncle?'

'Because, my dear, you are going to be presented to the Emperor of Rome and as a Roman citizen you should be properly dressed; to be otherwise would be an insult.'

'He still looks like a pompous arsehole to me,' Magnus commented to Vespasian as Gnaeus Domitius Corbulo, wearing his senatorial toga, entered Antonia's formal reception room. It was early evening and the house slaves had just finished lighting a myriad of lamps around the ornate and elegantly furnished high-ceilinged room.

'And I expect that you still look like an uncouth, illiterate oik to him,' Vespasian replied out of the corner of his mouth, whilst smiling at the approaching Corbulo.

'That's because he's a pompous arsehole.'

'Vespasian, how good to see you,' Corbulo said, grasping Vespasian's forearm. 'You've been back from Thracia for the last eight months, I hear – why haven't you come to visit me?'

'Good to see you too, Corbulo.' Vespasian was surprised to find that he genuinely meant it. 'I'm sorry but I've been kept very busy.'

'Yes, I heard. Sejanus is keeping the triumviri capitales hard at work at the moment.'

'I'm afraid so, but luckily he's not a literary type so we haven't had to burn any books.'

'Quite so, quite so,' Corbulo agreed vaguely; humour was generally wasted on him. He turned to Magnus and looked down his long nose at him. Despite the dangers that they had shared, Corbulo could not overcome the innate prejudices of his class and found it offensive that he should have to acknowledge someone so far beneath him. 'Magnus,' he said with a frown, as if only just being able to recall the name.

'Corbulo?' Magnus queried, staring back at him with nonchalant insubordination.

Sabinus' arrival brought their warm words of greeting to an end. The fact that his brother lived the closest to Antonia, in a newly rented house on the Aventine, but arrived last, led Vespasian to believe that he had been taking a long farewell of his wife. He suppressed a jealous pang at his brother's freedom and thought instead of Caenis and the likelihood of his seeing her that afternoon. Since he had been back in Rome Antonia had not summoned him and so, consequently, he had not seen Caenis. Neither had he been able to find out anything about Caligula's plan; Pallas had, of course, been a model of discretion on the walk from Gaius' house.

As he watched Sabinus' almost sycophantic greeting of Corbulo he was rewarded with the sight of his lover entering the room behind her mistress and Pallas. His heart jumped and he returned her radiant smile with equal measure.

'Sit down please, gentlemen,' Antonia said, seating herself on a well-upholstered couch and placing a scroll beside her. She arranged her crimson palla so that it fell gracefully from her head into neat folds on her lap. Caenis sat at a table behind her and arranged her writing things ready to take the minutes.

'We're still missing one person but I'll begin anyway as I don't want him to hear the first part of what I have to say.

'Over the last few months my grandson, Gaius, has managed to ingratiate himself with the Emperor on Capreae; he is now very much in his favour. This has been greatly helped recently by Sejanus staying in Rome. He has been in the city constantly since becoming Consul jointly with Tiberius. With Sejanus away from Capreae, Gaius has had the opportunity to get closer to Tiberius to the extent that he is now, Gaius leads me to believe, thinking of making him his heir. Sejanus knows very little of this as he is busy in Rome.

'This started me thinking. When Tiberius first announced that Sejanus would be his consular colleague, my first reaction was to think that he was just piling more undeserved glory upon him. However, I then thought about the timing. Tiberius didn't need to be Consul again this year, he could have made someone else Sejanus' colleague, leaving Sejanus free to come and go from Capreae as much as he liked whilst leaving his colleague always in Rome so that the business of government could carry on. But no, Tiberius, who hasn't been seen in Rome for five years, decides to be Sejanus' colleague, thus ensuring his absence from Capreae for the year. So, two months after Gaius arrives Tiberius effectively sends Sejanus away, with the double honour of a consulship and being the colleague of the Emperor himself to sweeten or perhaps disguise the fact. Now, why would he do that?'

Vespasian saw the logic of Antonia's argument and joined in her audience's mutterings of admiration about her mastery of the subtleties of imperial politics.

'Being unable to see into the mind of my brother-in-law,' she continued, 'I can only make an educated guess: Tiberius does want a member of his family to succeed him but has started to run out of options. I learnt recently that my eldest grandson, Nero Germanicus, has died of starvation in prison and that Drusus is unlikely to be released and will probably suffer the same fate. Tiberius Gemellus, the grandson shared by Tiberius and me, is too young and Claudius is too stupid, or so Tiberius still believes. That leaves Gaius as the obvious candidate. However, Tiberius has belatedly come to suspect that Sejanus has got his eyes on the Purple and has finally come to see him as a threat but is unsure how to counter him. If he tries to remove him quickly he risks a coup; he's now well aware that he is guarded by men as loyal to Sejanus as to himself, if not more so. So whilst he contemplates his problem he has put as much distance between himself and Sejanus as possible but without upsetting him because he's given him the highest honour: a joint consulship with the Emperor. Very elegant, I would say.'

There was a general murmur of agreement, as much for Antonia's reasoning as for Tiberius' handling of the problem.

'If I am right, then I believe that Tiberius will be very susceptible to what I have for him. With solid proof that Sejanus is conspiring against him he will be forced to act, and with the knowledge that elements within the Guard are loyal to Macro, he'll feel free to act.

'So, now that I've put a stop to my son Claudius' ridiculous intriguing with Sejanus and decided not to sacrifice him, what is the solid proof?' Antonia paused and looked around the gathering.

Vespasian enjoyed this insight into high politics by someone he knew to be a master of the art, in fact, almost as much as he enjoyed the stolen glances he shared with Caenis. 'The priest?' he ventured.

'Perhaps – but he had been fed the story that Asinius was behind the financing of the Thracian revolt.'

'Surely under torture he would be able to describe Sejanus' freedman Hasdro well enough for Tiberius to believe that Asinius had nothing to do with it and it was, in all likelihood, a scheme of Sejanus'.'

'That is not conclusive; I asked for Rhoteces to be brought

here when I was still compiling a range of evidence that, seen altogether, would be compelling. However, seeing as we have him in our possession it would still be worthwhile to take him to Capreae in the unlikely event Tiberius wants confirmation of Sejanus' strategy of destabilisation in the provinces in order to draw attention away from his plotting in Rome.' She picked up the scroll beside her and held it up for all to see. 'The content of this letter, which I will entrust to Pallas to deliver to him, will convince him of Sejanus' real and unimagined treachery. In it is a detailed description of Sejanus' plans as supplied to me by Satrius Secundus. He had not been quite as honest with you gentlemen as he'd led you to believe. Although he was trying to keep in both Macro's and Sejanus' favour, he was, from his own admission, doing a little more for Sejanus than he was for Macro, short of betraying him completely.

'One of the services he had recently been performing for Sejanus was administering small amounts of poison, not enough to kill but enough to make the victim seem ill and frail, to my grandson Tiberius Gemellus, the son of my vicious daughter, Livilla, and Tiberius' late son, Drusus. Now that I've blocked his route to power through Claudius, Sejanus' new plan is to murder Tiberius, make the under-age and sickly Gemellus Emperor and act as his regent; he would then marry Gemellus' mother, Livilla, before finally upping the dose to a fatal level. The sickly Gemellus would die, to no one's great surprise, and Sejanus would claim the Purple as the stepfather of the deceased Emperor.

'What would follow would be a bloodbath in which most of my family would be murdered. How do I know this?'

She paused again for effect. 'Enclosed in this letter is a list, procured, with a little coercing, by Secundus' wife, Albucilla. It comes from Livilla's study and is written in Sejanus' own hand; it contains the names of the sixteen people who would die. At the top of the list is Tiberius; I am next. Noticeably missing from the list is my daughter, Livilla, which, along with the place from which the list was taken, leads me to conclude that she is fully aware of the whole plot and, in order to become Sejanus'

Empress, has sanctioned the murder of not only most of her family, including her mother, but also of her own child.'

Antonia paused again; there was a stunned silence in the room. Vespasian found it hard enough to believe that anyone could kill a member of their own family, but knew enough of imperial politics to realise that it was becoming commonplace; but to kill your own child to secure your position was unfathomable. What could possibly justify a system of succession in a civilised state that involved infanticide? His thoughts on the subject were interrupted by the clatter of hobnailed sandals walking quickly down the corridor. Vespasian looked towards the door; in walked a huge bull of a man. Vespasian started; he recognised him immediately.

'Ah,' Antonia said, 'Tribune Macro, I'm so pleased that you could make it; I hope that you weren't followed.'

'Briefly, but it was dealt with,' Macro said brusquely, sitting down without waiting to be asked. As he adjusted his toga his eyes flicked around the assembled company and Vespasian detected a hint of recognition as they rested on him and then moved on to Magnus.

'You know Titus Flavius Sabinus, tribune,' Antonia affirmed, gesturing to Sabinus. 'This is his brother Titus Flavius Vespasianus.'

Macro gave a mirthless half-smile and nodded, whilst peering at Vespasian with dead eyes.

'And Gnaeus Domitius Corbulo,' Antonia said, carrying on the introductions.

Macro barely acknowledged Corbulo but continued staring at Vespasian and Magnus, who, much to his relief, was considered too insignificant to be introduced.

'So, gentlemen, to business,' Antonia said as if she had been waiting for Macro's arrival and the meeting had now only just started. 'Tribune Macro and my grandson Gaius have a way to get you on to Capreae without it coming to the attention of any of the Praetorian officers loyal to Sejanus.

'As you may or may not know, when Gaius was summoned to Capreae his two younger, unmarried sisters, Drusilla and Julia

Livilla, were moved to Tiberius' villa at Misenum, on the mainland, close to Capreae. Because Gaius has managed to inveigle his way so much into Tiberius' favour he has recently persuaded him that he should be allowed to visit his sisters for a few days each month; something that I do not approve of but happily works in our favour. The next visit will be in two days' time. Gaius is, of course, always guarded; but Tribune Macro, good to his word, has ensured that it is Clemens and a few of his men who always go with him on these trips. The tribune will explain the details of the plan.'

Macro roused himself from his thoughts and began to talk with ill-concealed bad grace, as if it were beneath his dignitas to act as a mere briefing officer.

'It's over a hundred and fifty miles to Misenum; because you will have to transport this witness in a cart, it will take you six days to get there.'

Vespasian raised an eyebrow as he realised why Antonia had started without Macro: he did not know about Secundus' and Albucilla's information.

'If you leave tomorrow morning,' Macro carried on, 'you'll arrive on the last scheduled evening of the visit. You will spend the night at Misenum – the guards there will be my men – and then you will leave the following day for the island. The ship that transports Caligula back to Capreae normally leaves around midday so that it gets back in daylight. Clemens will find a reason to delay it so that it gets to Capreae soon after dark. As it approaches the island, you will be dropped off in a rowing boat, unseen, near a small cove in the cliffs, just before the harbour. The ship will then carry on to the port where Caligula, Clemens and his men will disembark under the eye of the Praetorians guarding the dock, all of whom are loyal to Sejanus.'

'What about the ship's crew?' Vespasian asked, earning a glare from Macro. 'They would have seen us boarding and then going over the side.'

'I was coming to them,' Macro growled. 'The crew all come from Puteoli near Misenum; before you sail, their families will be rounded up to ensure their good behaviour and silence. The crew will get their families back alive once they have taken you off the island the following night.

'Two of Clemens' men will be waiting for you at the cove; they will show you where to hide the boat and then lead you up a steep path to the cliff-top; from there it's less than a mile to Tiberius' villa.

'The return journey, the following night, will be the exact opposite. The ship will be waiting half a mile off the cove, from midnight, burning one lantern; from the island it will look like a night fisherman. A few of my men will be aboard to keep an eye on the crew. They'll take you back to Misenum where you can pick up your horses and the cart, in the unlikely event that you should still need it.'

Macro sat back in his chair having evidently finished. His audience sat motionless, waiting to hear the crucial details.

Antonia broke the silence. 'Thank you, tribune. So, gentlemen, that's how you get on to and off Capreae. No doubt you're wondering what you will do whilst you're there?'

There were a few nervous nods. Antonia smiled. 'The truth is that I don't know but in the last letter that Gaius managed to smuggle out he said that by the time you got there he and Clemens would have a plan.'

Everyone looked aghast. Macro was outraged. 'I'm risking all this,' he shouted, 'and you're telling me that these . . .' He struggled for a word. 'These boys might easily be caught by Sejanus' men because there isn't a plan? It would be just a matter of time until they reveal my involvement under torture.'

'Tribune, please,' Antonia countered, raising her voice, 'we all have a lot to lose.'

'A lot to lose? I have *everything* to lose. You, on the other hand, will just go back to your scheming and plotting safe from Sejanus within the walls of this house.'

'You may have the most to lose, tribune,' Antonia said in a reasoned tone, 'but I would also say that, in terms of power, you also have the most to gain. I will just remove an enemy; you will be prefect of the Praetorian Guard.'

'And what if I think that it's too big a gamble to stake everything on an unfinished plan and decide withdraw my help? What then, eh?'

'Oh, I don't think you'll do that,' Antonia replied with a sweet smile.

'Why not?' Macro demanded, getting to his feet. 'You've got nothing to hold me to you, nothing at all with which you could convince Sejanus that I've been disloyal to him. I've been most careful on that point. I could just withdraw and pretend that this never happened.'

'I'm sorry to have to tell you that you're very wrong on that point, tribune; you see, I've got Satrius Secundus.'

Macro looked incredulous. 'Bollocks! He's dead; after he'd been missing for over ten days I had Albucilla questioned, she was convinced that he'd been killed doing some dirty work for Livilla.'

'I think we can all agree that a wife never truly knows her husband's whereabouts all of the time, tribune; I can assure you that Secundus is very much alive, with a fully functioning memory, and is secured in this house.'

'Prove it, bitch!'

'My dear tribune, if, when you become the Praetorian prefect, you're hoping to have a better relationship with me than your predecessor enjoyed, I suggest that when you address me you moderate your language. But this time I'll overlook your rudeness. Pallas, convince the tribune.'

Pallas walked across the room to the curtains concealing the small chamber, from where the brothers and Caligula had spied on Sejanus, and threw them open.

Macro gasped. Tied to a chair, securely gagged, evidently heavily drugged but obviously alive, was Satrius Secundus.

With a huge roar Macro leapt towards him, drawing a dagger from beneath his toga. Sabinus stuck out a leg and caught him as he passed. He crashed to the floor, spilling his dagger, which Vespasian quickly retrieved. Sabinus and Magnus pounced on his back and with some difficulty pulled his arms up behind it; Vespasian held the dagger to his throat.

'Now, my dear tribune,' Antonia continued as if nothing had

happened, 'I think that it's in everyone's best interest to carry on as planned, don't you?'

Macro struggled fiercely but, between them, Sabinus and Magnus managed to subdue him.

'Let him go,' Antonia ordered.

A nervous look passed between Sabinus and Magnus; then, with a degree of trepidation, they slowly eased their grip and stood up. Vespasian backed off, keeping the knife pointed at the prostrate Macro, who slowly rose to his knees. He looked up at Vespasian and glared at him.

'That's the second dagger you've had off me, boy,' he snarled to hide his humiliation. 'Keep it, like you kept the last one; one day I'll give you the third to make up the set.'

'There'll be no need for that, tribune,' Antonia snapped as Macro pulled himself to his feet. 'He's under my protection. You can hate him as much as you like but if you touch him you'll find that I'll be removing another Praetorian prefect.'

Macro glowered at her, hatred burning in his eyes; he began to say something but then thought the better of it and readjusted his toga instead.

'So we're all agreed then, tribune,' Antonia stated, her voice now full of harmony.

'My men will be there,' Macro said, drawing himself up and resuming his arrogant air. 'Make sure these boys are too, and pray to the gods below that Caligula comes up with an idea.'

'I wouldn't worry about that.' Antonia smiled. 'He was born cunning.'

Macro grunted, spun on his heel and walked briskly out of the room.

Vespasian looked down at the dagger in his hand and groaned.

'You've got to get out of the habit of nicking that man's daggers, sir,' Magnus said with a wry grin. 'It ain't a healthy hobby, if you take my meaning.'

Vespasian gave his friend a sour look. 'I'll try and remember that.'

'Before we eat, gentlemen,' Antonia said, sitting back down, 'and we can enjoy lighter conversation, there's one other thing that I want to say about this affair: should it become necessary for Tiberius to hear the priest's evidence the name of Poppaeus Sabinus is bound to come up. I want you to play down his involvement with Sejanus.'

Corbulo got to his feet, bristling with aristocratic indignation. 'Domina, it's to get my revenge on that treacherous little new man that I offered my services.'

'I understand that, Corbulo,' Antonia replied patiently, 'and at the time you offered them I was very grateful; but things have changed now. I don't want anything to deflect Tiberius' attention from the very real evidence that I've got against Sejanus. I know him; he's lost his decisiveness. If he has other traitors to think about he'll prevaricate; he will pick off the easier, smaller ones in the mistaken belief that in doing something he's dealing with the problem. I must keep his focus on Sejanus.'

'My honour demands revenge on the man who tried to kill me,' Corbulo insisted.

'And you will have it – on both of the men who tried to kill you, but Sejanus first. I will deal with Poppaeus and all of Sejanus' confederates in time. I find that revenge is best served regularly. If you're not content with that then I'd quite understand you wishing to withdraw; however, your testimony relating to the silver received by the Caenii may be of use.' The hardness of her expression did not match her conciliatory words.

Corbulo held her gaze for a few moments and then sat back down. 'No, domina, I won't withdraw.'

'Good. Let's eat. You will all stay here tonight so as to be ready to leave an hour before dawn; I want you out of the city and on the road before it's light.'

CHAPTER XVI

A SOFT BUT INSISTENT tapping on the door woke Vespasian from a deep, untroubled sleep. Caenis lay next to him, curled in the crook of his arm. He opened his eyes; it was still the dead of night.

'Who is it?' he asked in a projected whisper.

'Me, sir.' Magnus opened the door a crack and peered into the gloom. 'It's time we was going; I'm afraid that you'll have to leave that nice warm bed and its contents.'

'I'll be right out,' Vespasian replied as Caenis stirred beside him.

'We're meeting in the atrium; I've got your bag. See you there.'

Magnus closed the door leaving the room in complete darkness.

'Shit,' Vespasian said to himself, sitting up.

'What is it, my love?' Caenis whispered sleepily.

'I've got to go.' He leant down to kiss her, wrapping an arm around her warm body.

She responded and then gently pushed him away with a giggle. 'That's not going to help you get up.'

'It is.'

'I meant up and out of bed. Come on, I need to get up as well; my mistress will be wanting to see you off. I'll get some light.'

She slipped out of the bed and over to the chest. Vespasian heard her taking something out of a drawer and then striking a flint; within a few moments a glow softly illuminated her face, shortly after a flame burned at the end of the thin wick of an oil lamp.

'I always wondered how the house—' Vespasian stopped mid-sentence, feeling desperately uncomfortable.

'How the house slaves light the first oil lamp?' Caenis said, raising her eyebrows at him. 'It's all right, Vespasian, you don't have to be coy about my status; we both know that I'm a slave. I accept it; so must you.'

Vespasian grinned sheepishly and got out of bed. He knew that she was right; it was an unassailable fact, which, although it divided them socially, should never be allowed to come between them in private.

He took her in his arms and kissed her. 'I'm sorry, my beautiful slave girl.'

Caenis smiled up at him. 'There's a big difference between acceptance and rubbing it in my face,' she chided him gently.

A short while later Vespasian arrived in the sparklingly lit atrium; Magnus and Pallas were already there and Sabinus and Corbulo joined them almost immediately.

'Good morning, masters. We should get the priest and then leave at once,' Pallas said, taking command, despite his slave status. The brothers and Magnus did not question it but Corbulo bristled.

'As a senator and a member of the most noble family present, I should be giving the orders,' he said huffily. 'I'm certainly not taking them from a slave.'

'And so you shouldn't, master,' Pallas agreed smoothly. 'You will give the orders, but I'll decide what to do because I am acting in the Lady Antonia's name.' He held up his right hand; on the little finger was Antonia's seal ring.

Corbulo looked at the brothers. 'Do you accept orders from him?'

'I think that he knows better than any of us what is required,' Vespasian replied diplomatically.

Corbulo, realising the ludicrousness of a situation whereby he would just repeat Pallas' words like a herald, drew himself up and swallowed his pride. 'Very well then, Pallas leads.'

'Pompous arsehole,' Magnus said, not altogether under his breath.

Corbulo turned and glared at him but could not bring himself to acknowledge the insult. It was bad enough taking orders from a slave – he was not going to compound that by demanding an apology from an urban ruffian. He turned and followed Pallas out of the room.

'That didn't help,' Vespasian hissed at Magnus as they trailed behind.

Marcus grinned. 'I know, but it felt good.'

At the rear of the house they descended a stone staircase into a long, damp corridor lit by flaming torches in holders down one side of the wall; their acrid smoke partially obscured the low ceiling, staining it and the wall behind them black. On the opposite side were a series of sturdy-looking oak doors with grills in them at head height. The stench of urine, sweat and fear hung in the air. The clatter of their sandals reverberated off the walls and ceiling.

'Antonia has her own private prison, it seems,' Magnus observed as Pallas stopped outside one of the doors and inserted a key into the lock.

Vespasian chuckled. 'I suppose this is where you'll end up if you stop performing for her.'

With an echoing, metallic clunk the lock turned; Pallas pushed open the door, walked in and reappeared an instant later dragging a filthy, naked, skeletal body by the ankles: Rhoteces. His long, straggly hair and beard were matted with shit. He had evidently been asleep because, as he was pulled into the light, his head jerked up and his eyes opened. He immediately started screaming, grabbed the doorframe and held on whilst trying to kick Pallas away.

'A little help would be appreciated, masters,' Pallas requested politely, 'but don't knock him out, I need him to swallow.'

None of them reacted for an instant, unwilling to go too near to the disgusting creature.

'Fuck it,' Magnus said, stepping forward and grabbing Rhoteces' wrists he hauled them away from the doorframe.

The commotion had disturbed the other prisoners in the corridor and shouts emanated from behind rattling doors.

'Master Vespasian, would you mind taking these?' Pallas' voice rose against the noise as he offered Vespasian the ankles.

Vespasian took hold of the spindly joints; they were so thin they felt as if they would crack if he held them too hard. A couple of sharp twists from Rhoteces disabused him of that notion and he gripped them with all his strength. He felt a tremendous sense of satisfaction that the man who he had witnessed so happily sacrificing Roman prisoners in Thracia four years previously had been reduced, during the past eight months, to nothing more than an animal.

'Sit him up,' Pallas said to Magnus as he pulled a vial out of his shoulder bag. 'Master Corbulo, grab his head and force his mouth open; Sabinus, hold a knife to his throat.'

Corbulo winced but did as he was asked. Vespasian suppressed a grin guessing that Pallas had saved the most unpleasant job for him.

With his head held back, mouth forced open, baring his pointed, filed teeth, and with a knife at his throat, Rhoteces went still. Pallas approached him and opened the vial. 'This won't kill you if you drink it but that knife at your throat will if you don't. Understand?'

Rhoteces wild eyes showed he had. Pallas tipped a quarter of the brown, viscous contents of the vial into his mouth and quickly held it shut, pinching the priest's nose. He swallowed.

'That will keep him sedated for twelve hours or so once it's kicked in,' Pallas informed them, 'it's what was used on Secundus yesterday. Let's get him upstairs.'

Rhoteces had evidently accustomed himself to whatever fate was in store for him and had ceased to struggle.

As they pulled the priest along the corridor Vespasian noticed behind one of the grills a pair of eyes pleading with him from beneath a mono-brow.

He ignored them.

Out in the stable yard Rhoteces was pushed into the two-horse, covered cart that had transported him from Ostia; because he was drugged no one had to have the unpleasant job of travelling with him.

Antonia appeared in the torchlight on the steps leading up to the house. Caenis was behind her; she clutched her medallion and blew Vespasian a surreptitious kiss.

'Gentlemen,' Antonia said, 'Macro has sent eight men of his previous command, the Vigiles, to escort you to the Capena Gate. I will pray and sacrifice every day for your success in this task. May the goddess Fortuna travel with you.'

She took each of them briefly by the hand and then they mounted up. Pallas climbed on to the front seat of the covered cart and took up the reins. The gates were hauled open to reveal the eight Vigiles, all holding flaming torches aloft; heavy clubs hung from their belts. With a click of his tongue and a flick of the reins Pallas urged the cart's horses forward; the iron-rimmed wheels grated over the paved floor of the stable yard. Vespasian kicked his mount forward to follow the cart out. As he reached the gates he turned in his saddle and caught Caenis' eye; he raised his hand in farewell, and she returned the gesture as he passed through the gates and out of sight.

The Vigiles led the way down the Palatine Hill and turned left on to the Via Appia as it ran alongside the huge, shadowy façade of the Circus Maximus and then passed under the inelegant but functional arches of the Appian Aqueduct to exit the city by the Capena Gate. The official escort and Antonia's ring were enough to persuade the centurion of the Urban Cohort to let them pass without question. Now deprived of the Vigiles escort, who had left them at the gate, they had to push their way through the throng of farmers making their way to the city to sell their produce. Passing the public reservoir on their right they came to the junction of the Via Appia and Via Latina, close by the tomb of the Scipios; here they took the right-hand fork, staying on the Via Appia, and headed southwest as the first glimmers of dawn broke up the absolute darkness of the cloud-ridden night sky.

Progress was easy along the dead straight road and, in just two and a half days, staying at comfortable inns along the way, paid for by the generous travelling allowance that Antonia had given Pallas, they covered the almost seventy miles to Tarracina, where the road arrived at the coast on the edge of the Caecuban wine district. Here the road turned east and they followed it through the seemingly endless fields of neatly tended rows of vines. Sumptuous-looking villas on hills overlooking the crops that provided the money to build them demonstrated the wealth of the wine-producing families of the region.

Vespasian spent much of the journey time contemplating the problems of the transfer of power between generations or dynasties and how it had been effected by other peoples in the past. The history books that he had inherited from his grandmother had originally inspired his interest and then, in the last three months at Gaius' house, he had belatedly taken up his uncle's offer of the use of his good-sized library. With not much else to do in the evenings he had made his way through Homer, Herodotus and Thucydides as well as Callisthenes' account of Alexander's conquests – curtailed owing to the author's execution by his subject. He had finally read Caesar and the more recently published *History of Rome* by Titus Livius. All these and more had widened his knowledge and understanding of politics and confirmed a truth in life: power and glory for their own sakes were the only motivations needed for the men who had sought them, to keep them; history was not littered with men like Cincinnatus.

Having spent the third night at Fundi they followed the road southwest again back to the sea and then along the coast. The March days were warming up and the sky stayed clear of clouds. The Tyrrhenian Sea sparkled to their right; trading ships and galleys passed to and fro in the busy sea lane between Ostia and Neapolis, now reopened after winter.

Passing Mount Massicus, they entered Campania and the Falerian wine district. Here the style of buildings became noticeably more Greek, attesting to the mixed ancestry of the Roman citizens of the region.

They spent the fifth night at the town of Volturnum, situated on the river of the same name, and had a pleasant meal on a vine-shaded terrace watching the fishermen offloading their catch after the day's fishing at sea, just two miles downstream. Leaving early in the morning, they travelled the last few miles at a decent pace and, as the sun began to sink towards the sea, they passed the Portus Julius – home to the western fleet – and approached the rocky promontory of Misenum, which rose from the sea like the arching back of a mythical sea monster.

'They seemed to be expecting us,' Magnus commented as the gate to the imperial cliff-top estate was swung closed behind them by two uniformed Praetorians.

'Macro must have sent a message in advance of us,' Vespasian replied as they rode up the paved path to the villa at the tip of the promontory. 'He said that his men guarded Misenum.'

'I don't know whether being guarded by Macro's men should make me feel safe or not.'

Vespasian grinned at his friend. 'I know the feeling; but I can assure you that it's a lot safer than being guarded by Sejanus'.'

'Let's hope that it never comes to that,' Magnus muttered.

They came to the whitewashed wall surrounding the villa and rode through an arch. Vespasian, along with all of his companions, gasped at the beauty of the place: set almost at the cliff's edge, the single-storey, pink-marble-walled villa with its terracotta-tiled roof overlooked the glittering bay of Neapolis, which was speckled with ships and dominated by the humped-back mass of Mount Vesuvius rising over four thousand feet from the coastal plain. In front of the villa was a circular pool, fifty feet in diameter, surrounded by a colonnade studded with statues pillaged from Greece and Asia. At its centre was a marble fountain depicting the sea god, Triton; his human torso blended into a fish tail as he seemed to leap from the depths of the pool spurting a gush of water skywards from his upturned mouth whilst brandishing a conch shell in his left hand and, like his father Poseidon, a trident in his right.

Around the pool the gardens were laid out with a pleasing symmetry. Eight wide, shrub-lined paths emanated at regular intervals from the colonnade and terminated in the circular path, upon which they now stood, that encompassed the whole garden. The path was rimmed with acacias and cypresses with low, stone benches at their feet to provide a shady place to sit and read or just to contemplate the beauty of the setting whilst enjoying the soft sea breeze on your face.

A girlish scream brought the party out of their silent admiration for the place. Vespasian looked towards the direction of the noise and saw Caligula, on the other side of the pool, running down one of the paths, chased by two young girls; all three were naked.

As he reached the pool he jumped in and started to wade across; the girls followed him, cupping their hands and splashing water over his back. On reaching the edge he made a show of not being able to climb out and the girls caught him and, jumping all over him, pulled him under. There was a playful thrashing of lithe limbs breaking the surface of the pool until eventually Caligula surfaced and rose to his feet with the youngest girl draped around his neck. He looked towards where Vespasian and his friends sat on their horses and, instantly recognising them, waved.

'At last,' he called. 'I've been so looking forward to this. Come over.'

With a degree of trepidation Vespasian led the party to the pool's edge whilst the girls, with much giggling and squealing, hauled Caligula under again. Vespasian dismounted and approached his friend, who had managed to get to his feet again. Caligula divested himself of the young girls to reveal the most prodigious erection, almost as big as the false phalluses worn by actors in satyr plays: nearly a foot long and with a girth and scrotum to match.

'Vespasian,' Caligula cried, stepping out of the pool and grasping Vespasian's forearm; his sunken eyes beamed with delight. 'It's good to see you. Look, I'm still alive – how about that? Tiberius hasn't decided to kill me; in fact quite the opposite, he's going to make me his heir.' He gave a short, semi-hysterical laugh. 'When I'm Emperor I'll be able to play with my sisters all the time. Drusilla, Livilla, this is my friend Vespasian and his brother Sabinus; you must both be very friendly to them.'

'Drusilla,' the elder of the two said, holding out her hand; she could not have been more than fifteen. She had a small but not unattractive mouth and slightly chubby cheeks. Her ivory skin glistened with water and her thick black hair hung in damp clumps and stuck to her shoulders. She made no attempt to cover her nakedness and Vespasian was unable to help his eyes drifting over her firm adolescent breasts and down to other points further south. She looked at him with appraising brown eyes as he took her hand.

'I'm very pleased to make your acquaintance,' he managed to say, tearing his eyes away from her nubile body and meeting hers.

'And I'm Julia Livilla,' the younger sister said, stepping out of the pool. 'I enjoy making new friends, especially if they're friends of dear Gaius.'

'This is a nice Livilla, not like that gruesome aunt of mine,' Caligula said, stroking her cheek; she clasped her arms around Caligula's neck and gave him an affectionate kiss on the lips whilst pressing her belly against his persistent erection. She was about two years younger than her sister; she shared Drusilla's small mouth but had higher, more pronounced cheekbones and a longer, sharper nose. Her breasts had just started to bud on her skinny ribcage.

Caligula disentangled himself from his sister and greeted Pallas, who managed to act as if there was absolutely nothing amiss, nodded briefly at Magnus and then approached Corbulo, who was standing with his mouth open, goggle-eyed and positively brimming with aristocratic outrage.

'This is Gnaeus Domitius Corbulo,' Vespasian told Caligula by way of an introduction.

'Hello,' Caligula exclaimed, and then leapt back into the pool, leaving Corbulo even more speechless than before.

'We shall have dinner soon,' Caligula said, resurfacing. 'Back to the house now, my sweets.'

His sisters giggled, and then, each with a hand grasping his magnificent penis, led their brother back to the villa.

'I'll find the house steward,' Pallas said, climbing back up on to the wagon, 'and get him to organise our rooms and horses.'

He flicked the reins and the wagon moved off around the pool. Vespasian followed, leading his horse and hoping that Caligula and his sisters would dress for dinner.

Vespasian stepped out of his room into the courtyard garden to find Clemens sitting with Sabinus on a stone bench under a fig tree. The garden was enclosed only on three sides, the southern end being left open to afford a stunning view over the Bay of Neapolis; in the distance, with its sheer cliffs glowing red in the last rays of the sun, lay Capreae.

'It's madness over there,' Clemens said as he clasped Vespasian's forearm. 'The old man's gone quite mad. He's obsessed by sex, death and astrology to the extent that he thinks about nothing else, apart from the construction of the new villa that he's building: the Villa Iovis. It's only half finished but he's moved into the completed part and has filled it with porno-graphic mosaics and frescoes. I sometimes wonder whether it might not be a good idea for Sejanus to become Emperor. At least he has Roman values. There's nothing Greek about him; you wouldn't find him sodomising the young sons of his supposed friends. And he'd keep death where it belongs: in the arena or on the battlefield.'

'Or in the law courts,' Vespasian added.

'Yes, well, there's always going to be an element of that no matter who's Emperor; but Tiberius goes too far. Our Republican ancestors would fall on their swords for shame if they saw some of the things that I've seen in the last few months. One time he got over a thousand slaves and had one of them gutted in front of the rest, who were told that any man who didn't do as he was ordered would die in the same painful fashion. He then lined them all up and made them masturbate until they were all erect – his young catamites went along the line helping any of them who was having a problem – and then forced them into a long line of buggery; over a thousand of them in a row, can you imagine it?'

Vespasian, much to his consternation, found himself able to.

'Then,' Clemens continued, 'he had a century of Praetorians – infantry, not my cavalry boys – go up and down the line stran-gling the slaves as they orgasmed and reminding those who hadn't what would happen to them if they stopped, even if they were pumping a dead man's arse.'

'That's not really the action of a Scipio or a Julius Caesar,' Vespasian agreed.

'What was Tiberius doing whilst all this was going on?' Sabinus asked, mildly fascinated by the whole image.

'He had the fifteen-year-old son of Lucius Vitellius Veteris fellating him.'

'What about Caligula? Was he there?' Vespasian asked hoping for an insight into his friend's eccentric behaviour that afternoon.

'Oh yes, and positively encouraging the old man,' Clemens replied, shaking his head. 'He's worked out that to stay alive around Tiberius you've got to seem to be interested in his new hobbies. The first couple of months he was there he was in a constant state of terror, thinking that Tiberius was going to execute him on a whim at any moment, which I think has unhinged him a bit.'

'A bit?' Vespasian queried. 'He was having sex with his sisters when we arrived.'

'He's been doing that for the last couple of years,' Clemens replied dismissively. 'He just can't help himself when it comes to women, including his own blood. What I mean by unhinged is that he seems to find it hard to concentrate on any one thing for too long and he's become prone to hysterical laughter for no reason; but other than that he's still very much the same: sexually insatiable but good company and full of life.'

'Well, I'm pleased to hear it,' Vespasian said, strangely unsurprised by Caligula's relationship with his sisters; he now understood the reason for Antonia's disapproval of his visits to Misenum.

Further discussion of the subject was put off by the arrival of the house steward to announce that dinner was ready. They followed the steward into the villa as the sun finally disappeared beyond the horizon leaving the evening star burning brightly over the placid Tyrrhenian Sea.

'Tiberius doesn't like to be surprised,' Caligula announced as the *gustatio* was cleared away, 'even if it's someone with good news or even a present.' He took a sip of his wine and then laughed briefly, before putting his hand on Vespasian's, who was reclining to his left on the same couch. 'Last month a fisherman scaled the cliffs to bring Tiberius the largest mullet I've ever seen. The old man was so unnerved by someone being able to get into his presence unannounced that he ordered one of his guards to scrub the man's face raw with the scales of the fish.' He paused whilst he adjusted something on Drusilla's dress; she reclined on Caligula's right and had her back towards him talking with Corbulo, who was uncomfortably sharing the next couch with a very friendly Julia Livilla.

'Anyway,' Caligula carried on, happy with whatever adjustment he had just made, 'the fisherman showed spirit and despite his obvious agony managed to crack a joke.' He started to giggle almost hysterically and eased himself closer to Drusilla. 'He said . . . he said: "Thank the gods that I didn't offer Caesar the huge crab that I caught."' Caligula broke off into peals of laughter whilst seemingly trying to get himself comfortable on the couch. Vespasian joined in the mirth along with Clemens and Sabinus, who reclined on the couch to the left.

'But then . . .' Caligula continued as he managed to get himself under control, 'but then Tiberius orders the crab to be found and has the fisherman's face rubbed with that; it almost took all his features off.' Caligula dissolved into hysterical laughter, which ended with a sudden jerk of his lower body and an abrupt grunt of pleasure. He reached for his wine cup. As Caligula drank, Vespasian took the opportunity to raise himself up slightly and look over him at Drusilla. He looked away very quickly. Her stola was raised above her buttocks; Caligula had evidently penetrated her, but, judging from the angle of their bodies, it was not by the standard method. Drusilla was carrying on her conversation with Corbulo as if nothing had happened; from the look on Corbulo's face Vespasian could guess that he knew perfectly well what was going on.

'So I've made sure that Uncle Tiberius is expecting you, without unsettling him,' Caligula continued as the next course – two large platters of mixed seafood – was served. A soft sea breeze blowing through the open window gently billowed the slaves' tunics as they padded around the table.

'How?' Vespasian asked, selecting a crayfish.

'He has an old charletan of an astrologer living over there called Thrasyllus who, incidentally, is the father of the lovely Ennia whom I met at dinner at my grandmother's house.'

'Macro's wife?' Sabinus queried.

'I believe that she is; far too good for him, I've a mind to try her myself. Anyway, this Thrasyllus spends most of his time telling Tiberius that he is going to live to oversee the changes that will start when the Phoenix flies again in Egypt in three years' time.'

'What's the Phoenix?' Corbulo asked, anxious to be distracted from the outrage being perpetrated so close to him.

'It's a bird that has a life cycle of five hundred years, at the end of which it bursts into flames and a new Phoenix is born from its ashes heralding the beginning of a new age. Anyway, Tiberius likes the fact that he's predicted to live for at least another three years so he listens to Thrasyllus; so I've persuaded him to predict that I'll receive important news from my grandmother brought by a friend.'

'But how will we get to Tiberius?'

'Every morning, after he's finished his . . . er . . . exercises, Tiberius and I go down to the unfinished part of Villa Iovis to check on the progress – he's particularly interested in a frieze he's having done in what will be his bedroom. So if we hide you in that room overnight I can warn him that the predicted news from Antonia has arrived and that I feel it's so important that I think he should hear it; hopefully he'll consent to seeing you.'

'Just make sure that there're no mullets or crabs handy,' Vespasian said, breaking open the crayfish and rubbing his finger up and down the sharp shell.

Caligula laughed slightly more uproariously than the remark merited and adjusted his position against Drusilla. 'Crabs!' he guffawed, passing a whole grilled baby octopus to his sister, who was having trouble reaching the platters on the table.

Vespasian had noted with a good deal of relief that the siblings seemed content to remain surreptitiously coupled and were not writhing around next to him. Corbulo just carried on staring at them in disbelief and seemed not only to have lost his appetite but also the battle with Julia Livilla, who now rested a friendly hand on his thigh.

'My men meeting you at the cove will take you to the

perimeter wall of the Villa Iovis,' Clemens said, getting the conversation back on track. 'I'll join you there once I've taken Caligula back to his quarters, and escort you to the room. My men will guard the door to make sure none of the artisans see you in the morning. Once you've seen Tiberius you'll stay in the room until it's dark and then we'll get you back to the cove; that way you shouldn't come to the attention of any of Sejanus' men.'

Vespasian and Sabinus both nodded in approval.

'If you think that it'll work, Clemens,' Sabinus said, 'then I'm happy.'

'It'll work,' Clemens replied, breaking off a hunk of bread and soaking it in the seafood juice at the bottom of the platter in front of him. 'The problem's going to be Tiberius' state of mind.'

'But Caligula said that he would forewarn him – didn't you?' Vespasian nudged his friend, who was now engrossed in feeding Drusilla prawns.

'What?' Caligula asked, teasing Drusilla with a prawn.

'I said: you were going to forewarn Tiberius so he should be in a decent mood when he sees us.'

'Oh yes, yes, absolutely,' Caligula replied turning his attention away from his sister. 'He should be, but that's just the trouble. Recently, when he's in a good mood, he's taken to having people thrown off the cliff-top just for fun; he finds it very amusing. He's been doing it so regularly to people he's invited over to the island as guests that he's even had a unit of marines, armed with clubs, stationed at the base of the cliff to finish off anyone unfortunate enough to survive the fall; he told me that doesn't want his guests to suffer unnecessarily for his pleasure. That's why a lot of the people whom he invites over commit suicide rather than accept the invitation.'

Caligula gave a short high-pitched laugh and went back to feeding Drusilla.

Vespasian looked aghast at Sabinus and Clemens and wondered just how much of this Antonia had known before she had sent them to see this madman on Capreae.

CHAPTER XVII

'CAREFUL WITH HIM,' Vespasian whispered to a couple of frightened-looking crewmen as they lowered the semi-conscious body of Rhoteces down to Magnus and Pallas waiting in a rowing boat at the stern of the decked bireme.

'Got him,' Magnus hissed up from the gloom below.

The crewmen then lowered down the party's bags before helping Corbulo and Sabinus – fresh from another bout of retching – over the side. They were all unarmed as it was a capital offence for anyone but a Praetorian Guardsman and the Emperor's German bodyguard to carry arms into Tiberius' presence.

Caligula clapped Vespasian on the shoulder as he prepared to follow. 'Another fun wheeze, eh, my friend?' His white teeth were visible in the dark as he grinned at Vespasian. 'And, if this works, it'll clear the way for me to become Emperor; just imagine the fun we'll have then.'

Since finding out what Tiberius considered amusing, Vespasian had started to wonder just what Caligula's definition of fun really was. 'You just make sure that Tiberius isn't in a cliff-hurling mood,' he replied, swinging his leg over the rail.

'I will. I might even get little Vitellius to join us on the walk down; that always seems to soothe Tiberius.'

'Do anything you want if you think it'll help make him reasonable.'

'Reasonable? Now, there's a strange word.'

Vespasian smiled despite himself; he slapped Caligula's arm and, with a brief nod to Clemens, lowered himself down the rope and into the boat.

'I've had enough of boats for a lifetime,' Sabinus said miserably as Vespasian took his place by the steering-oar. Corbulo pushed the little boat away from the bireme, Magnus and Pallas took up the oars and they started towards the shore. Above them the forbidding cliffs of Capreae, haloed by the silver light of the moon rising beyond them, loomed menacingly; Vespasian swallowed hard, imagining the terror of Tiberius' guests as they were hurled from them for no apparent reason.

The bireme was soon lost from view, heading towards a flaming beacon, half a mile up the coast, which marked the entrance to Capreae's harbour.

With a sudden jerk, Sabinus vomited over the side. 'This is agony,' he moaned, keeping his head lowered towards the water.

'Not as much agony as last night,' Corbulo observed; he was still in a state of shock at the conduct of his hosts at dinner. As the wine had begun to flow more liberally, Caligula's and his sisters' behaviour had deteriorated from what already was (to Corbulo's way of thinking) an outrageous affront to anyone brought up with Augustus' ethics into a scandalous breach of all Roman moral standards and of the etiquette governing behaviour not only at the dining table but everywhere in the Empire, both in public and private. Livilla's lewd attack on him with a goose leg had been the final straw and he had managed to withdraw, without causing too much offence, claiming to have eaten a bad prawn. Vespasian, Sabinus and Clemens had been forced endure it a while longer but had eventually been able to make their excuses, after politely declining offers to join in, once the writhing that Vespasian had dreaded had started in earnest. By this point Livilla had begun to apply her goose leg to Caligula, and the three siblings had been too involved in their own strange world to be unduly worried by their guests' departures.

After a few hundred pulls on the oars Vespasian saw a couple of glowing points of light on the coast and steered the boat towards them. Not long later, guided by the torches, the boat's hull scraped on shingle and two Praetorians waded out into the gently lapping waves to help haul it in.

'Troopers Fulvius and Rufinus of the Praetorian Guard Cavalry, reporting on Decurion Clemens' orders, sir,' the older of the two said, snapping a salute to Sabinus as he climbed unsteadily but gratefully out of the boat, helped by the other trooper.

Sabinus staggered slightly as the solid ground caused him to sway. 'Thank you, troopers.'

Within a short time the boat had been secreted in a cave, Rhoteces had been loaded on to Magnus' back (with, naturally, a lot of moaning from Magnus concerning the state of the priest's personal hygiene) and, with their bags slung over their shoulders, they were ready to move. Fulvius started to lead them up a steep but passable path that traversed back and forth up the cliff, which was not quite as sheer as it had first appeared. The going was slow and methodical as the torches had been extinguished and they were relying upon the light of the moon, but eventually they reached the summit.

Following the cliff line, they made their way, in silence, east over moonlit, uncultivated land. To his left Vespasian could see the flickering lights of Pompeii, Heraculaneum, Neapolis and Puteoli reflecting on the swelling water; they were interspersed with fainter points marking the positions of the grand coastal villas of Rome's élite. Here and there in the darkness between the mainland and the island were dotted the solitary lamps of night fishermen. From below came the sound of waves breaking on the jagged rocks at the base of the cliff. A warm breeze blew from the west carrying upon it the scent of wild thyme.

After almost half an hour of steady walking they came to a high stone wall at the eastern tip of the island. Much to Vespasian's surprise Clemens was already waiting for them, sitting astride a horse.

'Any problems?' he asked, uncoiling a rope.

'None, sir,' Fulvius replied.

'Good; hold the horse,' Clemens said, pulling his legs up to kneel on the saddle. Steadying himself on the wall he stood up and threw one end of the rope over, then, grabbing the top of the wall, he pulled himself up and disappeared over the other side.

'It's secured,' he called over softly a few moments later.

Apart from a slight delay whilst they hauled Rhoteces up and over, they made it into the moonlight-dappled grounds of the Villa Iovis with ease.

'It's a fucking building site,' Magnus whispered in surprise to Vespasian as Clemens untied the rope from a huge oak beam lying on the ground. All around in the dim light Vespasian could see piles of bricks and cut stone; sections of columns lay on their sides amongst stacks of terracotta roofing tiles and wicker baskets. Magnus dipped his hand into one of the baskets and pulled out a handful of small marble squares.

'Looks like Tiberius has a few mosaics planned for his pleasure palace,' he remarked, letting them fall with a light clatter.

'This way,' Clemens whispered, leading them off crouching low and weaving through the construction detritus down a slope towards the massive hulk of the unfinished Villa Iovis just four hundred paces away. A few lights in the windows on the far side of the building showed that they were approaching it from the incomplete, uninhabited side.

With a hundred paces to go the building supplies petered out and Clemens halted them by the last heap of bricks. 'Stay here,' he ordered. 'There's normally a guard stationed close by; I'll draw him out.'

He stood up and walked purposefully towards the villa.

'Halt!' a voice shouted as he was halfway across the open ground. 'Stand and identify yourself.'

Two uniformed Praetorians appeared from the shadows and ran towards Clemens, who stood motionless.

'Decurion Clemens, first ala Praetorian Guard Cavalry,' Clemens shouted at the approaching guards.

'What are you doing out here, sir? You've no authority to be here at night, you'll have to come with us.'

'I was looking for you; I thought that I saw movement just up the hill,' Clemens replied, pointing in the direction of Vespasian and his comrades.

'Shit, he's giving us away, the bastard,' Magnus hissed as Clemens started to lead the two guards towards them.

'I find that highly unlikely,' Pallas said calmly.

Fulvius and Rufinus drew their swords; Vespasian automatically went for his only to remember that it was back at Misenum.

'Don't move,' Fulvius said, standing and pointing his sword at Corbulo. Rufinus stood over Vespasian and stuck the tip of his sword against his back. 'Over here, sir,' he called to Clemens.

Vespasian felt sick; unarmed and against five Praetorians they did not stand a chance and would surely be taken prisoner. He had a brief vision of being hurled off the cliff and swore vengeance on Clemens in this world or the next.

'Well, well, what have we here?' Clemens drawled, his pinched face leering over them through the gloom. The two Praetorians stood either side of him and drew their swords. 'Fish food would be my guess. Tie them up.'

'You little cunt, Clemens,' Sabinus spat. 'How much did Sejanus pay you to widow your own sister?'

Magnus made a jump for Fulvius, aiming his head at the Praetorian's groin. A sharp crack from the hilt of Fulvius' sword on the back of Magnus' head sent him crashing to the floor unconscious. Rufinus kicked Vespasian to the ground, stepped over him and with a lightning thrust planted his sword into the mouth of the Praetorian to Clemens' left as Clemens wrapped his right forearm around the other's throat and, with his left hand, grabbed the man's head and jerked it violently to one side; with a loud crack the neck snapped and the man went limp.

'You bastard, Clemens,' Sabinus growled, 'you had me there.'

'Sorry about that.' Clemens grinned. 'I wasn't expecting two of them and I couldn't take them both on. I needed help getting rid of them; they would have taken me to the guardhouse and I would have had some difficult explaining to do in the morning. Let's get the bodies over the cliff.' He grabbed a lifeless arm and started to pull it away; Sabinus, shaking his head, made to help him.

With adrenalin still coursing through his veins Vespasian helped Rufinus drag the other body the fifty paces to the cliff-top.

'How did you know to kill the two Guards?' he asked.

'I thought he was double-crossing you too,' Rufinus replied, 'until he ordered us to tie you up, then I knew what to do.'

'How?'

'Because, since a fisherman scaled the cliff, Tiberius' standing order is that all intruders should be executed on sight, no exceptions.'

'Well, I hope that he makes an exception of us tomorrow,' Vespasian said as they reached the cliff's edge.

'I've never known him to,' Rufinus said plainly.

They toppled the Praetorian over the edge. Vespasian peered over and briefly glimpsed the body spinning in the air before disappearing into the darkness; the roar of the waves crashing into the base of cliff swallowed any sound it made as it hit the rocks below. He turned to go with the sensation of falling preying on his mind.

Upon returning to his companions he found that Magnus was still unconscious and was obliged to carry him with Pallas; Sabinus and Corbulo took Rhoteces.

They quickly crossed the open ground in front of the villa and entered its dark corridors through an unfinished doorway.

With surprising speed Clemens navigated his way through the maze of passageways illuminated by faint moonlight seeping through open windows.

Eventually he stopped outside a huge door and pushed it open. They followed him in and found themselves in a cavernous room; their footsteps echoed off the high ceiling. Rhoteces was dumped unceremoniously on the floor.

'Fulvius and Rufinus will stand guard until Caligula brings the Emperor,' Clemens said. 'I will come too to share whatever fate he decides for you.'

'Thank you, Clemens,' Sabinus said, taking his brother-in-law's forearm.

Clemens returned the grip with a grin. 'There are plenty of workmen's buckets around to piss in. Good luck.' He turned and slipped out of the door followed by Fulvius and Rufinus.

As Vespasian and Pallas laid Magnus down he stirred, opened his eyes and then groaned. 'Shit! Now we're for it. They've got us,' he said, rubbing the back of his head.

'They've got us in more like,' Vespasian said, helping his friend up.

'What? I thought they were arresting us.'

'Well, you should have stuck around and seen what happened next instead of trying to play the hero and attacking the wrong person.'

'You mean Clemens was genuine after all and we're not in some prison?'

'Look around.' Vespasian waved his arm at the faintly lit room. 'If this looks like a prison to you, I think that Tiberius would be very pissed off; we're in his new bedroom.'

With the rising of the sun the room gradually filled with light that poured in from four windows high above the door and Vespasian could see the scale of it: it was a perfect cube with the high marble ceiling forty feet above him. Along the wall opposite the door was the unfinished frieze that Tiberius was taking so much interest in; after only a cursory glance at it Vespasian could understand why: it depicted every carnal pleasure known to man in a series of vivid scenes, involving adults, children and beasts, and left nothing to the imagination.

'Making mental notes, are you, brother?' Sabinus asked, catching Vespasian gawping at a cruelly used mule.

'You have to admire the workmanship,' he replied, ignoring yet again his brother's implication, 'even if the subject matter is somewhat obscene.'

'Somewhat? I've never seen anything like it,' Corbulo said, 'not even in the—' He stopped abruptly and blushed.

'In the brothels along the Vicus Patricius back in Rome?' Magnus questioned, helpfully trying to finish Corbulo's sentence for him.

Corbulo gave Magnus a foul look and then busied himself pulling his toga from his bag.

'I've got bread, salt pork and wine, masters,' Pallas said, walking over having gagged Rhoteces who was starting to come out of his drugged state in the corner. 'We should eat and then change our clothes in readiness for meeting the Emperor.'

*

An hour later they were sitting around on upturned buckets, each busy with his own thoughts and worries about the coming interview. There had been a couple of conversations outside the door as Fulvius and Rufinus had prevented workmen from entering, but the door itself had remained shut.

Suddenly there was the sound of feet coming quickly down the corridor; the door burst open and in walked an old but still vigorous man. Vespasian recognised him instantly; he was the most powerful and feared man in the Roman world: Tiberius.

They jumped up as one from their buckets and bowed their heads. At the top of his vision Vespasian could see Tiberius' hair-less legs protruding from under his pure purple tunic; they were traced with an extraordinary amount of varicose veins that wove their way around the open sores and dried scabs on the shiny, tight skin on his shin-bones. His feet were shod in a pair of regulation military sandals; his horn-like toenails were yellowing and ridged.

Tiberius strode towards Vespasian and stopped directly in front of him. Vespasian's heartbeat accelerated and he had to consciously stop himself from shaking; he found himself wondering why Tiberius did not have his toenails pared for him.

'Is this the one, my sweet?' Tiberius asked of someone standing at the doorway, out of Vespasian's field of vision. His voice was low and grated in his throat; it sounded distant, as though he was somewhat detached from the world.

'Yes, Nuncle,' Caligula's voice replied, 'that's him; he's my friend.' His voice was slightly strained, as if trying to appear light and nonchalant whilst concealing a nervousness born from the knowledge that a very important decision was about to be made.

'Your friend, you say?'

'Yes, Nuncle, my friend.'

'His name is Vespasian, is that right, my sweet?'

'Yes, that's right, Nuncle: Vespasian.'

'Look at me, Vespasian.'

Vespasian raised his eyes; large, rheumy, grey eyes peered back at him questioningly, as if trying but failing to focus on what was in front of them. Tiberius' face would once have been considered handsome but was now ravaged by the effects of heavy drinking: puffy-skinned and florid. His white hair was cut short at the fringe and above the ears but hung down in greasy strands over his neck. Flakes of dried skin peeled off his earlobes; there was a virulent pimple on the tip of his nose.

Tiberius placed his left hand on the crown of Vespasian's head and exerted a monumental pressure so that Vespasian felt that his thumb and forefinger would burst through his skull.

'He is still young enough for me to push my fingers into his brain, my sweet,' Tiberius observed, still staring into Vespasian's eyes with that questioning, almost puzzled look. His breath held the unmistakable reek of fresh human faeces.

'Yes, Nuncle, he is; but then I wouldn't have my friend any more.' Caligula's voice had risen slightly.

The pressure on Vespasian's head suddenly increased.

'But I'm your friend,' Tiberius abruptly shouted.

'Yes, Nuncle, you are; but you're my friend here. Vespasian is my friend in Rome; you don't go to Rome so I need a friend when I'm there.'

Tiberius released his grip. Vespasian had to stop himself from rubbing his throbbing head.

'But what happens if I come back to Rome?' Tiberius asked, still staring at Vespasian.

'If you do I won't need another friend in Rome, Nuncle, and you can push your fingers into his brain then.'

'In Rome then,' Tiberius said, suddenly cheerily as if a difficult matter had been finally settled by the simplest and most obvious of solutions.

Vespasian breathed a sigh of relief as Tiberius turned his attention to the other members of his party; he felt that he at least was safe for the time being. Caligula nodded towards him surreptitiously from the doorway, confirming his belief. Next to Caligula stood a very pretty youth in his mid teens; his hair had been decorated with flowers and his white tunic was embroidered with gold thread around the hem and sleeve. Behind him, between Fulvius and Rufinus, Clemens stood stock-still with his hand on his sword hilt, looking even more pallid than usual.

'What about these, my sweet? What are they?' Tiberius cast his eyes slowly over Sabinus, Corbulo, Magnus and then Pallas. 'Not more fishermen?'

'Of course not, Nuncle, you don't allow fishermen here any more,' Caligula replied, choosing his words carefully. 'These men have come with my friend with that important news that Thrasyllus predicted would arrive. One has a letter from Antonia to you.'

'They're not intruders then, come to destroy my peace of mind?'

'It's to help your peace of mind that they have come, Nuncle.'

Tiberius stared at Pallas for a while; nobody moved. 'I know you,' he said eventually, pointing his finger at the Greek. 'You're Antonia's steward. Your name is Pallas, isn't it?'

'I am honoured that you should even recognise me let alone know my name, Princeps,' Pallas replied, bowing. Even with the life-or-death tension in the air he still remained outwardly calm and composed; Vespasian was sweating freely despite the coolness of the morning.

'She would have given you the letter; give it to me.'

Pallas reached down into his bag; Tiberius jumped back. Realising his mistake, Pallas quickly removed his hand from the bag and tipped it upside down so that the contents fell to the floor with a clatter. It was the first time that Vespasian had seen the smooth Greek flustered and he found himself enjoying the sight.

Pallas picked up the scroll and offered it to Tiberius; the Emperor looked at it closely and then, evidently satisfied that it would do him no harm, took it.

'My mistress has sent her seal ring, Princeps,' Pallas said, holding up his hand, which was visibly shaking, 'to show you that the letter is genuine.'

Tiberius dismissed it with a wave. 'You're proof enough of that,' he said plainly, looking at the scroll and feeling its weight in the palm of his hand. His voice had become less detached as though the presence of a letter from his sister-in-law had helped to draw him out of the dark world in his head into which he had evidently deeply sunk. He looked at Sabinus as if seeing him for the first time. 'And you are?' he asked with almost genuine interest.

'Titus Flavius Sabinus, Princeps,' Sabinus replied hastily.

'Ah yes, tribune with the Ninth Hispana,' Tiberius said without pausing to think, 'served with distinction in Africa against Tacfarinas' rebellion; a good man according to the reports I read.'

'Thank you, Princeps,' Sabinus spluttered, stunned, as they all were, by the Emperor's sudden lucidity.

'You will all stay here under Clemens' guard whilst I read this letter; Vitellius will keep you company.' Tiberius indicated the pretty youth. 'He has certain talents. Come, my sweet; let's see what your grandmother has been up to.'

Tiberius swept out of the room; Caligula raised his eyebrows at Vespasian and followed.

When the sound of the Emperor's footsteps in the corridor had disappeared Vespasian and his companions all sank back down on to their buckets in exhausted relief.

They sat in silence for a long while, all contemplating how close to death they just had come. A loud moaning from the corner of the room brought them out of their reverie; Rhoteces had fully woken up.

'Do something about him would you, please, Pallas?' Vespasian said irritably; he hated the sound of the priest just as much as everything else about him.

'I'm afraid we have to keep him conscious for now, master,' Pallas replied, his composure returned. 'He may be questioned soon.'

Although that thought cheered Vespasian the increasing noise that the priest was making grated on his already taut nerves. 'Fucking shut up,' he shouted to no effect.

'Would you like me to soothe you, Vespasian?' Vitellius asked, walking over to him and laying a soft hand on his shoulder.

'What?' Vespasian exclaimed, looking up aghast at the youth. 'No!' He angrily brushed Vitellius' hand away.

'You're disgusting. Have you no sense of honour, boy?' Sabinus spat. 'You're a son of the Vitellii, an old and noble family; what are you doing prostituting yourself like a harbour whore?'

'If I don't then I'll die,' Vitellius replied simply. 'You've seen what he's like.'

'And you'd rather live in shame as his catamite than die like a man?'

'To me that seems to be preferable; shame doesn't matter to me. I've given up my honour and pride in order to live, just as my father did when he gave me to Tiberius in return for his life. This way, one day, I'll have my revenge upon all those who have abused me, or if they're dead then upon their families.' Vitellius looked at Sabinus with steel in his eyes.

Sabinus returned his look in full measure. 'I wouldn't suck another man's cock if my life depended on it, you degenerate.'

'I hope that one day your life will depend on it; then we'll see what you'll choose, Titus Flavius Sabinus.' Vitellius turned on his heel and walked out of the room.

'Whore boy!' Sabinus shouted after him.

'This place does weird things to people,' Magnus commented as the door slammed.

'It's not the place,' Pallas said, standing over Rhoteces and showing him a knife, which quietened him down, 'it's the power. Absolute power will reduce anyone who holds it to a state of depravity if they are weak-willed or morally flawed.'

'Then may the gods help us if Caligula becomes Emperor,' Corbulo said, shaking his head. 'I can't believe that I'm helping that eventuality to come about. Perhaps we should return to the Republic where two men shared that power for one year only.'

'It's too late for that,' Vespasian asserted. 'The wealth of the Empire is concentrated in too few hands; the days of the citizen soldier who fights alongside his neighbour to defend their small plots of land are long gone.'

'What's that got to do with it?' Sabinus asked dismissively. 'Every man in the legions is a citizen.'

'Yes, but now it's upside down: instead of fighting to defend his land in order to return to it after a summer of campaigning, the common legionary is fighting to gain some land after his twenty-five years' service.'

'What difference does that make? The army is still the army no matter what the motivation of the common legionary is.'

'We've already seen what a difference it makes during the years of civil wars, from the time that Gaius Marius made the army professional until Augustus created the Empire. Do you want those days to come again?'

'No, of course not,' Sabinus conceded grudgingly: he didn't like being bested by his brother, no matter how much the logic of his argument rang true. 'So what do you suggest, brother, seeing as you seem to have been thinking about it?'

'I have been thinking about it a lot actually; all the way down the Via Appia from Rome.'

'Enlighten us with your wisdom then.'

'I believe that there is a straight choice: either the Empire is ruled and held together firmly by one man; or it disintegrates as the legions in the provinces declare their support for any general who feels that his dignitas has been violated in return for him providing them with the best land available. If that were to happen then we'd either destroy ourselves completely through civil war and be overrun by Parthia from the East and the barbarian tribes from the North; or the generals would fight each other to a standstill and the Empire would break up into its constituent parts: Italia, Illyria and Greece, for example, then Gaul and Hispania, perhaps Africa, Asia and Egypt and so on – much as what happened to Alexander's Empire. They'd all be ruled by Romans but, like Alexander's successors, would always be fighting amongst themselves until they too would be swallowed up, in the same way that we and the Parthians gradually ate away at the Successor States.'

'How come you know so much about history all of a sudden?' Sabinus was incredulous.

'Because recently, brother, instead of spending all my spare time on top of a lovely young wife, I've been making use of our grandmother's and Uncle Gaius' extensive libraries; it may not be as exhausting but it's just as stimulating.'

Sabinus grunted.

'But what happens when the man who's supposed to be holding the Empire together goes mad?' Corbulo asked. 'As Tiberius seems to have done and Caligula almost certainly will if he inherits?'

'Well, that's what I've been thinking about,' Vespasian replied. 'If you accept the fact that the Empire needs an Emperor then you have to ask yourself how you choose him. As much as I like Caligula, his conduct last night was disillusioning and unacceptable. His obvious inability to discern appropriate behaviour makes him the worst possible person to hand unfettered power – but he's in line for it purely because he comes from the imperial family.'

'So do away with the imperial family?' Magnus suggested with a grin.

'Do away with the idea that the Emperor is succeeded by one of his family,' Corbulo said, nodding.

'Exactly. Look at the choices there are left to Tiberius from within his family: Caligula, Claudius or Tiberius Gemellus; which one would you want as your master?'

'None of them,' Sabinus answered wearily.

'So the Emperor should choose the best man in Rome to succeed him and adopt him as his son, for the sake of Rome not for the sake of his loyalty to his family. Then the idea of an imperial family – and the dynastic power struggles within it – would disappear for ever and, provided the right choices are made, we would be ruled by a man who can handle absolute power.'

'That all sounds very worthy, master,' Pallas observed, 'but how would you persuade the imperial family to release their grip on power?'

'That's the problem, I don't know,' Vespasian admitted.

'There'll be another war,' Corbulo said gloomily. 'Rome won't take someone like Caligula as Emperor for long.'

'Well, if there is,' Vespasian said hopefully, 'whoever eventually emerges as the victor would do well to follow that policy: forget the idea of forging a dynasty and adopt the most able man as his son and heir.'

'But what happens, master,' Pallas asked shrewdly, 'when by far and away the most able man in Rome is the new Emperor's own son?'

The door opened before Vespasian could answer and Clemens walked in. 'The Emperor has summoned you to his study,' he said almost apologetically. 'I'm afraid that means your presence here will no longer be secret.'

'What proof does she have?' Tiberius, waving Antonia's letter, demanded the instant they were let into his spacious study by a quizzical-looking German imperial bodyguard. Caligula was sitting on a window seat with his eyes closed, enjoying the warm sun on his face, seemingly without a care in the world.

Pallas took the lead as the door closed behind them. 'Princeps, that list is in Sejanus' own handwriting.'

Tiberius picked up the list, looked closely at it and then threw it back down on to the marble-topped desk. 'It may well be but it's just a list of names, it's not proof.'

'Nuncle, if everyone on that list were dead then who would be Emperor?' Caligula asked mildly without opening his eyes. 'No one from our family, that's for sure.'

'But Sejanus is going to be one of our family; I gave him permission to become betrothed to Livilla, my daughter-in-law.'

'I know, Nuncle, and you were so right to do that,' Caligula said soothingly, 'but perhaps it was a little bit rash. You told me yourself that you were worried about him; that's why you sent him away to be Consul.'

'Yes, I did, didn't I?' Tiberius gazed at a large pornographic picture adorning the wall between his desk and the window, as if he was reverting to the state that he had been in when he had first looked at Vespasian. 'But I need to be sure, I need to be sure; he keeps me safe, so safe, and takes so much of the load that I bear off my shoulders.'

'Princeps, may I speak?' Sabinus asked nervously.

Tiberius did not respond for a few moments but then turned his rheumy eyes to Sabinus; he suddenly jolted. 'Titus Flavius Sabinus of the Ninth Hispana, a good man. Yes, yes, speak.'

Sabinus told the Emperor of his discovery of the discrepancy in the mint and how the chests of denarii had ended up in Thracia.

Tiberius did not seem to be listening but as Sabinus petered out to what he feared was a flat ending to his story the Emperor became quite alert again.

'So who saw this money in Thracia?' he asked, looking around the room.

'I did, Princeps,' Corbulo volunteered.

Tiberius looked shocked for a moment, as if he had not noticed Corbulo before. 'Who are you?' he snapped. 'When did you arrive?'

'Gnaeus Domitius Corbulo, Princeps,' Corbulo replied proudly.

'You were a praetor early on in my reign. Never made Consul, though,' Tiberius responded.

'That was my father, Princeps,' Corbulo said, visibly pleased that the Emperor should know the name.

'Father, eh? You're the son? Never heard of you,' Tiberius said crushingly. 'Well, tell me what you saw.'

Corbulo gave his account, mentioning Hasdro's and Rhoteces' part but, as instructed, not Poppaeus'.

Tiberius looked at him dully when he had finished. 'So what were you doing in Thracia?'

'I was a tribune on Poppaeus' staff.'

Tiberius seemed uninterested. 'And who else saw this?' he asked dismissively, as if Corbulo's word was worth nothing.

'I did, Princeps,' Vespasian said.

'Ah, my sweet's friend,' Tiberius crooned. 'My sweet, your friend says he saw a box of money given by Sejanus' freedman to a Thracian tribe to encourage them into rebellion against me.'

'Then you should believe him, Nuncle,' Caligula said, still with his eyes closed, 'he's a very good friend.'

'But I do, I do!' Tiberius was now almost in a state of ecstasy. 'Yes, I can see that he's a very good friend indeed.'

'We have brought the priest with us, Princeps,' Vespasian ventured, 'so that you can question him yourself.'

Tiberius' joy was complete. 'Ahh, pain,' he moaned feverishly. 'Where is he? Bring him to me.'

Rhoteces' broken body lay strapped to a sturdy wooden table in the middle of Tiberius' study. He had just passed out for the second time, his right foot being no more than charred, smouldering bones, some of which had fallen off into the mobile brazier below. The stink of burnt flesh filled the smoke-enveloped room; a strong shaft of sunlight cut through the heavy atmosphere and fell on to the contorted priest.

Tiberius had administered the torture himself, taking, as Vespasian had expected, an inordinate amount of pleasure in Rhoteces' every scream and cry for mercy, as if he was listening to the most beautiful and relaxing music. Although he had told them everything that he knew the moment his foot was placed upon the brazier Tiberius had persisted in his pleasure.

'So this man says that it was Asinius whom he was working for,' Tiberius said. He was quite lucid again, looking with deep interest at Rhoteces' charred foot; he gingerly touched one of the blackened bones and, finding it still scalding hot, withdrew his finger quickly and sucked away the pain.

'Yes, Princeps,' Pallas answered, 'but he described Hasdro perfectly. Hasdro told him that he was working for Asinius to protect his master, Sejanus, in the eventuality that something like . . .' He paused, and waved his hand at what remained of the foot. 'Like this should occur.'

'I suppose that makes sense,' Tiberius agreed, 'but then what was Poppaeus' part in this?' He turned to Corbulo. 'You, you were on Poppaeus' staff, did you ever see him with Hasdro?'

'No, Princeps,' Corbulo lied; Vespasian could see that it stuck in his craw to do so.

'Well, I'll forget about him for the time being,' Tiberius said to himself, sucking his burnt finger again. 'But one day he'll pay for allowing his army to address him as "Imperator" – when he's no longer of any use to me.' He looked around suddenly, aware that he had externalised a private thought. 'So it seems that I was right all along,' he carried on cheerfully. 'Sejanus is a traitor. I knew it, but it takes my dear, dear sister-in-law to show me the evidence and you . . .' He held his arms out, encompassing them all; a look of deep emotion came over his face and Vespasian thought for a moment that he would burst into tears. 'You brave, brave, loyal men, good men, men with my peace of mind in the forefront of your hearts, you men have risked so much to bring it to me. You will go back to Rome and tell Antonia that I will act at once. Come, we shall all take a walk together.'

The gardens on the inhabited side of the Villa Iovis had been laid out on a slope that ran down to the cliff-top; a tall wall masking off the building works gave them privacy.

Tiberius led them, escorted by Clemens and his two men, down a set of grand steps lined with statues of naked gods and heroes on to a wide marble path that bisected the gardens and terminated, as far as Vespasian could make out, at the cliff's edge, two hundred paces away. On either side, shrubs and bushes were bursting into life encouraged by the spring sun and an irrigation system that pumped water at regular intervals through pipes directly into the beds.

This same system provided the water for the many fountains that fed ornamental pools set on descending levels so that the water cascaded downhill, falling from one pool into the next. The pools were surrounded by small, lifelike statues that, to Vespasian's amazement, came alive as the Emperor approached. The statues turned out to be children, adolescents and dwarves, who began to cavort lewdly around the pools' edges, occasionally jumping in, either in pairs or groups, to copulate freely in the shallow water.

'My fishies have awoken,' Tiberius cried, waving his hands with joy. 'Swim and play, my fishies; I will join you later. Will you come and play with the fishies with me, my sweet?'

'Yes, Nuncle,' Caligula replied with what Vespasian hoped was feigned enthusiasm, 'but after my friend and his companions have gone.'

'Perhaps they would like to join us?'

'I'm sure that they would, Nuncle, what could be more fun for them? But unfortunately they must return to Rome, as you've instructed.'

'Yes, yes, Rome; they must go back to Rome,' Tiberius said sadly.

'And you said', Caligula carried on carefully, 'that you would tell them what course of action you'll take against that wicked man, Nuncle, so that they can warn Antonia, who's your friend, and she can be ready to help you.'

Tiberius stopped abruptly and glared at Caligula, who looked momentarily afraid but then managed to cover it with a look of placid innocence.

'I didn't say that, you little viper!' Tiberius roared. 'Are you trying to upset my peace of mind?'

Caligula went down on to one knee. 'Forgive me, Princeps,' he said humbly, 'sometimes I'm just so happy here that I muddle things up.'

Although terrified and unable to take his eyes off the potentially fatal situation in front of him, Vespasian noticed that the fishies had become living statues once again; all had frozen in whatever act they were performing at the point of their master's roar.

Tiberius stared down at Caligula; rage burned all over his face and he clenched and unclenched his fists. He cocked his head a couple of times, clicking his neck, and then, gradually, he began to calm.

'Yes, yes, my sweet, I know,' he eventually sighed, 'it's so easy to muddle things up when one is so happy.' He held out his hand and helped Caligula up. Vespasian and his party, who had all been holding their breath, exhaled with relief simultaneously; the noise caused Tiberius to spin around and stare at them as if he had forgotten that they were there. After a terrifying moment his eyes registered recognition.

'When you get to Rome tell Antonia that next month I will resign my consulship,' he said evenly. 'That will force Sejanus to do the same and his person will no longer be inviolate. I will write to the Senate detailing his treacheries and demanding his arrest and trial; then I shall replace him. I know this Macro whom

Antonia has recommended in her letter; he's married to my good friend Thrasyllus' daughter Ennia. I'm sure that he is up to the job and and able to shoulder some of my burden; he's a good man.'

'He is a good man, Princeps,' Pallas confirmed, using a definition of "good" that Vespasian had never heard before.

'And his wife is a beauty, Nuncle,' Caligula informed him. 'I dined with her at Grandmother's house once; I'd like to see her again.'

'That settles it. I shall arrange for him to visit me here; he can bring his wife so that she can play with my sweet. Come and look over the cliffs with me.' Tiberius turned and walked purposefully down the path.

The fishies resumed their play.

At the end of the path a brown-skinned, grey-bearded man wearing a leather skull-cap and a long, black robe embroidered with astrological signs and symbols stood looking out to sea.

'Thrasyllus, my friend,' Tiberius called in Greek as they approached the cliff-edge, 'is it an auspicious time to make changes? I must know because a change needs to be made.'

Thrasyllus turned to face the Emperor. 'The stars say that you are the master of change, Princeps,' he replied in a melodramatic, quavering voice. 'You are here to oversee the greatest change of all: the dawn of the new age. Even now the Phoenix is preparing to fly to Egypt, the country of my birth, where in three years' time flames will consume it and it will be reborn from the ashes of its body; a new five-hundred-year cycle will commence. The world will change, and you, Princeps, through your wisdom and greatness, will guide the Empire through that change.'

'I'll wait three years then,' Tiberius said suddenly deflated.

Vespasian glanced at Caligula in alarm, concerned that the astrologer would deflect Tiberius from his purpose.

'You may find that the waiting will play on your peace of mind, Nuncle,' his young friend said; his voice oozed concern. 'I think that the venerable Thrasyllus was talking about major changes, not the little one that you plan now.'

'Of course he was, my sweet,' Tiberius agreed, relieved. 'If I don't do this now I won't live to see the firebird. Thrasyllus, consult your books.'

The astrologer bowed. 'I will have an answer for you by morning, Princeps,' he said theatrically. With a brief glance at Caligula he turned and headed back up the path.

Looking pleased with himself, Tiberius sat down on a stone bench that overlooked the narrow passage between Capreae and the mainland, dominated by the brooding Mount Vesuvius. Caligula went to sit next to him whilst the rest of the group placed themselves nervously behind them, uncomfortable at being so close to the cliff's edge in Tiberius' company.

It was past noon and the day had warmed up considerably; the sun beat down upon the Tyrrhenian Sea sending an ever-changing multitude of sparkles reflecting up off its deep blue, undulating surface. Gulls soared above them calling balefully as they rode the currents of the fresh sea breeze.

'I wish that I could fly like them, my sweet,' Tiberius declared, admiring the agile birds. 'There must surely be peace as you glide through the air.'

It was not the sort of conversation that Vespasian had hoped for in this situation.

'Yes, Nuncle, but we will never know it,' Caligula replied guardedly, as if he had had this conversation many times before and knew the conclusion.

Tiberius remained silent for a while contemplating the gulls. 'I hate the limitations of this body,' he said suddenly with passion. 'I'm master of the changing world yet I am earthbound.'

'We should go and play with the fishies, Nuncle,' Caligula said in an effort to change the subject.

'Ah, the fishies, yes, yes, we should,' Tiberius replied, rising to his feet. 'We must say goodbye to your friend first.' He turned to face Vespasian. 'Go with my thanks and prayers,' he said formally. 'Clemens will escort you to the port on my authority.'

They bowed their heads and, with communal relief, turned to go.

'Wait!' Tiberius shouted. 'Who is this?' He pointed his finger at Magnus. 'I haven't seen him before; he must be an intruder, perhaps even another fisherman. Clemens, have your men throw him off the cliff.'

'Nuncle, that is Magnus, he's a friend of my friend; he's been with us all the time.'

'I've not spoken with him, I don't know him; Clemens, do as I command.'

Caligula signalled them to remain silent as Fulvius and Rufinus grabbed Magnus' arms and pushed him forward. Magnus looked beseechingly at Vespasian as he struggled in their grip. Vespasian and the rest of them watched aghast as Magnus was forced towards certain death.

'I knew there was a reason for coming here, my sweet,' Tiberius crooned in pleasure. 'I do so enjoy the look of terror in a man's eyes just before he flies through the air.'

'Yes I know, Nuncle,' Caligula replied as Magnus was nearing the edge, 'but you also like to hear them scream as well; this one's a brave one, he's not screaming or pleading.'

'You're right, my sweet, he's not.'

'But I know one who will.'

'Then we should throw him over.'

'That's a good idea, Nuncle. Clemens, have your men fetch that priest immediately,' Caligula ordered.

Clemens understood. 'Fulvius, get the priest right now.'

Fulvius and Rufinus let go of Magnus, who was left shaking on the brink of the cliff, and ran back towards the villa.

'I'll say goodbye to my friend whilst we wait, Nuncle; he should go and take all his companions with him, to get your message to Antonia as soon as possible.'

'Yes, yes, my sweet,' Tiberius replied absently, his attention back on the gulls. 'And then we can play with the fishies.'

'Good idea, Nuncle,' Caligula said, whilst hurriedly pulling Magnus back from the edge. 'I'll see you there once they've gone.'

Caligula led them swiftly back up the path, past the romping fishies. Screams had started up inside the villa.

'Clemens, take them out through the main gate, they'll never get over the wall unseen in daylight,' Caligula said as Fulvius and

Rufinus appeared with a screaming Rhoteces between them hopping on his remaining foot.

'Thank you, my friend,' Vespasian said with heartfelt gratitude, 'I don't know how you manage to live here.'

'It's not all bad.' Caligula grinned. 'The fishies are fun.'

As they passed Rhoteces, Vespasian took a last quick look at his revolting weasel face and felt a huge surge of satisfaction.

'That's a fair swap,' Magnus said, still looking very pale, 'him for me. I'd take that any day.'

'It could have been any one of us,' Sabinus observed as they climbed the steps.

'Or all of you,' Caligula pointed out, stopping at the top. 'I've seen it happen. Pallas, tell my grandmother that I'll try and keep Tiberius focused on Sejanus.'

'I will, Master Gaius,' Pallas said with a bow.

'And don't worry about Thrasyllus, the old charlatan will declare it an auspicious time to make changes once I tell him that one of them is that his son-in-law is going to become Praetorian prefect. Now go quickly before he decides that he'd rather spend the rest of the morning throwing people off the cliff instead of playing with the fishies.'

Vespasian clasped Caligula's forearm and, as he turned to follow Clemens, he heard the sound that he had been looking forward to: a scream, long and shrill and gradually fading until it was abruptly curtailed.

PART VI

ROME, OCTOBER AD 31

CHAPTER XVIII

'THE SENATE ARE in a state of total confusion,' Paetus declared, throwing a heavy stuffed leather ball at Vespasian. 'One day Tiberius sends them a letter complimenting Sejanus for his loyal service and then the next he intervenes in a court case that Sejanus has brought against one of his many enemies, ordering it to be dropped.' He grunted as he recaught the ball and threw it back again, hard, at Vespasian. 'And not just dropped but also granting the defendant immunity against further prosecutions.'

'Yet he's conferred a priesthood on Sejanus and on his eldest son, Strabo,' Sabinus said, straining as he lay on his back on a wooden bench exercising his arms and chest by lifting two large, round lead weights above his head.

'Yes,' Vespasian agreed, throwing the ball so forcefully at Paetus' midriff that it almost knocked him over, 'but at the same time he conferred a more prestigious priesthood upon Caligula.'

'And now the latest rumour is that Tiberius is going to give Sejanus tribunician power,' Paetus said, throwing the ball violently at Vespasian's head and grinning as its velocity toppled his opponent, 'which would then make him inviolate even though he's resigned his consulship.' He walked over to Vespasian and pulled him to his feet. 'My game, I believe, old chap; two–one. Let's take a bath.'

They collected their towels and walked across the huge, echoing, domed atrium of the Baths of Agrippa, built fifty years previously by Augustus' right-hand man, outside the city walls on the Campus Martius. It was full of men, young and old, exercising, relaxing, conversing or having their bodies scraped and plucked within its circular confines, under the staring eyes of the lifelike painted statues that resided in semi-circular or rectangular niches embedded in its curved, glaze-tiled walls. The most famous of these, Paetus had told Vespasian upon their first visit there together, the *Apoxyomenos* by Lysippos of Sikyon – a four-hundred-year-old, beautifully proportioned image of a naked athlete removing the oil from his right arm with a strigil – had so enamoured Tiberius, ten years earlier, that he had it removed to his bedroom, leaving a copy in its place. He had been shamed into returning the original by chants of 'Return to us our *Apoxyomenos*' during a bad-tempered demonstration as he visited the theatre a few days later.

The noise in the atrium was deafening, amplified by the circular construction and the dome above: grunts of exertion from wrestlers cheered on by enthusiastic onlookers; laughter at a well-told, pithy joke; exaggerated but good-humoured howls of pain as men had their underarm-, chest-, leg- or groin-hair plucked by expert tweezers-wielding slaves; shouts of vendors selling food and drink; the pummelling and slapping of teams of masseurs toning the bodies of their masters: the citizens of Rome.

'So the end result is that no one knows any more whether to cultivate Sejanus or avoid him,' Paetus told them as they passed through a high door into a quieter, more relaxing square room lit by shafts of sunlight flooding in through windows high up in its frescoed walls. Here men dozed on couches or had a less frantic massage, having been through the bathing stages from the warm tepidarium, on to the hot caldarium, followed by the even hotter laconicum and rounded off with a plunge into the cold waters of the frigidarium.

'Perhaps that's what Tiberius wants: confusion, so as to isolate Sejanus without provoking him into rebellion because he too is unsure whether or not he remains in the Emperor's favour,' Vespasian suggested, wondering whether the bewildered old man was capable still of such a strategy.

Another set of doors took them out into the warm, mid-afternoon October sun, to a huge bathing pool – eighty paces long and forty wide – surrounded by a colonnaded walkway lined with stone benches crowded with men chatting, gossiping and rumour-mongering. On the far side of the pool, beyond the colonnade, rose the Temple of Neptune, built by Agrippa in thanks for his great victories at sea, firstly against Sextus Pompeius and then at Actium; however, this grand building was dwarfed by the dome of its neighbour towering over it: Agrippa's Pantheon.

'You saw him, brother,' Sabinus said dismissively, 'he wasn't capable of two relevant consecutive thoughts. He's lost his soul and his spirit is searching for it in the darkest parts of his mind.'

A large splash, like a ballista shot hitting the sea, as a particularly chubby citizen jumped into the pool with his arms around his knees, covered them in droplets of cool water.

'Oaf!' Paetus shouted at the submerged miscreant. 'I do think that they should raise the price of admission here; perhaps the standards of behaviour might go up with it.' He jumped into the pool in the same fashion, right next to the man just as he resurfaced and covered him with water as he drew breath, leaving him choking and spluttering; Vespasian and Sabinus jumped in after Paetus, compounding the fat man's misery.

'Well, whether it's a planned strategy,' Paetus said shaking the water from his thick brown hair, 'or whether it's the result of Tiberius' inability to think logically, or whether it's a pleasant mixture of the both, it's got Sejanus rattled and the Senate terrified, not knowing whom to back in order to stay alive.' He struck out with an attempted breast-stoke towards the far side of the pool, weaving his way through the bobbing citizenry; Vespasian and Sabinus followed, equally as unproficient in their swimming abilities.

'What about you?' Vespasian asked Paetus as they hauled themselves out to sit on the edge with their feet dangling in the refreshing water. 'Whom are you backing?'

'That's the beauty of my position at the moment,' Paetus replied with a grin. 'As one of the urban quaestors I just carry out the city's law business; I'm so junior that no one cares about what I think so long as I perform my duties.'

Vespasian smiled at Paetus, they had become friends during the last few months of working together – as a triumvir capitalis,

Vespasian worked directly for the urban quaestors – and they had come to enjoy their regular baths together in the afternoon after the business of the day had been completed. Since becoming a quaestor and entering the Senate, Paetus had taken pleasure in providing Vespasian with all the news and gossip that surrounded it – and then, a few days later, he would with great glee confirm the veracity of some and the utter unreliability of all the rest. Their conversations had provided Vespasian with a diversion from the nagging fear that had haunted him since his return from Capreae, seven months previously. Although Antonia and Caligula had both confirmed the opposite, he could not stop worrying that they had been identified by one of Sejanus' men and a painful question-and-answer session would eventually ensue. Antonia had also told him, on one of his few and pleasurable visits to her house, that the knowledge of a deputation of unknown origin reaching the Emperor but the lack of information concerning what had been discussed had only added to Sejanus' unease. She was also confident that Tiberius' vacillations were, in part, intentional and that the killer blow would be delivered soon.

Paetus, for his part, had never questioned Vespasian as to what had happened to him after leaving Thracia or where he had gone for fifteen days back in March. Vespasian judged that it was because his friend sensibly felt it safer, in this climate of fear and unease, to know as little as possible about the plots and schemes of the powerful.

Having completed all the stages of the baths, Vespasian, Sabinus and Paetus, with tingling skin and lightness of foot, descended the steps in front of the Baths of Agrippa into the graceful gardens that surrounded it: one of the few public oases of calm in an otherwise bustling and thronged city.

'How's your young daughter doing, Sabinus?' Paetus asked as they walked lazily past the small temple dedicated to Eventus Bonus and on through the gardens, enjoying the scent of lavender on the cool breeze. Sabinus had taken to joining them more and more often since the birth of Flavia back in May.

'She mewls incessantly,' Sabinus complained. 'Clementina is thinking of changing her wet nurse.'

'Yes, I can remember that problem with my boy Lucius,' Paetus replied sympathetically. 'Never could understand how the womenfolk tolerated it, but it seemed to keep them occupied, which at least was something to be grateful for.'

'Well, I'm finding it difficult to tolerate, that's for sure; I'm hardly getting any sleep. Clementina insists that the child sleeps close by her, and because our house is so small I can't move her to a bedroom far enough away from mine so as not to hear the noise unless she goes into the slaves' quarters, which she has flatly refused to do and I'm too soft-hearted to insist.'

'Get a bigger house,' Paetus suggested, in the manner of a man who did not have to worry about money.

'I've got the biggest one that I can afford at the moment,' Sabinus replied gloomily. 'And having failed this year, yet again, to get elected as a quaestor I'm forced to wait until next year when I surely will be elected and be able to use the position to bulk up my finances.'

'Quite so; but until then you're stuck, eh? Unless you would consider a loan,' Paetus offered. 'I wouldn't miss a hundred thousand or so for a couple of years; I wouldn't charge you much interest, say ten per cent for the duration of the loan.'

'That would be most kind, Paetus.'

Vespasian was shocked by the proposal. 'Sabinus, you can't!'

'Why not?'

'Well, for a start senators aren't allowed to participate in banking and I'd say that charging interest on a loan breaks that rule.'

Paetus guffawed. 'Vespasian, old chap, I don't know of one senator who's taken any notice of that since Marcus Crassus' excesses; he had almost everyone in the Senate in debt to him at one time or the other and his rates of interest were exorbitant. Besides, this is just a private agreement between friends.'

'What happens if you can't repay it?'

'You let me worry about that,' Sabinus said tersely, 'it's nothing to do with you. As Paetus said: it's a private agreement.

If the idea of taking a loan offends your miserly scruples then fine, don't ever take one out; I, on the other hand, have no problem with it. I intend to live comfortably and at the moment that means taking advantage of Paetus' kind offer, which I accept with thanks.'

'Live comfortably, yes, but live within your means. How will you be able to sleep at night knowing that you owe so much money?'

'I'll worry about that when I can't hear Flavia mewling.'

They walked in silence through the Gate of Fontus, in the shadow of the Capitoline Hill with the Temple of Juno towering on the Arx above them; here Vespasian bid a sullen farewell to his brother and Paetus, leaving them to go on to Paetus' house on the Esquiline Hill to draw up the agreement.

Walking quickly up the Quirinal to dissipate his anger he reached Gaius' house soon after. Upon entering the atrium he found his uncle sitting by the impluvium eating sweet pastries.

'Ah, there you are, dear boy,' Gaius boomed, spraying crumbs all over his lap. 'Have you heard the news?'

'No, Uncle, I've been at the baths.'

'Then I'm surprised that you haven't heard; it's finally happened, Tiberius has gone really mad.' Gaius wiped his moist lips with a napkin. 'He's asked the Senate to meet at dawn tomorrow at the Temple of Apollo. I think that I'll feign an illness.'

'Why, Uncle?'

'Because, dear boy, I don't want to be seen opposing a motion that I cannot in all conscience vote for; the rumour is that Tiberius has written to ask the Senate to confirm tribunician power upon Sejanus.'

An hour later, Vespasian and Gaius had just been called to dinner when there was a knock on the front door. After a quick look through the viewing slot the attractive new doorkeeper opened up; into the vestibule stepped Pallas and, much to Vespasian's surprise and delight, Caenis.

'Pallas, what brings you here at the dinner hour?' Gaius exclaimed, as always happy to see Antonia's steward but slightly nervous lest it should mean that she required a difficult favour. 'And in such beautiful company,' he added, casting a sidelong, knowing look at Vespasian. .

'Good evening, masters,' Pallas replied bowing, 'we're here, as you may well guess, on our mistress's business.'

'Then we shall discuss it over dinner,' Gaius replied, keen not to be parted for too long from his repast.

'Would that be appropriate, master?'

'Pallas, my friend, you know as well as I that now you've passed the age of thirty Antonia will reward you with your freedom sooner rather than later. When that day comes I have no doubt that you will become a man of considerable influence and it'll be I who will be honoured by your presence at my table; so dine with me this evening as a friend and let us forget our relative status.'

'In that case, master, it would be an honour that I shan't forget,' Pallas replied sincerely.

'And I'm sure that Vespasian could make room on his couch for you, my dear,' Gaius said, smiling at Caenis.

A vision of Caligula and his sisters flashed across Vespasian's mind; he banished it immediately.

'Thank you, master,' Caenis replied sweetly, 'although I'm sure that it'll be a bit of a tight squeeze.'

Gaius roared with laughter. 'Oh, very good, my dear, but shouldn't that have been Vespasian's line?'

'Only if he was thinking what I was thinking.'

Vespasian reddened and looked lovingly at Caenis: she really was perfect.

'So, my friend,' Gaius boomed, full of good cheer as the pretty slave boy Aenor filled his cup yet again, 'what is it that Antonia requires of me?'

The meal had been cleared away and fruit and sweet wine had been laid out on the table. Vespasian had eaten his fill and felt a sense of wellbeing steal over him. The hairs on his arm stood erect as it brushed against Caenis next to him and he was unable to resist subtly running his hand down her back. She smiled at him and popped a grape into her mouth.

'There are two things, master,' Pallas replied, sipping his wine rather than quaffing it in the manner of his host. 'Firstly: tomorrow the Senate meets at the Temple of Apollo on the Palatine; she naturally assumes that you will be present.' Pallas looked meaningfully at Gaius' now half-empty cup.

Gaius looked at his cup regretfully and put it down. 'At dawn, yes, I'll be there if she wishes, although I was planning on absenting myself through sickness.'

'She does indeed wish you to be there. She also wishes that Vespasian wait outside the temple in his official capacity.'

'But I'm due to be in the Forum,' Vespasian objected. 'There are three trials for treason to be held tomorrow, I may have some unpleasant duties to perform.'

'They will be suspended first thing in the morning. Antonia wants you near the Senate; Caenis will be with you.'

'Why?'

'All in good time; but seeing as Caenis will be accompanying you Antonia feels that it would be more convenient if she spends the night here. She hopes that it won't be too much of a problem.'

'I could always sleep on this couch,' Caenis said innocently.

Vespasian smiled at her, stroking her beautiful thick hair.

'Good,' Pallas continued, turning back to Gaius. 'The second thing she requires is that you make notes.'

'Notes? She can read the transcripts of the Senate's meetings and the results of the votes any time she wants, surely?'

'It's not what will be said that interests her, she already knows that; it's where senators sit and how long for.'

'I'm intrigued, Pallas,' Gaius said, taking just a sip of wine.

Vespasian managed to tear his attention away from Caenis and focus on what Pallas had to say.

'No doubt you have heard the rumour that Tiberius will ask the Senate to confirm tribunician power on Sejanus?'

'Of course, it's the talk of Rome,' Gaius replied. 'That's why I didn't want to be present.'

'Which I quite understand; however, it's no mere rumour, it's a strategy thought up by Caligula and adopted by Tiberius and my mistress.'

'To see who doesn't share my uncle's scruples?' Vespasian ventured, immediately seeing the beauty of the scheme.

'Exactly, master.' Pallas looked impressed that Vespasian had caught on so quickly. 'Tomorrow all Sejanus' known supporters will enthusiastically attend the meeting expecting to vote tribunician power for their patron and reap whatever rewards he has promised them. However, this rumour will also flush out the senators who have been a little more circumspect in their support for him; if they think that the man that they have been secretly backing is finally in a position to gain supreme power then they will want to be a part of that so as not to miss out on his favour.'

'And Antonia wants me to note who sits close to him?' Gaius asked, getting the gist of the ploy.

'In part, yes, but what really interests her is how long they sit with him.'

'What do you mean?'

'I'll come to that. For a start she wants the list, as soon as possible, of who is surrounding him at the beginning of the meeting. Caenis will be in the crowd outside the temple with Vespasian; once you have noted the names you will come out and dictate them to her.'

'But there may be as many as a hundred, perhaps even more,' Gaius complained.

'Don't worry about his open supporters, she already knows their names, just memorise the ones who don't usually associate themselves with him. Once Caenis has written down the list a slave will take it to Antonia.'

'Why does she want it so quickly?' Vespasian asked.

'I'm afraid that I'm not privy to all of my mistress's reasoning, she tells me only what I need to know.' Pallas turned back to Gaius. 'However, what I do know is that as Tiberius' letter is read out it will start by heaping praise on Sejanus but then it will, by degrees, become more and more critical and my mistress expects people to start moving away from him; note the order in which they do and at what point during the letter. Vespasian, as a triumvir capitalis, is allowed to enter the Senate if a member has summoned him; send for him regularly and pass on the names to him. Once Caenis has the complete list she'll return to Antonia's house.'

'But how will we know when the list is complete?' Gaius asked.

'Because by the time that the Senior Consul has finished reading the Emperor's letter there will be no one near Sejanus,' Pallas replied confidently.

'Shouldn't I escort Caenis back?' Vespasian asked.

'No, master, you will stay outside the temple. My mistress is hopeful that you will soon be busy as she believes that Tiberius will finish by asking the Senate to condemn Sejanus to death.'

'So Tiberius' vacillations have been no more than a ruse to unearth all of Sejanus' supporters,' Vespasian said to Caenis who lay, covered in sweat, in his arms. His bedroom was dark and the sweet smell of sex surrounded them.

Caenis nuzzled his neck gently. 'Not entirely. My mistress thinks that it was mainly because he was fearful that if he did act against Sejanus, his supporters would have their revenge on him. She dictated a letter to Caligula at Misenum – she's unable to get letters to Capreae without them being read by Sejanus' men – telling him that the names of all his supporters were well known. Caligula wrote back saying that Tiberius was fearful that there were more who as yet had not gone public with their support and suggested this scheme for rooting them out. My mistress thought it ingenious and told him to suggest it to the Emperor who embraced it wholeheartedly because he could carry on doing exactly what he had been doing since you left.'

Vespasian smiled in the darkness. 'Changing his mind, you mean.'

'Worse than that; he's actually written to Sejanus, a couple of times, saying that he's ill and on the point of dying and asking him to return to Capreae. Luckily, Caligula seems to have a lot of influence over him and on both occasions persuaded him, by reminding him of Thrasyllus' prophecy, to write again to say that he's now feeling much better and is in fact preparing a trip to

Rome, and that Sejanus should stay to meet him when he arrives.'

'I saw how Caligula deals with him; he's not having the easiest of times, one word out of place and he could be dead.'

'Yes, but he's managing to do the most important thing: keeping Tiberius away from Sejanus.'

'And tomorrow that'll be over.'

'Yes, my love, one way or another.'

'What do you mean? Tomorrow Tiberius will ask the Senate to condemn Sejanus to death.'

'Perhaps; I copied Caligula's latest letter for my mistress's records yesterday and in it he said that Tiberius didn't consult him whilst he was writing his address to the Senate nor did he get a chance to look at it; so no one can be absolutely sure what will be read out tomorrow.'

'But Pallas was confident that Antonia knew the contents.'

'Pallas only knows what she tells him; other than my mistress, only you, Caligula and I know the full truth.'

Vespasian sat up. 'Shit! He could've just as easily changed his mind and where would that leave Antonia and all of us?'

'We should sleep, Vespasian; it'll be a long and dangerous day tomorrow.'

Vespasian kissed her on the lips and lay back on the pillow. He closed his eyes but he knew that sleep would be difficult to find; tomorrow would be a bloody day – one way or another.

CHAPTER XVIIII

T HE EARLY-MORNING mist still clung to the lower reaches of
the city along the shores of the Tiber, shrouding the island
opposite the Campus Martius, as Vespasian, Caenis and Gaius
climbed the Palatine in the fresh dawn light. All around them,
groups of senators, carrying their folding stools, made their way
in the same direction, towards the Temple of Apollo on the
southern side of the hill; the mood amongst them was generally
buoyant but, here and there, small clusters of less exuberant
senators walked slowly with grim faces, the future weighing
heavily upon their shoulders.

The crowds grew thicker as they approached the Temple of
Apollo because the ordinary people of Rome, drawn by the
rumour of Sejanus' elevation, were gathering to witness the
day's unfolding events. Gaius' senatorial toga was enough to
clear a path for them as the deferential crowd parted to let the
senators through to the beautiful, octagonal temple set on a
podium, built by Augustus in thanks to his guardian god for his
victories.

Paetus met them at the foot of the steps leading up to the
temple doors and quickly got them through the security cordon
of a century of togate Praetorians. Gaius went ahead with Caenis
to find a place under the portico where he would be able to find
her again in a hurry.

'Why aren't you in the Forum, Vespasian?' Paetus enquired as
they mounted the steps.

'I've been asked to come here,' Vespasian replied simply as
scores of senators flooded past them into the building.

Paetus looked at him shrewdly. 'I needn't ask who by. So
things may not be going the way the rumours suggest, eh?'

'Perhaps not, Paetus. I really don't know. I'm in the rather unpleasant position of being used as a tool for a purpose that I don't fully understand.'

'It was ever thus for us junior magistrates. This is not a day to be in Rome, wouldn't you say, old boy?'

A loud cheer erupted from the crowd below and Vespasian turned to see both the Consuls, each preceded by twelve fasces-bearing lictors, cut two different swathes through the milling citizenry as if competing to reach the temple first.

'Well, this will be fun,' Paetus observed dryly. 'It's the first time the two Consuls have attended a meeting of the Senate together since Memmius Regulus took over from Faustus Sulla as Senior Consul at the beginning of this month; his junior colleague, Fulcinius Trio, hates him because he's the Emperor's man not Sej—' Paetus stopped abruptly and looked at Vespasian. 'Oh! I see,' he said slowly. 'This has been planned well in advance, hasn't it?'

'Yes, it has, but nobody except Tiberius knows what the outcome will be.'

'Well, Memmius Regulus must be pretty confident that he knows; he cancelled the three treason trials in the Forum this morning, all of which had been brought by Sejanus.' He turned to go. 'I'd better go in before the Consuls; I'll see you later in what will be a different Rome, one way or another.'

Vespasian watched him go with that uncertain phrase echoing in his head.

Regulus had won the race to be the first Consul to arrive and he mounted the steps with all the dignity befitting his rank, followed, a few paces behind, by a sour-faced Fulcinius Trio. As they disappeared into the temple Gaius returned, having left Caenis between the first two of the Luna marble columns of the portico, just to the right of the main door.

'I'd better be going in, my dear boy,' he said, sounding more than a little nervous. He indicated Caenis' position. 'You'd best go and join her. Good luck.'

Vespasian did not need a second invitation to vacate the entrance; as his uncle turned to leave, a mighty cheer broke out from the crowd and it parted to reveal Sejanus walking, in amongst a large group of his supporters, directly towards him.

Vespasian skipped behind the column to find Caenis ready with a wax tablet and bronze stylus in hand, but looking worried.

'Are you all right, Caenis?'

'I can't see the slave that I'm meant to hand the first list to,' she replied, scanning the crowd.

'Keep looking, I'm sure he'll turn up,' Vespasian assured her as Sejanus' party mounted the steps; when they reached the top Sejanus stopped.

'Friends,' he said, addressing the senators around him, 'go on in and reserve a place of honour for me; I'll stay out here a while until everyone is in and then I shall enter last, for maximum effect.'

His supporters cheered him and then began to make their way inside.

Vespasian peered out from behind the column and caught a glimpse of Sejanus; he did not look like a man confident of high honour. His square-jawed face seemed strained and he wore a heavy frown; his hands were fidgeting. He turned suddenly, feeling that someone close by was watching him, and caught sight of Vespasian as he ducked back behind the column.

'You there, what are you doing?' he shouted, moving towards Vespasian's and Caenis' position.

'Prefect!' A voice called from the bottom of the steps, stopping Sejanus in his tracks.

'Macro, thank the gods,' Sejanus exclaimed with relief in his voice. 'Has there been a message from the Emperor? I've heard nothing from him for eight days now; I don't want to go into the meeting unless I'm absolutely sure that he is favouring me and this isn't a trap.'

'There has been, sir,' Macro replied, taking the steps two by two, and taking a sealed scroll from the fold in his toga.

'Give it to me,' Sejanus ordered.

'It's for the Senate,' Macro stated, 'the seal is only to be broken by the senior Consul at the Emperor's express orders.'

'Who delivered it?'

'I did.'

'You've been with the Emperor,' Sejanus exclaimed incredulously. 'By whose authority?'

'The Emperor himself summoned me to Capreae two days ago. I saw him yesterday morning and travelled back overnight using our horse-relay service.'

'What? Why you and not me?' Sejanus asked with low menace in his voice.

'Because, sir,' Macro replied calmly, 'the Emperor felt that it would be inappropriate for you to carry this message to the Senate.'

'Do you know the contents, Macro?'

'I do, sir; let me be the first to congratulate you.' Macro clapped Sejanus on the arm. 'It's what we have hoped for: Tiberius is asking the Senate to vote you what you deserve for the services that you've rendered both to him and to Rome.'

'Tribunician power! Has he made me his heir?'

'The Emperor said to tell you that this letter contains almost everything that you deserve.'

'Almost everything?'

'Almost.'

'Then I shall be content with that for the present,' Sejanus said with relief in his voice. 'Come, my friend, let us enter together.'

'I'll only deliver the letter to the Senior Consul; then I'll go back to the Praetorian Camp to prepare the men for your welcome.'

'Do that, my friend,' Sejanus said as they entered the temple, 'you will not find me ungrateful.'

Applause burst out as they stepped through the doors.

Vespasian looked at Caenis with concern. 'What do you think?'

'I think that we have to wait to know for sure one—'

'Way or another?' he cut in, smiling at her.

'Yes, my love,' she said, squeezing his hand.

'Vespasian, sir, sir!' a familiar voice shouted from the crowd.

Vespasian looked round and saw Magnus with two of his crossroads brothers, Sextus and Marius, at the bottom of the steps. He quickly went down to them and, as one of the Vigintiviri, authorised them through the Praetorians.

'Antonia sent us, sir,' Magnus puffed as they went up the steps, 'something about a message to take to her.'

'You're just in time,' Vespasian said, seeing Gaius slipping out of the temple.

'The Consuls have just taken the auspices and pronounced the day as good for the business of Rome,' Gaius said as he approached Vespasian. 'It's quite an eye-opener in there; six new faces sitting with Sejanus including three ex-praetors and two ex-Consuls, Aulus Plautius and Silius Nervus. I'll call you in when it starts to get really interesting.'

He bustled off to give the names to Caenis.

'So why did Antonia send you?' Vespasian asked Magnus.

'She said that she was worried a slave would be intercepted and she thought that a bit of muscle was called for. Why, I don't know, but she's anxious about something – I can tell.'

'Getting to know her moods now, you old goat?'

Magnus frowned. 'Very funny, I'm sure,' he said as Caenis handed him the wax tablet with the names written on it. 'We'd best be going, sir. I'll see you in the Forum later.'

'Why?'

'I don't know; I just do what I'm told and that's what Antonia told me to do: go to the Forum with all my brothers and wait for you.'

'Well, it's always best to obey the last order. I'll see you there, I suppose.'

Vespasian watched Magnus and his brothers going back down the steps, with the growing feeling that he was a very small piece in a large and intricate game that he had little understanding of, and that he could just as easily be sacrificed as be used to make the winning move.

The sound of footsteps behind him made him turn; he came face to face with Macro.

'What are you doing here?' Macro snarled with barely concealed contempt.

'I'm here in my capacity of triumvir capitalis, awaiting the

Senate's orders,' Vespasian replied. He was determined not to be intimidated.

Macro laughed. 'Pray to the gods then that it's not your execution that you'll be overseeing.' He pushed past Vespasian and stood at the top of the steps, withdrew a further scroll from his toga fold and waved it in the air. 'Men of the Praetorian Guard, you know me, I am Tribune Naevius Sutorius Macro; I have here a warrant from your Emperor.' He unrolled the scroll with a flourish. 'He requires you to go back to your camp where I will read a personal message from him to all the members of the Guard concerning the events of this day; I can, however, tell you that it contains a promise of a largesse to every man.'

The Guards cheered and waved the loose ends of their togas in the air. Macro signalled to someone at the back of the ever-growing mob of spectators.

'The Senate will remain guarded,' he continued as a group of men started to push their way forward through the crowd, 'have no fear of that. Now follow me.' He walked down the steps and led the century away.

As the last Praetorian left the front of the temple a new body of men took their place: the Vigiles were now guarding the Senate.

Half an hour had gone by and the sun was now well above the hills to the east, casting a soft light over the rooftops of the city. The crowd was getting restless as no news of what was happening inside the temple had filtered out; a few late-arriving senators had gone in but no one as yet had left and the doors remained half-closed.

Vespasian sat with Caenis on a bench in the shade of the portico; he could hear the voice of the Senior Consul, Regulus, reading aloud, but his words were indistinct. Vespasian had started to become concerned about the outcome of the letter; if Tiberius was going to damn Sejanus after praising him, as Pallas had said he would, then he was taking his time over it. He was on the verge of sharing his worries with Caenis when one of the public slaves, used by the senators to run messages, stepped out of the door and approached him with a bow.

'The senator Gaius Pollo has requested that you attend him immediately,' he said with a thick Gallic accent.

Vespasian's pulse quickened as he stood up and, with a squeeze of Caenis' shoulder, followed the slave into the temple.

It was packed with senators all sitting on their low folding stools; at the far end, below a statue of Apollo, stood Regulus reading from a scroll. As Vespasian made his way behind the rear line of senators he heard the Consul declaiming in a high-pitched, clear voice:

'. . . and furthermore, Conscript Fathers, I consider his allowing of sacrifices to be made to him in public in front of the many statues of himself that now litter the city an affront to my position as your Emperor. I have made it clear on many occasions that I do not wish to be worshipped and have only allowed very few temples to be dedicated to me, and then only to bestow a mark of favour on the municipality that requested the honour if I consid-ered them deserving of it; yet he would have the whole Empire worship him if he could.'

The slave led him to Gaius' place at the rear of the left-hand side.

'It's started to happen, dear boy, look,' Gaius whispered, pointing to the other side of the room.

Vespasian craned his neck to see over the massed heads of the senators in front of him. Over to Regulus' right-hand side sat Sejanus with an impassive look on his face; as he was watching, two senators near Sejanus stood up and, picking up their stools, crossed over to Gaius' side. The others surrounding him were whispering to one another, with countenances full of confusion or fear.

'Tell Caenis: Aulus Plautius and Sextus Vistilius at "but what of his lesser qualities"; and those two, Silius Nerva and Livius Gallus at "have the whole Empire worship him". Go, and take the slave with you so that you can come straight back in.'

Caenis was waiting for him outside and he quickly relayed the names to her. 'It seems to be happening, Caenis,' he said excitedly as she finished writing. 'His supporters have certainly lost their triumphant demeanour.'

'If it is, then we've got a lot to thank Caligula for,' she replied seriously as he turned to follow the slave back in.

'"As to his divorcing his loyal wife Apicata five years ago…"' As Vespasian made his way back to Gaius to receive seven more names, Regulus read:

> '… on the assumption that I would let him marry my beloved son Drusus' widow, I considered that to be an arrogant move at the time, and still do. Whether it was because he genuinely desired her or whether it was because he felt that in marrying her he would further ingratiate himself with me I will leave to you, Conscript Fathers, to decide.'

Having just managed to recall all the seven names and give them to Caenis, Vespasian returned for a third time. Regulus was still holding forth:

> '… and through a weakness brought on by my recurring bouts of sickness, consented to the union last year. That, Conscript Fathers, was an error which I will now undo. I now formally dissolve the betrothal of Lucius Aelius Sejanus to my daughter-in-law, Livilla.'

At that point there was a mass migration away from Sejanus; the noise of stools folding and senators walking across the floor forced Regulus to pause as Vespasian once again reached Gaius.

'Well, that makes it easy, dear boy,' Gaius whispered to him, 'everyone else at "formally dissolve the betrothal". You might as well stay and watch what happens; no one will notice you in this atmosphere.'

Sejanus was left completed isolated with his head in his hands as Regulus continued reading the Emperor's words:

> 'I hope that you will agree with me, Conscript Fathers – whose opinion I have always valued – that these and the

numerous other offences that he has committed, including the bearing of false witness against many of your number, cannot go unpunished. I would therefore ask you, Conscript Fathers, to vote on whether or not he should be . . .'

At this point Regulus was forced to pause again as his voice was drowned by an eruption of howls of anger directed at Sejanus from all present. Even those senators who had until very recently been sitting close by him joined in, either through fear or because they believed that if they denounced him vehemently now their earlier support of the doomed man would somehow be forgotten.

Praetors, tribunes and quaestors, including Paetus, surrounded Sejanus but he made no move to flee to appeal to the crowd outside; he just sat in thought.

The noise died down and Regulus finished: '". . . whether or not he should be imprisoned."'

There was a stunned silence. Vespasian glanced around at the senators, all as visibly shocked as himself – Macro had not lied to Sejanus, the letter did ask for *almost* everything that he deserved.

Regulus rolled up the scroll. 'Conscript Fathers, I believe that we are as one in wishing to grant our Emperor's request.'

There was a general chorus of agreement; even the Junior Consul Fulcinius Trio was nodding his head slightly as he stepped forward. 'Seeing that you seem to be all agreed,' he said carefully, 'I believe that the Senior Consul need only ask one of you for your opinion because it will be the opinion of all of you.'

'So be it,' Regulus concurred as the suggestion met with approval. 'Lucius Aelius Sejanus, come here and stand before me.'

Sejanus continued sitting in thought as if he had not heard.

Regulus repeated the command; still nothing.

The third time he shouted Sejanus suddenly looked up. 'Me?' he questioned in the tone of a man surprised to be given an order after so many years of only delivering them. 'Are you ordering *me*?'

'I, in the name of the whole house, am ordering you.'

Sejanus looked around and with a dismissive sneer went and stood before Regulus.

'Senator Pollo,' Regulus called out, causing Gaius to almost fall off his stool, 'do you think that this man should be imprisoned?'

Gaius winced and then, with some trepidation, got to his feet. 'I do think that he should be imprisoned, Consul,' he said slowly and clearly.

'Then that is the will of the house. Take him to the Tullianum.'

'And just who is going to escort me there,' Sejanus drawled, 'through my Praetorians? Do you think that they'll let this happen? They'll slaughter you all first, like the sheep that you are.'

'Graecinius Laco, are your Vigiles all in position?' Regulus asked.

A tall man with a few days of thick black stubble on his face stepped forward from the far end of the temple. 'They are, Consul, and Tribune Macro has taken the Guard back to their camp.'

'What!' Sejanus roared, jumping forward and being restrained by at least four men. 'Macro! The filthy whore's whelp, I'll have him for this when the Emperor sees sense and releases me; just as I'll have every one you, you Convict Blatherers.'

'Take him away, Laco,' Regulus ordered. 'Consul Trio, you and I will now address the people together.'

Vespasian watched as Sejanus was led, head held high and shrugging off the restraining hands of his surrounding escort, from the Temple of Apollo.

Vespasian and Gaius squeezed out of the door through the crush of senators and gave the last and easy part of the list to Caenis.

'I should get back to my mistress now, my love,' she said as Regulus and Trio took up position at the top of the temple steps, ready to address the confused crowd, who had just watched the man who had held sway over them for the best part of the last decade taken away in disgrace.

'I'll come with you, seeing as my services don't seem to be required here now,' Vespasian said with genuine regret; it had been the first execution that he had been almost looking forward to.

'I'm going to listen to Regulus and then I'll follow you, I think.' Gaius looked less than pleased. 'I'm anxious to see what Antonia will do now. Go around the back of the temple – there's another set of steps there; you'll never get through this mob.'

As Vespasian and Caenis made their way around the temple they heard Regulus begin his address.

'People of Rome,' he declaimed, 'today your Emperor and the Senate have seen fit to protect you from a man who has sought to dominate you for too long.' A scattering of cheers rang out. 'A man who has grown too large for our city.' More substantial cheers greeted this remark. 'A man who, like Icarus, has flown too high and has now been burned by the sun. Is it not right, since our Emperor is like the sun to us, guiding us through this life, that this man, Sejanus, should have been brought down in the temple of the sun god himself: Apollo?'

Thunderous cheers drowned Regulus out as Vespasian and Caenis made their way down the back steps of the temple.

'He's certainly getting them going,' Vespasian observed as they headed towards Antonia's house, just two hundred paces away.

'He needs to,' Caenis replied, struggling to keep up with him. 'Sejanus has been very generous in sponsoring games. He's not unloved by all the people, by any means; if Regulus doesn't get them on his side they could well riot and try to free him.'

Vespasian shuddered at the thought but realised that Caenis' assessment was absolutely right.

They arrived at Antonia's door and knocked; a brief glance through the viewing slot was enough for the doorkeeper to let them in.

Antonia was waiting in the atrium with the first list in her hand. 'Vespasian,' she said disappointedly, 'so the Emperor didn't demand Sejanus' death.'

'No, domina, only his imprisonment.'

'I had a hunch that he wouldn't have the balls for it. He's still worried that Sejanus' supporters would resist a call for his execution and maybe even encourage him into open rebellion.'

'They were all shouting abuse at him by the end, domina.'

'Good, because I intend to use his supporters to encourage the Senate to do what Tiberius won't. It was for this eventuality that I had these lists drawn up. Give me that, Caenis.'

Caenis handed Antonia the second list; she scanned it quickly and compared it to the first. 'Ah, the ex-Consul Aulus Plautius is our man, last to show himself but then first out; he'll not be wanting that to come to the attention of the Emperor. I'll write to him immediately and in exchange for my silence on the subject I'm sure he'll be only too pleased to request the Consuls to hold another meeting of the Senate this afternoon, at which he will lead the calls for Sejanus' execution, supported by the others of that faction whom he can persuade to see sense.'

Vespasian shook his head in astonishment. 'Of course, force Sejanus' own supporters to call for his death; that is genius, domina,' he said admiringly.

'No, Vespasian, that's politics. There will be no risk of a rebellion if he is condemned by the very people who had hoped to gain from him. Now go to the Forum and wait to see whether I'm successful or not; you may still have work to do before the day is done. Come, Caenis, we're going to be busy, I also need to send a message to Macro.'

The Forum Romanum was heaving with people of every class, all thoughts of work or business having been put aside for the day as the citizens of Rome followed events and speculated as to what the final outcome would be. Rumour and counter-rumour circulated freely, from the reasonable (Sejanus would be banished or Sejanus would be released) to the outlandish (Tiberius was on the point of death or abdication and the Republic would be restored or Tiberius was returning to Rome to execute Sejanus himself), all of which held sway in different parts of the crowd.

Vespasian managed to push his way through to the Senate

House where he found Paetus and a group of senators in conversation with the two Consuls on the steps.

'I have left a guard of Vigiles around the Tullianum, Consul,' Paetus was saying. 'What are your orders?'

'We will keep him there until we are better able to discern the Emperor's wishes,' Regulus replied with uncertainty in his voice.

'We already know his wishes,' his junior colleague Trio snapped. 'The question is how long will the Praetorian Guard stand for it? If they come marching into the city to release him, I for one will not stand in their way; in fact I will lead them to the Tullianum and unlock the cell myself.'

'Then you will be going against the Senate and People of Rome,' Regulus shouted back.

'The Senate and People of Rome be buggered; the power lies with the Praetorians and whoever commands their loyalty. I intend to be on their side rather than lying dead on the Gemonium Stairs,' Trio replied, pointing at the steep steps that led from the Forum up to the summit of the Capitoline Hill.

'But you were a part of the meeting that condemned him,' Regulus said, shocked, 'how can you in honour go back on that decision?'

'I may have been a part of the meeting but I didn't vote, only one man voted, Senior Consul, and you chose him because you, like every other senator, knew him to be a supporter of Sejanus' greatest enemy, the Lady Antonia. That has left the rest of us free to keep our opinions to ourselves until such time as we see fit to express them.'

There was a murmur of agreement amongst some of the surrounding senators.

Regulus was outraged at being so outmanoeuvred. 'But it was your idea, which I went along with in the spirit of reconciliation, so as not to force men into voting against someone whom they had previously supported.'

Trio smiled thinly and shrugged.

Vespasian could see that the concord of the morning was starting to fracture; people were reassessing their positions as it dawned on them that the matter was far from resolved and that Trio had indeed left them room for manoeuvre.

Gaius came puffing up the steps towards the group; his usually carefully tonged hair lay flat on his head, lank with sweat.

'Consul Regulus,' he said, trying to regain his breath, 'may I have a word with you in private?'

'Very well.' Regulus stepped away from the group, with obvious relief, to join Gaius.

The senators split up into smaller clusters, muttering.

Paetus came over to Vespasian. 'It's all becoming a bit tricky, old chap. A bit of a mess, I should say,' he observed, beaming as if he was quite enjoying the situation.

'I think that the Lady Antonia has just forced the issue,' Vespasian replied, noticing a large group of senators cutting their way through the crowd and heading towards the Senate House.

Regulus broke off his conversation with Gaius, nodding his agreement at whatever he had been told, as Aulus Plautius led thirty or so of Sejanus' supporters to the bottom of the steps.

Plautius pulled back his broad, muscular shoulders and raised his head; the veins on his thick neck bulged blue. 'Consuls Regulus and Trio,' he called in his loudest voice so that the crowd of citizens all around him heard and quietened. The silence spread throughout the Forum as people became aware that the next move in the day's events was under way. Plautius waited until the hush was complete. 'I demand a full meeting of the Senate immediately, to address the unsatisfactory situation that we find ourselves in.'

'And I second that,' Trio immediately shouted triumphantly, 'unless you would prefer to do so yourself, Senior Consul? The day has already been declared auspicious for senatorial business, so you can't get out of it that way.'

Regulus looked to the sky and pointed at a skein of honking geese flying in a V formation, northwest, over the Temple of Concordia at the foot of the Capitoline Hill. 'I declare that to be a sign from the gods,' he shouted.

'You can't refuse a meeting because of a flight of birds,' Trio responded angrily.

'I could quite easily, there are many precedents for me to do so, but I take it as a positive sign: the saviours of Rome, who, whilst the dogs stayed sleeping, woke the defenders of the Capitoline Hill when the Gauls were scaling it at night, have shown us that the Senate should meet in the Temple of Concordia, the goddess of Harmony. Summon the Senate; there, in Concordia's sacred precinct, we shall resolve this matter.'

The crowd roared their approval of this patriotic reading of bird flight and parted to make way for the twenty-four lictors, who preceded the two Consuls to the Temple of Concordia.

Vespasian caught up with Gaius halfway across the Forum.

'What did you tell Regulus, Uncle?'

'When I went back to Antonia's house a message arrived for her from Plautius saying that he agreed to her demand and that over thirty of Sejanus' supporters, who were currently meeting at his house, would support it too, on condition that Antonia would intercede on their behalf with the Emperor. So she sent messages out to all the senators that didn't turn up to this morning's meeting, because they hadn't wanted to be a part of Sejanus' supposed victory, telling them to attend the Senate when the summons came. She asked me to come here as quickly as possible to ensure that Regulus didn't find an excuse to refuse a further meeting.'

'Like, for example, an ill-omened flight of birds?'

Gaius chuckled. 'Exactly. He could just as easily have declared the geese to be a sign that Rome's luck was leaving the city and no more business should be attempted today; we've all seen it done before.'

They reached the Temple of Concordia, set in front of the beautiful, arched façade of the Tabularium, where all Rome's records were kept. Gaius went in, leaving Vespasian by the doors.

For half an hour Vespasian watched as senators, many of whom had not been present at the morning meeting, appeared from every direction in answer to the Consuls' summons, each now believing that their faction would win the debate. Amongst the last to arrive were Corbulo and his father, who looked remarkably like his son. They both appeared very unsure of the situation.

'Vespasian, what's going on?' Corbulo asked nervously as his father went into the temple.

'Well, if you'd been at the debate this morning you would know.' Vespasian was going to enjoy toying with him.

'We were ill,' Corbulo replied huffily, 'we had some bad prawns last night.'

'You really must give up prawns: they obviously don't agree with you.'

'Yes, well,' Corbulo spluttered, remembering that he had used that excuse once before in Vespasian's presence. 'Tell me what's happening.'

'If you go in and vote for the motion you'll be fine,' Vespasian replied enigmatically.

Realising that he was demeaning himself by asking someone who was not a senator about senatorial business, Corbulo snorted and went inside.

'Conscript Fathers,' Regulus' voice carried out of the door, 'come to order.'

The chatter inside the temple immediately died down. The doors remained opened; Vespasian stood in the doorway to watch the proceedings.

'Although the day has already been declared auspicious,' Regulus began, 'we are now under the guidance of a different goddess and should therefore sacrifice to her.'

There were mutterings of assent and dissent from the opposing factions of senators; Trio instantly got to his feet but Regulus continued before he could take the floor.

'To ensure that there are no allegations of foul play in reading the omens I invite the Junior Consul to make the sacrifice.'

Trio accepted the offer gladly; he pulled a fold of his toga over his head and stepped up to the altar. Because a flight of geese had led them to the Temple of Concordia a goose had been chosen as the most propitious sacrifice. Trio hastily despatched the bird, saying the prayers over it in a most perfunctory manner, then slit it open to examine the liver, which he quickly declared to be perfect and a sign that the good goddess of harmony favoured their endeavour.

'Thank you for your diligence, Consul,' Regulus said, without a trace of irony, as he took the floor again. 'Senator Plautius has asked for this meeting, I therefore call upon him to speak first.'

Regulus sat back down on his Consul's curule chair as Plautius stood to speak.

'Conscript Fathers.' He held out his right arm and, in a dramatic gesture, swept it around the room to include all the seated senators. 'I have asked for us to meet again today because I, like many of you, feel that we haven't rightly interpreted our Emperor's wishes and in not doing so we have created a very combustible situation.'

There was a general murmur of agreement; neither faction could dispute that.

'I therefore propose to examine more carefully what he meant. He asked us to vote on "whether or not he should be imprisoned"; we all took that to mean that the Emperor wanted Sejanus imprisoned, did we not?'

Again both factions found themselves agreeing.

'Yet imprisonment of a citizen has never been a punishment recognised by the State, so was the Emperor really asking us to mete out a punishment that doesn't exist?'

Frowns and puzzled looks passed over the faces of his fellows.

'Let us look again at the words "whether or not". In using that form of words Tiberius was deferring to the Senate; he was leaving the decision as to what to do with this man to us. However, Conscript Fathers, we took him too literally; it wasn't just a choice between imprisoning Sejanus or not. No, the Emperor is sometimes too subtle for even his loyal Senate to follow.'

Another chorus of unanimous agreement rose from the senators. Vespasian smiled to himself; he could see that that sycophantic line had been put in with the Emperor's reading of the meeting's transcript in mind.

'The choice our beloved Emperor was giving us wasn't nearly so narrow; he in his wisdom knows that to have Sejanus locked up here in Rome could only lead to ill feeling, riots or even civil war. It was not just imprisonment or freedom that he was giving us the choice of, it was also imprisonment or loss of all honours previously voted him; imprisonment or confinement to his house, either here in Rome or one of his many country estates; imprisonment or denial of fire and water within three hundred miles of Rome; imprisonment or banishment to an island or a faraway town.' He paused as the truth of what he was suggesting began to sink in to his audience and senators started to call out for their preferred punishment or for clemency. Plautius raised his strong voice and drowned them out. 'Or, Conscript Fathers,' he declaimed, 'imprisonment or death. And I call for death – but not the death of a Roman citizen that he has denied to so many of his victims. No, let it be the death of an enemy of Rome: strangulation.'

There was uproar, but Plautius stood his ground, raised his arms in the air and waited for the commotion to die down.

'But let it not be just I who expresses his view,' he carried on once the noise had abated enough for him to be heard again, 'let us do this properly, unlike this morning, so that there can be no doubt as to the will of the Senate. Every senator should speak and give his opinion, and then the motion should be put to a full vote. If you agree, Senior Consul, I would have you call my colleague, Silius Nervus, to speak next as is his right as an ex-Consul.'

Plautius sat back down whilst Regulus retook the floor.

'Consul Trio, do you agree that we take this to a full debate?'

Trio was in no position to argue, having insisted upon the meeting and having taken the auspices himself. He stood and mumbled his agreement, shocked by such a high-profile desertion from his faction.

'Very well then, I call the ex-Consul Silius Nervus.'

A round, middle-aged man waddled forward and took the floor. 'Conscript Fathers, I too demand death by strangulation, and also *damnatio memoriae*, let his name be removed from all monuments and history,' he said simply, before waddling back to his stool.

There was a communal gasp from all sides as the senators realised that this had been an ambush and Sejanus now had no chance of reprieve. Vespasian watched with an increasing sense of awe at Antonia's political finesse as Regulus called every senator in order of precedence, from ex-Consuls down, to speak. With a few exceptions, who pleaded briefly but ineffectually for either death by decapitation or one of the more innocuous punishments, they all called for death by strangulation.

By the time the most junior of the more than four hundred senators present had spoken the sun was getting low in the sky and it was time for the presiding Consuls to wind up the debate.

Regulus took the floor. 'Conscript Fathers, it now only remains for the two Consuls to speak before I call a vote. I call Consul Trio.'

Trio rose slowly to his feet and walked unhurriedly into the centre of the Temple. He had the look of a beaten but unbowed man determined to pursue the only course of action left open to him.

'Conscript Fathers, we have over the centuries witnessed many a man who has for one reason or another exceeded himself.' His voice was slow and flat; there were angry growls from the senators as they immediately saw that this was the beginning of a filibuster. 'Coriolanus, Gaius Marius, Sulla, Tarquinius Superbus, Appius Claudius . . .'

The list went on and on and Vespasian, like the senators, began to worry that he would talk until sundown at which time the debate would be talked out and no vote could be taken.

'It is time to consider what manner of a man is Sejanus,' Trio continued, having named scores of ambitious historical figures and being forced to raise his voice against the growing clamour of his furious colleagues. 'Is he the sort of man who—' A stool hit him full in the face, gashing his right cheek and almost felling him. He stood back erect with blood flowing on to his toga and opened his mouth to speak again; before he could get another word out he went down under a sustained salvo of brutally hurled stools and was forced to crawl from the floor and seek shelter behind his curule chair.

'Thank you for your opinion, Consul,' Regulus said, nodding to his bloodied and bruised colleague as if nothing was amiss. 'I too demand death. The house will now divide, those in favour to my right, those against to my left, on this motion: That this house would condemn Lucius Aelius Sejanus to death by strangulation and that his name be expunged.'

There was almost a stampede as the senators all struggled not to be seen to be the last man standing on the left. Within a few moments the only man not to Regulus' right was Trio, who was still cowering behind his chair; he gingerly poked his head up and looked around to see that he had been utterly defeated.

'I declare,' Regulus called out, 'that the motion is—' He stopped mid-sentence with his mouth open, staring through the doors, past Vespasian and out into the Forum.

Vespasian spun around to follow his gaze; fifty paces away, resplendent in blazing white togas, scything through the panicking crowd with ease and heading directly for the Temple of Concordia, marched a cohort of the Praetorian Guard.

CHAPTER XX

'ME AND THE lads are down here, sir,' Magnus' voice called from the crowd. Vespasian turned to see his friend, at the bottom of the steps to the side of the temple, surrounded by his crossroads brothers, all bearing cudgels and staffs. Behind them the Gemonium Stairs rose up the Capitoline. 'I think that it may be time for dinner, if you take my meaning?'

Vespasian paused and looked with concern towards the central steps; the front rank of the cohort's first century had just begun to mount them with Macro at their head. Had Macro been unable to persuade the Guard to change allegiances and there-fore changed sides himself to save his own life? Vespasian did not know but reckoned he would be safer surrounded by Magnus and the brothers. He turned to withdraw.

'Triumvir capitalis!' Macro roared. 'Come here or I'll have my men cut you down.'

With no chance of escape Vespasian did as he had been ordered. Macro clamped a massive hand on his shoulder and propelled him forward into the temple.

Inside the senators stood aghast as the Praetorians clattered in and, on a command, came to an abrupt halt.

'What is the meaning of this, tribune?' Regulus barked as Macro walked forward, leaving Vespasian next to the front rank of the century.

'Have you taken your vote, Consul?' Macro growled.

'We have.'

'And what was the outcome?'

'I was just about to announce it when you so disrespectfully interrupted me.'

'Well, I suggest that you announce it now, Consul.'

All the senators huddled together fearing that they had just made the wrong decision. Trio came out from behind his chair looking triumphant.

Regulus swallowed. 'The motion before the house was: that this house would condemn Lucius Aelius Sejanus to death by strangulation and that his name be expunged.' He paused and looked at Macro nervously. 'And I declare that the motion is carried,' he said in a thin voice.

There was silence all around the chamber as the senators awaited Macro's reaction. No one moved.

Macro slowly clapped his hands together three times. 'I congratulate you, Conscript Fathers, for once you have made the right decision.'

The senators exhaled with relief.

Trio's face fell.

'I'm pleased that you should think so, tribune,' Regulus said.

'You will address me as prefect from now on, Consul; I have a warrant from the Emperor appointing me prefect of the Praetorian Guard,' Macro said, brandishing two scrolls. 'I also have a request from the Emperor demanding the same punishment that you have voted Sejanus for this man. Bring him forward, centurion.'

The Praetorian centurion pulled a young man out from the middle of the century; his hands were manacled. He held his head high and had a proud, contemptuous look on his square-jawed face.

'Who is he, prefect?' Regulus demanded.

'He is Sejanus' eldest son, Strabo. The Emperor is sparing the two younger children.'

'What is the charge?'

'That he is a traitor's son.'

'We can't just condemn him for his family ties; that would be going back to the excesses of the civil wars.'

'You will do as the Emperor wishes if you want this matter to rest, Consul. If you don't I will see to it that the Emperor understands exactly why the Guard was forced to execute Strabo and not the State.'

'You leave us no choice then,' Regulus said, drawing himself up. 'The motion before the senate is: that Strabo, the eldest son of Sejanus, should share his father's fate. Those in favour stand to the right of me, those against, to the left.'

The senators remained where they were; only Trio moved, realising that he could perhaps regain some favour with the Emperor if he joined the rest of the Senate on Regulus' right.

'I declare the motion carried,' Regulus said sorrowfully.

To Vespasian's surprise the Praetorian century cheered; the cheers rippled down its ranks and out to the rest of the cohort outside

'Summon one of the triumviri capitales,' Regulus called over the growing tumult as the news of the Senate's decision spread from the Praetorians to the massive crowd in the Forum.

'I found one lurking outside,' Macro informed him. 'Vespasian, step forward.'

Vespasian joined Macro in front of Regulus. 'I'm Titus Flavius Vespasianus, Consul, one of the triumviri capitales.'

'I charge you to do the will of the Senate of Rome, triumvir,' Regulus said formally. 'Take this man to the Tullianum and oversee his immediate execution by strangulation and that of his father, Lucius Aelius Sejanus. The bodies are to be exposed on the Gemonium Stairs.'

Vespasian led Strabo, guarded by two Praetorians, out through the temple doors and left down the steps. The noise was deafening; the huge crowd had begun angrily tearing down the many statues of Sejanus set about the Forum and the surrounding area. Fights had broken out and blood began to flow as citizens turned on men suspected of being part of Sejanus' large network of informers and stooges.

Magnus and his brothers shielded Vespasian from the mob as he crossed the Gemonium Stairs towards the entrance of the Tullianum, just the other side, guarded by the Vigiles.

'Strabo! Strabo, my son,' a woman's voice shrieked from close by, 'what are they doing to you?'

Vespasian turned to see a desperate-looking woman, with

tears streaming down her face, holding her arms towards his prisoner in supplication.

'Let her through,' Vespasian ordered Magnus, realising that she must be Sejanus' ex-wife Apicata. 'She should be allowed a farewell,' he added, looking sternly at the two Praetorians.

Apicata rushed up to her son and flung her arms around his neck.

'There's nothing that we can do, Mother,' Strabo said, unable, owing to his manacles, to return the embrace. 'It's over. Father will never be Emperor and neither shall I.'

'But why are they condemning you? You've done nothing,' Apicata howled.

'I've done enough, Mother, believe me. Besides, if I were in Tiberius' position I would do the same. You have Capito and little Junilla to console you; keep them safe and get them out of Rome.'

'We must go,' Vespasian said, pulling Apicata's arms away from her son.

'Goodbye, Mother. I shall die well and with no complaint,' Strabo said, kissing her forehead. 'Remember me.'

'I will, my son,' Apicata called as Vespasian led Strabo away, 'and I vow to tell Tiberius that, just as he took a son away from me, his son was taken from him.'

Vespasian unlocked the low door to the Tullianum and ushered Strabo in. Strabo paused. He took a last look at the clear blue sky and a last breath of fresh air and then, lowering his head, walked through the doorway. The drop in temperature was sudden and Vespasian almost shivered, as he did every time he entered the prison.

The room was low, small and windowless; in the centre of the floor was a wooden trapdoor. Three gaolers sat at a table on the far side playing dice by the light of a single oil lamp; they got up as the Praetorians closed the door behind them, leaving Magnus and his brothers outside with the Vigiles.

'Another one for the cell, Vespasian?' the oldest gaoler asked, grinning a toothless grin and wiping his hands on his greasy tunic. Vespasian found the evident pleasure he took in his job revolting.

'No, Spurius,' Vespasian replied, 'you've to execute him immediately along with his father.' Vespasian indicated to the trapdoor.

'Sejanus' son, eh? Well, well, a family do, that's a novelty.'

Spurius' two mates sniggered.

'Cut or twist?' Spurius asked, examining Strabo's neck as if he were a sacrificial ram. Strabo remained erect and dignified, disdaining to notice foul creature in front of him.

'Twist,' Vespasian almost shouted, fighting to keep his temper. 'Now get on with it.'

'That's good, less mess to clean up afterwards, eh, lads, just a bit of shit and piss. Find a couple of twisters and I'll get old matey-boy up.'

Spurius lifted the trapdoor and threw down a rope attached to an iron hook in the ceiling. 'Up you come, sir,' he called down with mock politeness.

The rope immediately went taut and an instant later Sejanus hauled himself, arm muscles bulging, out of the hole, wearing only a loincloth. Despite the straw sticking to his sweat-slicked torso and powerful thighs, he exuded an aura of dignity and power and Vespasian had to restrain himself from taking a pace back. Vengeful malice burned in the dark eyes locked on his gaoler.

'The Emperor and the Senate have seen sense at last, you filthy maggot,' he growled, sticking his face into Spurius'. 'I'll not forget your hospitality.'

'I'm afraid not, Father,' Strabo said.

Sejanus spun round to see his son, manacled, between the two Praetorians. For a moment his hauteur faltered as the reality of his predicament sank in; he nodded his head in comprehension, half smiling to himself. 'Ah! I see. It's come to that, has it?' He looked at the Praetorians. 'How much did Tiberius pay the Guard to betray me?'

Neither of the Guardsmen replied; they just stared straight ahead.

'Ashamed to say, are you?' Sejanus sneered. 'Let me guess: twenty gold aurei per man.'

The Guards remained mute.

'Thirty then?'

The two men started to look uncomfortable.

Sejanus' eyes widened in disbelief. 'Less than twenty? You cheap whores.'

'It was ten, father,' Strabo informed him, 'they were boasting to me about it as they brought me to the Senate.'

'Boasting! Boasting about ten pathetic aurei, two hundred and fifty denarii.' Sejanus burst out laughing. 'The Emperor bought back his Empire for less than a year's wages per man of the Praetorian Guard. What a bargain – at that price soon everyone will be able to afford to become Emperor.' He spat at the Guardsmen's feet. 'Let's get this over with.' He looked at Vespasian, frowned suddenly, and pointed at him. 'I know you; you were skulking behind a pillar at the Temple of Apollo this morning. If you're one of the triumviri capitales, what were you doing waiting outside a senatorial meeting that was expected to give me tribunicial power?'

'I was told to,' Vespasian said, looking Sejanus in the eye.

'By whom? Macro?'

'No, Antonia,' Vespasian replied, seeing no point in concealing from Sejanus the instigator of his downfall.

Sejanus smiled grimly. 'That bitch? It was her then, not Macro?'

Vespasian nodded, still staring Sejanus in the eye.

A deeper recognition flashed across Sejanus' face. 'I've seen you once before, haven't I?'

'That's right.'

'On Livilla's wall five years ago; you were part of the group that freed Antonia's secretary, weren't you?'

'I was.'

'That was bravely done.'

Vespasian continued staring back at Sejanus, giving no sign of acknowledging the compliment.

Sejanus studied him in silence for a while; no one else in the room moved as they sensed the intensity of the look that passed between the two men. Vespasian squared his shoulders back and drew himself up, suddenly no longer afraid.

'I can recognise something in you, young man,' Sejanus said eventually, 'something that I have in myself: an iron will. Antonia must see it too as she is still using you to do her work five years on. She normally discards people after a few months; she must think that you have potential. Antonia's champion yesterday, Rome's executioner today, but what tomorrow for you, I wonder? What's your name?'

'Titus Flavius Vespasianus.'

'Well, young son of the house of Flavius, I'll give you some advice; remember it well, it's the last that I shall ever give. I am here for one reason and one reason alone: I didn't take power when it was within my grasp. When I was Consul I should have rebelled. The Guard were mine, the Senate, for the most part, was mine and the people would have been mine – but I hesitated. Why did I hesitate when I'd been chasing that power for so long? Why? When I've been trying to manoeuvre myself for years, as I'm sure that Antonia's told you, into becoming either Tiberius's heir or regent to his heir, by marrying Livilla and disposing of rivals until the choice left to Tiberius would have been Claudius, Tiberius Gemellus or me?'

'What about Caligula?'

Sejanus sneered. 'That warped little scorpion? Why do you think I persuaded Tiberius to summon him to Capreae? I judged that the mad old man would have him thrown off the cliff within a month; I was wrong, although it may still happen. But if it had, no one could've accused me of his death; just as no one can accuse me of any of the other potential heirs' deaths. People may have their suspicions but there is no proof; if there were I would already be dead. I have been very careful not to be seen as the murderer of my rivals because I didn't want to take the power; I wanted it given to me. I foolishly believed that if I seized power then someone would come and grab it from me in turn; but if it was given to me legitimately then I would be able keep it to pass on to my son.' He looked proudly at Strabo and, placing a hand on the back of his neck, pulled his head forward and kissed him full on the mouth.

'So what is your advice, Sejanus?' Vespasian urged.

'Advice? Yes,' Sejanus said slowly, patting his son's cheek, 'my advice is when you come within reach of power, don't hesitate, you must seize it immediately. No one will give it to you, so if you don't grab it when you can then whoever does will destroy you and your family for coming so close to what they now so jealously guard.'

'Why tell me this?'

Sejanus gave him a mirthless smile and shook his head. 'Now put an end to it; come, Strabo, my son, we face the river together.'

'I do so gladly in your company, Father.'

Sejanus took Strabo's hand and they knelt on the floor; he pushed his head forward whilst his son remained upright.

'It's not the sword, Father.'

'No, it's the twister,' Spurius said, coming forward with one of his mates. Both brandished a garrotte.

'Lucius Aelius Sejanus and Lucius Aelius Strabo,' Vespasian said, 'the Senate has sentenced you both to death by strangulation; do you have anything to say?'

'I've already said it,' Sejanus said as nooses of rope were placed around his and his son's necks.

Strabo shook his head.

'Spurius, do your duty,' Vespasian commanded.

The two gaolers each placed a short oaken rod into the rope nooses at the back of their victim's necks and then twisted them around until the slack had been taken out of the ropes and they were tight, biting into their skin.

Spurius looked at his mate and nodded. Slowly and methodically they twisted the rods around, each turn tightening the garrottes. Hand in hand Sejanus and Strabo submitted to this slow death. First their eyes started to bulge and a strained gurgling sound emanated from their throats. Then their tongues protruded, waggling unnaturally far out of their drooling mouths and a pool of urine appeared about their knees. Their faces became almost purple, their heads went back with bulging eyes staring maniacally at the ceiling and lips curled up over their teeth; but they still clasped hands, their knuckles whitening. The gurgling stopped and the smell of fresh faeces filled the air. With a look of straining agony contorting their faces their hands fell away from each other, their heads lolled to one side and their bodies slumped forward, held up by the bloody garrottes now embedded in their throats. The executioners let go of the rods and the bodies fell into the pool of their own waste.

Vespasian looked down at the man who had come so close to breaking the Julio-Claudian grip on power. Their final conversation echoed around his head; why had he told him these things? How would he ever be in a position to sieze power? Then the last line from the prophecy of Amphiaraos came unbidden into his mind: 'So to gain from the Fourth the west on the morrow.' Was he the one who would gain? He shook his head and tore his eyes away from the man who had failed to gain the west. 'Throw the bodies on to the stairs, Spurius,' He turned and walked to the door.

Outside, the Vigiles, along with Magnus and his mates, were having trouble holding back the crowd from the prison door. Vespasian and the two Praetorians joined the security cordon and helped them push back the surging mob enough for Spurius and his colleagues to drag the bodies of Sejanus and Strabo unceremoniously out of the Tullianum and fling them in a contorted heap on to the Gemonium Stairs before beating a hasty retreat back into their cheerless domain.

At the sight of Sejanus' and Strabo's lifeless bodies the citizens of Rome roared out their pleasure and rushed towards them, each eager to be the first to desecrate the corpses. The entrance to the Tullianum was left clear.

'I think it really is time for dinner now, sir,' Magnus suggested again.

'I think that you may be right, Magnus,' Vespasian replied, breaking into a run.

They made it to the relative safety of the Senate House steps and looked back into the Forum. In amongst the chaos, elements of the ever-growing crowd had now turned their attentions to the cohort of Praetorians, with Macro at their head, who were trying to make their way out of the Forum and back to their camp. Pieces of broken statues, sticks and stones and other improvised missiles were being hurled into their ranks, felling a few of their number as the crowd vented their anger on the men who had maintained Sejanus in power for so long.

At a roared order from Macro the cohort stopped and drew their swords from beneath their togas. Macro bellowed another order and they turned outwards to face the mob on both sides of them.

Then they charged.

Showing no mercy for their fellow citizens, they cut down those nearest to them and stepped over their bodies to get at those behind. The howls of hatred and abuse from the crowd swiftly became screams of terror and pain as the mob turned and fled in all directions, with the pursuing Praetorians pitilessly cutting down those not swift enough to avoid their blades.

On the steps of the Temple of Concordia those senators brave enough to emerge watched helplessly as the massacre progressed, seeping out of the Forum Romanum into the Forum Boarium and on into the surrounding streets.

Vespasian looked over to the Gemonium Stairs, now deserted apart from the two broken bodies and a woman, Apicata, tearing at her hair and rending her clothes in furious mourning.

From beyond the House of the Vestals at the far end of the Forum came a massive roar and the sound of thousands of hob-nailed sandals pounding on stone tore Vespasian's eyes away from Apicata. A quick look at the source was enough to make him turn and run.

'Definitely time to go,' Magnus shouted as he and his brothers pelted after Vespasian down the steps in the direction of the Quirinal Hill.

Behind them the rest of the Praetorian Guard spilled into the Forum and fanned out across the city to exact their vengeance on and reassert their authority over the citizens of Rome.

CHAPTER XXI

'How's the house coming along?' Vespasian asked Sabinus as they took some afternoon refreshment of chilled wine and honeyed cakes in Gaius' courtyard garden.

'We should be able to move in very soon,' Sabinus replied. 'The sooner the better, in fact, as Clementina is pregnant again.'

'Congratulations.'

'Thank you, brother. I want her to be settled as soon as possible; you know how stressed women get when they move house.'

'Yes, indeed,' Vespasian lied.

'I've been waiting for things to quieten down, though. Now that the Senate is finally meeting again today we should see a degree of law and order return.'

'I certainly hope so,' Vespasian replied, thinking of the violence that had recently engulfed the city.

For two days and nights Macro had allowed his men to loot and pillage Rome, before recalling them to their camp outside the city's walls, leaving its citizens poorer and subdued but in no doubt as to who was the real power within the city.

It had taken half a dozen more days for life to get back to normal, although there had been sporadic outbursts of violence, aimed mainly at Sejanus' supporters, whether real or imaginary. After a few more days the Senate had managed to reconvene, most of the senators having fled Rome for the safety of their country estates during the Praetorian Guard's occupation of the city.

'Did you get on the list of prospective quaestors for next year?' Vespasian asked, changing the subject; he had only enquired after Sabinus' new house out of politeness and was still in fact deeply disapproving of the way that his brother was financing it.

'Yes, I did,' Sabinus replied gloomily, 'but there seems to be a candidate from every patrician family on it this time. Plebeians like us don't stand a chance. I've a nasty feeling that I'm going to fail for a third time.'

They were interrupted by Gaius bursting into the garden accompanied by Aenor, who was trying to relieve him of his toga.

'I sometimes think that my fellow senators are a bunch of brainless sheep,' he boomed furiously. 'Aenor, bring me a cup.'

The young German boy scurried off; Gaius plonked his ample behind down on a bench next to Sabinus and reached for a calming honeyed cake.

The brothers waited whilst their uncle devoured the tasty morsel and was served a cup of unwatered wine.

'The idiots were debating whether to censure Macro for letting the Guard loose in the city,' Gaius continued, thumping his half-empty cup down on the table and spilling a lot of its contents, 'when Aulus Plautius stands up and says that rather than censuring Macro, we should be praising him for managing to restore order in such a short period of time. Short period of time, my flabby arse! Two days we were barricaded in here with murder and mayhem going on out in the streets.' He swilled down the remainder of his wine and held his cup out for Aenor to refill whilst reaching for another cake. 'So he proposes a motion that Macro should be voted the rank of an ex-praetor even though he is not a member of the Senate, which everybody jumps at as being an excellent idea; the house then divides and the motion is carried unanimously.'

'Unanimously, Uncle?' Vespasian queried as Gaius took a large bite of his cake. 'Didn't you vote against it seeing as it's so infuriated you?'

'Of course not,' Gaius replied testily, spraying crumbs all over the table. 'I didn't want to be seen as the only person opposing it – that would hardly have been wise!'

'If everyone thinks like that then it's no surprise if the Senate votes for outrageous motions.'

'Well, that wasn't the most outrageous motion today,' Gaius said. 'I'm afraid the retribution has started and, in order to deflect attention away from himself, it's being led by Aulus Plautius. He had three of Sejanus' closest supporters in the Senate condemned to be thrown from the Tarpeian Rock, and as if that wasn't bad enough he had them dragged up there immediately and threw them off personally. I'm afraid that you are going to be quite busy over the next few days, dear boy.'

Five days later Vespasian stood on the steps of the Senate House, in the warm mid-morning sun, awaiting the latest senatorial decree in the ongoing purge of Sejanus' supporters. He and his fellow triumviri capitales had indeed been busy, as Gaius had predicted; in the last couple of days they had overseen half a dozen beheadings, four garrottings and one more unfortunate senator being hurled from the Tarpeian Rock. Over a dozen more had managed tocommit suicide before the executioners had got their hands on them, thus preventing their estates from being seized as well. None, however, had had the benefit of a proper trial in the Forum; their executions had been sanctioned by an executive order from the Senate at either the written request of the Emperor or after a motion put to the house by Aulus Plautius.

That morning another long letter from Tiberius had been read out by Regulus; Vespasian had not bothered listening at the Senate House's open doors as he was bored with the frequent diatribes against Sejanus' supporters with which Tiberius had been haranguing the Senate.

The noise of the ongoing debate floating out of the doors subsided and Vespasian guessed that the House was dividing. He smiled to himself at the use of that word; during the recent debates the Senate had never been divided, it had always voted unanimously for death. There were a few moments of silence then he heard Regulus pronounce the motion carried and a huge roar of agreement from the Senate.

Vespasian braced himself ready to do his duty and wondered which hapless senator Paetus would be escorting out to him and what form of execution had been decreed. To his shock and consternation Paetus came rushing out with Gaius.

'Surely not you, Uncle?' he called, running up the steps to meet them. How could he possibly oversee his own uncle's execution?

'What?' Gaius replied momentarily confused. 'Oh! No, dear boy, not me,' he laughed. 'Tiberius has just snared his biggest prey yet: Livilla.'

'Livilla? How?'

'The Emperor's had proven what most people have long suspected: that Livilla poisoned her own husband, Tiberius' son Drusus, to clear the way for Sejanus to marry her. Her physician and one of Drusus' body slaves, who are both freedmen now, were tracked down and confirmed it under torture. I've been charged by the Senate to inform the Lady Antonia of her daughter's sentence. I can't say that I'm looking forward to the conversation.'

'I've got to oversee the execution of a woman?' Vespasian asked, not liking the idea in the slightest despite Livilla's blood-thirsty reputation.

'No, no, old chap, the Senate hasn't pronounced a sentence,' Paetus informed him cheerily, 'you and I have just got to secure her. Out of respect for Antonia, Tiberius asked that Livilla be handed over to her; he felt it proper for the mother of the woman who murdered his son to decide the manner of her daughter's punishment. Personally, I think that he's been too lenient; what mother would order the execution of her own child?'

Four centuries of the Urban Cohort had surrounded Livilla's property on the Palatine to prevent her escape, although as far as Vespasian knew news of the Senate's decision had not yet come to her ears. He and Paetus walked up the grand set of steps leading to her front door accompanied by an Urban Cohort centurion; behind them the century that was covering the front of the house formed up. Paetus pulled a chain and a bell sounded inside.

The viewing slot opened.

'Quaestor Publius Junius Caesennius Paetus, here to see the Lady Livilla at the request of the Emperor and the Senate,' he said slowly and clearly.

The slot closed but the door remained shut.

'It seems that the good lady is not too keen on seeing us,'

Paetus observed after a few moments. 'Can't say that I blame her. Centurion, break it down.'

'Sir!'

At a barked order from the centurion four men came rushing forward with a small battering ram. After a half a dozen resounding thumps the door burst open; Vespasian and Paetus walked through the vestibule, followed by the centurion, into a lavish atrium. Vespasian had never seen so many gold and silver ornaments. Vases, statuettes, candelabras and bowls, all of differing sizes, were placed around on low, polished marble tables with ornate legs, again of either silver or gold; chairs and couches, upholstered in deep reds and golds, punctuated the room and echoed the colours of the frescoes that adorned its walls, depicting the bloody wars of the Titans in the days before the coming of man. Four towering black marble columns, streaked with grey, supported the ceiling at the four corners of the impluvium, in the centre of which was a huge bronze statue of Saturn castrating his father, Caelus, with a sickle.

'How dare you break into my home,' a low, female voice said threateningly.

Vespasian and Paetus spun round to see a beautiful, slender woman in her mid-forties glaring at them from one of the many doorways off the atrium. She was unmistakably Antonia's daughter, fine boned and haughty; but whereas Antonia's eyes were clear and wide hers were dark and mean; the lines that ran from their corners curved down from frowning, not up from smiling. Her mouth was small and her lips full, like her mother's, but they were set in a sneer that seemed to be permanently fixed upon her ivory-skinned face.

'We are here to escort you to your mother's house,' Paetus replied, stepping towards her.

'On whose authority and for what reason?' Her voice had become wary and even lower.

'On the Emperor's and the Senate's authority; you are to come with us immediately.'

'I will do no such thing until you tell me for what reason.'

'You have been found guilty of your late husband Drusus'

murder and are to be handed over to the Lady Antonia so that she can decide your fate,' Paetus answered, stopping just in front of her.

She fixed him with a vicious glare. 'I am dead then.'

'Not at the hand of your own mother. Tiberius has shown mercy by giving you to her.' Paetus layed a hand on her shoulder. 'Come with me, lady.' Livilla's right fist came up from her side and thumped into Paetus' chest; she turned and ran, leaving Paetus standing motionless, his hand still stretched out. Vespasian instantly sprang forward and, constricted as she was by her silken stola, caught her by the hair within a few paces. Shrieking like a harpy and writhing like a Babylonian whore, Livilla tried to break from his grasp; long nails slashed at his face and sharp teeth drew blood from his arm. Behind him men of the Urban Cohort came flooding in through the door to hold back members of Livilla's household rushing to their mistress's aid. As he wrestled with her she forced him around until he could see Paetus over her shoulder. He had sunk to his knees. Blood soaked his tunic and toga and he gazed down incredulously at the golden hilt of a dagger that protruded from his chest.

With an animal roar Vespasian tightened his grip on Livilla's hair and pulled back his right fist, causing Livilla to go limp in submission; a look of terror filled her eyes. Vespasian pulled her upright by the hair, looked at her in blind fury and spat in her face; with a rolling snarl of hatred he slammed his fist into her full lips. Blood exploded from her, covering her face and splattering his as his blow split her lips in several places and shattered her front teeth. He let her drop and she crumpled, howling, to the floor; savagely kicking her belly in the hope that she might be pregnant, he stepped over her as Paetus collapsed slowly onto his back.

Kneeling down, he lifted his friend's head in his hand; his skin was waxen and pallid.

Paetus looked up at him with fading eyes. 'Bit of mess, eh, old chap,' he whispered. 'Keep an eye on young Lucius for me, won't you?'

'I will, my friend,' Vespasian replied with tears welling up in his eyes. 'I'm so sorry.'

'Silly me, I thought that she was just a woman.' The breath left him in a slow rattle and his eyes glazed over. Vespasian laid Paetus' head down and passed the palm of his hand over his face to close his eyelids.

'Have some of your men guard his body until his wife comes to claim it, centurion,' he ordered, 'then follow me and bring that bitch with you.'

Vespasian stepped out into the warm sun and descended the steps with Livilla, bloodied, face swollen, moaning, walking unaided behind him, escorted by the centurion and four of his men. His eyes were hard and set in a fixed stare as he tried to control himself; all he wanted to do was to rip Livilla's throat out with his teeth. How could Tiberius have been so merciful towards her?

'Livilla!' shrieked a shrill female voice from across the street.

Apicata stood behind the screening century of the Urban Cohort brandishing a long, thin-bladed knife. Her clothes were in tatters and her cheeks and arms were covered in fresh, deep scratch marks; blood lined her fingernails.

'Livilla, look at me, you Gorgon's miscarriage!'

Livilla looked up and focused through puffy eyes.

'I did this to you, Livilla,' Apicata screamed triumphantly. 'It was me. I wrote to Tiberius. I told him how you got the poison from your physician Eudemus, and how Drusus' body slave Lygdus administered it. They were both tortured and confirmed it.' She cackled hysterically and waved the dagger at Livilla. 'You took my husband and caused the death of my son and now they've taken my other two children from me, but I don't care, Livilla, I don't care because I've got you – you're finished, Livilla, finished! And this is what I think of you.'

She lifted the knife above her head, placed both hands on the hilt and, with another high-pitched scream, forced the blade down and under her lower rib; she convulsed and doubled up. Then she lifted her face to Livilla, blood seeping from the corners of her mouth and her nostrils.

'This is what awaits you!' she howled and, with a look of wide-eyed, manic concentration, she forced the blade up into her heart and died without another sound.

*

Gaius was waiting for Vespasian in Antonia's atrium looking agitated.

'Where's Paetus?' he asked as Vespasian stepped through the door.

Vespasian made no reply. One look at his expression and a quick glance at Livilla's ruined face was enough to tell the story.

'Oh, I see,' Gaius mumbled. 'I'm very sorry, dear boy.'

Vespasian nodded in acknowledgement as Livilla was led past him, now visibly shaking. Vespasian stared at her with hatred. 'She deserves to die, uncle, but she'll only get banished to live out her days on some island. No mother would order the death of her child.'

'This is an unnatural day,' Gaius said, almost apologetically. 'I have to go back to the Senate. I'm afraid you're going to have to join me once you've delivered Livilla to Antonia.'

'As you wish, Uncle,' Vespasian replied numbly. 'What's happening now?'

'It's rather unpleasant but I can't see how it can be avoided,' Gaius said, shaking his head and walking out.

'Bring her this way,' Pallas said, appearing through the columns at the far end of the atrium. 'The Lady Antonia is waiting.'

'Thank you, centurion.' Vespasian walked forward and took hold of Livilla's arm. 'I can manage her now. Wait for me outside.'

Vespasian, leading Livilla, followed Pallas through the house until they came to the door that led down to Antonia's private prison where Rhoteces and Secundus had been incarcerated. Pallas pushed it open and descended the damp stone steps.

Livilla started to struggle as she caught the scent of fear and desperation that wafted up from the forbidding, dank corridor below. 'Where are you taking me?' she shrieked, squirming in Vespasian's strong grip.

'To see your mother, bitch,' he growled, pushing her through the door.

Antonia was waiting for them in the low corridor outside what had been Rhoteces' cell.

'That it has come to this', she said, shaking her head and regarding her daughter with cold, menacing eyes, 'grieves me more than you will ever know, Livilla.'

'Mother, Mother, please,' Livilla cried, breaking away from Vespasian and running to kneel at Antonia's feet and clasping her knees. 'Please, Mother, forgive me.'

With a sharp crack Antonia slapped her daughter across her broken face. 'Forgive you? You, who killed your own husband; you, who would have tortured Caenis, the daughter I should have had, had I not intervened; you, who were prepared to see your own son die to achieve your aims. You ask me for forgiveness?'

'I beg you, Mummy.'

'Don't you dare be familiar with me, whore!' Antonia screamed, pulling away from Livilla's grasp. 'There is no love between us any more, nor will there ever be again.' She swung open the door of the cell. 'Get in there.'

Meekly, Livilla obeyed and crawled whimpering into the fetid cell. Antonia pulled the door shut behind her and locked it. She threw the key to Pallas.

'Keep it, Pallas. Don't give it back to me even if I beg you to; Vespasian is your witness to my order,' she commanded, pulling a stool in front of the door and sitting down.

'What are you going to do, domina?' Vespasian asked.

Antonia folded her hands on her lap. 'What I must.The Emperor lost his only son because of my daughter. Livilla was prepared to sit by while her son died through poison; so, to end it, I will do the same. Bring me food and water once a day, Pallas; I will sit here and wait for my daughter to die.'

At these words a long screech erupted from the cell and fists pounded at the door.

Vespasian stepped forward. 'But domina, to kill one's own child goes against all tha...' Pallas' hand clamped over his mouth, silencing him and pulling him back. Vespasian turned to face him and saw for the first time an expression written over the Greek's normally neutral face: anger.

'It shall be as you command, mistress,' Pallas articulated deliberately whilst staring into Vespasian's eyes. He turned and pulled

Vespasian back up the steps. As they neared the top Vespasian glanced back. Antonia sat, hands clasped in her lap, impervious to the cries of her daughter behind her, staring fixedly at the smoke-blackened wall.

Pallas escorted Vespasian back through the house as Livilla's screams echoed around the corridors.

'Vespasian,' Caenis called, running up to him as they re-entered the atrium, 'what's happening?'

He wrapped his arms around her and nestled his head in her hair. 'A demonstration of your mistress's strength of will: she has passed a death sentence on her own daughter and is acting as the executioner herself.' He let go of Caenis and jabbed his finger repeatedly towards of the source of the now hysterical screaming. 'No matter how much she hates her,' he shouted at Pallas, 'how can she do that?'

'She has to, master,' Pallas said, his face now a study in neutrality. 'If she doesn't then she knows that for honour's sake Tiberius will have his revenge for his son in far more terrible way. Claudius, Caligula and Gemellus will all die and with their deaths he will take away her power.'

'If that's what it takes to hold on to power in Rome then I want to go back to my estates.'

Caenis looked up at him, shaking her head slowly as the screams continued. 'No, my love, you stay here and learn from her strength. Pallas is right: she cannot afford to force Tiberius into a position whereby he is honour-bound to kill the rest of his family.'

'Why not? Caligula is my friend and I wish him no harm, but I've seen what he's like and I know that he will be the worst kind of emperor. It would be for the greater good if Tiberius were free to choose a suitable man to succeed him.'

'Do you really think that he'll do that? Or will he just choose someone infinitely worse so that he's remembered, by compar-ison, in a better light? A *real* tyrant,'

Recollecting the unstable old man on Capreae, Vespasian did not need to think long about the answer. 'He'd choose a tyrant and it would amuse him, because . . .' He stopped and a look of comprehension slid over his face. He began to relax. 'So we're better off having someone like Caligula, however profligate and base he may be, because at least he will have the restraining influence of Antonia over him?'

'I would think so, master, which is why I would not have you try to change her mind.' Pallas held up the key to Livilla's cell. 'I won't give this back to my mistress until she has done her duty to Rome. It's better for us all this way.'

Vespasian stared at the key; with a shock he realised that giving it to Pallas was an admission by Antonia that she could not trust her maternal instincts not to overrule her sense of duty. 'She doesn't want to do this, does she?'

'Of course not, would you?'

'And there is no other way?'

'Not unless she took the knife to her daughter's throat. But she couldn't do that – who could? So she must bear her daughter's screams as she slowly dies. She will see it as her punishment for infanticide, but she is willing to take that punishment in order to fulfil her obligation to Rome.'

Vespasian looked back towards the screaming. 'Yes, I think I can see that... and I must applaud her for it. She's paying a high price indeed, but a necessary one, I suppose, to fulfil her duty.'

Pallas shrugged. 'She has the strength and, in the end, it's no more than she can afford.'

'For that I suppose she must be grateful.' Vespasian looked back at Caenis and sighed. 'Now I should find the strength to go and do my duty.'

Caenis reached up and stroked his cheek. 'You'll find the strength to do it, my love; one way or another.' She smiled.

He stood back and gazed at her. He wanted nothing more than to bury himself deep within her and cleanse himself of the cares and horrors of the day, but he knew that it was not yet over. 'Pallas,' he said quietly, 'would you be so good as to have Caenis escorted to my uncle's house – I don't think your mistress will have any use for her services over the next few days.'

'I shall see to it personally, master.'

'I'll see you later, my love,' Vespasian said, raising her chin and kissing her gently on the mouth.

'Where are you going?'

'To the Senate House to do what my uncle thinks may be a very unpleasant duty. I don't know what it is but it will seem as nothing compared to what Antonia is doing.'

He kissed her once more with passion and then, with Livilla's screams still resounding in his ears and the image of his benefactress sitting, waiting placidly for her daughter's death in his mind, he walked away, steeled by Antonia's unselfish resolve.

The Senate was in uproar as Vespasian looked through the open doors. Standing in front of the two Consuls at the far end, and flanked by rows of baying senators sitting on their folding stools on the stepped levels that ran down either side of the house, were two children: a boy of about fourteen and a small girl of no more than seven.

'And I ask you, Conscript Fathers,' Consul Trio was bellowing at the top of his voice, 'how can we be seen to pass such a sentence on two children, so obviously innocent of any crime.'

He sat back on his curule chair and Aulus Plautius rose to his feet from within the disorderly ranks of senators.

'Conscript Fathers, I would have your attention,' he shouted and then paused whilst the furore died down. 'Innocent of crimes they may be,' he said, looking down his nose at the two frightened children, 'but innocent of name they are not. When we voted for Sejanus' death we also voted for damnatio memoriae, wiping his name from history as if he had never existed. What is the Senate, Conscript Fathers, if it refuses to act on its own will? It is our will that the name of Sejanus be eradicated and they' – he pointed a damning finger at the two children – 'they carry his name. So do your duty and condemn them.' He sat down with a dramatic flurry of his toga to absolute silence as the senators tried to mentally refute the logic of his argument. None could.

After a brief pause it became obvious that no one else wished to speak. Regulus got slowly to his feet.

'The motion before the house is: that the children of Sejanus,

Capito and Junilla, be executed in the same manner as their father in accordance with the previous decree of damnatio memoriae. The house will divide.'

Vespasian's heart sank as the vast majority of senators passed to the right of Regulus.

'So be it,' Regulus said wearily. 'I declare the motion carried. Summon a triumvir capitalis.'

Vespasian walked with leaden feet into the House and stopped just behind the two children.

'You heard the sentence?' Regulus asked him.

'Yes, Consul.'

'Then do your duty.'

Vespasian steeled himself. Rome, it seemed, was asking much from everyone today. He put a hand on the shoulder of each child; the boy looked up at him with cold, dead eyes and brushed the hand away.

'Where are we going, Capito?' Junilla asked her brother.

'To Father,' Capito replied, taking her hand.

'But he's dead.'

Capito nodded.

'What does execution mean?'

Capito squeezed her hand and led her calmly, with his head held high, towards the open doors.

Vespasian followed. The senate was silent as they passed.

As they descended the steps into the Forum Gaius caught up with Vespasian.

'I'm sorry that it has to be you, dear boy,' he mumbled.

'Why did Aulus Plautius do that? Hasn't it gone far enough already?'

'It wasn't Plautius, I afraid.'

'Then who proposed the motion, Uncle?'

'I did.'

'You? Why?'

'On Antonia's orders,' Gaius replied, obviously distressed. 'She had the children seized in vengeance for Apicata writing to Tiberius; she knew that Livilla would have to die, Tiberius expected no less, and although she hated her she couldn't in honour let it pass without retribution. So she demanded that I asked the Senate for Apicata's children's deaths. I tried to refuse her but she threatened me.'

'What with?' Vespasian asked wondering what Antonia could have on Gaius that would make him do such a thing.

Gaius looked his nephew straight in the eye. 'My life,' he said simply and walked away.

He slowly shook his head as he watched his uncle go, wondering whether Antonia really would have taken Gaius' life if he had not done her bidding. Then he remembered her sitting resolutely waiting for her daughter to die. He knew the answer and he understood why: what was Gaius' life to her compared to what she was forced to do for honour and duty?

Vespasian turned and followed the two children as they walked hand in hand, escorted by the Urban Cohort centurion and his men, the short distance across the Forum towards their deaths in the Tullianum.

As he walked he again remembered his grandmother sipping her wine from her treasured cup and saying: 'I advise you to keep out of politics that you don't understand, and to keep away from the powerful, because in general they only have one goal and that is more power. They tend to use people of our class as dispensable tools.' He had seen the reality of that warning: Gaius was as dispensable as he, Vespasian, could one day be.

The centurion rapped on the Tullianum door; Spurius opened it after a brief pause.

'Well, well, what do we have here?' he drawled, surveying Capito and Junilla and licking his lips.

'You will do your duty with dignity and remain silent, Spurius,' Vespasian hissed, 'or by all the gods I will see to it that you will be the next victim of this purge.'

Spurius looked at him, taken aback by the venom in his voice, and seeing the steel will in Vespasian's eyes slowly nodded his acquiescence. He stepped back from the door and allowed Capito to lead his young sister in.

'What place is this?' she asked her brother, looking around the chill, shadow-ridden room.

'This is the place where it ends, Junilla,' Capito replied softly. 'Be brave.'

'Cut or twist?' Spurius asked in Vespasian's ear.

'Twist,' he replied, although the word stuck in his throat. 'Make it swift.'

One of Spurius' mates quickly procured two garrottes whilst Spurius made the children kneel. The nooses were placed around their necks; Junilla started to cry softly as she realised what was happening.

'Wait,' Spurius said suddenly, 'we can't do this to the girl.'

'Why not?' Vespasian snapped. He was shaking with tension. 'It's the will of the Senate.'

'She's a . . . you know . . . ' Spurius spluttered, trying to be discreet, 'and we can't . . . it's against the gods.'

Vespasian closed his eyes and put his hands over his face.

'Do the boy then,' he ordered swiftly.

Junilla watched in frozen horror as the wooden rod was inserted in the noose behind her brother's neck and twisted until the slack was taken out. Spurius looked back at Vespasian who nodded reluctantly.

A silent scream was written over the young girl's face as the noose squeezed the life out of her brother and his face and body contorted in agony. She buried her face in her hands and shuddered uncontrollably.

Capito's lifeless body fell forward with a splash into the pool of urine that surrounded it and Junilla threw herself, heaving with sobs, on to it.

'What shall we do with her then?' Spurius asked.

Vespasian felt weak and sick. He thought of Caenis and wanted only to lie in her arms.

He turned and walked to the door. 'The Senate has decreed that she must die,' he said, opening it. 'If you can't execute a virgin then make sure that she isn't one.'

He walked out into the sun, slamming shut the Tullianum door, as Junilla let out a long, terrified shriek.

AUTHOR'S NOTE

THIS HISTORICAL FICTION is based mainly on the writings of Suetonius, Tacitus and Cassius Dio.

The Getae were Thracians noted for their horsemanship and use of horse-archers – as well as the wearing of trousers! Whether I owe their shades an apology for my less than complimentary assumptions about their personal hygiene I don't know, but I somehow doubt it. They originally lived along both banks of the lower Danube but successive invasions, notably the Celts in the third century and the Romans in the first century, confined them to the northern bank from where they raided Moesia from time to time. There is much debate as to whether they were the same people as the Dacians, Rome's great enemy a century later, or whether they were originally a separate people and were eventually assimilated by them. The outline of the fourth century BC Getic fortress at Sagadava and the Roman camp next to it can be best seen, at the time of printing, on Wikimapia.org 44.2414329 N, 27.8540111E.

That Romans used slaves as oarsmen is a fallacy that is still given credence by repeated showings of the excellent film *Ben Hur*. I chose to have the Thracians use slaves for the purposes of the plot but have been unable to find out whether they did so in reality. If this turns out to be a massive historical blunder on my part then I apologise to the Thracian navy – if indeed there was one still extant at the time.

The ruins of the Temple of Amphiaraos and the surrounding sanctuary and theatre are still there. The preferred method of receiving guidance from the Hero was to sleep inside the temple after making your sacrifice; I moved Rhaskos outside so that Vespasian and Sabinus could be alone with the priests.

Clemens was in the Praetorian Guard and a distant relative of the Flavians through their grandmother, Tertulla. Sabinus did marry his sister, Clementina, at around this time but probably not in the circumstances described.

Josephus' *Jewish Antiquites* mentions Pallas acting as Antonia's messenger, taking her evidence of Sejanus' treachery (no doubt written down by Caenis) to Tiberius. Satrius Secundus is said, by Tacitus, to have disclosed the damning evidence to Antonia but neglects, like Josephus, to say what it was. In *To Marcia,* Seneca states that Secundus was Sejanus' client, but I decided to put him with Macro as well and have his wife, Albucilla, who was notorious for her many affairs, in Sejanus and Livilla's bed as a means of gaining the evidence that Antonia needed. Whether or not Caligula helped Pallas avoid the notice of Sejanus' men guarding the emperor is not known; however, he was on Capri at the time and had a vested interest in Sejanus' fall. Vespasian, Sabinus and Corbulo accompanying Pallas is of course fictitious.

Tiberius' 'hobbies' of hurling people from cliffs and general sexual depravity are spoken of by various sources. Suetonius tells us of the unit of marines stationed at the foot of the cliff to finish off any survivors. He also mentions the 'fishies' or 'minnows' as they appear in Robert Graves' translation. However, the most chilling detail, to my mind, is the snippet were Suetonius tells us that Tiberius' left hand was 'so strong that he could poke a finger through a sound, newly plucked apple or into the skull of a boy or a young man'. I can only assume that he must have practised the art on a regular basis for it to be remembered as one of his party tricks.

Caligula's incestuous behaviour towards his sisters is documented by Suetonius who goes on to tell us that his habit when reclining at banquets was to place his wife above him on the couch, i.e. to his back, and his sisters 'all below him in turn'. Whether Caligula has suffered a bad press over the years, as one recent German biography very interestingly argued, is hard to say; however, I have chosen to use the more colourful version of this fascinating emperor for the obvious reasons.

I have taken the events surrounding the fall of Sejanus primarily from Cassius Dio's account, Tacitus' being almost completely lost and Suetonius' vague. For the sake of the narrative I have condensed some of the action: Strabo was not executed together with his father, but a few days later, and the two younger children were executed a couple of months after that, not days. Both Cassius Dio and Tacitus mention Junilla's rape before her execution. Apicata did get her revenge for the deaths of her children, before committing suicide, by exposing Livilla's murder of Drusus. Whether Antonia starved Livilla to death is uncertain; Cassius Dio just states that he heard a rumour to that effect. Aulus Plautius being a supporter of Sejanus and then turning against him is my fiction; I wanted to introduce him into the story before we meet him as the general in command of the invasion of Britain. However many senators would have behaved as he did in order to save themselves.

Pleasingly, according to Suetonius, Vespasian's father, Titus, did end up as a Helvetian banker and no doubt, like his modern day counterparts, did very well. Titus Pomponius Atticus is recorded as having had banking interests amongst the Helevetians after their defeat by Caesar. Pomponius Labeo being his grandson is fictitious but seemed to be a good way of getting Titus to his historically correct position.

Again, I have taken the dates for Vespasian's career from Barbara Levick's excellent biography *Vespasian*. He would have become one of the Vigintiviri at around this time if he served his full four years in Thrace but whether he was one of the triumviri capitales is not known. Barbara Levick points out that if he had been involved with the hideous executions of Sejanus' younger children it would surely have been used as propaganda by his enemies against him during the Year of the Four Emperors and on into his Principate, which it was not. However, the possibility is still there and I chose to use it rather than have him involved with roads, which would be more logical, taking into account his future career; I doubt a road-related ending would have been very interesting.

My thanks again to my agent, Ian Drury at Sheil Land

Associates, without whom I would still be standing in muddy fields in the freezing cold or stuffy film stages at the height of summer, trying to get the next shot completed so that we can move on the next one, and so on and on. Also thanks to Gaia Banks and Virginia Ascione in the foreign rights department and Lucy Fawcett in the film and TV department.

Nic Cheetham, my publisher, has made it an extremely exciting year for me and my gratitude goes to him and his fine team at Corvus: Mathilda Imlah, Laura Palmer, Becci Sharpe, Nicole Muir and Rina Gill to name but a few. Congratulations, Rina, on the birth of Amahra Grace McQuinn.

Again it has been a pleasure to work with my editor, Richenda Todd; my thanks to her for being incisive, logical and really good at the job. (Sorry, Richenda, I think that was telling, rather baldly, not showing!)

Finally, thank you, Anja, for your love and support whilst I changed the direction of my life and wrested back a degree of control over it; and, of course, for listening to what I write every evening.

Vespasian's story will continue in *The False God of Rome*.